T0354594

Journals of a Revolution

The Citizen's War

Robert A. Binger

Order this book online at www.trafford.com
or email orders@trafford.com

Most Trafford titles are also available at major online book retailers.

Printed in the United States of America.

ISBN: 978-1-4669-5085-6 (sc)
ISBN: 978-1-4669-5084-9 (e)

Trafford rev. 08/13/2012

www.trafford.com

North America & international
toll-free: 1 888 232 4444 (USA & Canada)
phone: 250 383 6864 • fax: 812 355 4082

To the family that's supported me
through this endeavor and will stand
behind me the rest of my life.

PRELUDE

In the eighteenth century, after being oppressed by the British Empire for years, the thirteen colonies of America stood up for themselves. Their actions included such historic acts such as the Boston Tea Party and the manifesting of the Declaration of Independence, along with a general rebellion against the monarch's laws. Though they had been a nation for a short time, the people, with the exception of some loyalist jerks, they fought back and took their nation from the British.

As time went on, the nation grew to unprecedented heights. The nation established its own government under its new constitution and ruled itself through the contributions of every citizen. As the nation continued to grow, the people expanded west and discovered what the modern American terrain consists of.

With new developments in technology coming with every moment, the people continued to advance, making America one of the most powerful nations in the world. Through time, America fought against the tyranny of dictators and the evil of the sickest humans to walk the earth. For a while, things were going in America's favor.

However, as the years continued to pass, the nation that had once been a place of envy to the rest of the world began to slow its advance to the top. As the leaders began ignoring the calls of the people and secret missions began to come to light, the people began to look at their leaders with disgust.

Over the years, the people had been lied to and had their rights abused left and right. The constitution that had protected them for years began to disintegrate in front of them. The powerful government and its minions had taken control and ignored the cries from the people, so they could continue to fill their pockets and maintain their own interests.

The wars led by this great nation began to become shrouded in conspiracy and their motives became unclear. The tragedies of the nation began to appear to be inside jobs to those that had seen what the government was capable of. The economy took a turn for the worst, and the ones that led the nation continued to line their pockets through big businesses' donations and high pay. Meanwhile, the citizens of the nation sat wallowing in self-pity.

Some sat on the sidelines of this catastrophe and accepted their condition as "not that bad." They ignored the crimes that were committed every day by the government that they had put in place to protect them. They maintained the mindset of "well it could be worse."

Others decided that enough was enough. Those that saw the government's blatant refusal to cooperate took to the streets to scream sense into the heads of the nation's leaders. Numerous states' citizens led protests to the deepest parts of their cities and demanded change. The nation seemed to have been on a track for change, until the police showed up.

The ones that had once been there to protect the rights of the people began arresting everyone that demanded change. The camps that had been set up and had become symbols of the people's power were torn down and the defeated citizens went back to their homes. The people had been defeated, but their hope hadn't ceased.

The constitution tells us that it's the people's responsibility to overthrow the government, should it ever become corrupt. As conditions in the federal government continue to become worse and worse, many have begun to wonder if a revolution could be the next step in our nation's history. As it was in the previous revolution, many will have the desire for change, and many will not.

As I look at this situation, I wonder, what kind of spark would be needed to fuel a revolution? How far do the people of this great nation need to be pushed before they push back? How long will it take before the people realize that there are millions of us and only a few leaders?

This book is meant to be a fictional description of a possible scenario that could come about in the nation. This is the story of a new American Revolution, and what could happen, should the revolution ever take place. I'm not recommending that people ever follow what is entailed in this book, I'm simply presenting a possible scenario in an entertaining manner. It will seem realistic to some, but I must remind the world that people will act in whatever manner they see fit, and if they do, it's not my fault.

I say one more time, I don't condone what takes place in this book, so don't send me to Guantanamo please. And to the people that read this and become inspired, I don't blame you for wanting to act, but please, if you choose to act, don't do so recklessly.

CHAPTER ONE

ELECTION DAY

"Marisa, turn it up will yah'?" Brian mumbled through the bagel that filled his mouth while simultaneously reading the paper and watching the news. Danny's dad always did enjoy multitasking. It's something that comes naturally from working in the military.

"Give me a second," Marisa replied. She put down the papers she was organizing and turned up the television with the remote next to her. She then returned to the pile of papers she had to review before the workday as was her morning routine.

"After the poll done on our website this past month," the anchorwoman began, "Presidential candidate Stewart Marshall is predicted to receive seventy percent of the vote, a staggering advantage over candidate David Stone."

"Good," Brian said. "Guy's a fuckin' idiot." He took another bite of his bagel.

Marisa flipped her brown hair out of her face and looked at his dad with a shocked expression that would lead one to believe that she had never heard a word like that in her life. "Brian, don't say that in front of Danny."

"Kid's twenty-one. He's heard worse, Marisa. Like pu . . . "

"Brian!" Marisa yelled, cutting Brian's vulgarity short. You could see a vein popping form her forehead. Danny continued to eat his cereal as if he hadn't even heard the discussion. His eyes rolled at the argument that was about to ensue.

"The kid's almost done with college. You can't keep babying him," Brian debated.

"Well, he's still my baby, no matter how old he gets," Marisa replied.

Danny looked up from his cereal, mouth full. "Seriously, mom?" he mumbled.

Marisa stood up from her station and walked to Danny's spot at the table. She bent over and kissed him on the head and wrapped her arms around him. "Of course, baby. You always will be," she said

"Ugh, come on. I'm trying to eat," Danny said as he nudged his mom away.

Marisa let go and walked back over to the couch next to her papers and coffee. She seemed indifferent to Danny's behavior until she said, "Look Danny, just because you'll be living on your own in a few months doesn't mean you can act like you own the place. You're still under my roof."

"Sure thing, mom," Danny said as he turned his attention back to the cereal.

"Will you two quit bickering?" Brian interrupted. He turned back to the television screen and adjusted the volume to compensate for his family's conversation.

"More arrests in the recent protests in Boston," the television told them. "A hundred protesters were hauled off to jail after refusing to move from the highway leading from Boston at around three in the afternoon yesterday. The protesters had been warned multiple times that they would be arrested if they continued to refuse and the officers held true to their promises. Still, some are saying that the arrests are unjust."

Brian chuckled. "Here's where they find the biggest moron in the crowd who ends up all over the internet for his 'inspirational' rant," he said.

Sure enough, the television went to an interview with some scrawny hipster with an unkempt beard. "We can't allow the public to vote ignorantly like we always do! David Stone is a coward and a criminal! Just because they couldn't find proof that he had a part in the war crimes committed by others in his platoon doesn't make him innocent! Myself and everyone else here will be damned if we let that guy run our country!"

"Told you," Brian said. "Guy's dumb, but he's no murderer. Arrest all of them, I say. They always get in the way of my morning commute anyways. It would probably clear up the damn coffee shop too." Danny's dad finished up his bagel and grabbed his jacket. He lifted his suitcase from the corner of the room and walked across the living room to Marisa. "I'll see you after work, sweetie."

Marisa grabbed hold of the back of Brian's neck and gave him a kiss. She backed her head away and smiled, "Alright, you be careful out there! I love you."

"Love you too. Catch you later Dan," Brian said as he gave Danny a solid punch on the arm and began to walk away. Danny tried to swing back, but his dad was already a meter away smirking at him and waving.

"Yeah, I'll see you," Danny said. He took another bite of his cereal and looked back at the television. "Why can't these people find something better to do with their time, like working? They're just wasting everyone's time."

"They're just standing up for what they believe in Danny," Marisa said from the couch. She was still trying to get her papers organized and it was obviously flustering her. She took a break and sipped at her coffee. "There's nothing wrong with demanding change or keeping something from changing. Maybe you should go to a protest at some point. You might learn something," she continued.

"I wouldn't waste my time on stuff like this," Danny said. "It would be easier to just keep your beliefs to yourself and just roll with the flow. A lot less people hate you that way." Danny was never into politics, and it showed whenever he tried to present an argument. It also showed in his history and political science grades.

Marisa looked worried and in a sense, hurt. "Surely you don't believe that. Do you Danny?" she asked.

"Of course," Danny said as he took another bite. He never broke eye contact with the television. "It works in college, why wouldn't it work in the real world?"

"Danny," Marisa said as she took a sip of her coffee and proceeded to cross her hands in her lap as if she was preparing to give a lecture. "If you never stand up for your beliefs, it doesn't matter how many people you befriend, nobody will ever stand with you when you really need them and that's a fact. People will just see you as another student and you won't stick out as someone with an opinion like you should. If you don't agree with something, you need to stand up against it, or it may never change."

Danny slurped down the milk from his cereal, not giving anything Marisa said a second thought. "I'd love to chat about beliefs and junk, but unfortunately I've gotta get to class and do that," Danny said as he put his bowl in the sink and went to his room. He opened the door and started rummaging through the avalanche of clothes to find his book bag. He moved every article of clothing around, but to no avail. "Dammit," he mumbled. "Hey, mom! Is my bag out there?"

He could hear his mom put her paper down and walk around the living room, then a few soft bumps on the wall. She looked behind the couch and yelled back to him, "Yeah, it's behind the couch." He walked out and to her outstretched hand with a book bag on the end of it. "You need to start keeping track of your stuff better. I won't be here to find it for you forever." She lowered her head to give him that look that moms love to give to their kids when they try to teach them a lesson.

"Of course you will," Danny said with a smile. "Love you, mom." He gave her a kiss.

"Love you too, honey," Marisa said as she gave him a hard hug as if it was the last time they'd see each other. Danny heard her speak softly in his ear, "Don't grow up too fast, baby."

Danny headed out the door and across the front lawn towards his car. He looked to his left and saw the neighbor doing the same. He was an older guy, didn't look like he had a job to get to. He was too old for that. His wife came shuffling as quickly as she could out of the door yelling at him for forgetting his wallet. Looks like the guy had the same problem Danny did, old women yelling at him for forgetting his stuff. Danny smirked and continued across the lawn.

To his right, he saw a house that had been abandoned for a few months now. It still had the foreclosure sign in the front yard with some realty company's name on it. His mom would always complain about kids from his old high school breaking into the house and doing things that hoodlums do. He couldn't exactly say he was exempt from that group. He knew he had some good times there during winter break.

He started to think about his friends waiting for him at college. It finally hit him that he'd be graduating in a few months, and he'd probably never see any of them again, unless he needed to call in a favor for something. They'll all get their degrees and be unified for a small ceremony, and the next day, they may never see each other again. They'll all go back to their respective states and try to find a job in this poor job market. It was a dark future, but he was sure that he'd gotten the education he needed to be one step ahead of the pack.

He got into the driver's seat and threw his bag in the back. There were a bunch of fast food bags and other pieces of litter sitting back there from however many days ago. He knew that he should probably clean it up, but who has time for that stuff anymore? He couldn't put his life on hold simply to keep things clean. He put the keys in and got on his way to school.

Danny thought to himself, "I've got pretty good grades and I've got a decent amount of job experience, right? Sure, I'll have some loans to pay off, but if worse comes to worst, I could just join the army, or maybe the navy. Besides, companies love veterans. I can get a job in a snap after that, and there'll be no rush, cause all of my loans will be paid off by the military."

He pulled up to a stoplight and reached into his pocket for his phone. He checked the time. It looked like he'd get to class with plenty time to spare. "Maybe I'll just stop by Charlie's for a bit before class and then walk over to Dame Hall," he thought to himself. He dropped Charlie a text while someone honked behind him. Danny looked up from his phone to the rear view, and of course it's that old guy that had been leaving his house. Apparently he did have somewhere to get to in a hurry. Danny took a few more seconds, just out of spite. He managed to go halfway through the yellow light so the old man got stuck at the red light. Danny chuckled to himself and continued down the road.

After a ten minute drive, Danny had arrived at Charlie's dorm. He walked over to Charlie's window, but of course Charlie was still sleeping, like always. Danny banged as hard as he possibly could on his window and took great joy in the shocked expression on Charlie's face as he dropped to the tile floor from his bed. He looked up at Danny, clearly very upset. He stormed around and opened the front door of the house for Danny to come in.

"Do you realize what time it is?" Charlie asked him.

Danny chuckled and looked down at his phone. "It's about fifteen minutes to class time, bro," Danny said.

Charlie looked down at his phone and freaked. "Shit," He said as he ran faster than Danny had ever seen that kid move back to his room. Danny followed behind him laughing and taking his time.

"You're such an idiot, dude," Danny said. Danny looked to the stairs in time to see Amanda coming down them. She was looking as beautiful as he had remembered her being. She took great pride in her appearance. They'd discussed before that it took her hours simply to get ready for an average day. Kinda weird that someone goes through all the effort she does to look good at eight in the morning while most kids just pull a Charlie and fall out of their beds only moments before class.

Danny waved to her. "Hello, m'lady," he said.

"Danny!" she yelled. "Hey, how are you doing?"

"Pretty solid I'd say," Danny said as he gave her a quick greeting hug. Just to add to Danny's attraction to her, she smelled like a new perfume today. "How are you doing?" he asked.

"Solid as well I suppose!" she said. "Did you study for the exam today?" She held her books in front of her, looking very interested in Danny's answer.

Danny pretty much peed himself. "Exam?" he asked.

"Don't tell me you completely forgot, dude," Charlie yelled from the bathroom. Danny and Amanda looked towards the bathroom door, and then back to each other.

"Crap, I did," Danny said as his heart sank. There goes his day. "Dang. What was it on?" he asked as Charlie came running out of the bathroom with his stuff. His hair had found a way to slightly straighten itself in the time he was in the bathroom.

"It's fine, Danny," Amanda said, shaking her head. "I'll quiz you a bit on the way there." They started off on their journey to Dame Hall. "Basically, it's all going to be on the election today, and the sides of the candidates." Danny tried to think back to who he saw on the news this morning.

"Wasn't it like, Stewart something and David Stone?" he asked. He pretty much knew that he was wrong. Charlie laughed to himself and Danny shot him an angry glance in response.

Amanda giggled a bit. "Well, David Stone and Stewart Marshall," she said. Of course. "Now, Stewart Marshall's a libertarian, and the first one to actually be a frontrunner in, well, ever. He's got an economic plan of making everyone's taxes directly comparable to how much they make. He wants to get the government out of businesses as much as possible in order to avoid corruption of government officials, as we've been seeing a lot recently. He mentioned that he wants to cut spending on unnecessary policies, enough so to save the U.S. billions every year, possibly even trillions."

"Sounds like a pretty great guy," Danny said, not really remembering what Amanda had said. He couldn't even pay attention when it would be the only chance to save himself from failure. With college being that close to ending, how could anyone concentrate on anything?

"Oh he is! He's really inspirational!" Amanda said. She always took so much joy in discussing politics.

"And he wants to legalize pot," Charlie chimed in. "Just sayin'"

Amanda looked as if she'd never heard of marijuana before, as her jaw dropped. "Charlie!" Amanda snapped. "He said he wants to cut the money spent on the police force's 'drug war.' It's bigger than you just getting your fix."

"Either way, it makes him better in my eyes," Charlie smirked as he lit up a cigarette. "I don't see anything wrong with approving of him because of one of his policies. Do you?"

"You're such a loser," Amanda said, shaking her head.

"Look," Danny interrupted. "We're like two minutes away from class and I still don't know jack."

Amanda turned back to him and said, "Sorry, Danny. Anyways, then you have David Stone. He's definitely a hardcore conservative, almost too much so for most republicans on a lot of issues. He's wanted to set up a nation-wide language and religion, wants to make gay marriage illegal, basically get rid of all gun laws, and he wants to spend even more on our military than we're already spending. He's basically just some gun-toting redneck with a stick in his bum."

"Bum?" Charlie laughed. He almost burnt himself on his cigarette.

"I don't cuss as freely as you and Danny do, Charlie," Amanda scolded. They were walking into the building as they spoke more about the exam's material. "But yeah, he's definitely not going to do anything good with our country, like most republicans."

Danny turned to her and noted, "I'm a republican."

Amanda opened the door for Charlie and Danny. She turned and gave Danny a smirk. "Key word: most," she said. Danny walked in and sat in the seat that he always chose: three seats back, and two from the left wall, right next to Charlie and behind Amanda. The professor still wasn't in the classroom so Danny took out his papers and started studying ferociously. He looked over every little thing he had copied from the most recent debate, or at least half of the debate. He studied every single policy that they wanted to change, and every number that was mentioned. It was quickly becoming a hopeless effort.

He must have been sweating over his papers for a while when Charlie said, "Isn't it ten minutes for professors and fifteen for doctors?"

A voice chimed in from across the room in the front row, "Well, he's a doctor, and skipping another class isn't going to help you get over your mental disability,

Charlie." Of course it was Melissa, the class smart ass. She studied every night while everyone else was having fun and dedicated the life story of every professor to memory. It was doubtful that she even knew what color vodka is.

"Thank you, Melissa," Charlie yelled across the room with his head raised slightly. He turned to Danny and whispered, "I'm not staying here all day, dude. I'll see you after class." Charlie stood up and opened the door of the classroom to leave.

"Ah, getting the door for me, are you Charlie?" Professor Ivan said from the other side of the door. Everyone laughed as Charlie walked back to his desk and sunk down in his chair. The professor looked especially excited today. His hair wasn't even parted over his bald spot in the front like it normally was. He put down his briefcase in a hurry and immediately looked out to the class. "I've got some good news for you all today!" he announced. "As you know, today's election day, and you all have an exam today."

"Don't remind me," Charlie muttered with his head still resting on the desk in front of him.

"So I decided last night on something with one condition," Professor Ivan said. "You all are not required to take the exam today, unless you really want to." Danny's heart rose back up into his chest and a stupid smile formed on his face. Charlie's head shot up and his face took the same shape that Danny's had. "Only condition, go out and vote. Also, I'll be cancelling class today in order to give you all the opportunity to go out and vote! So I'll see you all next Thursday."

Charlie practically ran out of the room. Danny stood up with a huge grin on his face and looked to Amanda. "Lucky break, huh?" he laughed.

She glared at him. "Easy for you to say. You didn't study all night," Amanda mumbled. They met up with

Charlie in the hall and began walking back to Charlie's dorm.

Charlie was jumping around in the hall. "I've never been so happy in my life." He said through uncontrollable laughter.

Amanda smirked, and Danny just laughed and shook his head. "What a pathetic life you must live," Amanda told him.

"You're just pissed because you and Melissa studied together all night while Danny and I just enjoyed the night," Charlie said while giving Amanda a wag of his finger and resuming his happy gait.

"Exactly," Amanda pointed out. "And don't rag on me for studying for Melissa. The chick knows what she's talking about."

"Whatever," Charlie said. "The point is, we're going home and I'm getting trashed!" It really was sad how much Charlie looked forward to getting drunk on a Tuesday. Then again, it had been his tradition all through college.

"Don't forget we still need to go vote, Charlie!" Amanda reminded him. "Danny, can you drive us there?" Amanda asked him with a smile. Who was he to deny her a ride to the voting booths?

"I don't see why not," he told her. The entire walk back to Charlie's dorm, Charlie was bursting from the inside with happiness. He'd go run for president himself if it meant that he didn't have to go to that class. They dropped their bags off in Charlie's room. It smelled like some sort of cheese and there was an empty tequila bottle sitting on the fifteen inch television. Charlie was living the high life.

They loaded up into Danny's car and started down the road. "Yo, Danny, can we listen to some music?" Charlie yelled from the back.

"Yeah, I'm down," Danny told him. He handed his music player back to Charlie and Charlie started scrolling away. He looked as if he was reading the most exciting book of his life.

"Are you guys excited to vote?" Amanda asked with a smile on her face.

Danny leaned back in his seat. "I mean, I guess," he said. "I didn't really know anything about these guys until an hour ago so definitely not as much as you."

"Maybe you should start researching these things," Amanda scorned. "It's your responsibility as an American!"

"Chill, Amanda. We're not all political science majors," Danny joked.

Amanda just shook her head. "Ha!" Charlie yelled, "I know what we're listening to!"

A familiar breakdown came out through the speakers, and Charlie rocked out in the back seat as he often did. A bunch of guitar riffs and screams just drove Charlie to the point of insanity the entire ride. Amanda looked out of the window, obviously annoyed by Charlie's feet kicking the back of her chair. She looked to Danny for some sort of solution, but he just sort of shrugged and laughed as if he was trying to say, "That's Charlie."

They drove into the parking lot and turned off the car. Their little entourage walked up to the front doors of the elementary school turned voting center. There were campaign signs literally everywhere. Every step they took led them to another sign, and everywhere they looked, they saw another five. "Stone for President!" "Marshall 2020!" There were a few protesters there as well yelling about Stone like the ones on the news had. They kept yelling the same things about how he shouldn't be allowed to run because of some crimes he might have committed. Danny thought about what his dad said this morning about them and laughed to himself.

They walked in through the front door and went to their respective booths. Danny looked down at the computer screen in front of him. This would be the first time he had ever voted, and it hadn't hit him at all. He picked up the little pen and tapped his chin. Danny thought about what he had heard from Amanda. Danny definitely wouldn't mind his tuition getting lowered a bit, so he checked the box next to "Stewart A. Marshall."

He walked out of the booth and met up with Amanda. Charlie took much longer, as usual. Danny picked up a little sticker that said, "I voted!" He figured that the professor would probably need some sort of proof that they actually voted and didn't just say that they did . . .

Once they got out of the building, Amanda asked, "So who did you guys vote for?" as if she couldn't wait to find out, or as if she didn't already know.

"I just chose Marshall," Danny told her. "From what you told me, he sounded a lot better than Stone."

She got all excited. "So did I!" she yelled as if it was a surprise. "How about you Charlie?"

"I wrote myself in," he responded, looking down at his shoes. Amanda and Danny looked over at him with the most puzzled looks, then to each other, then back to him.

"Are you serious?" Amanda asked.

"Yeah," Charlie replied, looking very proud of himself.

"There's no chance you'd ever win, Charlie. Why would you do that?" Amanda questioned.

"You never know, Amanda." Nothing could ever beat Charlie logic.

"I know that nobody else in this country knows who you are and the people that do would never vote for you, even if you were the only candidate."

"Harsh. I'll keep that in mind whenever you tell me something that you dream of doing. Then I'll crush those dreams like you just did mine." Charlie got in the back seat and turned on some more music.

Danny drove back to the college with his friends and dropped off Charlie at his dorm. "I'll see you later, Charlie," he yelled out the window to him.

"For sure, dude," Charlie replied. He bent down and looked in at Amanda. "Are you coming?"

"Nah," she replied. "I'm heading over to Danny's to watch the tallying of the votes."

Charlie smiled, then looked at Danny. "Get some," he said, reaching out for a fist bump. Danny laughed and gave Charlie his fist pump. Amanda tried to look mad, but she couldn't help but chuckle.

"Get out of here, Charlie," Danny told him, trying not to burst into uncontrollable laughter. Charlie walked towards his dorm room and gave a final finger point to the two and walked into the front door. His hair was blowing all over the place, so it was doubtful that he even knew where he was going.

"What a loser," Amanda said to Danny.

"It happens," he told her. He stepped on the gas and started back to his house. Amanda turned on some music and they drove down the road listening to some pop-punk and enjoying the day.

CHAPTER TWO

THE SPARK

Amanda and Danny walked inside Danny's front door to an empty house. They looked around the entryway, seeing nothing but their shadows in front of them. Danny shut the door, and the two put their bags on the coffee table. They moved to the couch and sat to reflect on the day. "So when are the polls closed?" Danny asked.

Amanda looked down at her phone and checked the time. "Probably not for a few more hours," she said.

Amanda began to text a bit and Danny stood back up. "Cool. Do you want anything to eat or drink?" He asked as he opened the pantry and looked around. Nothing but ingredients for dinner and things that didn't look appealing in any way.

"Nah, I'll be fine, you good host, you," Amanda joked. Danny looked over his shoulder and smiled. He returned to scanning the pantry hopelessly for anything edible, but it was proving to be a hopeless battle.

"I'm actually pretty pumped to see who won the election," He told Amanda, as he examined a random box of noodles.

"You should be!" Amanda said. "It's a piece of American history, not to mention our future."

"I guess so," Danny said, not really listening. He finally fixed his eyes on some chips and returned to the couch. They opened the bag and started fulfilling their cravings for junk food. For the longest time, they basically just sat in silence, occasionally interrupting it with the crunching of a chip. They reflected on the unexpected events of the day, making their own predictions on what the night might bring. Danny looked around the house from the couch trying to figure out what they could possibly do, aside from sit awkwardly on the couch eating junk food.

Amanda broke the silence with, "So, what do you normally do around here?" She took some chips from the bag and began to eat them bit by bit.

Danny tried to answer while simultaneously stuffing his face with as much food as he could hold in his hand, "Well . . . this," he said as he ate his handful of chips.

"What a life you live."

"Eh, it's not as glorious as you think. I get bored every once in a while. I usually just head over to Charlie's." Danny could tell that Amanda was getting bored. Amanda continuously looked back down at her phone, as if she was waiting for a call.

"Seems pretty chill. However," she grabbed the bag from his hands, "I think we should do something else." She smiled at him and took closed the bag.

"What did you have in mind?" Danny asked. He smiled at her a bit. It was obvious what he had in mind.

"Let's see what's in your room," Amanda said as she stood from her seat. "You forget that you haven't even given me the grand tour."

"Ah, how rude of me! Right this way," Danny said as he stood. They walked past the wooden stairs that led to the basement, Amanda looking at all of the baby pictures on the walls the entire time. She would occasionally stop and giggle at an embarrassing photo of Danny from school or as a baby. They made it to the end of the hall, and went to the door of the last room they reached. "This would be my parent's room," Danny said.

Danny opened the door and the two entered. Amanda looked around in amazement at all of the antiques Danny's parents clung to in order to fill up their room. She went to one side of the room and began picking up small items sitting on the dresser. "What's this thing?" She asked as she picked up a small eagle statue standing on a branch. The eagle had an American flag sitting behind it, the entire scene in some sort of stone.

"That would be an eagle," Danny pointed out.

Amanda shot Danny an angry look. "Thanks. I mean is there any significance to it?" she restated.

"You're asking the wrong guy. I didn't even know half of this existed," Danny responded.

"Some tour guide you are." Amanda returned the eagle to its spot and turned to Danny.

"I try," Danny said with a shrug of his shoulders. They left the room, and Danny shut the door behind Amanda. They walked to the next door on their tour. Danny opened the door to the bathroom and Amanda peered inside.

Like the bedroom, Amanda began to pick up an item sitting on the back of the toilet and turned to Danny while examining the item closely. "What's th . . . " she began.

Danny cut her off. "Don't tell me you're about to ask me questions about the bathroom," he said.

"Am I not allowed to do that? Man, not only are you a terrible tour guide, you're a jerk," Amanda pointed out.

"My mistake," Danny said in the most sarcastic way possible. He began to point at every item in the room. "This is the toilet, often used to 'take care of business' as most Americans have been known to say," he said in an obnoxious tour guide voice.

Amanda pushed Danny out of the way. "You're an ass," she said. She walked into the hallway and began walking away.

"Wait! I didn't get to show you the sink!" Danny said while chasing her down the hall, laughing at how clever he thought he was along the way. She ended up opening the door to his room and stood in the doorway. She saw the mountain of clothes, the dirty mirror, and the king-sized bed with messy covers on it. She put her hands on her hips and looked around as if she was at the top of a hill looking down.

"Man, you really do live a life of luxury," Amanda said, standing in the doorway looking around, almost scared to step any further into the room. "I never knew."

"Hey, you don't hate on a guy's room. That's like if I insulted the music you love so much," Danny said. He knew how dumb the analogy that had just slipped out of his mouth sounded and began to scratch the back of his head.

"How does that even make sense when we listen to similar music?" Amanda asked with a confused expression. She ignored his stupidity and turned back to the task at hand. Finally overcoming her fear of Danny's room, she stepped further in, almost falling over the clothes.

"It just does," Danny pointed out, even though the conversation had ended. He walked into the room behind her and said, "So now that I've given you the grand tour, what would you like to do?"

"I mean," Amanda said, looking over to the bed. "I would like to take a nap on this nice bed of yours." Score! Amanda climbed into the bed and got under the covers. Danny's excitement reached a boiling point, but he attempted to keep his composure throughout his smooth series of moves.

"Yeah, I could go for a nap," he said as he started to lift the covers next to her.

He got one leg in before Amanda interrupted and put her hand out. "Hey! If you want to take a nap you can go somewhere else!" she said as she pulled the covers over her shoulders.

"Seriously? I mean, it's not my bed or anything," Danny said as he began to get out of the bed slowly.

"Yep. Go to the couch, sir," Amanda commanded.

Disappointment took over Danny. "Wow, you're fun."

He began to walk his way to the couch downstairs when Amanda yelled after him, "Maybe you'll be a better tour guide next time!" Danny stopped for a moment and contemplated making a sarcastic remark, but nothing came out so he continued his walk of shame. He walked down the wood stairs and grabbed a blanket from the closet. He went to the couch and laid down.

The election popped into his mind. He was curious of who was going to win, but no more than one would be curious about what kind of soda the nation prefers. It seemed as if an election took place every other day, or at least that's what it seemed like to Danny. Before he knew it, he'd bored himself to sleep.

As he dreamt, he saw himself sitting in front of his house enjoying a beautiful day. He was sipping on some sort of drink and watching a man walk down the street with his dogs on a leash. Danny waved to the man and he waved back. The dogs barked at Danny, but he didn't pay them any mind. They didn't seem threatening.

Danny woke up to the sound of the front door opening. He squinted his eyes open just enough to make out the figure of his mom standing in the doorway with a bag in each hand. "Hey there, honey!" she said as she bent down and kissed him on the forehead. Danny simply tucked his face into the blankets, trying to get back to the dream he was just enjoying. "How was school today?" she continued.

Danny grumbled and turned onto his back, eyes still closed. "Pretty good," he mumbled. "We got out of class early because the professor wanted us to vote." Danny rubbed his eyes and then pulled the blanket up to his chest.

"Oh!" his mom said. "And did you?"

"Sure did, for Marshall," he said with as much enthusiasm as his tired body could muster.

"Ah! That's my boy! I really like that Marshall. I know you're not really into politics, but he's a really smart guy, and I really feel like he can turn this economy around." Marisa looked at Danny and noticed his lack of enthusiasm. "You don't seem very excited about the election."

Danny gave a sigh and turned his head to just barely make out his mom in the peripherals of his vision. "You should talk to Amanda about all of that stuff," he suggested. "She's a lot more into it all than I am." He turned back onto his stomach and attempted to go back to sleep. He let out another sigh into the pillow and closed his eyes tightly, telling himself he wouldn't open them again until he was asleep.

"Is she here?" his mom asked, now putting the bags on the coffee table.

"Yeap," Danny said into the pillow.

His mom practically jumped in place, almost knocking the bags off of the table. "Oh! Where?" she asked.

"Upstairs," Danny grumbled.

"Alright, I'll let you sleep," Marisa said. He heard Mom go upstairs and knock on his door. After a short break from the noise, he heard her yell, "Amanda! How are you?" Danny could only imagine what a fun way that was for Amanda to wake up. He just sat on the couch arguing with himself about whether he should get up or just go back to sleep. After hearing his mom talking for the longest time, he finally heard Amanda's voice as they walked down the stairs to the living room.

"Yeah," Amanda said. "I think Marshall is so much better than Stone. I mean, he's never been accused of murder for one thing, and he's not just another politician. I feel like he's one of us."

"I try to tell Brian that all the time," Danny's mom said, holding Amanda's shoulder as they walked. "He likes Marshall, but still just sees him as a candidate." As they walk into the room, Danny decided to sit up and attempt to be social. "Ah! You've decided to join us!" his mom practically yelled at his face.

"Danny, your bed's amazing," Amanda said with a smirk. His mom let out a bit of a chuckle. She always did think that Amanda was hilarious, then again, she thought that about all of his friends.

"Yeah, I know," he told her while rubbing his eyes vigorously. "It would've been nice to have slept there instead of this couch." His neck gave way to the weight of his head and he leaned back against the couch.

"Well," his mom said. "I'm glad that you gave it to her like a gentleman." She gave Amanda a little elbow bump. She always ganged up on Danny whenever Amanda came over. It was a habit that she never seemed to notice when Danny pointed it out.

Brian stormed into the house, scaring everyone in the room, and changing entire mood of the room completely. "I can't fucking believe this," he kept muttering, stomping around as if he was on a mission of the highest importance.

"Honey, what's going on?" Marisa asked, trying to walk to Brian and calm him down.

He went storming over to the couch. "Move Danny," he commanded. He picked up the remote and turned on the television. He was sweating profusely and looked as if he had just ran over someone on the way into the driveway. His lack of a response to anyone's statements was worrying to say the least.

"Dad," Danny muttered, much louder now, but still very slowly. "Seriously, what's going on. You're freaking me out." Danny turned his head until it was basically right in front of his dad's face.

His dad flipped through the channels as quickly as he could until he got to the news station. They passed a few commercials and eventually came to the same channel they had been watching this morning. What they all saw next, left everyone in the room with mouths agape. They all knew the seriousness of what was unfolding on the television in front of them. Instantly, all of their hands rose to their mouths, their heads, or their eyes, rubbing them in disbelief.

They saw images of a large crowd outside of the White House. They all seemed to be waiting on something. At first, they thought it might be a protest, but they soon realized how wrong they truly were. Many pictures of Stewart Marshall from his campaign began filling the screen in a sort of slideshow with reporters speaking behind them. "Still no reports on how it took place, but officers are looking for answers," the reporter said. "The entire situation is unfolding in a manner that the country has never seen in its history." They kept repeating the same things, all with a sense of disbelief in their voices.

Danny read the headline at the bottom of the screen: "Candidate Stewart Marshall Found Dead."

The room was completely quiet. One could hear footsteps a block away, had the television not been on. None of them could believe what they were seeing. They listened to the anchorman speaking with the images still filling the screen. "All we know right now is that Stewart Marshall is indeed dead, found with a bullet wound to his skull in his campaign bus. The body was discovered about a half an hour ago by one of his campaign managers. Officers are refusing to comment right now as they are still investigating possible leads. We'll go to our reporter Steven near the White House now where a large crowd has gathered to both mourn and to get answers as they are delivered from the front of the White House. Steven, do you have any idea what's going to happen with this change in the political race so close to the decision?

"Well Dan, since there was no official vice-president, we can't go to Marshall's choice for vice-president. Basically, unless Stone wins the presidential election, we'll be stuck with the current incumbent for a while as new candidates are lined up and a decision is made on who will be president based on another vote. The real kicker, is that the deadline has not been met for voting, so people can still go out and vote. They are now met with the decision to either try to get Marshall to win and then force our country into this big situation of trying to choose another president, or vote for Stone and get a president as soon as possible. It's a situation that this country has never been met with."

Danny's mom put her arm around Amanda to comfort her, both still had a look of shock filling their faces. The anchor continued the conversation with the reporter, "Would you recommend that people vote for Stone at this point? It seems to me like the other option could bring this country into chaos."

"I mean, it's just my opinion, but it would definitely help out the country a lot more than keeping our current president who hasn't done much to improve our country in most people's eyes in the past year and most just want out of office as soon as possible. Stone has been a politician for a while and knows what he's doing so it would be the people's best bet. I wish that there were more options, but at this point, it's second best, or chaos."

"Thanks Steven, it's certainly a dark day, and we'll continue to deliver updates as soon as we get them."

The silence they all maintained was suddenly broken at the end of this bit of information. "This is bullshit," Brian yelled. He punched the couch and put his face into his hands. He seemed as if he was on the verge of tears, seeing his country thrown into such an amount of confusion. It was probably frustration getting to him. It was a feeling that they could all share.

"Brian," Marisa tried to reason with him. "What's so bad with just getting Stone? He's a lot better than . . . "

"It's not about if Stone's better than nothing," Brian said as he looked up to her with a face filled with sorrow and anger. "We voted for who we voted for and now we're basically stuck with one candidate or something that could wreck our country. We're stuck and there's nothing we can do because our government isn't prepared. Our democracy just went out the window and you're trying to tell me that we should settle for second best?"

"It's not that bad," she said in a lowered tone. She got down to his level on the couch and put her hand on his knee. "Stone's a pretty good politician," she pointed out. "We might not agree with everything he says, but it's better than nothing."

"I don't give a damn how he's a decent politician!" Brian said. "If we don't want him in office, we should have the other guy, but he was murdered by some asshole that obviously doesn't care about the outcome that could potentially destroy our country." Danny's dad stood up and left the room, not being able to handle the situation any longer.

"He's right," Amanda said. "This isn't right. We need to find other candidates to vote for. We can't have this sort of totalitarian election where we're going to get one person whether we like it or not." She was just looking at the floor shaking her head, trying to make sense of it all.

"There's nothing we can do," Marisa said. She cupped her hands over her mouth and walked out of the room. She got on the phone in her bedroom and made a phone call to her mom to talk about what just happened. Danny looked over at Amanda. She was sitting on the floor against the wall and looked deep in thought. For the first time in Danny's life, he could say that that was concerned with politics. He couldn't believe that he was alive to see a politician assassinated before he even got a chance to take office. It was shocking.

The room remained quiet, besides the reporters and anchors continuing to relay the same details over and over. Danny thought the whole situation over in his head. It was all starting to hit him. The country was without a president, and the only person able to step up was someone that every earlier was said to have no chance of winning. Was it really better than nothing? Should the country have to settle for someone that had been accused of horrendous war crimes, but had a political background? Surely there had to be something else. Unfortunately, the news did nothing in terms of helping Danny convince himself of this.

They waited in this silent tension for hours until the polls closed and the ballots were counted. Danny watched as the states on the anchor's map began to light up with the color red. One after the other, the states turned, as if it was a disease spreading across the map at an alarming rate. Finally, the anchor came over the air saying, "We have the results for the 2020 presidential election. After counting up all of the votes, David Stone has won almost every state in the United States, one of the biggest blowouts in history. In the case of the investigation, the police have a main suspect in custody. He was found with a gun of the same caliber as the one that killed Marshall minutes after the assassination by a hotel maid. The maid then called police and the suspect has been arrested. The name is not being released, but we have heard word that the suspect has no connections to Stone in order to quell any that have that thought in mind. We'll keep you updated."

"This can't be real," Amanda said, still sitting on the floor, still retaining the same amount of shock that she had before.

"I wish it wasn't," Brian said. He had returned to the room after calming down to watch the events unravel. He had his arm around his wife, as if to give her relief as she watched these horrific reports. "This is insane."

They sat around the television all night as more updates about the suspect and the election were coming through. At the end of the night, they were just as confused as they were in the beginning.

Amanda headed back to her dorm and attempted to brush off all of the shock of the night. She watched more of the reports and ended up breaking down. She'd been into politics for the longest time, and everything she thought she knew was thrown out the window. She researched Marshall's views to a point that she thought she knew him. She took it much harder than Danny had.

Marisa eventually gave up on trying to stay awake through all of it. Her emotions had worn her out and she still needed to go to work the next day. "Are you coming to bed, dear?" she muttered to Brian. He simply shook his head with his hands on his chin. She moped her way up the stairs and into her room.

Danny looked over to his dad and gave him a hug. He could feel his dad's frustration flow between them. Danny began to get emotional at seeing the ones he loved hurt as much as they did. He didn't give a damn about politics, but the pain that politics was causing his parents was too much for him to handle. He tried to transfer sympathy over to his father in the hug, but to no avail. His dad just returned to the couch and stared down at the floor, thinking about what was going to become of the country that he had worked so hard for all his life.

Danny went upstairs and went straight to bed without even changing. None of them got any sleep that night. Odds were, nobody in the nation did.

CHAPTER THREE

THE SEARCH FOR THE TRUTH

"The protests in Boston have been continuing, despite the death of presidential candidate Stewart Marshall," Danny and his family heard on the news a while after election day. "Everything continued as they normally have been. Many camped out in public parks and marches that resulted in arrests as usual, however, it seems that protesters have been met with a new group in their midst. A group calling themselves 'The Truth Committee' have been showing up at protests throughout the country. They have claimed that the death of Presidential Candidate Stewart Marshall was in no way an act of random violence. The group says that the assassin was hired by President David Stone in order to win the election and several members of congress were paid to suggest that David Stone take power as president within minutes of Marshall's death. However, investigations into the murder show that the assassin didn't have any connection to Stone, which would lead us to believe that it's just another group of conspiracy theorists."

"What did they call themselves?" Marisa asked the family at breakfast. "The Truth Committee? Sounds like something from a movie." She flipped through her papers as usual.

"As if the protests weren't already dumb enough," Danny said. "Now they've got these dumb asses walking around yelling about something that doesn't make any sense in the slightest."

"Yeah, I mean, they did an investigation into the killing," Marisa commented. "And they said that there's no connection between the murderer and Stone. Crackpots will be crackpots I suppose. I guess we shouldn't be so surprised that someone would question something that we already got the answer to."

"That's what I'm saying," Danny said as he ate his breakfast.

Brian was silent on the couch with his hands on his chin. He had been taking the murder to heart, almost as if Marshall was his brother. "Dad are you alright?" Danny asked him, moving over to the couch to sit next to him with his breakfast accompanying him.

Brian looked to the side to see Danny in his peripherals. "Danny," his dad began. "Why do you insist on saying that this group is completely wrong?"

Danny was confused. "I mean, the investigators said that there was no connection between the killer and Stone," Danny said. "Those guys are trained to look at any lead possible and they didn't find anything that suggested that Stone was involved. So why wouldn't I?"

Danny's dad leaned back in the couch and sighed. "Danny, you can't follow what the media tells you like it's always the truth," he said. "They've been proved wrong countless times. I raised you to be open-minded, and I want you to grow up staying that way."

Danny was speechless. "Dad, are you agreeing with the protesters?" he asked. Marisa seemed interested to hear the answer as well.

"I'm not agreeing, but I'm not disagreeing," Brian said. "I just don't know, but I'm not going to immediately discredit them just because the media does." He took a quick pause to look up to the ceiling and collect his thoughts. Marisa had stopped sorting her papers and had turned her full attention to the conversation. Brian looked back to Danny and just smiled. "Would you like to go play poker with me and some of the guys when I get home from work tonight?" he asked. It was a horribly random question.

"I mean," Danny paused, still very confused. "I suppose so."

His dad gave him a pat on the shoulder and said, "Good. I've got to go to work now though." He gave his wife a kiss and left the house. Danny just sat on the couch trying to collect his thoughts. He looked over and his mom had a similar, confused, expression.

"Do you think we offended him?" Marisa asked, looking down at the counter. She too was attempting to figure out what had just happened.

"I think so," Danny said, feeling ashamed. "I've never seen dad like that. It was weird."

"Yeah," Marisa said before they sat in silence for a bit. "But you've got to get to class. Get your stuff and head off." Danny grabbed his stuff and drove off to school. The world seemed so much different to him. It's as if the death of Marshall was really putting a shroud over the country. The morning sunlight seemed to be a bit more dim than usual, signaling to everyone that hadn't heard that something horrible had happened . . . The trees on Danny's way to Charlie's seemed a bit less green and even Danny's complexion didn't seem as bright as it usually was.

Danny pulled up to Charlie's dorm and Charlie came to open the door for him. Amanda came downstairs and they sat in Charlie's room waiting for Charlie to get ready. They had their usual talk about schoolwork and how much college sucked, and then sat in silence. Danny wanted to talk to Amanda about what his dad had said this morning, but he felt so weird just thinking about it. There was no way that Amanda would ever agree with what his dad thought.

"Amanda," Danny finally got the strength to say.

"Yeah?" she responded, looking over at him.

"Um . . . have you heard of that Truth Committee thing?" Danny asked, attempting to let out no signal that would point out that he knew anything more than he should.

Amanda sat looking at the floor near Danny's feet for a bit. She seemed very unsure of her answer for some reason, even though it was just a yes or no question. "Yeah, it's a really weird concept," she finally responded. "It seems like any time that something tragic happens a conspiracy springs up, though. It'll probably be gone soon."

Danny looked forward, feeling a bit better that he asked. "Yeah, you're probably right," he said. Truly, he didn't know how to feel. His own father seemed to stand up for something that so many others seemed to think was some sort of joke. In a way, he felt sort of ashamed of his father. He was disgusted with himself for feeling this way, but how could he not? He just kept telling himself that his dad didn't agree with them, he just didn't put the idea they presented down immediately.

"Alright, go time," Charlie said, finally getting out of the bathroom. Danny put on a fake smile and they all walked to class.

They walked the entire way in silence. Danny just stared at the ground the whole time, very deep in thought. Amanda was looking around at everything they passed as if she was looking for something. Even Charlie wasn't as full of energy as he would normally be. They were a depressing sight. They got to the door of Dame and Charlie asked them, "Are you guys feeling okay? You haven't said a word the entire way here." Danny and Amanda just smiled and nodded. "I don't understand you guys," he said as he held the door for his odd friends.

They walked into class and waited for the professor. He was late once again. When he finally came in, even he was acting depressed. "Well everyone, today we're going to cover some current events," Professor Ivan said as he put his suitcase down quickly. "As you may know, there has been this movement rising up called the Truth Committee." Of course he had to talk about that. Professor Ivan wrote their name up on the board in big letters. "Now can anyone tell me about this movement?" he asked, turning his attention toward the class.

Melissa was the first to raise her hand, as always. "They're a group of conspiracy theorists that think that the assassin that killed candidate Marshall was hired by candidate Stone in order to win the presidential election," she belted out with pride.

"Alright," the professor said. He wrote what she said under the previous writing. "Does anyone want to add onto that?" Another kid raised his hand on the opposite side of the room.

"They're a bunch of nut jobs," the student told Professor Ivan. The class couldn't help but laugh at the outburst. This only made Danny feel even worse that his dad defended had them.

"But Tyler," the professor responded. "Don't you think that people have a right to speak their minds, even if the masses might not agree with it?"

"I mean, they can," Tyler said as he prepared another smartass remark. "Doesn't mean they should." The class laughed again.

A kid near Danny nearly snapped. "How can you be that ignorant?" the student asked.

"What? Are you a part of the Committee, Brandon?" Tyler laughed.

"I am, and I guarantee anyone in that group could destroy you in a debate about politics, Tyler," Brandon defended. "Everyone that I tell that I'm in that group thinks I'm some dumb ass that doesn't deserve to speak up and it's completely contrary to what we're taught by our founding fathers. We fought for our independence so we *could* speak our minds freely, and it's people like you that make everyone else scared to do so. I can guarantee you that there are other people in this room that believe that Stone had something to do with the death of Marshall and they're just scared to say it because they know that their intelligence will lose credit that they've worked hard to gain."

Tyler was completely quiet after that. "Very interesting point, Brandon," the professor said to break the awkward silence following the conflict. "Well, everyone in this room should understand that we're here to learn, not be judged. You're all open to speak your minds, whether other students may agree with it or not, like Brandon said." He took a quick pause. "Is there anyone else here that side with Brandon on this one?" Nobody raised their hands. "Come on, I promise that I'll make sure you can have your say without someone else in this class cutting you down." Still nobody raised their hands. Professor Ivan looked around, just waiting for someone to raise their hand so he could give them a pat on the back. "Alright, well if nobody . . . " he stopped short. He let out a small smile. Danny looked around and in front of him to see what fool raised their hand. Then he noticed that Amanda was raising her hand. "Ah, Amanda. I'm proud of you for standing up for what you believe. Do you have anything you'd like to contribute to the discussion?"

Amanda looked more nervous than Danny had ever seen her. He felt like she could tell that he was shocked that she believed in the Committee's ideals after that morning's discussion. "Well," she began. "I just feel like there's so much evidence that points to David Stone having something to do with it. The murder itself could have just been an unfortunate event, but the fact that immediately after, congressmen were saying that Stone should become president since the other way to go would leave us without a good president for a while is really suspicious to me. From the moment that the media was pushing voters to go out and vote for Stone even while there was a tragedy taking place, I knew that Stone had to have something to do with it. I think it's just a matter of time before we find out the truth."

Danny just sat in his seat stone-faced. He suddenly felt so much better about his dad defending the Committee. Maybe defending a group for not following what they're told all the time was actually really wise of his dad. Danny couldn't help but smile. It seemed like a lot of other kids in class also seemed very stunned to the point that they found themselves smiling.

Professor Ivan even seemed very impressed. "I'm so glad that I have students as wise as the ones in this room," he said with a smile. "I'm very proud of you all for doing your research and promoting free speech."

Before long, class was over and Danny's eagerness to talk to Amanda was at a boiling point. "So I thought you didn't support them?" he asked as they left the building once he managed to catch up to Amanda.

"Actually," Amanda said. "I said that it probably won't last long."

"Why do you think that?" Danny asked.

Amanda was hesitant. "Because of people like Tyler," she said. Danny suddenly felt terrible about himself. He had acted just as Tyler did about the situation. He'd believed that the protests were a joke, and the Committee was a joke. "It's just so frustrating to try to get people to listen when everyone has their hands over their ears," Amanda continued. "I support the way that the Committee is trying its hardest to get people to lower their hands and listen up. If anything, I wish people would just take their opinion into account rather than immediately shutting the Committee down."

Danny felt a lot more understanding of his dad now. "I can see where you're coming from," Danny said, meaning it a lot more than Amanda realized. "It's gotta be hard trying to spread a message that nobody agrees with."

Amanda looked at Danny and nodded. She then looked away, then back. "Hey, Danny, what are you doing tonight?" she asked.

He got excited, but then realized he had already promised his dad that he'd go with him tonight. "Oh, I've gotta go hang out with my dad tonight. Sorry," he said with his head down.

Amanda only looked slightly disappointed as she said, "Dang, well it's okay."

"I mean, I'll go," Charlie butted in with a smile.

"No, Charlie," she responded quickly.

"Damn, you just love cutting me down." Charlie said, seeming pretty pissed off.

"It's not that I don't want to hang out with you Charlie," Amanda began. "It's just that I don't think you would want to join me in what I'm planning on doing tonight."

"Well what are you planning on doing?" Charlie questioned.

"It's not important," Amanda spit out quickly. "Just know that you would hate it." She seemed a lot more nervous than anyone would expect someone to be over such a small question.

"Fine," Charlie said. By this time, they had gotten back to Charlie's and Danny was heading towards his car to go home.

Danny took a moment to collect his thoughts before leaving. So many things were flying through his mind. Where was Amanda trying to go? Why couldn't Charlie go? What would his dad think when he told him that Amanda was a part of the Committee?

He arrived home and sat around, anxious for his dad to get home. He really wanted to treat his dad differently than he had this morning. He was eager to make sure his dad knew that he supported what his dad was doing when he had defended the Committee. Until then, Danny just turned on the news and watched more footage of the protests that were now taking place in other states.

"Protests in Washington D.C. got violent today when protesters attempted to surround the White House. Many members of the Truth Committee had attempted to jump the fence of the White House and ran to the front door to sit and wait for answers, all of whom were arrested, many of which were either tazed or pepper sprayed."

"Well," Danny thought. "Looks like they're gunna be called crazy some more."

After a while, Danny's dad walked through the front door. "Are you ready?" he asked immediately. He didn't even take a moment to get himself settled.

"Yeah, I'm pumped," Danny responded.

"Good! Let me just go grab my other suitcase," Brian said. Danny waited in the living room. He put together everything that he would say to his dad when they got into the car. His dad returned and they started their drive to his dad's friend's house.

For a while, Danny sat composing his conversation in his mind until he found himself ready to speak. He looked to his dad and took the shot. "Hey, dad," he said to gain his attention. "Guess what we were learning about in class today."

"What were you learning about in class today?" his dad asked with enthusiasm that seemed fake.

"We talked a lot about the Truth Committee," Danny said.

"Did you now?" Brian asked, his enthusiasm seeming very real now. "Did any students support it?"

"Yeah, a couple kids stood up for it like you had and spoke against a kid that called it stupid," Danny said proudly. "They really seemed to defend the fact that the Committee stood for freedom of speech and said that people shouldn't be scared to speak their minds. It was really inspirational. Even Amanda said that she supported the Truth Committee."

"Huh," Brian said as he rubbed his cheek. "So do you still feel the same way you did this morning about them?"

Danny saw this as his golden opportunity. There was a spark in his dad's voice and Danny wasn't about to miss his chance to regain his father's love. "Nah, I can definitely see where the Committee is coming from," he said with confidence. "They're definitely educated and they have every right to stand up for what they believe in, whether I agree with what they say or not. They're really brave."

Danny could see his dad smile with pride. "Well I'm glad you think that way, son," Brian said. "It makes an old guy proud." Danny was so happy that he could make his dad feel better.

"So where's your friend at?" Danny asked to break the silence following his dad's statement.

"He's actually right here," Brian said as he pulled the car into his friend's driveway and he and Danny got out and walked to the front door. The house was really nice. It was only one story, but the lawn and the porch were really nice. There was a small wooden swing that looked like it had just been put up today surrounded by a few small trees that were potted on the porch. The windows had dark curtains over them, so all Danny could see was light, until one of them moved showing someone's face trying to see who was outside.

Soon after, the door opened and a tall man was standing there smiling. "Brian! How are you doing?" the man asked.

Brian gave the guy a hug. "I'm doing great, how are you doing?" Brian asked the guy.

"Well I'm doing pretty well myself," The man said before he paused and looked at Danny, then back to Brian.

"Oh, this is Danny," Brian said as if he'd completely forgotten that Danny had been next to him. "He's my son."

"Ah," the man said. "Nice to meet you Danny. I'm Adam. Your dad and I work together."

"Nice to meet you too," Danny said.

"Well everyone's in the basement, I'll meet you guys there," Adam said as he let the two into his home. Danny and his dad went downstairs to meet the rest of the people there. There was a round table in the middle of the room and some chairs along the wall.

Danny's dad went around greeting people and introducing them to Danny. Then his dad stopped at a guy making coffee and pointed to Danny. The man turned around, and Danny saw that it was his uncle Chuck. Most people just called him Champ. It was some high school thing.

"How have you been, Danny?" Champ asked.

"Pretty great, how have you been Uncle Chuck?" he responded.

"Pretty damn good, despite all of this political shit," Champ said. He always had let his vulgarity make up for his lack of an advanced vocabulary. "I'm glad that your dad invited you to this. It will be a good experience for you."

"Yeah," Danny responded. "I just hope I don't lose all of my money." Danny let out an awkward laugh, but soon realized he was the only one in the conversation laughing.

Champ looked confused and asked, "What do you mean?"

"Well, I'm not that great at poker," Danny said nervously, hoping that his uncle would laugh to relieve the awkwardness.

Champ stood there with the most confused face on. He turned to Brian and raised his hand as if he was trying to say, "What's wrong with this guy?"

Brian said, "I'll explain it to Danny. I told him we were going to play poker tonight."

Champ suddenly completely understood what was going on, but Danny just took on Champ's confused look. Champ turned to Danny and nodded as if he didn't notice the dumbfounded look that Danny had on his face.

"Do you want me to explain it to him?" Champ asked Brian.

"I think it would be better if I did, but don't go too far," Brian responded. Champ looked away and started talking to someone else in the room. "Danny, follow me, I need to talk to you about something," Brian said as he began to walk away.

"Dad, what's going on?" Danny asked, looking very concerned now.

"Just come to the other room with me and I'll explain it to you," Brian said as he continued to walk.

"No, dad," he grabbed Brian's arm and stopped him. His dad turned around and looked at him. "What the hell is going on?" Danny asked.

"Danny, you don't want to talk about it in here." Brian tried to walk further from the crowd and closer to the door he had been going towards.

"Dammit, dad," Danny said as he grabbed Brian's arm again. "I want you to tell me now. I'm not going anywhere until I know why we're here."

At this point, everyone in the room was looking at Danny and his father. Brian looked around, looking very embarrassed and concerned. "Brian! Are you telling me you brought this kid not even knowing that he wanted to support this? Are you fucking insane?" someone yelled from across the room.

Someone else yelled, "How are you going to be that reckless? Do you not even care if we all get thrown in jail?"

Danny started becoming nervous and realized that maybe he should have just kept walking. Brian shared his emotions to an equal extent and looked at Danny with frustration. Champ stepped in and said, "Guys, it's his kid. I know the boy. He's not going to tell anyone, trust me. Before the end of the night, the kid will end up helping us out." Everyone began to back off and going back to what they were doing before the eruption, but the tension remained in the air.

"What did I tell you?" Brian told Danny, his voice filled with anger and embarrassment. "Now come on. Champ! You come too." Champ, Danny, and Brian went into the other room where there was a table waiting for them. They all took their seats and Brian began talking with, "Danny, do you remember how you felt when we watched the broadcast saying that candidate Marshall had been killed?"

Danny thought back to the night when he hardly got any bit of sleep. He remembered how upset everyone in the house was. "Yeah, I remember," he said. "It was pretty scary."

"And do you remember how I had taken it harder than most in the room and even after you all went to bed, I remained downstairs to watch the news?" Brian added on.

"Yeah, what's the point?" Danny responded, getting impatient. His search for answers didn't seem to be going very well.

"Well, Danny. When I had seen Marshall lose his life, I knew that there was something wrong," Brian said. He took a pause and prepared his lecture. "Back in '63, I was in the same position you're in right now. The day that Kennedy was shot dead going down the road, my dad had the same reaction I had that night. Your grandpa was more concerned than I had ever seen him. He got to the point that he began crying his eyes out. Danny, in 1963, Kennedy wasn't just shot because someone wanted to be famous, he was shot because his fellow politicians wanted him out of the way."

Danny couldn't believe what he was hearing. His embarrassment at his father's beliefs was reinstated in his mind. "How could anyone know that?" Danny asked.

"Because an advisor to the man that wanted him dead at the time had come to us filled with guilt and told us himself," Brian pointed out. "He was an advisor to a group of congressmen that wanted the Vietnam war to escalate. We weren't in Vietnam to fight communism, Danny. We were there for our own imperialistic reasons. We weren't there to liberate, we were there to control. In 1963, that group caught wind that Kennedy wanted to pull us out of Vietnam. Instead of letting him do that, they demanded that he be killed. When Lyndon B. Johnson took control as president, he didn't even want to escalate the war, but by November of that year, he jumped on board and we stayed in Vietnam for even longer, attempting to control a nation."

Danny was dumbfounded. He just sat in his seat staring down at the table trying to take all this in. "At that time," his dad continued. "Your grandfather joined a society like this attempting to expose the government for what it had done. He tried his best to speak out to people in order to build up some sort of rebellion against the government to end its tyranny. However, the society failed and your grandfather was called an idiot, along with everyone else that tried to stand up. Then, ten years later, Allende, the president of Chile, was killed in a bloody CIA-backed coup. This was all done so Milton Friedman and his

'Chicago Boys' could test out their economic theories on Chile. My father tried to start up another society. Within a month, he had taken me to something similar to what you're at right now. When he told me that we weren't there for what he had told me, I reacted exactly as you did just now. I felt betrayed by him, and naturally, I felt very scared. I tried to help him after he told me all of the stories and I understood that something needed to be done. Unfortunately, we failed, and now Milton Friedman is being called an economic hero for his work there."

"So you thought that another society should be made this time as well?" Danny asked.

"Yes, Danny. That's why your uncle and I wanted you to come here."

Danny tried to take all of this in at once, and asked, "But dad, how do you know that something can actually be done this time?"

Brian and Champ looked at each other, then Champ spoke, "We know something's going to be done, because this time, we're not going away." Danny was shocked at how determined his family members looked. They were completely confident that this time they would expose the murderers for what they were.

"But Danny," his dad started. "This time, the government knows about us. They saw us the previous times that we had attempted to tell the public what was happening. The first time, we were shot down. There are still people today trying to expose the government for its part in the Kennedy assassination, but they're simply called fools and a cold shoulder is turned to them. The only ones that got close to exposing it have been killed. The ones that attempted to expose the government in '73 were tolerated a lot less. People were taken from their homes quietly and erased from existence. Families went to police trying to find out what happened, and were told that nobody knew or had any leads when they had just gotten done murdering them. This time, the government was bold in the actions they took to take control, and they know that we're going to be here to expose them. They know that we're tired of being defeated and they're going to begin killing off anyone that tries to expose the government for its part in Marshall's death."

"That's why everyone was so worried that you were here and I didn't even know if you'd help us out," Brian continued "We're taking a bigger risk than we've ever taken. It's going to be dangerous, Danny. I won't lie to you about that, but if you want to stay free in this country, free from fear, free to express yourself, free to walk to class knowing that you aren't going to be picked up off the street and killed, you must stand with us. So I ask you, my son: will you join us?"

Danny just sat staring at the table. Everything his father and uncle just told him was a lot to take in. He couldn't believe everything he heard. It countered everything he thought he knew about the world. But, if they were right, then something really did have to be done. "Alright, but I want to sit through this meeting to be completely sure," he finally said.

Champ and Brian. "I knew I could count on you, son. I'm so proud of you," Brian said. Danny and his father stood up and hugged. Champ, Danny, and Brian went into the other room and everyone looked to the door, completely silent. "He said he'll help us," Brian said proudly. The room cheered. People began coming up to Danny and giving him pats on the back and handshakes. Then Danny saw someone he would have never expected to see.

"Amanda?" he started. She pulled him in for a hug. Before Danny could realize what was happening, she backed up and kissed Danny. She held his shoulders and just smiled at him.

"Danny," she began to explain. "I was brought here by my mom. She had been in a society like this with your dad years ago against Pinochet's rule in Chile. I assume he told you about that by now?"

"Yeah, it's crazy stuff," he said. "But he didn't mention that he was in it with your mom, and you never told me that you were in this."

"Yeah, well this is where I wanted to take you tonight, Danny," Amanda chuckled. "I knew that you would be willing to help us. Brandon's here with his dad too. We arrived while your dad was talking to you. I'm so glad that you decided to help out." She gave him another hug, this one harder than the first.

"Alright everyone," Brian, who was standing near the round table, began. "It's time to get started." Everyone moved to their seats. Danny, Amanda's mom, and several others that Danny didn't recognize sat at the round table. Everyone else filed in around the room. Danny sat next to Brandon and Amanda.

"I'm glad that you're here to help, Danny," Brandon told him. "We're going to change the world." Danny definitely hoped so. Even though the meeting wasn't about him, he was enjoying all of the attention he was getting.

"Alright," Adam continued. "To begin, I have some bad news. We lost two members today at the protest. Sebastian Jentowski and Steph Balin were taken by the police today for demanding answers about the assassination and asking others to stand up for said answers. Their families have no idea where the two are and every police station near the protests have no record of the two ever being there. It's assumed that they're gone. Someone that met Steph at the protest is here to talk to us."

Adam sat down, and a woman came to the small stage in the center of the room near the round table. Things were getting very real, very quickly and the severity of the situation was making itself known. The woman looked very upset, understandably. "Well, I met Steph at the protests in D.C. today," the woman began. "She told me about how she thought that Marshall was murdered by someone hired by Stone and I told her that I shared the same belief. When the protesters began running to the White House, Steph . . . " the woman stopped, and began tearing up. "Steph told me that she wouldn't be returning home and I would never see her again. She handed me some papers and gave me a hug. She then ran to the White House and attempted to get inside. She was tazed and carried off." The woman was now sobbing. "I looked at the papers and a man approached me in the crowd. He told me that he was supposed to give her this piece of paper," she was now holding up a paper that looked like a conversation on paper. "It's a chain of e-mails showing a conversation between Stone's campaign manager and a relative of the man that killed candidate Marshall. Based on the e-mails, it definitely looks like Stone's administration has connections to the assassin's family." The room cheered as the woman handed the paper to the round table. "Another paper had the address of this meeting. The other paper was for Steph's kids, telling them that she loves them and to grow up and make her proud. I gave it to them today. Thank you for listening, and I'll be here to support this society until I die, and I'm doing this for that woman that died for what she believed in today."

The woman stepped off of the stage and headed back to her seat with everyone in the room cheering. She received the same pats on the back and hugs that Danny had received shortly before this. Adam stood up and began speaking about the e-mails, "Well, after looking at this, these e-mails seem legitimate, and they'll serve as some good pieces of evidence for recruitment. We'll be copying this in order to hand it out, which brings me to my next topic: it's time to phase one of our revolution.

We need to begin getting more people to our side. Each of you will be given a copy of these e-mails that we have received today. Start out getting only your most trusted friends and relatives to listen to your argument. Show them this conversation and they'll most likely agree with your side and join us. Everyone, I can not stress enough how dangerous this is. It's important that you don't show anyone that you can't trust with your life. That's about all we have for tonight. Thank you all for coming."

The room stood and put their hands on their hearts. They began to recite the same words with the rest of the room:

We as the Truth Committee will always stand
To bring about a society that understands
That we are the ones that run this nation
And we'll spread that truth like a conflagration
We know that tomorrow we may die
But our dreams will live on up high
One day our people will be truly free
And it's up to us to plant the seeds that will grow into a tree
The people, united, will never be defeated

Danny was moved by this oath that everyone in the room recited and took it to heart. He was on the verge of tears seeing his father recite the words that could end up growing into a nationwide revolution. The two left the house and got into their car and drove home. Danny's dad looked to him and said, "So are you sure you want to stand with us Danny?"

"Definitely, dad," Danny reassured him without skipping a beat. Danny's dad rubbed Danny's head.

Danny looked over to his dad moments later and saw tears strewing down his face, "I'm so proud of you, son," Brian said. Those are words that Danny would love to hear again.

CHAPTER FOUR

GET TO IT

"Police presence in Boston has been heightened as officers say that they've caught wind that today's protests may be much more confrontational than the previous days. President Stone had this to say: 'I encourage citizens to speak out if they want change, but violence for the sake of violence will not be tolerated and any protesters committing a crime at the protests will be prosecuted to the full extent of the law.'"

Danny sat watching the news the next morning during his small breakfast. He moved through every bit of cereal with his spoon as if looking for explanations somewhere in the milk. Every move with the spoon illustrated pictures of being called a nut job for believing in a conspiracy. Every piece that moved seemed to represent another friend moving far away from Danny because they thought he was insane.

How was he supposed to accept everything he'd heard? He'd been exposed to new ideas in college, but even the most radical of professors could never stand behind what the Committee was saying. It was just a weird coincidence and a tragedy that Marshall would be killed so close to the election. Danny felt almost disgusted with his father, but he was willing to stand behind him despite what was going on, and despite his thoughts, simply to make his father happy.

Danny poured the rest of his cereal down the sink and got ready to leave for class. Like he was cued to do so, Brian walked into the room. "Morning," he told Danny, smiling. He'd obviously found some new pride in his son and Danny hated it, but he would never show it.

"Morning," Danny muttered, feeling sick for putting up a front simply because would please his father.

Brian stepped in front of Danny as he moved to grab his stuff from his room. "Danny," He said as he stood looking at Danny as if he was trying to hold in a birthday surprise. "I've got your first job for the Committee."

"What?" Danny said with confusion.

"Well you didn't think that just talking to other people in the Committee would get anything done did you?" Brian said with a laugh and a shake of his head. He reached into his suit pocket. "I need you to drop this off to a guy in Boston after class." Brian handed him an unmarked package and a piece of paper with an address and a name.

"Dad," Danny began attempting to pull out of the situation.

"Danny, you're not rethinking this now are you?" Brian asked. His face immediately took on a look of disappointment. It was always a shock at how well he could read Danny's thoughts.

Danny paused and muttered, "Well . . . no." Danny tried to come up with a quick excuse, and all that came out was, "The protests in Boston are supposed to get bad today."

"No they're not Danny. Just go to downtown Boston after class, drop this off in the coffee shop off of 3rd and just come right back." Brian put his hand on Danny's shoulder and gave him a reassuring look. "Nothing's going to happen to you if you just get it to the right person and don't talk to anyone." Sounded simple enough. "The guy's name is Burke. Get to it. Love you, son." With that, Danny had the package and his first 'job' or whatever the Committee wanted to call it.

Danny walked outside in a nervous slump and got into his car. He put the package in his passenger side seat and leaned back into his chair. He let out a sigh, shook his head in disbelief at thc situation, and got on his way.

The drive to Charlie's dorm was a dreadful one, full of thought and doubt. Danny wanted nothing more than to just throw the package from his window and just go to school and have a normal day. He just prayed for a chance to go back to his dull life and pretend like he'd never even gone to the meeting. Guess it was too much to ask for a normal life.

Danny pulled into Charlie's parking lot and saw Amanda and him already standing there waiting. He grabbed the package and threw it towards his back seat. After recovering, Danny looked down at his phone to check the time. He was actually earlier than normal, which made it even odder that they were waiting for him to arrive. He opened his door and stood up next to it. "What are you guys doing ready this early?" Danny asked.

Amanda looked somewhat concerned, Charlie just looked excited. "So buddy, what's going on today?" Charlie said as if he was playing some joke that nobody let Danny in on. His suspicious behavior was definitely bothersome.

"Why are you acting so weird?" Danny asked.

He looked over to Amanda and Amanda looked back at Danny. "I told him," she said with a sight. Of course she did. Of course she did something that would put them in danger and limit Danny's chances of having a chance to leave the Committee.

"Yep!" Charlie said, looking very proud of himself. Danny joined them in front of Danny's car. "So when do I get to be a secret agent?" Charlie chuckled.

Danny pushed him a bit and the three started walking toward class. "Why would you tell him, Amanda?" Danny questioned. He was frustrated, and Amanda could spot it right away.

"Hey!" Charlie said, moving a bit in front of the group. "I thought we were all friends here. I have the right to know." It was much more difficult to read Charlie. If a normal person had said that, one would believe that they were upset, but Charlie masked his emotions with a wall of stupidity and random sarcasm.

"Charlie, this isn't some fucking game," Danny said, looking very serious now. "You obviously don't see the severity of the situation. We could get into mountains of trouble for what we're doing."

Charlie stopped walking and brought Danny to a stop with him. He stared Danny down and clearly stated, "All you're doing is going around telling people what you think is the truth and putting down what could actually be the truth. The news doesn't lie all of the time, Danny." Charlie had matched the seriousness of Danny. "Besides, you won't get in trouble for speaking your mind. It's the first amendment. Read a damn book." Charlie began walking away.

"Dammit, Charlie," Danny said while attempting to catch up to Charlie. "There have already been people arrested for doing what the group is doing within the past few months. The government sees this group as a threat, unlike before." Danny actually felt like a true member of the group, like his dad. This seemed to be the only time he's stood up for the Committee.

"Look, guys," Amanda said. She asserted herself to the middle of them to slow the conflict. "The only thing that matters now is that we all know, so we're all in this together at this point. Danny, you need to accept that Charlie's going to be a bit skeptical at first. You can't tell me you aren't too." Danny was shocked that Amanda might actually know what he'd been thinking. It freaked him out. "And Charlie, this is serious," Amanda continued. "We let you into this, so now you're obligated to help and tell nobody about what's happening. Now can we just go to class and have a nice day?"

The two looked at each other a bit longer. Danny still didn't trust Charlie with this information as much as he could with a pointless secret. He knew it would wear on his friendship with him, but he had to attempt to look past it. "Eh, I suppose so," Charlie said before Danny could decide if he wanted to trust Charlie any longer. He gave Danny a spiteful hug and the three moved to their classes. Danny could feel the arrogance flowing from Charlie the entire walk away from him.

Danny was sitting in his psychology class now. He absolutely hated this class. There were too many people, the room was hot as Satan's furnace, and the professor spoke with a monotone the entire time. Sometimes the guy's brain would give out on him and he'd repeat the same thing for the next half hour.

The class seemed smaller than it normally did today. It was the middle of the week and it wasn't sunny outside, so there weren't many reasons to skip class today. It was the perfect amount of absences for it to be noticeable. It was probably just a random phenomenon.

They were about halfway into the class when the professor got onto his computer as the students were copying down notes. He looked a bit concerned as he scrolled and felt the need to look up to the class. "Well, students," he said, interrupting their thoughts. "Looks like you're getting out early today. The movements in Boston are getting heated and we've been told to let you all get back to your dorms."

Everyone seemed happy, except for Danny. Now not only would he have to be inconvenienced with his delivery, but he'd be in danger. Even the university knew that it was so dangerous in Boston that a college near Boston couldn't even take the risk of staying open. At least he might get a chance to see a few people get arrested.

Danny walked out of the class and noticed Charlie was waiting for him right outside. "Hey, Charlie," Danny greeted. "What's going on?"

"Not much, man," Charlie said as he shook Danny's hand. "Well I'm out of class and have nothing to do. Do you wanna hang?"

Danny remembered the package and said, "Nah man, sorry."

"Look, Danny, I know we argued earlier," Charlie started. "But that's no reason for things to get weird."

"It's not that," Danny confessed. "It's just . . .I've got something to do." Charlie looked at Danny in an accusatory manner. He felt as if Danny definitely wasn't telling the truth, and Charlie always followed his gut.

Danny thought about the situation. What could it hurt if Charlie came along? He already knew that Danny was in the Committee anyways. "Alright, Charlie," Danny said. "You can come with me, but I'm trying to get out of there quickly so please don't do anything that will slow us down."

"Awesome!" Charlie nearly shouted. "Where are we going?"

"Boston," Danny said as they began walking towards the car.

Charlie got really excited, and then looked horribly confused. "Why are we going to Boston?" he asked.

"I've gotta . . .drop off a package for the Committee," Danny said. He awaited the freak-out that was about to take place.

"Aw yeah!" Charlie said. He was ecstatic. "Fun, fun, mission stuff."

Danny shook his head, knowing the situation he'd just put himself in. They got to his car and drove off.

Danny always loved going into Boston. Aside from New York City, it was the biggest city he'd ever been to. They listened to music the whole ride up, as they normally did. As they entered the city, Charlie looked at Danny and asked, "Why don't we make a band?"

Danny considered the proposal and quickly said, "Because we don't have any talent."

Charlie looked stunned. "I can play drums pretty well," Charlie said. "We just need to find other people."

"And what would I do, Charlie?" Danny said with a sarcastic smirk on his face. He'd might as well humor the idea to give Charlie the benefit of the doubt.

"Can't you sing?" Charlie asked.

He wasn't completely wrong. Danny wasn't a half bad singer and for the genre they would probably end up doing, he'd probably be doing a lot more screaming than anything else. However, he didn't have time for that. With school and now the Committee surely filling up his time, he wouldn't have the time for a band. "I'm not that great, Charlie," Danny lied.

"That's where practice comes in," Charlie pointed out. "I'm not exactly sick at drums, but I'm willing to put in the hours to practice."

Danny figured that he'd might as well agree, simply to end the pointless conversation. "Alright, if you can find the other people, we'll do it," Danny said.

Charlie was beyond excited. "This is gunna be sick, dude," he said. "Just imagine if we ended up playing huge shows across the United States! I'm telling you, bitches for days, dude."

Danny shook his head, but couldn't help but smile. He advised, "Don't count your chickens before . . . " Danny's window was hit with a rock. He swerved and eventually regained control and parked on the side of the road. He'd narrowly missed popping the curb out of fear.

"Dude, what the hell just happened?" Charlie yelled, running out of the car and encircling it as if it was on fire.

"I think some asshole just threw a rock at my car," Danny said in confusion. He was visibly angry as he stormed of his car to look at his window. He looked around him and didn't see anything. They started walking back to where the window got broken and saw the culprit: a protest. "Dammit, dude," Danny said, looking back at the glass on the ground from his window.

"Who did it?" Charlie asked, standing on his toes to try to somehow find the one person in the massive crowd of people that could have done it.

"I don't fucking know, Charlie," Danny said. "There are people everywhere. How do you expect to figure out who did it?"

"Damn, dude," Charlie said. He kicked at the ground a bit to show his frustration.

Danny looked back at his car parked on the side of the road. "Well let's just drop off this package so we can get out of here," he said.

They started walking towards the coffee shop which was conveniently only about a block away. "What's in the package anyways?" Charlie asked.

"I don't know," Danny said, starting to spin the package around. "It's not really heavy, but it's not all that light either. I don't really care. I just want it out of my hands." Danny kept looking behind him and watching the protest. They were really loud, but they didn't look like they had reached the point of violence yet, aside from the person that decided to bust his window. The only thing that seemed odd was that they weren't moving in any direction. They were just standing in the road facing away from Danny.

The two walked into the coffee shop and saw just one guy sitting at a table. Danny assumed it must be the Burke guy and walked over to him with the package in hand. "Hey, I'm Danny." Danny put his free hand out to shake the guy's hand.

The man looked a bit concerned, but still shook Danny's hand. "Hello, Danny," he said.

"So I'm guessing you're the guy with the Committee?" Danny said. He felt a sense of excitement through the fear that he'd previously felt. His first goal in the group, completed. Just then the cashier came out from the back and walked to the register.

"Can I help you guys?" he said loudly across the room.

"Oh, sure," Charlie said. "Do you want anything, Danny?" He reached into his wallet to prepare his cash.

"Nah," Danny answered from in front of the man he'd just met. "I'll just finish up here and we can go."

Charlie nodded and walked up to the counter. "Hey, I'll just get a medium vanilla iced coffee," he said.

"Sure thing," the cashier said. The cashier then leaned forward with great speed and pulled Charlie close. "Get your friend and get the hell out of here," he whispered.

"What did you say?" Charlie asked as he attempted to pull away from the crazed cashier.

"That's the wrong guy," the cashier answered. He was looking from Charlie to the man at the table sporadically.

"What?" Charlie's fear levels shot up.

"That guy's with the Boston P.D. You were supposed to give the package to me."

Charlie shuddered and walked over to Danny as fast as he could without looking suspicious. "So what's in this package anyways?" Danny asked the guy.

"Oh, don't worry about it," the man said. "I'll just take it to my higher up. I'm supposed to come get it for him."

"Alright then," Danny said as he stretched his arm out and handed the man the package. "It was nice meeting you," he yelled after the man as he started to turn around.

Charlie grabbed Danny's arm. "Danny," he whispered. "That's the wrong guy, dude."

Danny turned to him and whispered, "Are you serious?"

"Yeah," Charlie responded. "You were supposed to give it to the cashier."

"What the hell do we do?" Danny asked.

"Go get it!"

"How?"

The man was walking away. "I don't know! Just get it!" Charlie said.

Danny ran over to the man and yelled, "Hey!"

The man turned around and said, "I thought we were done." He looked a bit scared. It was doubtful that he was filled with as much fear as Danny was.

"That's the wrong package!" Danny said as quickly as he could. He reached into his book bag and found a letter he was going to send after they were done at the coffee shop. "Here," he said as he held the letter out.

The man reached out and took the letter. He examined it and looked back up to Danny. "This says it's going to a college just outside of Boston."

"Well . . .yeah!" Danny said. "Nothing suspicious about college mail. The cops would never know!"

The man looked a lot more settled and he said, "You've got a good head on your shoulders. I'll go get this to my superior and maybe I'll see you in the future."

"Sure thing!" Danny yelled as the man walked away. Danny now had the package in his hands and was sweating profusely. He sat down in the coffee shop and put his head on the table.

"Quick thinking," the cashier said. He walked out from behind the counter and locked the front door. "Come on," The cashier told Danny as he began walking to the back of the store . . .

The three walked into the back behind the counter and to the manager's office. They passed a few employees on the way there that looked at Danny and Charlie oddly, but nothing that seemed threatening. "You guys can go ahead and sit down." The cashier let them in and shut the door behind them. He came over and sat down across from them at his wooden desk. "I'm Alan."

"I'm Charlie," Charlie shook the man's hand.

"I'm Danny," Danny did the same. "I thought that your name was Burke?"

"That's what I go by before I know I can trust someone," Alan said. "It's my middle name." He let out a sigh and held the package in his lap. "It's a good thing I got you to stop in time. Almost gave me a heart attack, kid," Alan said, chucking nervously a bit.

"Yeah, sorry about that," Danny said. He rubbed the back of his head and continued. "So what's in that package anyways?"

Alan opened the package and looked inside of it. He began removing things and naming them, "A bunch of pamphlets, the map of Boston I wanted," Alan stopped. "Holy hell. Good thing you didn't let him get this." Alan held out a list with a bunch of names and phone numbers on it.

"What are those?" Charlie asked.

"It's a list of phone numbers from everyone in your chapter," Alan said. Danny and Charlie looked at each other after Alan said it. "Yeah, that would've been pretty bad," Alan pointed out.

"I don't even know how I could be dumb enough to not ask the guy who he was," Danny shook his head as he spoke. He felt like an idiot.

"It's an easy mistake to make," Alan reassured him. "Just don't do that again. We've got to be careful." Alan reached into his desk and pulled out an envelope. "Here."

Danny reached out and took the envelope. It was blank and said "payroll" on it. "And this is?" Danny asked.

"It's the records of brainstormed ideas from our chapter," Alan responded. "And take these too." He reached into another drawer and pulled out a stack of flyers. He put them into a drawstring bag and handed it across the table to Danny. "Go to the protest and see if you can't hand some of those out. Just don't get caught or hurt. We'll probably need you in the future."

"Alright, it was nice meeting you, Alan," Danny said as he put the bag on his back.

"Same," Alan said as he shook Danny and Charlie's hands.

"Nice guy," Charlie said as they walked out of the shop.

The pair walked outside and started to make their way to the mob that they he seen earlier. Danny looked over to make sure his car was still intact. Still no window, but at least no further damage had been done while they were inside. Danny reached into his pocket and grabbed his phone to call Brian. After a few rings his dad picked up. "Hello?" Brian said into the phone.

"Hey, dad. It's Danny," Danny said.

"Oh hey," his dad said in a surprised tone as if he didn't expect to get the call. "How'd it go?"

"Well, we had a bit of a mix-up, but we got the guy the package."

"Awesome! He's a pretty cool guy. Right? He'll probably be joining our chapter to help it get up to the status that the Boston chapter is."

"Oh yeah. He seemed to like us, so I guess that's a plus."

"Who's us?"

"Oh yeah. Well Charlie sorta knows now, but don't worry. He's in this with us."

"Are you positive?" Brian didn't seem to be as trusting as Amanda had been, and he shared Danny's skepticism.

The two were moving closer to the group of people. "Well, yeah," Danny said. "He's been my friend for a while now. I can trust him." He didn't actually fully trust Charlie, but if he told his dad anything different, who knows what could happen.

"Alright, Danny," Brian still sounded concerned. "Well just please make sure that he doesn't go around telling everyone about this. I don't want you getting into trouble for something I got you involved in."

"Dad, don't worry," Danny reassured him. "Charlie's a good guy."

Charlie chimed in with, "I'm a good guy Mr. Bruce!"

"Haha, alright," Brian told Danny, a bit louder so Charlie could hear. He seemed to have lightened up to the idea of Charlie knowing because of that simple outburst. "Well what are you doing now?"

"Alan told us to go to the protest and hand out a few flyers," Danny responded.

"Be careful as hell, Danny. You heard what that woman said at the meeting. They'll get you if you're not careful."

Danny just shook his head and attempted to finish the conversation with, "Alright, dad. I'll talk to you later."

"Alright," Brian said. "I love you and I hope you can join us for dinner tonight."

"Actually, I was thinking I might stay over at Charlie's dorm tonight," Danny said "It *is* a Friday after all."

"We haven't had dinner together in a while, Danny," Brian said. He was starting to sound like his mother. "Your mom is gunna make us some steaks. Can't it just wait another night?"

"I mean, I'm going to be wiped after today," Danny pointed out. "I just kind of want to chill out. I'll definitely come home and have a big dinner with you guys tomorrow though."

"I guess you do stay at home a lot. Alright. Just try to be home early tomorrow."

"Thanks, dad. You're awesome."

"I try, Danny. I try."

"Haha. Alright, love you. I'll see you tomorrow."

"Love you too, Dan."

Danny hung up the phone and returned it to his pocket. At this point they were a few meters from the protest. "Your dad talks forever, dude," Charlie told Danny.

"Yeah," Danny said. "What can yah' do?"

The two got to the back of the protest. It was horrendously loud in front of them. There were so many chants going on at once that they couldn't even tell what anyone was chanting about. Danny jumped a few times to see what was going on over the crowd. Everyone was just standing there shouting and looking in one direction.

"What's happening?" Danny asked Charlie.

"I dunno," Charlie answered. He tapped a bearded guy in front of them. The man turned around and tilted his head up a bit. Charlie moved the hair from his face and asked, "What's happening?"

The man turned around after giving his sign to another guy next to him. "The police are up ahead and aren't letting anyone through," the guy said. "We've been marching all day, but they won't let us get into the center of town."

"What's everyone trying to do in the center of town?" Charlie asked him.

"Well, it's more of a symbolism thing and it's a much better way to get heard," the man stated. "The media will focus on the pure numbers of our crowd in the middle of town and other people will probably end up joining in the future because of it."

"Makes sense," Charlie said before he turned to Danny. "Hey, do you wanna try to get further to the front?"

Danny gave a pamphlet to the bearded guy and his friend and turned to Charlie saying, "I don't know man. I'm not trying to get arrested today."

"Don't worry," Danny said, brushing off the danger of the situation. "We aren't going to get arrested just for standing there."

"You guys should definitely get further in," the bearded guy interrupted. "I've looked into this 'Truth' stuff you're handing out, and it's definitely got some valid points in it. Plus, it's good for younger guys to get involved in this sort of stuff." The guy made a space for Danny and Charlie to enter. "You guys be careful."

The two started moving through the crowd. Charlie was pushing quicker than Danny as Danny would occasionally get stopped by people asking for a pamphlet. They had gotten very close to the front of the group and looked over a few shoulders and heads to see the front. There was a line of police officers with riot shields and barricades up.

"Danny," Charlie said. "Put those away." He pointed at the pamphlets. "If your dad's right, they'll arrest you in a heartbeat." It was the first good idea that Charlie had in a while, but at this point, Danny didn't have much fear left to spare for the situation.

"My dad's just taking this too seriously," Danny responded. He put the pamphlets in his book bag. "It's reminding me of a movie, the way he's acting. We'll get taken in by the guv'ment for treason for handing out pieces of paper."

The pair stood around, just watching the chaos for a while. This scene was crazy. People were screaming for the police to move. They were calling them pigs, dictators, tyrants, every word that Danny's ever heard a hippie call a cop. The police up ahead just stood in their spot, completely motionless, as if they couldn't hear anything. An officer stepped up to the barricade, obviously one of the head guys. He held up a megaphone and began to speak.

"By order of the Boston Police Department," he started. "You're all ordered to turn around and clear the area. You are allowed to protest, but not in a public road. If you fail to leave, action will be taken and you will be arrested." The officer was stern and very serious about everything he was saying. He stood in his spot with his officers behind him and his arms crossed.

"Should we leave?" Danny asked Charlie. His paranoia was starting to act up.

"I think so, man," he answered. "This is getting way too serious for me right now. We got enough of those things passed out, we're good for today."

A lady behind them grabbed them by the shoulders and said, "How are you two going to hand out those pamphlets, yet you're not going to actually stand up for what they say?" The lady looked much older than them and had a pamphlet in her hand. "I've been involved in protests my entire life and never once have I backed down because of what the ones I'm protesting threaten to do to me."

This lady spoke in such an inspirational tone. "How old are you?" Charlie asked. Danny looked at him and gave him a disapproving look as if he should have never asked such a question to her.

"I'm seventy-three," the woman said, putting the two into a state of shock. Such an old woman and she was still trying to make a change. "It's our right to stand up for what we believe. These are *our* streets that *we've* built and we're surrounded by houses that *we* live in. They have no right to tell us that we can't be here. If they want to stop us, they'd have to cut out our tongues." Graphic imagery, but inspirational nonetheless. "You boys need to stay and make yourselves heard."

The crowd behind the woman began chanting, "The people, united, will never be defeated." Danny remembered that from the thing everyone said at the end of the Committee meeting. Maybe they weren't the only ones that believe in the message. Then again, they probably don't all think that Marshall was killed by Stone's guys.

"Do you hear that, boys?" the woman said, interrupting Danny's thought. We're all thinking the same thing. We all want a change. Whether that be because we're not satisfied with how things have been run, or because we're here for the cause that you boys are advertising, we're all part of the same purpose: we want change. I know a lot of people in this crowd that are asking the questions your pamphlets ask. It's your responsibility as an American to stand with them."

The chants were only growing louder. Danny and Charlie looked at each other for a moment, as if trying to communicate telepathically. Charlie turned to the front of the crowd and joined the chant. Danny looked down and thought to himself. This was so inspiring. Danny felt like he was actually in the process of making a change, like his presence mattered. He too turned to the front and joined the chant, which was now becoming deafening.

Danny watched as the head officer moved behind the officers in riot gear. The officers on the ends began moving the barricades from the front of them. There was now nothing between the officers and the protesters. Danny felt a sense of intense fear, but his inspiration pushed him to stay. He felt some people brush by him and move to the front of the protest. Most of them were wearing bandanas on their faces. They stood at the very front and made a wall between the police and the protesters. They interlocked arms and stood there, still chanting as loudly as their throats would allow.

The officers shot a couple of canisters of tear gas to the front of the protest. One of them landed only feet from Charlie. Charlie started backing up to get away and pushed Danny with him. Someone reached down and threw the canister back at the officers. The other had also been thrown back.

Everyone recovered and the officers began moving closer to the protesters with their shields. An officer attempted to grab one of the people in the wall and arrest him, but the ones around him refused to let go. Some people behind them summoned the courage and grabbed onto the guy to make sure the officers would have to take many more of them to get to one guy.

The officers began swinging away at protesters with batons. Danny could see one man with a bandana on his face lying on the ground bleeding. Another protester helped to make sure the man was okay. Both of them were grabbed by officers and hauled away. The officers trying to pry people off of the people in the wall moved back to their line. Everyone got back to their feet and the wall now grew a few layers with more protesters.

The officers now shot a substantially larger amount of canisters into the crowd. People began to scatter, including Danny and Charlie. They ran as fast as they could as the officers now began to run full speed at the crowd. People in front and behind the two were falling and essentially being trampled under the crowd. The people that had stood so strongly were now running with all of their ability with their tails between their legs.

Danny could hardly breathe through the gas. He looked around him through blurred vision. All he could see was movement of people around him trying to get out. Some ran back to help others that had fallen. Danny could see a concerned wife screaming out for her husband. It was heartbreaking to see a crowd that had been so united now trying to simply get away from the danger. It made Danny feel like an ant amongst many, attempting to scurry away from a child's magnifying glass.

Danny managed to get out of the gas and turned around. He thought about he old woman that had talked to Charlie and him and he looked franticly to make sure she was okay. He looked and saw the wall of protesters still standing as strong as ever, some of them crumpling down to baton hits. Danny looked towards the middle and his heart almost fell out of his chest. The old woman was standing at the front of the wall, interlocking arms with other protesters. Danny simply turned his head, as the old woman fell with the rest of the wall.

Charlie was a bit ahead of Danny, both of them now sprinting to get back to Danny's car. People were all over the place. Some were running back, some were walking home, and some were going to start another march in a different direction. Danny was relieved to see that his car was untouched by the running crowd. He and Charlie got into the car and their muscles gave up on them. They were exhausted. Danny looked at the roof of the car panting and running the day's events through his mind.

"Dude," Charlie said to Danny, also panting.

" . . .What?" Danny responded.

"Let's get the hell out of here," he said before he returned to panting with his head on the seat rest.

The two drove back to campus in silence. The entire way back, neither of them said a word, and neither of them played any music. Both of them were prisoners to their own thoughts. Charlie was stuck thinking about how tired he was and how insane that entire situation was. All Danny could think about was what happened to that old woman, but his only conclusion made him sick.

They arrived at Charlie's dorm and went inside. They sat on Charlie's couch and continued to think. Nothing could have ever been as comfortable as that couch at that particular moment. Charlie eventually turned on some TV when he summoned the strength to lift the remote.

Charlie was the first to break the silence with, “I can’t even believe we just saw that.”

Danny continued to stare at the ground, but said, “I know. Definitely isn’t what I was expecting to do today.”

“You should probably call your dad and tell him you’re alright.”

Danny thought about it for a second. He looked at the clock and saw that it was a few minutes from midnight. “I’ll send him a text,” he said. “I highly doubt that he’s awake right now.”

“Alright, man,” Charlie said. Danny sent a text to his dad, letting him know that he was okay.

“What do you wanna do now?” Danny asked as he put his phone back in his pocket.

The two sat in silence for a while. They looked at the TV a few times, then back at the floor. Charlie finally spoke up. “You tryinta?”

Danny looked at Charlie with one of those “What the hell” faces. Charlie just laughed. Danny started chuckling and looked down at the floor, then back at Charlie, “Why not?” he laughed.

Charlie left his response at, “My man.”

CHAPTER FIVE

NIGHT

Danny and Charlie headed out of Charlie's room and walked outside. "Where should we go?" Danny asked Charlie.

"I know an awesome spot," Charlie reassured. They walked for about five minutes across campus. Danny hadn't really been on campus all that much, so he enjoyed looking around at everything. Every time, he finds something that he hasn't seen before.

After the short walk, they made it to a field that a bunch of kids usually play football on when it's not cold. Danny and Charlie were both wearing a couple of jackets and a beanie their heads. They found a good hill where they sat and looked to the sky.

The two sat in darkness, exploring their minds, each of them getting more and more in tune with the parts of their thoughts that are usually never touched. The only break in the silence would be a cough from the cold air or the resonating effects of the tear gas. Charlie's eyes were still bloodshot from the gas that had filled the street in Boston. Danny felt a burning in his chest still remaining from the lack of oxygen that he'd experienced.

Both were so enveloped in thought, that they had forgotten each other's company. Charlie was sitting up examining the ground around him, as if he'd lost something and he was making a mild attempt at finding it. He considered how crazy of a day he'd experienced. He could almost picture himself telling his friends about everything that had happened. His mind was preparing the speech that he'd give when he ran into a friend in the future.

Danny, on the other hand, was still feeling remorse for the manner in which everything had happened. The image of that old woman that had guided them in a way that would likely change them forever. She was still trying to help get the message across, even after seeing such an unfathomable amount of days, and then had her body beaten by people that would never be able to imagine all that she had probably been through throughout her life of experiences. It didn't seem human, the way that the officers had acted. To strike down your fellow man with such borderline happiness, was unbelievable.

He looked to the sky and allowed his mind to wander. He observed every star glistening in the sky, each lying millions of miles away, completely unaware of the life that sat in observation. Orion's Belt manifested images of the wall of unbreakable brotherhood that the protesters had shown for each other. The bow reminded him of the batons that were so freely used against the ones that wished only to help their friends. Even the face of the moon reminded him of the faces of everyone that were now looking at the same sky, or were wishing they could have the freedom to do so.

They sat for so long in an unreeling silence that the feeling of the other's presence had completely disappeared. They had been put through too much to even think of speaking to their neighbor. Their minds were pulled out of concentration only by a cough from Charlie's damaged lungs.

"You okay man?" Danny asked Charlie as he patted him on the back.

Charlie coughed a few more times and mustered the strength to say, "Ugh . . . Yeah I'm good." before he shook his head and laughed.

Danny smiled and looked back to the sky. The stars continued to glisten and throw his mind into deep thought once again. He finally began to speak when he wished to hear about what his friend had been thinking. "Charlie," he said.

"Yeah, man?" Charlie asked as he was pulled out of his thoughts.

"What do you think of what happened today?" Danny asked.

"It was crazy as hell," Charlie said. "That's what I think." He chuckled a bit, but didn't hear a response from his friend. He looked over at Danny who was still staring at the sky. He could tell that something was troubling him. "What's wrong?" he asked.

Danny glanced over to Charlie, then back to the sky. "I just can't understand how all of that happened," he admitted. "Like, I don't get how people protesting without causing any harm should be subject to all of that."

Charlie looked at the ground and took a breath. It finally didn't burn to breathe. "Well Danny," he said. "The world's a pretty fucked up place if you haven't noticed by now." Charlie looked to see if Danny was still looking at the sky, which he was. "Police are supposed there to protect us, but in times like this when the people aren't satisfied with what's been happening, they're put out to protect the silence that the politicians have been used to."

"What do you mean?" Danny said as he finally looked at Charlie.

"Well . . . You know how when there's no sort of trouble brewing anywhere how cops are usually pretty cool? Like you'll get pulled over and they'll just say 'Have a nice day' and they don't make a big deal of anything?"

"Yeah."

"Well now they're put in a situation where they're being told, 'Don't just pull them over, get them for breaking the law.' Basically politicians like it when we just sit around and don't ask questions. But once they're threatened, they try to teach us not to stand up.

The cops just get caught in the middle and they get a sort of mentality from their bosses that we're the ones that need to be put down. They make protesters sound like criminals that have to be dealt with. Everyone's up to something and they need to be arrested."

"Then why would they just beat people down and shoot tear gas at innocent people that weren't doing anything wrong without questioning their orders? If we can stand up, then why can't they?"

"They didn't want to do it, Danny. Trust me." Charlie seemed so confident, and had finally seemed intelligent.

"How can you tell?" Danny aasked.

"The guy that was shouting commands was the one that made them think we were criminals. I guarantee he told them all that they needed to uphold the peace and we were breaking that peace. When he shouted out on that megaphone, I could tell he hated us and all he wanted was to see us bleed. But I looked at one of the guys on the end. I could see his face. That guy didn't want to be there. He was staring at the ground. I saw him move the barricade and move back in line. When cops started moving, he was the last to move. The ones in the center went quickly to show their commander they were there to help, but they definitely didn't put in a lot of effort once they had to arrest people. Things just got out of control and then they felt threatened and started swinging. I know they didn't want to at first, but with your boss at your back and people yelling threats at your front, people just tend to blow up."

Charlie had never been this insightful. Danny was blown away. "Charlie, that's probably the smartest thing I've ever heard," Danny said.

"You forget my dad's a cop," Charlie told him. "But not gunna lie, what I saw today definitely made me uneasy. This stuff's getting serious."

"Yeah, and you can bet the media isn't gunna take it as seriously as it should be taken. I don't think anyone could even portray how messed up all of that was."

"Yeah."

"Do you remember that old woman that talked to us?"

"Yeah. She inspired the hell out of me," Charlie said. "I've never felt so motivated to do something in my life."

"Do you know what happened to her?"

"Nah. I was gone before those cops got to me. Do you?"

"Well, the last I saw her, she was with all of those people interlocking arms," Danny said slowly.

Charlie looked up quickly. "Are you serious?"

"Yeah, exactly."

Charlie was in awe. He started looking at the sky as well. "She's hands down the bravest person alive," he said.

"I don't think it was bravery," Danny said. "I think she just has seen so much in her life that she knew something needed to happen. She was tired of backing down."

"I could see that making sense," Charlie said as he nodded. "Danny, I need you to be honest with me for a second."

"Sure thing."

"Do you really believe Marshall was assassinated by someone Stone hired?"

Danny never expected this question to come up. He knew his answer, but he was too ashamed to ever tell anyone. He just prayed that nobody would ever ask. However, it was finally time to see what his response would be. "Well, I definitely didn't at first. In the beginning I just thought it was some crazy conspiracy theory. But now that I saw how quickly the protests are being fought, it's starting to seem likely. Before

Marshall's death, the cops didn't really care that much about protests. Now they're actively hunting protesters. Then there was some woman at the meeting I went to with my dad the first time and she was so convinced that someone she met in the Committee was taken by cops or . . . whatever. I'm really starting to believe."

"Man," Charlie paused. "I was thinking the same thing. I just really want to see some actual proof so I don't feel crazy talking about it. My dad shut me up when I ran the idea by him and told me not to be going around spreading that nonsense."

"My dad believed it from the beginning. I thought he was pretty crazy," Danny admitted.

"That's probably how most people think about people that believe it," Charlie pointed out. "That's why there needs to be proof."

"Yeah." Danny took a break to look at the sky. "I really feel bad for thinking the way I did about him. Like, I was almost ashamed of him."

"Damn, dude," Charlie said. "That's pretty low."

"Yeah. It made me feel like hell and it still hurts to think about it. I just didn't want everyone else to think my dad was crazy, I guess."

"Well are you happy he believes it now?"

"I'm definitely getting there," Danny said as he picked at the ground. "I just need to talk to him about it so he can kinda give me his perspective and reasons. We used to talk all the time, and now I just take him and my mom for granted. You never really realize how important they are and I'm finally getting there. We're having a family dinner tomorrow so there will probably be quite a bit of talking."

"Does your mom know that you two are in this?"

"I'm not sure," Danny said. "I'd have to ask my dad."

"Solid," Charlie said as he fell back on the ground with a thud.

"It's awesome having you in this with me, dude. I needed someone to talk to about this craziness."

Charlie looked over and laughed. "Yeah, man, definitely," he agreed.

The two continued to stare at the sky and talk about life and everything that happened. They joked about school and helped each other to forget about the day. After the chaos of the day, the night became the only peaceful moment they had.

CHAPTER SIX

THE GAME'S CHANGED

"Protesters clashed with police yesterday in downtown Boston. Hundreds of protesters were arrested and many others injured in what has been called the biggest crackdown on the protest since its beginning. An elderly woman was also reportedly killed in the riot. She has not yet been identified. The finger is being pointed at the officers, but the police department assured in a statement that she was trampled when protesters ran from officers."

Danny woke up on Charlie's couch under a pile of blankets. He adjusted his eyes to the room and turned on the TV. There wasn't much on. There were a bunch of news reports on the protests from the day before, and not much else.

After a while of flipping through channels, Charlie came out of the bathroom. "Smells pretty awful in there," he warmed Danny.

"Thanks Charlie," Danny responded as he put his face into the pillow.

Charlie ran over to Danny and shook him. "Come on, man," he said. "You told your dad that you'd be home early today and I want to go get some breakfast from the dining hall."

"Just go by yourself," Danny said as he rolled over. Charlie ripped off the blankets, and threw them onto the floor. Danny pulled himself to a sitting position and glared at Charlie. "What time is it?" he mumbled.

"It's like nine thirty or something," Charlie said.

Danny reached for his phone which was sitting on a nearby table. He checked it and didn't see any text messages, but he did notice that Charlie was correct on the time he gave. Danny wouldn't have to be home for a bit longer, so he decided he'd go to get some food while he still had time. "Where do you want to eat?" Danny asked as he put his socks on.

Charlie rubbed his face as he answered. "Probably just gunna eat on campus," he said. "You down to join?"

"I suppose," Danny said. He put on his shoes and the two left the room. "Should we go get Amanda and see if she wants to go?" Danny asked. He was constantly rubbing his eyes in order to somehow give himself some energy to continue.

"Get out of her ass!" Charlie joked. Danny pushed him into the wall and laughed. They walked up to Amanda's room and knocked on her door. "She's probably still sleeping," Charlie said. "Do you want to just go?"

Amanda opened the door. She was dressed as if she had been awake for a few hours. "Hey, guys," she welcomed them.

They all exchanged hugs and Charlie asked, "Do you wanna go get something to eat?"

"I mean," she began. "I'm not really hungry, but I'll go for the company."

"Solid," Charlie responded as they began walking. They went to the nearest cafeteria and broke up. Danny headed over to get an omelet as Amanda and Charlie just grabbed some sandwiches. The beauty of college dining halls. Danny met up with Amanda and Charlie with a pile of omelets in hand.

"Are you serious, Danny?" Amanda asked.

"Hey, I like my omelets," Danny responded.

The three sat down at a table and began eating. "So what did you guys do yesterday?" Amanda asked while preparing to put food in her mouth.

"Went to the protest in Boston," Danny answered. He began cutting his omelets into tiny bits.

"Oh, I heard it got pretty dangerous yesterday," she responded.

"Pff yeah," Danny said. "Then again the news and my professor told us that it would be."

"Why did you guys go if you knew it was gunna be bad?" Amanda questioned.

"Eh, just wanted to check it out."

"Danny," she said, with a very condescending look. "Have you already forgotten I'm in this with you?"

"Why does everyone act like we're going to die if someone knows?" Charlie asked. "I've heard kids talk about it in class and I don't think twice about it."

"Dude," Danny said, obviously concerned. "We've gone over this. Don't tell anyone. I'm not trying to get picked up by secret police or something."

"It's not even a big group yet," Charlie said after swallowing his food. "Why would they care about it?"

"Because they've tried to get people to do something about government corruption before and now the government's actually going to try to shut them down."

"Danny, if the group never made something work, how would you think they can change anything now? The government's definitely not worried about them, so how do you figure that they'll get something done?" Charlie took a sip of his drink.

Danny leaned back in his chair. "Why are you acting like such a prick? Why take any chances?"

"I'm not being a prick. I'm trying to get you guys to stop freaking out over something that doesn't matter. It's boring hanging out with people that are too scared to even talk to each other."

"People have been taken Charlie. I heard a woman tell us about a woman that she met at a protest that was abducted during it by police. This isn't some bull shit game."

"That's bull, dude. That woman's probably just being a woman."

"Charlie!" Amanda yelled.

"What? Women over exaggerate shit," Charlie responded. He took another bite of his sandwich.

Danny was getting thoroughly angry. "Charlie, if you can't take it seriously then get the fuck out of it," he belted.

"Fuck you, Danny," Charlie said, dropping his food. "You don't even believe in this shit either, so don't act like you're suddenly such a big believer." Charlie stormed out of the restaurant without looking back.

Danny watched Charlie leave and shook his head. Amanda stared at Danny, mouth agape. "What?" Danny asked.

"You mean, you don't believe in anything that the Committee says?" she asked.

"I mean . . . " he muttered. "Not really at first, but I'm getting there."

"So you're lying to your dad, everyone in that place, and now you're just going to lie to me?"

"I said I'm starting to believe it. I just don't have facts to back it up. It's possible, but not necessarily true," Danny said. He was attempting to extinguish the situation, but to no avail.

Amanda got up. "You're just like everyone else Danny. You're too scared to think for yourself unless you have all of the facts. You can never put your faith in anything. I've been made fun of countless times because everyone thinks I'm an idiot and I thought you were on my side. Should've known you were just like Charlie." She began to walk away.

Danny ran after her. "Amanda," he pleaded.

"Stop it, Danny."

"Amanda, look. I'm sorry that you've been put through this. I know you don't think I want anything to do with the group, but I'm in it because I'm willing to give it a chance. I want other people to think about the ideas the groups presents, but I can't stop myself from thinking about them at the same time. I don't know if it's completely true yet, and it puts doubt in my head when I try to think of telling someone about the group. That's why I want something to back up the accusations so I can defend the claims that I'm willing to make. I just feel like such an idiot when someone knows I'm in it and I felt dumb when I had first found out that my dad believed it. I know it's hard, and you're right, I am scared of getting insulted because of this group, but, I'm here until something gets done. I'm not quitting on this and I'll defend you every time someone attacks you for believing in something, regardless of what I ever believe."

Amanda and Danny just stood there staring at each other. Danny felt like he might've just put more on the table than he should've. It felt like he just said the wrong thing again.

Amanda started to talk, "Danny." She paused and looked around. "It . . .it feels good to hear you say that." She smiled. "I'm glad you're there for me and you're finally starting to open your mind." She reached out and gave Danny a hug. Maybe Danny did say the right things. "Ugh. So what are you gunna do today?"

"I'm having a family day, basically," Danny told her, still feeling tension from the argument.

"Ah, bummer," she laughed. "I'm gunna be bored all day, I guess."

"Eh I mean you have other friends and such in your hall," Danny pointed out.

"Yeah." She looked back at the table. "I suppose. Well I guess I'll see you later then! I'm going to go to the library to study a bit."

"Alright. I'll see you later then," Danny said as he gave her another hug. He walked away from the cafeteria feeling very proud of himself. He knew that he'd definitely avoided a problem. He walked back to his car and began the drive home. Things always seemed so weird to look at in his neighborhood when he wasn't in class. It felt almost like he shouldn't be there. He drove in front of his house and pulled the keys out.

Danny got out and started walking up the lawn, staring at the ground as he walked. It was a bit nippy today, more than it had been all week. He got to his front door and looked up. Then he found a very alarming problem with what he saw: his front door was kicked in. "What the hell?" he mumbled.

Danny walked in and started looking around cautiously. There was random stuff strewn all throughout the living room and the kitchen. He walked further into the house and saw their things literally all over the halls. "Mom! Dad!" Danny started yelling. He didn't get an answer. He started to panic and ran through the house yelling, "Mom!? Dad!" Then Danny realized another problem: his parents work.

Danny felt a huge deal of relief, despite the house being wrecked. He grabbed his phone and called his dad. He continued to look around the house as the phone rang. He found some of his stuff sitting in the living room. He thought that it might've been thrown there, and then realized that he had done that on his own. His dad didn't answer the phone. He pulled the phone from his ear and called his mom's cell phone.

He walked further through the house while the phone rang and rang. He walked to his parents' room and looked at the damage. This room looked similar to all of the other ones. He opened the door to the bathroom and almost dropped the phone as he slipped. He fell hard on the ground and hit his head on the counter. "Ah!" he yelled as he grabbed his head. Then he looked on the floor and found a small puddle of blood with his shoeprint freshly formed in it. Danny's jaw dropped. The phone rang once more, and nobody answered.

Danny ran into the living room and called the police. It rang a few times and an operator picked up, "911 operator."

"Hello! This is Dan Bruce!" Danny attempted to say, though he was out of breath. "I live on Mechanicsville Road . . . in."

"Sir, are you okay?" the operator asked.

"Yes I'm fine, but my parents are gone, the house is trashed and I saw blood on the floor," Danny panted.

"Okay police have been dispatched to your location. Remain at the house until they get there."

"Alright, thank you."

"Are you injured?"

"Well, yeah. But that's just because I fell."

"Do you need a paramedic?" the operator asked, along with all of her other questions.

"No. I'll be fine."

"Okay, is the suspect somewhere in the house?"

Did she expect him to look for some criminal in his house? "Um . . . I don't think so. I walked around a bit."

"Have you checked all of the bathrooms and bedrooms?"

Danny walked to the one bathroom he hadn't been in. "I don't know. I'll check." He felt the fear of wondering if there was still be someone there. He tried to plan how he would fight the guy, but nothing came to mind. He opened the door as quickly as he could and saw another bathroom, also trashed. "Nope. I don't think he's still here."

"Alright. Well where will you be in the house to wait so the officers don't think you're the criminal?" the operator asked.

"I guess the living room."

"Ok sir. The police should be arriving soon."

"Th . . . " Danny paused. "I didn't give you my address."

"The police will be arriving soon, sir."

"You said that, but how do you know where I am?" Danny was getting suspicious. Then the call ended. How did she know where he lived? Danny thought maybe it was some sort of GPS that they used on calls, but he never knew it worked on cell phones. He sat in the living room and a few minutes later, officers were in his driveway.

The officers entered the front door looking around and then walked to Danny. "We got a call?"

"Yeah, officer," Danny said. "Someone must have broken in and I don't know where my parents are. They won't answer my calls and there was blood on the floor in the bathroom of their room."

"Okay and you're Dan Bruce?" the officer attempted to confirm as he approached Danny who was still sitting on the couch.

"Yeah, I am," Danny responded.

The other officer walked to Danny, looked down at him, and said, "I'm going to need you to stand up for me, sir."

"For what?" Danny asked. He was getting even more suspicious.

"You're under arrest for conspiracy to commit a terrorist act," the officer said.

Danny's heart stopped and felt as if it had been filled with lead. He couldn't find the strength to stand up. "Are you serious?" he asked. "What did I do?"

"We were told there's a warrant out for your arrest. Now come on." The officers pulled Danny up and cuffed him. Danny couldn't believe what was going on. He called them and now they were arresting him. What did he do? Did it have something to do with the Committee? He was thinking so much, the time he didn't notice him walking out of his house and before he knew it, he was in the cop car getting his read to him.

Danny sat in the back of the car almost in tears the entire ride. He was humiliated at every stoplight and just distraught the entire drive. The time that passed in the cop car went by much slower than it would if he had driven there himself. It was almost like a parade and the cops were going just slow enough to show Danny off to the world.

They finally arrived at the police station and the officers got out. They walked to the back door and helped Danny out. He walked into the station wearing the same clothes as the day before. The wind was blowing hard as they approached. Danny looked around at all of the people staring him down. People in other cells, other people getting arrested, visitors, they all looked at him as if he was scum. They made the dreadful walk to the desk. Danny had his prints and his photo taken as they prepared him for life in a prison.

"Sit here," the officer told him, pointing towards a chair beside a nearby desk. Danny sat there, his mind wandering, searching for the reason of his arrest. He thought of literally every bad thing he had ever done, scanning his petty crimes for which one landed him in jail. He thought about his friends and family, his college, everything that he had. Even insignificant things like the trees near his house seemed so sacred now. He looked and saw that he wasn't that far from the door. He could see himself getting up and making a mad dash for the door, or simply walking out. He considered just running and never looking back. Skipping town, changing his name, and living somewhere else.

By the time he might've had any courage to do that, the officer was back. "Stand up, we're going to the interrogation room," he said. Danny felt ashamed, but at least now he had hope that he might find out why he was in this place. The officer unlocked the door and led Danny inside. The officer sat him in a chair in front of a table with a chair on the other side of it. It didn't look anything like the movies, but it was just as scary as he could imagine it being. He imagined the scenes with good cops and bad cops and the criminal getting beaten senseless. He pushed that thought away and sat in silence, mouth still slightly open.

After what seemed like an eternity, a man in a suit walked in. He stood across the table from Danny and threw a folder on the table. Now it was starting to seem like a movie. "Hey, Dan, can I call you Danny?" the officer asked with a demented grin on his face.

Danny looked up slowly. He was confused by such a simple question. "I guess."

"Alright then, Danny," the officer said with a smile. "Do you know why you're here?"

Danny tried to come up with a good answer. "I was hoping you could tell me."

"Well, Danny, we've heard that you got caught up in this whole Truth Committee business," the man said as he went through some papers.

"Is it a crime to question what we were told about the assassination?" Danny said, feeling bold. He instantly regretted saying it.

"Not at all," the man assured him. "It is, however, a crime to try to start a revolution or even just a riot."

"How are you accusing me of starting a revolution?" Danny questioned.

"Well, one of our officers told us that you tried to give him a package thinking that he was in the Truth Committee. You instead gave him a letter intended for your college with your name on it." Danny felt like a complete idiot. "Can you tell me what was in the package?"

"Do I have to tell you what was in a package that I was trying to give to a friend?"

"You do if you don't just want to be put in a cell right now." Danny then felt very obligated to start talking. "You see, Danny, I don't want to see a young bright kid go behind bars. I just don't want you to fall into this whole business that the Committee's spreading like your dad unfortunately did."

"What did you say about my dad?" Danny grew concerned. "Do you know where he is?"

"Let's not start asking questions we already know answers to, Danny," the man said with the same demonic and unsettling grin.

"Do you know something about him?" Danny asked, sounding helpless. "Do you know where he is? Please tell me."

The guy looked at Danny and put his hand on the table. "Look Danny, I hate to separate kids from their parents, but . . . "

Danny freaked out and yelled, "Where the hell is he?" He started to stand up, but the officer that had brought him in sat him back down.

"Danny, your dad was involved in a dangerous group. You are too, but I know you can change. Your dad's in another prison."

"Which one?" Danny pleaded.

"A government prison."

"What does that mean?"

"It means he's a homeland security threat so he's having eyes on him at all time."

"Can you tell me the name of it?" Danny asked.

"It's classified."

"You can't just keep my dad locked up somewhere and not tell anyone where he is," Danny complained. He was getting nowhere with this guy and it was frustrating him to no end.

"Danny, if you keep talking like that you'll be going to thc same place, and that's not a place you want to be. I will let you out today if you simply tell me what you know about the Committee."

Danny looked down to the floor. Should he do as that old woman told him and stand up and suffer the consequences? It would be the right thing to do, but then he wouldn't be able to do anything to speak out. Nobody would even know where he was. The only thing he could really do was spill the beans and get out of there so he could warn others. "All I know is that the package had numbers of people that were in the Committee and some pamphlets," Danny confessed.

"Who was the package intended for?" The officer asked, now sitting down taking notes.

"For some guy I was supposed to meet there," Danny said. "I don't know who he was."

"The officer said you gave it to gave it to someone else."

"No, the officer was gone and I left shortly after. My friend got a coffee and we left."

"Who was your friend?"

"He has nothing to do with this. He's an idiot and someone I just met. I wouldn't trust someone like that with that information about the package and the Committee," Danny lied. He thought that it might have worked, but he couldn't be sure.

The officer wrote down a few more things. "Okay, last thing: have you been to or know of any meetings?"

"No, my dad just told me about it," Danny lied again. "He hasn't even been to any meetings for anything. We aren't in any big underground operation like you think we are. You can let him go. We were just trying to get other people to think about it. I didn't even think it was that big of a thing."

"So you just believe in what the Committee says, but you don't go to any meetings?" the man asked.

Danny tried to think of a good lie to say, "Do they have meetings for that sort of thing?" he asked.

The officer looked at Danny and pushed his tongue to his cheek. He thought for a few moments and stood up. He nodded to the officer across the room who then uncuffed Danny. "Well, Danny, you're free to go," the man said. "And don't go spreading that business about your dad or we'll get you back here. Whether you want to believe it or not, he's a criminal and there's nothing you can do about that. I'm sorry it had to happen to you, but that's the way things are." Danny wanted so badly to hit him in the face, but he couldn't even mutter a last word. He was so confused and so angry that his basic abilities had become disabled.

The officer led Danny outside and to the parking lot outside. "Do you need a ride to a family member's house?" he asked. This was the only time that Danny had actually looked at the officer. He was a really large guy and seemed to be of Latino descent.

Danny thought about it. He could always just go to Charlie's and figure out what to do. He didn't have much of a choice. "Can you just take me to my college?" The officer nodded and led Danny to the car. They both got in and started to drive out of the parking lot.

The officer stopped at the end of the lot and turned around to Danny. "Look, Danny," he said. "You need to get your uncle and get somewhere safe."

Danny was stunned. "What?" he asked from the back.

"They're going to be going to get your uncle very soon," the officer said. "They know that he's a part of the conspiracy and you need to get him and hide as soon as possible."

Danny didn't know what to say. Was he ready to trust an officer when he was just completely betrayed by the police department that was supposed to protect him? "How do they know where he lives?" Danny asked.

"You know your uncle has been in run ins with cops before," the officer said. "I know your uncle. Most people just call him Champ?"

"I mean . . . " Danny began.

"Look, Danny. Just tell me where he lives and we'll get him out of here. You have to trust me. I know this whole situation is really messed up and confusing, but you need to get him out of here. I don't know what I can say. All I can say is that you need to trust me."

Danny thought about it for a while. He didn't have much of a choice, seeing how the officer was probably going to keep pushing the issue. "Alright, I'll trust you," Danny told the officer. He gave him his uncle's address and leaned back in his seat.

"Thank you, Danny" the officer said. "I know it's got to take a lot to trust anyone nowadays. Believe me when I say I hate this whole situation too. I've considered joining the Committee, but if I was caught, well I work in the police station so it would be pretty detrimental to me. They would think I was a traitor and probably kill me. Regardless, I'm here to defend the citizens and your group is included in that."

They were almost halfway to Champ's house. They had just been talking about the Committee and the protests. Danny told him about the old woman and about the wall of people at the protest. He could almost tell if this guy was genuine.

They eventually stopped talking and Danny just started thinking about his dad. He felt terrible that he wouldn't even give a night with friends up to see his family. He thought of how proud his dad was of him when he heard that Danny would be in the Committee with him. He thought of his mom who had always been so inspirational and always told him to keep his mind open. Then he thought of how much blame should go onto his shoulders for making such a dumb mistake. His failure had gotten them taken from their normal lives forever and he couldn't bear to know it.

By the time he looked up, they were pulling into Champ's driveway. The officer and Danny walked up to the door and the officer knocked. They waited a few moments and Champ opened the door. Danny feared that the officer would grab his uncle and take him back to the station. To his relief, Champ yelled, "Rob! Holy hell! How have you been!" Then he looked and saw Danny. "Danny, why are you with a cop and why were you in a cop car?" He looked back at Rob and asked, "Is he in trouble."

Rob looked at Champ sternly and said, "We need to talk a bit."

"Well come on in you two," Champ said as he backed out of the doorway. Danny walked in behind Rob and sat on Champ's couch. The officer sat to the right of him and Champ sat across.

"So what happened?" Champ asked as he held a beer from earlier in the day tightly in his hand.

Rob looked at his hands for a second. His fingers were interlocked with his elbows on his knees. He then looked at the table between him and Champ. "They took Brian and Marisa for their Committee activity."

Champ sat without showing a reaction. He looked away and then fell back into the couch cushion and sipped his beer. "How did they know they were involved?" he asked.

Rob didn't say anything. He sort of looked at Danny and then back. Champ looked at Danny and realized what he was trying to explain. It would be a lie to say that Champ didn't feel a great deal of disappointment in his nephew. Rob nodded his head. "It was a mistake," he said. "He messed up on delivering a package and long story short the cops figured it out. They got them last night around midnight or so."

"Those sons of bitches," Champ said as he got up and threw his empty beer at a wall.

Rob stood up and said, "Champ . . . they're coming for you in less than an hour."

Champ spun around in a fury and yelled, "What the hell? Why?"

"They associated you with him. We need to get out of here. I'll drive you guys anywhere you need."

Champ ran and packed a few pieces of clothing and ran back in the room in less than a minute.

"Sons of bitch government assholes trying to fucking kill me," he was rambling. Danny was now standing from his spot and Rob was heading for the door. They all walked as fast as they could to Rob's cop car. Rob told Champ, "You're gunna want to lay down in the back so nobody will see you. And once the car turns on, nobody talk. The dash cam rolls when the cars on and I don't want to get myself locked up." Champ and Danny nodded. "So where can I take you?"

Danny and Champ thought for a bit. "Can we go to that place where the meetings were?" Danny asked.

Champ thought about it for a moment. "Alright, I'll send Adam a text or something and let him know that we're coming." Meanwhile, Danny told Rob the address and they got on their way. The silence on the way to Adam's was horrible for Danny to have to hear. He continued to think of everything that had happened with his parents and continued to feel horrible for everything that he'd done to cause their abduction. All he wanted was a chance to hug them and tell them he loved them. It was a horrible feeling knowing that he couldn't even have that luxury.

They drove a short way from Champ's and found Adam's house. Danny got out and Champ gave Rob a handshake. Rob did the "call me" thing with his hand and Champ nodded. Danny and Champ walked to Adam's door and knocked. Adam opened the door quickly and said, "Hey guys, come on in." Adam looked as distraught as everyone else.

Danny and Champ went into the kitchen and sat at the table. Adam brought them some steak that he had made. "Thanks, Adam," Champ muttered.

"Sure thing," Adam answered. "You guys have been through hell. It's the least I can do. You guys can stay as long as you please. Hopefully we can figure something out."

"Yeah," Champ said. The three looked down at their meals and started eating.

Adam looked up at Danny, who was barely eating. He stopped eating and said, "I'm sorry to hear about what happened with your parents. They were great people, and we'll make sure we do all we can to get them out."

Danny looked up. All he could mutter was a small, "Thanks."

"Do you want to call anyone?" Adam asked. "Any friends or something? They're welcome to stay to keep you company tonight."

Danny thought about it for a bit. Charlie was probably still too angry to contact. It looked like Amanda was the only other person he could call. "Yeah, I'll call my friend Amanda," he said.

"The phone's right over there," Adam said, pointing to the phone. Danny took it to the other room and shut the door.

Danny typed in the number very slowly and finally got the phone to his ear. It rang a few times and Amanda answered, "Hello?"

"Amanda, it's Danny," he mumbled. "I need you to come to hang with me tonight."

"What?" Amanda asked. "Why? Where are you?"

"I'm at that place where the meeting was," Danny said. "Just get here as quick as you can. I need someone to talk to."

"Okay. I'll leave right now."

Danny put the phone down and went back to the kitchen. "Where can I sleep tonight?" he asked Adam.

Adam said, "You can sleep in the spare bedroom downstairs."

"Thank you," Danny said. "It means a lot." Danny headed downstairs and waited for Amanda on the bed. Until she arrived, he was a prisoner to his thoughts.

Less than a half hour later, Amanda knocked at the door. Danny could hear Adam letting her in and saying, "He's right downstairs."

Danny listened to the footsteps as they went down each stair. Then he listened as Amanda walked to the door of the bedroom. She knocked twice. "It's open," Danny told her.

She walked in and gave Danny a hug and asked, "What's wrong?" Amanda took off her jacket and set it on the floor.

Danny could do nothing but stare at the floor. He felt the emotions starting to boil over inside. He fought as hard as he could to hold them back. He forced the words to come out of his mouth, "They took my parents."

Amanda sat confused and asked, "Who took your parents?"

"The cops took my parents for being in the Committee," Danny said.

Amanda sat in shock. She couldn't believe what she heard. She couldn't even think of what to say to Danny. All she could say was, "Oh my God . . .Are you okay?"

Danny broke down and cried, “No I’m really not, Amanda. I just lost my fucking parents.” He started sobbing.

Amanda threw her arms around him as the tears filled his face. The constant pressure finally got to him. The fears of what happened to his parents finally surfaced. The pain of how his life had taken a turn for the worst had finally forced him to his breaking point. “When did they take them?” she asked.

“Last night,” he sobbed. “And I couldn’t even make the time to have a damn dinner with them. I refused to put what I wanted aside in order to just give my parents time with their only son. I’m supposed to be their pride and fucking joy and all I do in return is get them thrown into a prison in God knows where.” He cried even harder.

“How did they find out they were even in it?” Amanda asked.

Danny explained everything through tears. He told her how he had mistaken the cop for Alan and how the police tracked them down. He told her about the protests. He told her about everything that had happened today and how his uncle was now on the run because of him. “All I did was fuck up and now everyone I love is in trouble,” Danny admitted.

“Danny, we all make mistakes,” Danny said. “You can’t blame yourself.” Amanda was starting to get emotional as she watched one of her best friends fall apart. “I know the effects were greater than most people’s mistakes, but it was an honest mistake. You can believe everyone in the Committee will help to find your parents. They’ll be fine.”

“How can you even believe that? The government thinks my parents are terrorists, there’s no way they’re going to just let them go,” Danny explained. “It’s fucking hopeless, Amanda.”

Amanda sat back for a moment. She didn't know what to say to calm Danny down. He had given up any sort of hope. He was nothing like what he usually was. "Danny, I know you don't know what to do. I know you feel like you can't do anything, but trust me, nobody's going to let your parents go down without some sort of a fight being made about it," Amanda told him. "Any support you need while we all try to figure out what to do, you'll find it with me. I love you Danny. You're my best friend and I can firmly tell you that I won't let you feel this way without something being done to help."

"Thanks, Amanda," Danny mumbled. His tears were starting to subside and he was feeling worn out. He looked over to her and asked, "What do you think they'll do to help them?"

Amanda thought for a second, "Well they'll definitely make sure nobody forgets about your parents and they'll make sure that everyone knows about them. They're not going to be stuck in there without the whole country asking to see them. The Committee won't let them get hurt and they'll make sure you get them back. But for now, you need to stop blaming yourself. That isn't going to fix anything, it's just going to make the battle to see them again much harder."

"What else can I do?" Danny asked, wiping the tears from his eyes. "I don't know how we'll find them. They're lost."

"You can be thankful that we're all here to help you through this and help to help your parents. It's all you can do right now. And they're not lost, Danny. We don't know where they are, but we'll definitely find out. There are a lot of smart people in the Committee and I guarantee at least one of them will know how to find them."

Danny looked at Amanda and smiled. He'd found out that at least he had some genuine people left to help him through the toughest part of his life. Amanda smiled right back. Danny felt like he could truly love this girl. She was the first person he called in the toughest moment of his life. She was the one that had always been a person that he could turn to, and he loved her for it.

Danny leaned in and kissed her. She moved to him and held him firmly as ever. They had quickly figured out that they were both in this together. They embraced the love that they could find in times of tragedy. Danny's sorrow subsided as best as it could for the time being and he enjoyed the company, and the love, of someone that truly cared about him.

CHAPTER SEVEN

REBUILD

"A house on Mechanicsville Road was broken into yesterday night. Officers said that the home, owned by the Bruce family, was broken into at some point between Friday night and Saturday morning. The two parents Brian and Marisa Bruce have recently gone missing as well. This suspected kidnapping was one of hundreds in the past month. Police urge anyone with information on this crime, as well as the other recent crimes, to contact them with information."

Danny woke up early in the morning the next day. He had gotten little to no sleep last night, and no matter how tired he became, he couldn't find the ability to close his eyes. Too many thoughts were racing through his head for sleep to have been possible.

As he laid in his bed, he looked over and saw Amanda still sleeping, very deeply from the looks of it. Without waking her up, Danny got out of bed and walked to the bathroom. The room was still dark, but he could tell that the sun was beginning to rise. It had been a long night, and he was just happy that the others would be awake soon to keep him company.

Danny closed the door behind him and paced around the bathroom for a bit, looking for something to do to take up time. He walked to the sink and looked up at the mirror at the distraught face that peered back. He knew that there was no way that he would ever see his parents again, and it killed him inside. The entire cause revolved around the same problem: he was involved in the Committee. Danny thought hard about it, and came to the conclusion that he would have to leave the Committee. He didn't want to hurt anyone else. He'd rather just continue to live his life in the way that he used to.

From the beginning, he knew that joining the group was a bad idea. He didn't like the sound of it then, and he decided to follow what would please his family rather than his gut. Even when he knew the risks of being in the organization, he continued on. Now that the only ones that had kept his desire to remain in the group alive were gone, there was nothing holding him to his previous decision.

Danny moved to the door and walked out of the bathroom. He walked to his clothes he had worn yesterday and put them back on. Amanda rustled around in her bed. It seemed that Danny had woken her up. She looked a lot more tired than Danny, even though she had gotten a substantial amount more sleep than he had. Amanda pulled the blanket off and sat up. She looked up to Danny while simultaneously rubbing her eyes. "How'd you sleep?" she mumbled.

Danny was now checking his phone for any new texts or calls. "Not all that well," he said with much more energy than he had. "Gotta say."

Amanda stood up and walked to her suitcase. She opened it and grabbed a new outfit to change into. "I'm sorry to hear that," she said. Danny just looked down at the floor while putting his phone back into his pocket. He stood in the same spot, completely motionless, as Amanda went to the bathroom to change. He rubbed the back of his head and looked around the room. It was full of stuff he'd expect to see at his grandmother's house. A bunch of useless vintage glassware covered every nook and cranny. Even the smell reminded him of his grandmother's house.

Danny heard footsteps coming down the stairs. He moved to the other room in order to meet them. As he opened the door, he saw Champ walking to the door. "Oh hey!" Champ said. "I was just on the way to wake you two up. We've got breakfast going upstairs."

"This early?" Danny responded.

"Yeah, Adam wanted to get up early for some reason and woke me up a half hour or so ago," Champ said.

"I'll come up whenever Amanda's done in the bathroom," Danny told him.

"Cool. Just don't take too long. Nobody likes cold bacon." Danny always loved bacon in the morning, but it didn't have the same appeal that it normally had, then again nothing really did. Amanda finished up in the bathroom and walked back to her suitcase. She threw yesterday's clothes in and pulled out a few small details to add to her outfit.

Amanda looked over to Danny as she put her hair up. "You really should go get some more clothes from your house," she said as she looked at his wrinkled clothes.

Danny thought about home. He remembered the horror that he faced when he found the place completely ransacked. Danny turned to Amanda and said., "I don't want to think about home right now." There was no way he'd be going back any time soon.

Amanda looked to the ground. She knew Danny was still upset, but had no idea how to help him. Not many people know how to comfort someone that had lost the closest family they have, and she was no exception. She felt as if she was in a helpless situation. "Well . . . do you want to go get some breakfast?" she asked.

"I guess," Danny told her. She smiled at him and they walked upstairs.

The smell of breakfast filled the entire floor. The smell of perfectly cooked sausage, soft pancakes, and crispy bacon rushed the groups' noses. Danny moved up the stairs at a groggy pace and Amanda followed closely behind, almost stepping on his heels with every step.

The two entered the kitchen and saw Adam and Champ sitting at the table in the dining room. "Morning," Adam greeted them with a smile. "Help yourselves to whatever you want. I made a lot so don't be scared to help yourselves."

"Thank you very much, Adam," Amanda said with a smile. Her and Danny walked around the counter, filling their plates with piles of food. They covered every bit of food with salt, pepper, syrup, whatever they thought would enhance the flavor. Danny sat across from Champ and Amanda across from Adam. The four looked at each other's plates, investigating what the taste buds of the table were thinking. Champ was finishing up his first plate, and, from the look of his speed, he would soon be filling another plate. Adam was picking around his plate, trying to find the best morsels to feed himself. Danny ate with a hesitation that confused the rest of the table.

Danny's depression was bringing an uncomfortable silence to the table, and it didn't go unnoticed. When they could see that Danny wasn't looking, the rest of the group would exchange glances, sympathizing with their friends' confusion. It was an odd time, and Adam attempted to alleviate the situation.

"So what's the plan for the day?" Adam asked the table in the cheeriest voice he could muster. Everyone continued to sit and pick at their food. They had only partially understood due mostly to the distractions sitting on their plates and in their minds. Champ was getting up for that next plate when Adam asked, so he had no time to respond. Adam looked around, "Anyone doing anything today?" Again everyone took a while to register what Adam had just said.

"You two have school tomorrow, right?" Champ said from the plate of bacon, disregarding what Adam had said.

"Yes, sir," Amanda replied politely.

"Well then you two should go out and enjoy the day," Champ suggested. "I'm sure Adam can show you guys a good time!"

Adam looked a bit blindsided by the accusation. He glanced around the table and Danny's morbid demeanor caught his eye. "Yeah," he said, nodding his head. "I'll make sure you guys can enjoy the day before school tomorrow."

"Sound good to you Dan?" Champ asked. He was now turned around with bacon in his hand. The rest of the table looked up to see how the wreck of a child would respond to the suggestion.

Danny looked up from his untouched plate. He reached down and put a piece of bacon into his mildly agape mouth. "Yeah," he said. Danny continued to stare at his food and started to finally pick at it. He was having a hard time eating, and thought that maybe this would be a good time to tell everyone that he didn't want to be a part of the Committee anymore. Then again, why spoil such an extravagant breakfast that Adam had prepared.

Danny continued to eat, now picking up the pace. The small social interaction was making him a bit more comfortable, but by the way he was behaving, nobody would have been able to tell. Amanda stood up and walked over to Champ. She tapped on his shoulder and began to whisper in his ear as Danny continued to dilly dally around his food. After their exchange, Champ and Amanda left the room.

Adam looked over at Danny again. The room was getting awkward again and Adam wanted nothing more than to lift the spirits of it. "So, Danny," he began, fishing through his mind for something to say. "What would you want to do today?"

Danny finished up his last piece of bacon and moved to his eggs. "I don't know," Danny said. "I kind of want to just stay in."

Adam felt like he had to try to help this sad kid. As everyone feels when they see a friend in need, Adam felt like it was his responsibility. He was one of the kindest people in Massachusetts and it showed in situations like these. "Do you want to talk about what you're thinking, Danny?"

Meanwhile, in the next room, Amanda and Champ were talking about Danny's behavior. "I just don't know what to do," Amanda told Champ.

"I feel like I should talk to him," Champ told her. "I might be able to cheer him up a bit."

"About what?" Amanda asked. "It's understandable that he's upset, I just don't know what to do. Should you talk to him about his future in the Committee?"

"Hmm . . . That's definitely an issue we need to talk about. I would think the kid would want to do something to get his parents back, but I think he's given up all hope. He probably just wants to live the life of a normal kid. He's had his life turned upside down, so I'd think that he would just want the closest thing to normal that the world can offer him at this point."

In the kitchen, the conversation wasn't much different. "I just don't think that I could go on working with you guys," Danny told Adam.

"Danny," Adam stopped eating. "I understand your frustration, but wouldn't it make sense to continue so that one day we can get your parents back? We'll do everything we have to do to make it happen, believe me on that, but we'll need your help."

"I just want to go back to my normal life," Danny said. "It's this group that caused all of this to happen and I just want to get back to what I was doing before this. I'll just move in with my uncle or something and I'll just finish up at college and buy a house."

Adam felt defeated. There was nothing he could say to him to make him feel better or to even persuade him to continue to work for the group. "Well . . . I can't force you to do anything," Adam muttered. "Well is there anything I can do to try to convince you otherwise?"

"I really don't think so, Adam," Danny responded. "I respect what you guys are doing, but I don't want any part in something that ruined my life."

Guilt hit Adam like a freight train. Being the kind of person he was, he took on the full load of responsibility, regardless of the reality of the situation. "Well, I'd still like to take you and Amanda out somewhere to cheer you up a bit. It's the least I can do."

Danny looked up at Adam's defeated face. He could tell that Adam really just wanted to make Danny feel better, and Danny felt obligated to give him a chance. "I think that's a pretty good idea," he said.

Adam's face mustered a small smile. "Awesome," he said, returning his eyes to the food.

In the other room, Amanda and Champ were finishing up their conversation. "You should really go out with all of us tonight too, Champ," Amanda said.

"I really wish I could," Champ confessed. "But they're out looking for me. There's nothing I can do."

"Alright, Champ. I'll try to talk to Danny about the Committee today."

"Thanks, Amanda. Mostly just make sure the boy's okay. I feel so bad for him."

"Well how are you handling all of this?" Amanda asked. Nobody had really asked Champ how he felt about the loss of his brother and sister-in-law.

He looked at Amanda with a saddened expression. "It really upsets me and pisses me off," he said. "But right now, I'm just more concerned with taking care of my brother's son than my own emotions."

Amanda and Champ made their way back into the kitchen, completely unaware of the conversation that Adam and Danny had shared. Adam greeted them again with, "Hey. We came to the conclusion that we're gunna go into Boston for the day. I'm sure we can find something fun to do there."

"Sounds awesome," Amanda told him. She picked up her plate, dumped the scraps into the trash and washed her plate. The rest of the group followed suit. Danny wasted much more of his portion than the rest of the group.

Once everyone had cleared their plates, Adam clapped his hands together and said, "Alright, let's hit the road then!"

"Okay," Champ said. "You all have a great time. Let me know how it goes."

Adam walked outside to his car, followed by Amanda and Danny. It was much brighter out than Danny had thought it was from his room downstairs. The three got into the small car to leave for their destination. Danny sat in the front passenger seat and Amanda sat in the middle of the back seat. Adam turned the car on and tried to turn the heat on right away, but all that came out was a brisk breeze of cold air. It looked like they'd have to drive a ways with no heat.

Adam started up conversation immediately to avoid the awkward silence that had taken place at the table inside. "So are you excited, Danny?" he asked.

"Yeah," he replied. "I just need to want to take my mind off of everything and start feeling better."

Adam turned to him and said, "Yeah. Me too, buddy." Then the awkward silence began. Sensing it's arrival, Adam sprung into action. "So what's your college like?"

"It's so amazing," Amanda said. "The professors are great, and the classes are interesting, and just everything about it is so great." It was a much longer and sporadic response than Adam had expected, but that's what you get from Amanda, no matter the conversation.

"What do you think of it, Danny?" Adam asked.

Danny stared out of the window. "It's pretty cool," he said.

Adam waited for more, but got nothing. "Is that it?" he asked.

"I mean, there's a lot to do," Danny responded. "I don't know what else to say."

Nothing was getting through the wall of depression that Danny had up.

"What do you want to do when we get into Boston?" Amanda asked Danny.

"Whatever you guys wanna do," Danny said.

Adam couldn't take it anymore. "You really want your parents back, don't you?" Adam asked.

Danny looked at him, knowing that he should already know the answer to that. "Of course, more than anything in the world," he said.

"Well you seem to think that they're gone forever," Adam said. "You realize that chances are they're very much alive and they're probably not far from reach."

Danny shook his head. "I highly doubt it," he said. "I want to hope, but I have no strength to do so. I want to believe that they're still alive and they're just waiting to be rescued, but with how everything's gone, I wouldn't be surprised if I never saw them again."

Adam became frustrated by Danny's attitude. "Why think like that?" he said. "Why can't you just believe that they're okay? It's clear that everyone else thinks that they're fine and we can still get them back."

"Because I don't want to be upset when I realize that they really aren't coming back," Danny concluded.

Adam had been defeated by Danny's doubt. It was impossible to argue with someone that had given up all hope in what another was trying to persuade them of.

Amanda took the reins. "But Danny," she started. "What if you did see them again?"

"I'd be the happiest kid in the world," Danny said. "But I have no reason to believe that it'll ever happen. I keep saying it, but I don't think you guys are getting it."

"I'm not saying you don't have a reason to believe that," Amanda said. "But why don't you think about how happy you would be if you saw them again, and hold onto that feeling?"

Danny turned towards the back of the car. "What do you mean?" he asked.

"I mean, why don't you make the happiness that you'd feel your incentive for fighting?" she said. "Why don't you fight to find them in order to feel the happiness that you know you'll feel?"

Danny hesitated. "I don't know," he said. "I just don't want to cling to something that might not ever come."

"Well at the very least, just keep that thought in the back of your head," Amanda said. "I'm sure it will help you to feel much better."

"Eh," Danny said. "I guess."

The car remained silent the rest of the ride. They'd tried to help Danny, but he wasn't having any of it. It was clear that he preferred to be miserable. Some people are just like that.

Once they arrived in Boston, Adam drove them to the front of the coffee shop that Danny had made his fatal flaw at. Adam was completely oblivious of that. "I'll be right back, guys," he told the two. "Just got to drop something off."

Adam left the two in the car and went inside with a book bag. Danny stared up at the building from his seat. He could remember the fear that he'd felt when he screwed up, and the stupidity he felt when he'd gone the extra mile to make his situation even worse.

Amanda noticed his interest in the building and decided to ask, "Are you alright, Danny?"

Danny looked back at Amanda and told her, "This is where I messed up the package delivery."

Amanda realized the significance of the building. She looked at the building and imagined the situation that Danny had been put in. It was then that she'd noticed a point that Danny hadn't. "Didn't you say that the package had important information regarding everyone in our chapter of the Committee?"

"Yeah," Danny replied. "A total for like forty people's addresses and whatnot."

"And you gave it to the wrong guy, but still went to him to try to get it back, and did so successfully?" she added.

"What are you trying to get at?" Danny snapped. "I didn't do it successfully. I fucked up and it cost me my parents. Did you not understand that?"

"Danny," Amanda paused. "You don't even realize what you did."

"What do you mean?" Danny asked as his interest took precedence over his sadness.

"You saved the lives of everyone in the chapter," Amanda said. "You don't even see that your choice to get the package back rather than just turning the other cheek saved all of us. If they had gotten that information, everyone would've been taken. Me, you, Adam, your parents, all of our families. You're a hero, Danny."

Danny thought about it. There was no arguing with Amanda's logic. Danny would have lost his parents either way. It was a classic ethics situation. Sacrifice a few to save the rest. It still hurt to know that he lost his parents, but at least now he could rest easy knowing that he did save the entire chapter.

"Amanda," Danny said.

"Yeah, Danny?" Amanda responded, very hopeful.

"How did you manage to get as smart as you are?" he asked.

Amanda chuckled and said, "I guess some of us just study more than others." Danny smiled. "So are you feeling better?"

Danny laughed a bit, "A lot better." He turned around and smiled at Amanda, "Thank you."

"It's what I'm here for," Amanda smiled.

Danny turned back around and saw Adam walking back to the car. He looked pretty happy. He entered the car and let out a joyful yelp. "So guess what I just got!" he challenged them.

"What?" Danny asked.

"Well we've had some people in the D.C. chapter watching President Stone and his secretaries as closely as possible," Adam began. "Well the Secretary of Defense William James was followed by one of them. Take a wild guess where he went."

"Where?" Amanda asked.

"He went to the prison where the gunman that killed Marshall is being detained," Adam continued. "After an hour inside, guess who he came out with."

"Don't tell me the gunman," Amanda guessed.

"Spot on," Adam smiled. "And our guy got a great picture of them walking together out of the prison." Adam reached into the book bag and held up the picture. "So the plot thickens."

Adam started cracking up. Amanda quickly joined in and patted Adam on the back. Adam looked at Danny. Danny wasn't smiling as much as they were. "Aren't you excited, Danny?"

Danny knew this changed everything. The Committee actually had some proof that Stone had something to do with the assassination. Danny looked over to Adam, "Hell yeah I'm excited." The three started cracking up and high fiving each other.

"Does this mean that you're gunna stay with the Committee?" Adam asked.

Danny thought about it for a second, "My mom had always told me that I can't just follow others blindly. My dad told me to always be open-minded. We have solid proof that Stone was involved. I have to stick around, for them."

"It's great to hear," Adam said. He gave Danny a hug. "Your dad would be so proud of you."

"I'm so glad you're gunna stay, Danny," Amanda contributed. She gave him a hug as well.

"So what's next?" Danny asked.

"We need to get this picture on the internet, in people's hands, everywhere." Adam told him. "Let's enjoy today, and we'll get to work tomorrow."

"Sounds good," Danny said, still smiling. He was feeling so much better. It was unbelievable.

"Well, let's get out and go have some fun," Adam said as he opened his door. The others got out as well and they began their walk on the sidewalk. "Alright so here's my plan: We'll go see a movie, and then we'll go out to a nice restaurant. All of it on me."

"Are you sure you don't want us to give you some money?" Amanda asked.

"Don't worry about it," Adam told her. "You two just worry about having a good time.

"Thanks," the two told Adam. They started their short walk to the movie theater.

Danny couldn't believe how much his mood had changed. Every step had a bit of pep in it now. He was so much happier. He knew where they were going and he knew that he would be making his parents proud. When he finally found them, they would be ecstatic about how much he had taken their advice.

As they walked through Boston, it seemed almost like the city was full of a brightness that was bettering the moods of everyone they passed. Maybe it had something to do with the luck that they had been having. Hell, maybe it was just the weather. It made Danny a lot happier to think that the day's luck was making the day that much brighter.

After a few blocks, the group had reached the theater. They paid to see an action film and went in. Adam bought everyone some popcorn and they entered the room to take their seats. Danny sat in the middle of the two and sat back and relaxed for the first time since he'd been forced to leave his home. As the previews started to roll, Danny started thinking how crazy of a movie his life would be. Everything that had been happening would have made for quite the movie. The movie would only be getting crazier, and the three knew it.

"That was a hell of a movie," Danny said as they left the theater after the show. They started walking to a restaurant right down the street.

"Yeah it was," Adam added. "The action scenes were insane. Then again, that's what always happens when I see a movie with actors like that."

"Yeah definitely," Danny concluded.

"Man," Adam began. "Looking around, you would never know that something this big was going on underground. You would never see Boston like this and think that there was a revolution of sorts rising up."

Just as Adam said that, they rounded the corner and saw police officers breaking into a house across the street. The three could hear a huge ruckus coming from inside. They heard things breaking and suddenly heard a woman screaming. Shortly after entering, the officers brought a young couple out of the house. They were both screaming asking what they had done. The only answer they got were rifle butts to the back of the head as they were thrown into the cop car. As soon as it had started, it was done.

"Well I take that back," Adam said. The three continued to watch as the cop car drove away. The front door of the house was still on the ground. "Well let's get to the restaurant. I suddenly don't feel that safe."

They entered the restaurant and were quickly greeted by a hostess. "Welcome, how many today?"

"Three," Adam told her. "And we'll be having someone else joining later."

"What?" Danny asked.

"I'll explain when we get to the table."

"Alright, just follow me," the hostess said as she motioned forward. They walked to a table in the far right corner.

"I always sit here," Adam told Amanda and Danny.

"Can I get you all something to drink?" the hostess asked them.

"I'll get the best beer you've got," Adam told her.

"I'll get tea," Amanda said.

"Come on," Adam told her. "We're celebrating. Live dangerously."

The table laughed. "Okay," Amanda said. "I'll get a margarita."

"There you go!" Adam laughed.

"And for you, sir?" the hostess said to Danny.

"I'll get what he's having," he told the hostess as he pointed to Adam.

"Good choice," Adam added. The hostess walked away and the three started talking. "Alright so I'm meeting a guy soon so he can make copies of the picture and put them everywhere on the internet. And he even knows a cameraman at the local news station. So that guy will push the picture onto the news. We're looking at a huge increase in membership."

"Whoop whoop," Danny joked.

Adam laughed and added, "Which brings me to my next point. Danny, I'm going to need to ask a huge favor of you."

"Go on," Danny said. He had no idea the suggestion that was about to come out of Adam's mouth.

"We need to use your house as a safe house," Adam told him.

Danny was expecting something small. This was a pretty big risk, though. "What would I have to do?" he asked.

"Well the way I see it, the city has no idea where you are right now. They thought you were going to your uncle's, but now he's missing in their eyes as well. They are going to think that house is uninhabited. You just board up the doors and windows like they usually do to abandoned houses that are deemed unsafe to live it. This will ensure security and it will guarantee that nobody will be coming by trying to buy the house."

"What about when it's all boarded up?" Danny asked.

"Well, we'd be hiding people that are running from the government. Also, we'll try to run some operations through that house. We will have an old ham radio set up so we can communicate back and forth with other chapters. Then whoever is in our group can come up with further plans, if that's okay with you."

Danny didn't really have to think much. Once this picture got out, the police would be trying to get everyone that was joining the Committee. He had to do it to help the cause. "Alright. I'm down," he said.

"Awesome!" Adam said. "Wow, great timing." Danny turned around and saw a guy walking up to their table. "John! What's going on, man?" Adam yelled.

"Not much," John said. "I can't stick around long, I've gotta get going so I don't get arrested."

"Ah, of course," Adam said. "Well this is Danny and his friend Amanda."

"Nice to meet you two," John said as he shook their hands.

"Yep," Adam started. "Danny here will be using his house for a safe house."

"Is that so?" John asked.

"Sure is," Danny told John with a smile.

"Awesome," John replied. "Is it okay if I lay low there for a while? My house is actually getting raided as we speak. I have all of my important stuff in my car."

Danny felt pretty awesome getting asked something like that. It was his first person to help out! "Sure thing!" Danny told him. "Just let me write down the address and I'll see you there when we're done here."

"Ugh thank you so much," John said. "Well I'll just get that picture and be on my way."

"Oh yeah," Adam said. "Here you go." Adam gave John the picture.

"Wow," John exclaimed, looking at the picture in awe. "This is really good quality. I'll get this copied and sent around once I get to the house. Alright I'll see you guys. I'll have that radio and such set up by the time you get home, Danny."

"Alright, see yah," Danny and the others said in their own ways. John left the restaurant looking left and right to make sure he was in the clear.

"Well guys," Adam said as their drinks arrived. "I'm going to have to discuss something with you."

"Are you guys ready to order?" the hostess asked.

Adam was a bit put off that he was interrupted and said, "Um . . . yeah just get us some steaks."

"Alright, and how would you all like them?" the hostess asked.

"Rare," Adam said.

"Well done," Amanda decided.

"And I'll get mine medium rare," Danny told her.

"Alright I'll put this into the kitchen," the hostess said as she walked away.

Danny took a sip of his beer. He reeled back a bit and said, "Damn. That's good, but it's strong."

"Yeah, it's a lager," Adam laughed. "Alright now back to business. I'm afraid that tomorrow is your guys' last day of school."

Danny and Amanda traded confused glances. "Why?" Amanda asked.

"Because once this stuff gets going, kids are going to start getting pulled out of that school. It's the easiest place for the police to find you, besides your house."

Amanda was obviously more distraught than Danny. "Isn't there another way?" she asked.

"I'm afraid not. You'll still have your books if you want to continue to learn, but you can't go there anymore. Tomorrow, find any kids that you can trust and get them to Danny's house."

"Awesome!" Danny yelled. "This is going to be awesome. I honestly can't wait to never see that school again."

Adam laughed and added, "I understand that. But don't think that you don't have to work hard anymore. You'll be working even harder now."

"Alright, Adam," Danny said. The steaks arrived and the three chowed down. Amanda was obviously still upset, but she got over it. The three had a real bond going. Adam had become somewhat of a second father for the two of them.

The three left Boston pretty late. Adam took Amanda by her house so she could tell her parents about the situation. They were excited, but upset that they had to see their daughter give up college so close to graduation. Amanda's parents got working on setting up their radio and making sure they added some security to their home.

Adam went and picked up Danny's uncle and drove Danny and Champ back to Danny's house. Danny walked up to the now boarded up front door. His house looked so odd, and in a way, almost demonic. John had gotten to work quickly. He already had all of the windows and doors boarded up from the outside. For a second, Danny didn't know how they were supposed to get in. Then while in the back yard at the bottom of a hill, John opened the boarded up back door.

"Man, that's really convincing," Champ told John.

"Thanks," John said. "I was an eagle scout back in the day, so I know a lot of useful stuff. We just need to board up everything from the inside as well."

"I'll get on that," Champ volunteered.

"Alright," John said. "Then Danny, you just get all of your stuff organized upstairs. Whatever you don't need here, put it all in one room."

"Why?" Danny asked.

"So we know where to go if we need something," John explained. "If we need clothes, blankets, whatever, they should all be organized in one room."

"Alright," Danny told him. With that he went upstairs and started organizing. It took him almost all night. The ransacked house finally looked clean, but empty. He filled the spare bathroom to the brim with random stuff. The toughest part was cleaning out his parents' room. It was crushing seeing their things again, but not them. However, he felt good that he would soon be able to return this room to them.

He took a few of his dad's clothes and put them into his own room. After getting everything organized, Danny went downstairs to see how things were going.

"What have you guys been doing?" Danny asked.

"Well," Champ started. "I got everything boarded up and John got the radio working perfectly. I did a bit of organizing down here as well."

John told Danny, "I got the picture onto the internet via every social network and every forum about government conspiracies. I sent it to the cameraman I know and he said that everyone at the station's been freaking out trying to report on it and such. Tomorrow's gunna be a big day."

"Agreed," Danny told him. "But for now, I've gotta go to bed."

"Alright," John said. "Goodnight, Danny. And thanks again for letting me stay."

"Same here," Champ said. He gave Danny a hug.

"Any time," Danny told them. He went upstairs and got into his bed. He was out before he could even start to think. He dreamt of what tomorrow would bring when he watched the news in the morning and went to class. It would definitely be a crazy time.

CHAPTER EIGHT

Last Day of School

"A shocking photo has been released from the Truth Committee depicting current president, David Stone's, secretary of defense, William James, escorting Anthony Darrell, the man that shot and killed Presidential Candidate Steward Marshall, out of the penitentiary in Virginia where he was being held. President Stone said in an interview, 'I have no reason to believe that anyone in my cabinet would be at all involved in assisting a criminal who has been accused of assassinating a presidential candidate. Americans need to understand that anyone with a camera and a computer can make it seem like something's happening that really isn't. Secretary James was sent to the prison to ensure that the accused criminal was being held securely with no chance of fleeing before his trial.'

"The Virginia penitentiary has refused to comment on the matter. Despite President Stone's explanation of the situation and denial of the photo's validity, protests have grown exponentially with people asking for the impeachment of President Stone. Increased police presence has been brought to protests in both Boston and Washington D.C. with the chance of violence heightening. The photo has since spread throughout the internet. We will be interviewing Secretary of Defense William James tonight at eight to discuss the allegations."

"Danny, get up!" Danny awoke with Champ yelling in his face.

Danny turned to Champ, then back into the comfort of his bed. "What do you want?" Danny mumbled into his pillow.

"Today's your last day of school and you slept through your alarm. Now get the hell up," Champ informed him. Danny looked up at his clock quickly and noticed the time: 8:37. He had class in twenty-three minutes. Danny jumped out of bed and grabbed whatever clothes he could find on the ground. Within five minutes, Danny was dressed and in his car.

Danny drove the way to Charlie's that he always took. He had completely forgotten about what had happened between him and Charlie, but realized it halfway along the ride and saw the mistake he was about to make. Danny attempted to conjure up a method of getting to Amanda's room without Charlie seeing him. Perhaps he would just take a different hallway to avoid Charlie's door altogether. Then again, Charlie would probably still be sleeping, as he usually was, thus making a plan unnecessary.

Danny pulled up in front of the dorm and turned off his car immediately. As he got out, he made sure to close his door quietly, just from the paranoia of being in Charlie's vicinity. Danny walked into the front door of the dorm and took the hallway opposite Charlie's. He walked up the stairs like a sneaky husband sneaking home after a night of adultery with a woman of the night.

As Danny walked up the stairs, he was happy to see that Amanda was already walking out of her room. "I thought you weren't coming!" she yelled across the hall.

"Nah, I just slept in a bit," Danny replied. As Amanda walked closer, Charlie walked out of her room behind her. Danny's heart sunk and a feeling of annoyance overwhelmed him. Just the sight of him made Danny want to go home and skip class altogether, but he knew that his uncle would probably be upset if he did so.

"Well let's get moving so we're not late to our last class," Amanda told Danny. She could sense the tension in the air, but didn't take the time to acknowledge it. Charlie stared at the floor and Danny looked at all of the walls surrounding them, rather than shooting even one glance in Charlie's direction. Amanda looked at both of them, shook her head, and started walking between them on the way to class.

After walking out of the building and still no conversations manifesting themselves, Amanda made an attempt to strike up some conversation. "So your last class of college is an ethics class, right, Danny?" she asked.

Danny looked up quickly after realizing that Amanda was talking to him, "Oh, yeah," he said. "Professor Peter Sanford. Pretty smart guy."

Amanda realized Danny would be of no help in making the walk less awkward. Perhaps Charlie was the guy to go to. "What classes do you have today, Charlie?" she asked.

"I've got philosophy and film," he said without breaking eye contact with the ground.

Amanda was annoyed by their reluctance to talk to each other, or even talk in general. "Come on," she tried to begin. "You guys are best friends. Just because you fought once doesn't mean you have to be pissed off forever. Get over it."

The two didn't say a word. Amanda just shook her head and walked ahead. Danny and Charlie continued to look at the scenery and went to their separate classes without saying a word to one another. Neither of them could muster the strength to suffer through the inconvenience of speaking to the other.

Danny walked into his class five minutes late and took a seat near the back. "Mr. Bruce," Sanford announced in the middle of his lesson. Danny looked up. "Why don't you come up to the front? You missed part of class already, and I don't want you missing any more." Danny reluctantly stood up and took his stuff to the front row. The eyes of the class felt as if they were staring into his soul as he passed. He sat all the way at the bottom of the stairs of the lecture hall right in the middle. He could feel himself heating up from embarrassment and annoyance.

"That's better," the professor said. Danny could feel himself getting more annoyed with every moment. "So back to the discussion at hand: education and the human instinct. So we were just getting done talking about how we've advanced very quickly as a species as a result of rapid knowledge intake. We've gotten to this high point where we have all of these amazing technologies that have been used to fix conditions that would have killed someone years back. We've made the internet which I'm fully aware many of us would not be able to live without today.

"So can anyone tell me why we've seemed to have stopped growing as a species, and have actually started declining in our amount of intelligence as of recently?" The class was quiet, as with many lectures. Many students were already asleep and the others were distracted by something else.

"Alright, then. We've gotten to a point in our existence where we've begun to concern ourselves with other people's problems, superstitions, and intolerance. We hear people complain about how Susy did this and Eric did this, and then we go back and think on it rather than blocking out rumors and actually learning something from a situation. When we hear about things such as drug legalization or religion, we block it out because of what our friends have said or what our parents have told us as children. We've grown into these close-minded fools that hold their opinions so close that we refuse to listen to what anyone else has to say. Educated opinions are blocked by ignorance and now we're at a time of constant war because nobody can relate to anyone else, because they don't want to take the time to deal with their opinions.

"What are some common ways you all resolve your problems?" The class sat mostly quiet once again.

Now, however, a few more students were interested and volunteered their answers.

"I usually just ignore the problem and go back to living my life." "I clear my head on the internet." "I talk to my friends about it and end up not avoiding the source altogether." Were some of the answers the professor heard.

The professor stepped in front of his desk and began again, "Has it ever occurred to you all that you could simply try to relate to the person that has a problem with the situation? Do you ever try to simply talk to them?" This related way too closely to Danny's own life for him to slump back in his chair. "What we never realize is that we are all very, very different people. We all come from different backgrounds, religions, ideas, families, schools, everything about us is different from someone else. We never try to think 'well maybe they have just been exposed so much to my situation that it's grown intolerable for them and they needed to speak out.' We think about ourselves and how resolving a problem shouldn't inconvenience us for anything to get done."

The class was now very interested in Sanford's enthusiasm. "The biggest danger that knowledge faces today is the existence of close-minded people. Intelligence's biggest fear lies in those whose heads it attempts to fill. Our blatant disregard for the problems our peers or even our greatest enemies face will be the source for the extinction of knowledge and the flourishing of ignorance."

"In terms of religion," the professor began again. "Why do we tend to deny the religions of others so quickly?" He paused for a moment and looked at a couple hands go up. "Ok. It's because we cling to our own ideas with a much greater strength than we should cling to the thought of being open-minded. Countries and regions wage holy wars against each other because they refuse to even believe that other people may have a different idea in things such as creation or the afterlife. It kills us to think that our religion isn't the only one. When it comes to atheists, they refuse to have faith in anything other than science. All of these clashes in ideas cause some of the biggest breaks in our society. What the religious refuse to admit is that there are other people that don't agree with us and that we need to accept that. What the atheists don't want to admit, is that religion is based on faith. This is no reason to discredit it as some of the most ingenious scientists have been religious, and the bashing of what someone believes in simply because you fear what religion has caused in the past whether it be to you or to the world will never be something that anyone with sanity can accept. We need to all realize that we are of one species and in order for us to live in harmony, we need to accept others for who they are and the foundation they were built upon."

Everyone in the class had their laptops shut with their heads facing Sanford with unbreakable attention. "When you leave this class and this college, I want you to be immersed in the minds of others, and not just your own. My goal as a professor is not to teach, it's to help you all embrace ideas, not just from me, but from everyone you meet. I guarantee you, if you will simply give everyone a chance to explain themselves and you accept them for them, you'll make it further in this world than anyone that shuts the doors of their mind in order to disrupt the flow of other people's opinions."

Danny had never been in a class like this before. It was nothing but discussion, but he was actually interested. He was actually starting to freak out on the inside in a weird way.

The professor stepped back behind his desk and instructed the class, "I'm going to call attendance. When I call your name, I want you to tell the class something difficult that you've made it through that has changed your life and how."

Danny became instantly nervous, as he had during every time he had to speak in class. Should he tell all of these people about the situation with his parents? He'd probably end up breaking into tears just talking about it. As he thought about it, he tried to think of something random that he could name.

The professor continued, "And when someone speaks, I want everyone to listen. Nothing that is said in this room will leave this room unless the student that says it tells us it's okay to talk about. If you're going to anyways, at least have the decency to keep it anonymous. When a person is done speaking, I want for you all to give them a round of applause for trusting you with something that has been one of the biggest trials of their lives."

Danny began to think more. There's been nothing else that has changed his life more than what just happened on Friday. It's either he says this, or he's just left sitting there like a moron.

"Melissa Adams," the professor called out.

Everyone turned to see the blonde girl sitting in the middle row on the left of the aisle. She looked around a bit and hesitantly started to speak, "Here. Well . . . my freshman year I tried heroine for the first time in my life." A lot of people in the class were visibly shocked. Even Danny had seen this girl as a pretty innocent and intelligent girl. "Only a few months after trying it, I was addicted. Now that I'm clean, I've learned that addiction can be solved with belief in oneself and with the help of friends that will stick with you, even through the worst time of your life."

Everyone clapped for her, some people even stood up. "Very good, Melissa," the professor said as he was clapping. "It's impressive that someone coming from something as challenging as addiction can become someone as intelligent as yourself." Danny was getting the inspiration he would need to speak, but not completely. "Brandon Allen."

It was the same kid that had flipped out in class the day after Marshall's assassination. The kid announced to the class, "I'm here. The assassination of Stewart Marshall has probably been the most influential thing on my life thus far. It's taught me that you can't take everything you see on television as the truth and you have to think for yourself."

Many students clapped, but not everyone. The professor questioned Brandon for a bit, "If you don't mind me asking, would you consider yourself a part of the Truth Committee?" Danny's heart just about stopped. If the kid actually talks, Danny knows exactly what's going to happen to him.

Brandon spoke very confidently, "Yes I am. It might get me in trouble to admit, but I'm not ashamed."

The class was silent. They turned from Brandon to the professor to observe his reaction. The professor just smiled, "Well then that makes two of us." Danny couldn't believe what he had just heard. This stuff was spreading, rapidly. Even one of the smartest professors he'd ever had affiliated himself with the group. The professor continued, "And don't worry, this doesn't leave the class. So you can rest easy tonight knowing nobody's pulling you from your house." He continued down the list. "Samantha Brooks?"

A brown-haired girl spoke up, "Here. I haven't really had to deal with any big trials. I've always been happy with myself and have always hah friends to keep me that way."

Nobody clapped. "You've been through no challenge in your life, and you expect me to believe that?" the professor asked.

The girl looked confused and said, "I mean, yeah. I'm a strong person by nature."

The professor looked offended and told her, "Don't take this the wrong way, Samantha, but nobody gets strong having gone through no trials. We all go through something, and we are made the people we are today through it. You've never been disturbed by something you've seen, you've never been inconvenienced by something, and you've never had someone around you struggle with something that you've had to help them with? Is that what you're telling me?"

"Yeah. I've never had something I've had to deal with and my friends don't complain about little stuff."

Sanford looked back down at his attendance sheet and shook his head. He finished with, "Then I hate to see how you end up when you're finally hit with something and you refuse to talk about it."

Samantha looked like she was about to blow when she yelled, "Just because I take care of my body and don't let things get to me doesn't make me a bad person."

The professor put his pen down and looked back up. "Yes, but lying and creating a wall that people can't penetrate just to get you to take a serious discussion, well, seriously can do so very easily."

The girl looked embarrassed now. "Alright, so I used to smoke cigarettes a lot. I guess I don't get pulled into doing stupid things anymore."

The class clapped and the professor smiled. "See, it's not that hard," he said. "You've just got to be more open and you'll drop tons of weight off of your shoulders." He looked back down at his list. "Danny Bruce."

Danny was so distracted by that back and forth that he didn't even prepare himself to talk. He looked up slowly and said, "Here." He took a quick pause to bring himself together. It looked like it was time to come clean. "My parents were taken from me on Friday."

The class looked at Danny so quickly their necks looked like their necks would snap. The professor looked at him and removed his glasses. "For what? If you don't mind me asking," he asked.

Danny took a while to say it, but finally opened his mouth and let out, "My dad was arrested for being a part of the Truth Committee and my mom just happened to be home when it happened. I don't know where they were taken because nobody will tell me and I don't even know if they're still alive. It's taught me to be more careful in the way I go about my life and it's taught me to trust others only after they've clearly earned it."

Danny's eyes started to tear up. The professor spoke to him, "Oh my God." He took a long pause. "Are you sure you're telling us the truth?"

Danny got more upset. He tried his hardest to keep the tears in. "I was taken in and the officer that interviewed me told me that they were terrorists and they were taken to a classified prison," he said. "He then told me that if I told anyone I would be arrested and taken to the same place. I wouldn't lie about my parents, professor. I know now what it's like to lose someone you love and I wouldn't joke about something like that. Now that I've told you all about it now, I'm probably not going to be going here anymore."

The class stayed quiet waiting for the professor to begin talking. "You don't have to be scared, Danny," Sanford said. "I told everyone not to speak about all of this outside of class."

"Trust me, professor," Danny chuckled a bit through teary eyes. "Like I said, I don't trust anyone anymore."

The professor took a moment to look back down at his paper. "Well then all we can give you is that round of applause and wish you the best," Sanford said. The class clapped, some even stood. Danny felt happy with himself that he actually spoke up and told everyone, but now he got very scared. He stood up and walked out of his seat with his book bag. As he prepared himself to ascend the stairs to the top of the lecture hall, he stopped by the professor's desk and shook his hand. The professor said in a soft voice, "One day, this world will be free of intolerance, Danny. That's when we'll finally be free. If you ever need anything, I'm in the Boston chapter. And I'll take your words to heart, it looks like I won't be able to teach anymore."

Danny looked at the face of Peter Sanford for the last time. His eyes were glistening as it looked as if he was holding back tears as Danny had been. His face was rugged with age. His mouth curled into a smile of satisfaction, one that could only be obtained when someone has seen the end and has realized that they tried their best. In a way, his face saddened Danny. It was a shame that someone that loved teaching as much as he did would have to stop because of the intolerance he preached about. It was like a cruel joke was being played. Danny only prayed he would be able to see this professor again.

Danny turned and began making his way up the stairs of the lecture hall. Students on either side of him reached out to shake his hand. He shook them for what felt like the last time and made his way out of the room.

He walked back to where his car would be waiting for him. He thought about everything he had heard in the class. Suddenly, Danny felt like it was up to him to make things right with Charlie at this point. He guessed that Amanda was right, a single disagreement shouldn't end a friendship.

Danny made his way to Charlie's room to wait for Amanda. She would be leaving college today as well to live at his house along with her parents. She seemed stressed earlier in the day, but hopefully by the end of her class today she'd be fine. Leaving home isn't necessarily easy on stress.

As Danny walked into the building, he heard a bit of a commotion coming from Charlie's dorm room. He was probably having a few people over for some midday drinking. That was going to make it a lot more awkward than it had to be.

Danny opened the door, and of course there were a bunch of people in there. They all looked at Danny quickly as if he had just walked in on them doing something illegal. With it being Charlie's room, it wouldn't be all that surprising. Danny nervously said, "Is Charlie in here?"

Charlie came from his bedroom into the living room saying, "Who left the door propped?" Charlie walked past Danny, unpropped his door and closed it with the lock in place. "What's up?" he asked.

Danny was a bit hesitant now after being confused by that odd chain of events. He looked to Charlie nervously and asked, "Can we talk?"

Charlie looked at everyone in the room, who were still standing like deer in headlights. "You guys chill for a sec, I'll be back," he told them. The two walked past a couple of the people and went into Charlie's room. Danny walked in and Charlie locked the door behind him. "What's up?" he asked.

Danny began, "It's about that fight."

"Don't worry about it," Charlie told him. He put his hand on Danny's shoulder. "Look, Amanda told me what happened. I'm sorry I doubted you, man."

"It's fine," Danny said. "I was gunna ask you, do you want to come with Amanda and I to the safe house?"

Charlie looked like he was really considering it, but said, "Sorry, dude. I was going to actually start a chapter here. All of those people in there? They're here for the second meeting."

"Really?" Danny asked. He was highly doubting Charlie's capability to run something like this.

"Yeah," Charlie said with a grin. "Except we're not beating around the bush with this stuff. We're going to start a full blown revolution, and we're starting at the protest tomorrow."

Danny was shocked. "What do you mean?" he asked. Danny was very hesitant, and very scared to hear what Charlie was about to tell him.

"Well," Charlie started as he walked away a bit. "We're fighting any cops that come to hurt the protesters. Hopefully people will see what we're doing and will join in. Then we'll have a revolution to start."

Danny was dumbfounded. Charlie didn't realize the trouble he could get into, but what could he really say? At least Charlie finally understood the severity of the situation and was taking it seriously. Then again, Danny felt like he had to say something. "Are you sure that's safe to do?" he asked.

Charlie chuckled. "Of course it's not safe, but it has to be done," he said. "If that old woman was willing to go down for the safety of everyone else, there's no reason I can't. Besides, this time we're going to have guns."

Danny couldn't believe his ears, but there was nothing he could say to dissuade the radical that Charlie had become. "I just want to make sure you're completely sure, Charlie."

Charlie walked back over to Danny, "Trust me. I know what I'm doing and so do the rest of us. We're going to do all of this, you just worry about making sure you guys keep doing what you're doing, and do it well."

Danny just accepted that there was no changing Charlie's mind. He just hoped that what Charlie was doing wouldn't hurt the cause. Danny gave Charlie a hug and told him, "Well, good luck then."

"You too, man. I'll see you around the bend." Charlie walked and unlocked the door. He walked back into the living room and started talking to everyone again. Danny walked to the front door and heard people walking in the hall outside of the door. Maybe one of them would be Amanda.

Danny thought that it would be funny to try to scare Amanda, so he planned to open the door and scream when she passed, if she was passing. He was chuckling a bit to himself and looked into the peephole with his hand on the knob to make sure his timing was perfect. As he touched the doorknob, he felt it move.

Danny looked through the peephole and saw police officers in the hallway. This didn't scare Danny as much as the officers' clothing did. They were all wearing helmets and masks as if they were about to rescue a hostage. Danny immediately backed away from the door.

"What's wrong, Danny?" Charlie asked as he noticed how Danny was acting. Danny continued to back up, his skin quickly turning to a pale white, as Charlie walked to the door. He looked through the peephole and had the same reaction. Charlie pulled his head away from the door slowly while everyone in the room was staring at him anxiously. Charlie turned to look at Danny as someone knocked on the door. Charlie stared at Danny in a way that showed more fear than Danny's ever seen in someone's face. All Charlie could do was mouth the word "run."

Danny turned and sprinted into Charlie's room. As he entered the doorway, he could hear another knock, this one much louder, but no one answering.

As Danny opened Charlie's window, he heard a huge bang on the front door. Danny jumped out of the window and started sprinting as quickly as he could away from the dorm. He wasn't even slightly concerned about his car remaining in the parking lot. He could hear the door of

Charlie's room bust down and the yells of officers. Danny fought back the urge to help as he ran as fast as his legs could carry him.

He heard a quick volley of gunshots ring out behind him. Just as quickly as they had started, they stopped. There were a few more yells that he could hear faintly, but none that he recognized. As much as he didn't want to believe it, he knew that his friend had just died. He continued to sprint as quickly from the building as he could.

Danny could see the police cars sitting in the parking lot all around his car when he stopped in a gas station across the street. He composed himself so that nobody inside would think that he had just ran from there. He watched as people were pulled out of the building and loaded into cars. As some were put into police cars, an ambulance pulled up to take the rest. It struck Danny hard in the heart, but there was nothing he could do.

The cars drove past the station and Danny watched them go with everyone else in the store that had sat watching in wonder. "I wonder what happened at the college. I hope nothing bad," the cashier said to another curious customer. "It's just one of those places where people should be able to have peace of mind. I guess it's not like that anymore."

They had no idea, and Danny knew it. The game had changed and nobody was safe anymore. He wished he knew what happened to Charlie, but there was no way of telling without getting himself into trouble. He was losing everyone around him and it was really taking a toll, but he had to get back home to warn everyone.

Danny checked his pocket and saw that he had some money left. He asked the cashier for the number of a cab and called. After about half an hour of awkwardly sitting in the corner of the gas station, the cab finally pulled up. Danny got in and told the cab driver where to go. As they pulled into Danny's street, he told the cab driver to just stop at another house on the street so the driver wouldn't wonder why Danny wanted to go to a boarded up house.

By this time, it was already afternoon. Danny got out and paid the cab driver. He walked the rest of the way to his house. He was only growing more and more paranoid with everyone around him getting taken. It was at a point where he could no longer feel heartache from it, he just had to make sure the ones he could keep safe stayed that way. He approached the house, but he still continued to look over his shoulder for the police that he had convinced himself were coming.

As Danny walked into the back yard, Champ was putting up signs that said things about not trespassing due to fire damage. "Very clever," Danny told him.

"Ah, thank you," Champ replied. "Did you enjoy your last day of school?" He went to put up another sign on another boarded up window.

"Well," Danny said as he got nervous as he thought about his day thus far. "A bunch of students got pulled out of a dorm by the police."

Champ stopped putting up the sign. "For what?" he asked.

"Charlie was having a meeting to start his own chapter of the Committee."

Champ put his face into his palm. "Are you serious?" he asked.

"Yeah."

"Does he know that there's a chapter here?"

Suddenly Danny felt a horrible sense of fear. He was almost certain that Amanda had told him. "Is there a working phone inside?"

Champ looked at Danny with a confused glance. "I believe so. Why? What happened?"

Danny ran by Champ and went to the upstairs of his house. He found Adam in the living room taking a break. "Adam!" Danny yelled.

Adam looked up quickly and asked, "What?"

"Where can I find a phone?" Danny asked as if he'd never known where the phones were in his house.

Adam threw Danny the phone, but still looked worried. "What happened?" he asked.

Danny ignored Adam and called Amanda. The phone rang and rang. On the verge of going to voicemail, Amanda picked up with a, "Hello?"

"Amanda," Danny said. "It's Danny. Did you tell Charlie that we were using my house as a safe house?"

Amanda paused for a while. Champ and Adam were now behind Danny asking what happened. "No, I figured I'd wait," Amanda said. Danny felt like a truck just got off of his chest.

"Ok, Charlie doesn't know," Danny told Champ. Champ almost fainted from relief and told Adam the situation. "Alright, I'll see you when you get here."

"What happened?" Adam asked Danny.

Danny walked slowly to the couch and sat down. "Well, after class I went to visit Charlie to make sure everything was good between us," he started. "Apparently he's been trying to start his own little chapter, but he told me that they weren't going to be as wary as we've been in the past."

"What does that mean?" Adam asked in a confused tone.

"I guess he was going to get violent instead of trying to do things in a pacifist sort of manner," Danny said. "When I was about to leave, I saw a bunch of cops in the hallway wearing helmets and carrying some pretty serious guns. Charlie told me to get out so I jumped out of his window and ran as fast as I could."

Champ freaked out for a moment. "Were you followed?" he asked as he looked around at the boarded windows.

"There's no way," Danny told him. "I ran to a nearby gas station and waited for the cops to leave. Then I called a cab and got dropped off way down the street and walked the rest of the way home."

"Alright," Champ said. He walked to the kitchen and poured himself a glass of water. "Do you guys want anything to drink?"

"I'll take a water," Danny said.

"I'm fine," Adam said.

Champ brought a cup of water to Danny who was sitting on the couch in shock. Danny took down the water in a few large gulps. Champ sat next to him and did the same. "Things are getting crazy," Danny said.

"You're tellin' me," Champ told him. "We've got to get a meeting going as soon as we can."

"Definitely," Adam said from the other side of the room. "I'll start calling everyone and get them over here tonight if at all possible." With that, Adam left the room and began calling everyone in the chapter.

Danny's mind was overwhelmed with the severity that this situation had reached. Everyone he knew was getting taken from him at an alarming pace. After only about a couple months or so, the entire country was reaching a suspicion level that could cause a full-blown uprising. Danny and the only family he had left besides his grandparents in Maryland were hiding out in a boarded up house. John was downstairs setting up a radio just so nobody would get caught on the phone. It was like Danny couldn't even live in a secure setting that he used to call a home. Within such a short span, everything had changed. He never imagined that one day he wouldn't be able to go to school and he'd have to live in a boarded up house.

Champ interrupted Danny's thoughts with, "Danny."

Danny looked up. "Huh?" he quickly responded.

"I asked you if you wanted to go see how John was doing on the radio," he answered.

"Oh . . . yeah."

Champ shook his head. "You've got to stop thinking so much, kid," Champ said. "It's bad for the brain." Danny sat with a look of confusion on his face. Before he could point out Champ's flaws in logic, Champ was getting up and waving for Danny to get up. The two walked down the hall and Champ opened the door to the basement. Danny took the lead as they descended the stairs.

Danny got to the bottom and looked around the corner. John was fiddling with the knobs on the radio. "Hey, John!" Champ yelled.

John nearly threw the radio across the room from the surprise. "What the hell, Champ," he said, trying to catch his breath with his hand on his chest.

Champ just laughed. "Scared yah' did I?" Champ asked through the chuckles.

"Just a bit," John told him. "What brings you down here?"

"Curiosity," Champ answered. "How's the radio thing going?"

John looked down to the radio. "Well, it's working," he said. "We just need to get everyone else on the channel and we'll be all set. I got connected with the chapter in Boston. Apparently they have three chapters going there already."

Champ looked surprised. "Really?"

"Yeap. Apparently that picture's really got people riled up. A lot more than I had expected, actually."

"How many?"

"Well, in Boston alone, it's going on about a thousand people." Danny and Champ's mouths dropped. "They've got safe houses all over the place there."

"Hear that, Danny?" Champ asked.

Danny could hardly speak. "That's crazy," he said.

John and Champ chuckled. "We're going to try to have a meeting tonight," Champ told John.

"Good plan," John said, turning back to the radio. "It's supposed to snow for the next two days so it would be good to get everyone's situations figured out before it hits. I'll call the Boston chapters and let them know." John started fiddling with the knobs a bit more and started telling the chapters about the meeting. The chapter communicators told him that they would hold meetings that night as well.

"Well, I'm going to go upstairs and have a few beers," Champ told Danny. "I guess just bum around for a while and I'll get you when we're going to start moving stuff around for the meeting. We'll probably have to make sure we have enough bedding supplies for anyone that's going to be staying here for a while."

"Alright," Danny told Champ. Danny went to his room and sat around. There wasn't much to do since they didn't have any internet or cable. He just decided to go to bed until the meeting.

CHAPTER NINE

Time To Go

"We are joined now by Secretary of Defense William James. Mr. James, how are you doing today?"

"I'm great, how are you?"

"Can't complain. Now we're going to cut right to the chase because our viewers have been asking a ton of questions about this. What's your opinion on the validity of the photo depicting you and the alleged murderer of Presidential Candidate Stewart Marshall walking out of the prison together?"

"It's a complete farce."

"Really?"

"Of course. Look, we're in an age where computers can alter a photo to look like anything. If someone really wanted to, they could make a picture look like I was walking an elephant out of the prison. Besides, the guy's having his trial tomorrow. How would I manage to get him out and then get someone else to go to the trial in his place? It's impossible."

"You don't seem to be taking these allegations very seriously."

"Why would I? They're ridiculous. What reasoning would I have for helping someone that killed a presidential candidate?"

"Well groups such as the Truth Committee say that President Stone hired the gunman to kill Marshall."

"People will believe anything nowadays. Anything that sounds controversial, people just eat it up."

"So are you discrediting those allegations too?"

"Yes. They have no credit, no proof, no backing, nothing. I used to be a lawyer, and when there was a trial that had no proof to accuse someone of something, then the accused would be set free. That's how things work. So how would I allow myself to just let people continue to believe this?"

"Okay. And there have been allegations that government officials have been abducting individuals that have been accusing President Stone or hiring the gunman. What do you say to those claims?"

"Once again, just a bunch of mumbo jumbo that only people who have watched too many movies would believe."

"There have been a series of disappearances involving many people that have affiliated themselves with the Truth Committee, though."

"So? Officers from all parts of the United States have told us that they've done everything they could to help find those individuals and they couldn't find them. They probably left the country since they seem to hate it here so much."

"Don't you think you're being a bit insensitive?"

"Those people don't treat me with enough respect to just let me do my job, which involves making sure that they stay safe. What else am I supposed to do? Look, there's no big government cover-up going on here, as much as everyone likes to think that there is. I would like to just move from this and get on with my job."

Danny awoke to the sound of Champ downstairs yelling. It sounded like he was greeting a big group of people as more shouts joined in. Danny checked his phone and saw that it was a bit after eight in the afternoon. Great, nobody even woke him up to allow him to get ready for the meeting.

He got out of his bed and changed into something a bit more presentable than the clothes he was sleeping in. He could hear a bunch of people walking into the downstairs of his home so he quickened his pace. Just before Champ came into Danny's room to wake him, Danny finished changing.

"Hey, Danny, wake up!" Champ yelled as he burst into the door.

"I'm already up," Danny told him.

"Alright, good," Champ said. He seemed a bit drunk already. "We're all ready downstairs. We're just waiting on the rest of the group and we'll be ready to start so hurry up." Champ closed the door and walked back downstairs. Danny walked into the hall and into the bathroom. He emptied his bladder and splashed some water on his face. After a quick look in the mirror, he started his walk through the house.

Danny walked to the door that led to the stairs and opened it. A rush of noise came pouring into the hallway. Danny started his slow descent into the basement. Something odd was taking place, though. Every step he took, the basement seemed to get a lot quieter. By the time Danny was at the bottom of the stairs, the entire room was quiet. Everyone was staring at him as if they were at his funeral and he'd just gotten out of the casket.

"Hey," Danny said, looking utterly clueless. He looked around and people began to turn back to each other to continue their conversations, a lot quieter this time around, though. Danny walked slowly to Adam who was talking to John and a couple of other people. "Adam, what's going on?" he asked.

Adam shook his head a bit and said, "Everyone heard about what happened with your parents. They're shocked to say the least. The fact that you're still walking around took them by surprise, I suppose."

Danny felt embarrassed. Having almost forgotten that he was now an orphan, this shock back into reality caught him by surprise. He wasn't used to the spotlight being on him, or even people feeling bad for him. It was an odd thing for someone to get used to, but Danny was getting used to things changing rapidly.

"Alright everyone," Adam announced. "Let's get this meeting underway." Everyone walked to the seats around the room. There were a lot more people than Danny had remembered being at the last meeting. Instead of one row around the room, there were now a few with a spot to speak in the center. Danny definitely didn't remember having ever owned this many chairs either.

He took a glance around the room at the large crowd. Unlike it had been last time, people were completely silent at the start of the meeting and every face had a very stern expression. It was obvious that those committed to the cause were taking the conditions they had been put into very seriously

"So," Adam began. "As you all know, a lot of us have had some loved ones and friends taken from us. We all know why they were taken, none of us really know where they were taken. Those of you that don't know, Danny's parents Marisa and Brian Bruce were taken a short time ago." The woman next to Danny gave him a small rub on the back. This was getting a bit weird. "Danny's still staying with the Committee though and has offered us this house as a safe house for anyone that doesn't feel safe in their own homes. It will act as a sort of headquarters for our chapter as well." The group clapped for Danny. He didn't really know how to react, so he just sort of bobbed his head. A lot of them stood up as well which caught him off guard even worse than the clapping did.

"This brings me to my next point," Adam continued. "We're in a time where we can't walk around speaking about the Committee openly. You're all here because we know that you can be trusted. It's your duty as a member to recruit only those that you know will join us and will be willing to sacrifice their lives if needed and will keep their mouths quiet to those that cannot be trusted." The room clapped again. "Also, we should probably not clap anymore because we haven't soundproofed the house yet and it would be a bit odd if a bunch of noise was coming from a house that people believe to be unoccupied. I understand that Danny's neighbors have joined us here, but we still can't be too careful." Danny looked around the room. Sure enough, the old couple next door were sitting in the back row across from him.

"Now, we're going to skip right to the most important part of this meeting. We need to figure out where we're going to go from here. We already have that superb picture that I know you've all seen on the news and around the internet. This would be perfect if Stone and his cabinet didn't have their silver tongues. So we'll need to figure out where we're going to go from here. Any suggestions?"

The room was quiet for a second besides the murmurs of members talking to their friends about the question. Some people would raise their hands slightly and then shoot them back to their laps after realizing how preposterous their idea was. Danny's mind was pretty much blank. It seemed like nobody knew where to go next. Adam just stood in the middle of the room looking around in disappointment. "Look," Adam said. "You can suggest whatever's on your mind. We're here just to brainstorm and your idea might not be best, but it could lead to an idea that is best."

Finally someone raised their hand. Adam pointed to them and said, "Yeah? Come up here and let us know what's on your mind." An elderly man got up and scooted to the middle of the room. After the full minute of the room watching him struggle to get to the center, he finally began.

"Hi, I'm George Herman," the man spoke. "Well, I think we should focus on getting some good evidence on Stone. I don't know how we'd do it, but if we could get something that shows that Stone communicated with the gunman, then there's no way that other people wouldn't join us." The old man walked back to his seat just as slowly as he had walked from it.

Rather than waiting for him to make the journey, Adam called on another person to make their suggestion. This time it was a woman from Danny's neighborhood. She walked quickly to the center of the room and began to speak right away by saying, "I'd like to start by thanking Danny for allowing us to use his home, even after all that he's been through. My name's Nancy Herman. No relation." The woman chuckled a bit. She was obviously a lot happier than everyone in the room.

"Well, going off of what George said, we should find something that shows that a reward was given to the gunman. The man wouldn't risk his freedom for no sort of payment."

"How the hell would we do that?" a man yelled from the front row. He stood up to make his point even clearer. "The only way we'd be able to do that would be to find the gunman, which would prove impossible considering he'll be in a courtroom in tomorrow, and after that we'll have no idea where he'll be. It would never work."

"Well, Peter," the woman began again, this time much more serious than she had been when she first walked up. "We're already taking a risk by being here. We're here to expose the truth, no matter what the consequence. Why should we just sit around and do nothing instead of taking a risk that could boost our cause exponentially? I thought we were all committed." The room began to look at each other and nod or shake their heads. Her question of their commitment got everyone on edge.

"If I may," another man said as he stood. "If we're here to take a risk, I don't see why we don't just take down Stone and all of his officials. We should start a revolution, not just attempt to convince everyone that Stone's bad. If he's proven to be guilty of the allegations, then what? We'll have to take him down at some point. I heard that Boston already has enough people to make an army, so why don't we just get some guns and go take Stone down? I'm tired of waiting around wondering if I'm going to get taken like so many others have been."

"If we tried to stand up, we'd be put down very quickly," someone else yelled. "How do you expect a few civilians to stand up to the entire army, police force, and who knows what else? We can't exactly just go buy some tanks and storm D.C."

"Well it's a better plan than sitting around all day," the man responded.

Someone else joined in, "We could get some people in the army to join us. I bet that some of them have family here that have been taken."

"But they'd be killed by the other soldiers before they could do anything," someone called out.

"Well we'd might as well try"

"Why go for broke when we can take things slowly and improve our chance of success?"

"Yeah. There's no reason we have to rush into things."

"Just because some of you are too scared to act doesn't mean the rest of us shouldn't."

The entire room was in an uproar. There were opinions coming from every direction and nobody knew who was doing the talking. It seemed like the room was about to break into a war itself. Every single person with a mouth was yelling about something, besides Danny. He was just sitting back in shock at everyone's behavior. It was crazy how the people that were in such an endeavor together were so ready to snap each other's necks. It got to the point that Danny thought his house might cave in from the noise.

Danny looked across the room and saw Adam looking over at him. Adam gave Danny a bit of a nod. Danny didn't really know how to take it, but figured Adam meant that he had to do something.

He stood up and walked into the center of the room which had remained unoccupied. Everyone seemed unaffected by his presence. Danny looked at Adam who began to look around, trying to think of a way to get everyone to stop. All he could think to do was begin yelling. He walked into the center of the room and began screaming at the top of his lungs. Only a few people looked over. Those few people were focused on Danny. Danny figured he'd join in too if he was supposed to be the one to talk. He yelled once and more people began to look at him. One by one, everyone began to shut their friends up and turn their heads towards Danny.

Before long, everyone was quiet and focused on Danny. Danny felt like he had when he first entered the room. It was awkward once again, but at least people took pity on him enough to allow him to speak. Then Danny realized that he hadn't even prepared anything to say. He was too focused on getting everyone quiet. With everyone staring and their patience obviously still short, Danny decided to just start talking and see where his words took him.

"Hey, I'm Danny Bruce," he said. "As you've heard, my parents and just today, my best friend were taken from me." It was then that Danny noticed Amanda and her parents sitting in the back row. "The way I see it, I've been affected more by this movement than many of you here. I've seen what the government is capable of. They've taken everything that mattered to me. Now I'm left with a boarded up house and a few loved ones left. To say the least, I have next to nothing. If it wasn't for those few loved ones, I'd probably be gone by now." Danny looked around the room. He noticed Rob, the officer that took him to Champ's house. That shocked him more than anything else. The guy that had told him that there was no way he could join the Committee because of the risk decided to show up. Danny was as inspired as he had been when he had met that elderly woman at the protest. Then he figured out exactly what to say.

"Before I lost all of that, I had gone to the Boston protests. There I met an elderly woman that told me that if you believe in something, it's your job to risk your life for it. My mom always told me that if you aren't willing to think for yourself, nobody will ever stand with you. My dad told me that you've got to be willing to think outside the box and not take everything you hear as the truth. All of those people were willing to die for what they believed in, and for all I know, they might have." The room was an unspeakable kind of quiet. It was as if someone could close their eyes and believe they were alone. Danny could see some people beginning to tear up. The old woman that lived next door to him was sobbing.

"I've lost the people that taught me the most about how to live, but in it, I've gained a whole now outlook on life. I never cared about politics, and now I'm having a big group of people here that want to stand up for what they believe in. I'm surprised, to say the least, but I'm happy at the same time. When Adam asked if I wanted to still do this, I knew I had to for them. If I didn't, I know that my parents, wherever they are, would be ashamed of my choice." Danny could feel himself starting to get emotional as well.

"I know you all have loved ones that would push you to stand up for what you believe in. I know a lot of you want to simply go straight for the heart of those that stand in the way of your way of life, but we unfortunately can't right now. I know I'd want nothing more than to charge right into Washington. Then again, I know that there's no way I could. We need to deal with this situation with cool minds, but fierce hearts. We need to act with everything we've got, but do it in a manner that won't kill us."

Danny could see a lot of people nodding with everything he said. "Right now, I think the best thing for us to do is stick something good on Stone, and recruit at the same time. By the time Stone's argument that we're liars has taken a turn for the worst, we'll have an entire army ready for him. I don't know where to go, but I know that's how we've got to act. Thank you." Danny returned to his seat. Everyone around him gave him pats on the back, even hugs. He was feeling good as if he'd accomplished much and had given everyone a good idea of how to come up with a reasonable plan.

Champ stood up and walked to the center of the room. "I think I know what will please all of us. We need to get the gunman after the first day of his trial. That's the only lead we have and it's a risk we have to take. If we can get him in our hands and can figure out from him how to prove that Stone's administration was involved, we'll be in a good spot."

The Peter guy asked Champ, "How are we supposed to do that? There will be cops everywhere."

"Like it has been said before, those cops have minds of their own. They have families that probably believe in what we believe in. We would just need to get enough of them on our side to control the convoy and drive the gunman out of there, whether it be with stealth or violence. Who in here is a cop?"

Rob and a couple others raised their hands, very reluctantly. They felt threatened and horrible with the knowledge that they have been involved in arresting people from the Committee. "Alright then," Champ continued. "You all need to figure out who is transporting the gunman and make sure that the people transporting him will get him to us, or at least tell us how to find the people in the convoy so we can take them out and get their vehicles. It's going to be difficult and risky, but it's got to be done."

Rob stood up and said, "I'll be driving a car in the convoy. I'm good friends with a lot of people in the force in D.C. and we all talk about if Stone did hire this guy or not. I think I can convince most of them to help us out. The ones that don't that are still going to be driving will just have to be incapacitated in some way. It's going to be tough and we'll probably need a lot of help from you all. If you're willing to make sure the officers can't drive, and you can get the cars to the courthouse, my friends and I will do our part. Don't kill them, but just make sure they won't make it. Knock them out, whatever you have to do. I promise we'll do what we have to in order to get the gunman."

Champ smiled, "Well there we go. We'll get some of those in our group prepared to incapacitate the officers and Rob will figure out where the officers doing the transports live and will let you all know where they are. Then you all do the rest."

Someone stood up from behind Danny and said, "What are you going to be doing in the meantime, Champ? Isn't it kind of unfair that we're going to be risking our asses out there and you'll just be here doing God knows what?"

Champ just smiled and said, "I'll be taking care of our guest when he gets here." Seeing his uncle like this was a really odd experience for Danny. Seeing everyone in this light came as a shock to Danny in general. This whole situation really brought out who people really were. His fun-loving uncle seemed like some movie badass, and even his elderly neighbors seemed like the heroes of epic tales. This was just one of those situations that nobody ever expects to be in, and it brought out people's true selves.

Adam took the center of the floor again. "So who's going to be staying in the safe house from now on?" he asked. People turned to their loved ones and began to discuss. Adam allowed them a good amount of time to weigh the options as he and Champ discussed the future plans. Danny sat in silence like he had most of the meeting, just contemplating all of the current events. A lot of people around him seemed to be getting overly emotional. Leaving one's home is never something that comes easy, but in times of danger, it was just something that needed to be done.

On one side of the room, the elderly couple living next door to Danny were comforting each other at the thought of leaving the home that they had lived in since they had first gotten engaged. They thought of the good times that they had, as well as the bad. The trials of raising children all took place in that one house. They had shared every day of their long marriage in the same place. Now, when everything seemed to be against them aside from this one group of people and their significant other, they didn't have much of an option. They would have to leave a place that was more than just a house, it was a home.

Amanda persuaded her parents to leave behind the house that they had raised her in. They recalled, in their minds, the great times they had when she was just a child. That house was the place where everything that Amanda had become was fostered. It was the birthplace of every thought that she had. She had gotten her acceptance letter to her university in that house. They had shared in the great times there. Her graduation party, just before she left her crying mother and proud father to pursue her dreams had been held in that very spot. Now the dangers of what the world had become was going to force them to flee their memories.

After about fifteen minutes, which was a very short time to make such an important decision, Adam asked the question again, "So who will be staying in a safe house?" At first only a few had immediately risen their hands, including Amanda's family and a few other spouses and families that had quickly come to terms with what they'd have to do. Then, the reluctant others put their hands in a midway point compared to the others. They were the ones that were much more nervous to leave the place that they had called their homes for such a long time. Then the final ones, that only had the strength to raise a single finger through the emotions, made their decision clear. Danny looked around the room.

Every person in the room had their hand raised. Those that couldn't raise them through their tears had their loved one holding them in one arm and the other one speaking for them. Danny's heart sank at the realization that the horrors of what was happening behind the scenes was crushing everything that these people had known. They all had to leave the norm and enter a world of conflict.

Even Adam seemed heartbroken as he looked around the room at all of the hands. He wanted time to deal with this emotional toll that everyone was paying, but he had to represent a sort of leadership in a time of turmoil. "Okay," he began, very slowly. "We'll see how many can stay here, but due to the size of this house, we'll need some of you to let others into your home."

Most were reluctant to let almost strangers into their homes. The ones that rose their hands to volunteer were the ones that couldn't bear to leave their homes. Someone that lived down the street from Danny had volunteered, as well as a few other families. The way it looked, there would be about twenty or so people in every house. Not preferred amounts of people, but it would have to do, considering the conditions.

"Alright then," Adam continued. "Everyone break yourselves off into groups based on whoever lives closest to you when we conclude the meeting." Adam paused. The emotions were hitting him harder with every moment spent in that tense room. "When you get to your new homes, board up the doors and windows, put up false eviction notices, basically make it seem like the house is in no condition for people to live in. Tomorrow, get a sort of radio so we can all stay in contact. Work together to gather the supplies you'll need, and overall, just be careful out there. I think we're ready to conclude, unless anyone has anything else to say."

Adam looked around the room. Everyone looked at either Adam, the floor, or their loved ones. After the pause, Adam continued, "Alright then, let's say our final motto and get out of here." The room stood and spoke:

We as the Truth Committee will always stand
To bring about a society that understands
That we are the ones that run this nation
And we'll spread that truth like a conflagration
We know that tomorrow we may die
But our dreams will live on up high
One day our people will be truly free
And it's up to us to plant the seeds that will grow into a tree
The people, united, will never be defeated

Some couldn't utter the words, and others spoke them through the sadness. Everyone dispersed to gather their belongings and make their way to their new bunkers. The only ones left in the room were Adam, Danny, John, Champ, and Danny's neighbors. Adam walked to the elderly couple and asked, "Do you want some help moving your things?"

The old woman spoke, "That would be lovely." She had a smile on her face, but you could tell she was struggling to keep it. "I'm Mary."

"Nice to meet you, I'm Adam," he told her. "Danny, John, come with us and help out. Champ, you help everyone that comes back to get adjusted if they show up before we're back."

"You've got it," Champ told him. He walked to the radio and took a seat. He picked up a beer he had opened just before everyone had gotten there and resumed drinking it.

The three of them and the couple walked over to the house. The couple's car was in the driveway and it would soon be filled with their belongings. "Well, this is the house," Mary said. "Come on in and we'll let you know what we want to bring. We'll try not to take long."

Adam put his hand on Mary's shoulder and said, "You two take as long as you need." Mary smiled at him and opened the front door. Danny walked in after Adam. The house was reminded him a lot of his own. The smell a lot less so, but it was very homey.

"Come on with me, Danny," the elderly man told him. "I'm Greg by the way."

"Nice to meet you," Danny told him. They walked back to the master bedroom together. The walls were covered in family photos. Greg looked around at them all and then grabbed a suitcase out of his closet to begin filling it. Danny helped to grab clothes from the closet and fill the suitcase. It filled quickly and they needed more things for storage. "Do you have any boxes or anything?"

"Eh, this will have to do," Greg told him. "I don't need that many clothes, and Mary will fill her suitcase when she comes back here. She'll probably take a lot longer than I will." Danny sat on the bed. Greg began to walk around the room looking at the pictures. He pulled a picture off of the wall and walked to Danny very slowly, constantly staring at the picture. "Here," he said as he handed the picture to Danny.

The picture showed Mary and Greg looking a lot younger. Greg still had a full head of brown hair and Mary looked untouched by age. They were in front of the home they were currently sitting in with three others. One was a tall boy, he looked to be in his late teens. He was wearing a navy uniform with a couple of medals on his jacket. Next to Mary was a girl much younger than the boy. She looked as if she had just entered middle school. She was wearing a plaid dress and knee high socks. Her hair was down at her shoulders. She looked like a girl from the fifties. Mary was holding the last child. A baby that couldn't have been any older than a few months, all wrapped up in a blanket, sat sleeping in her arms.

Greg began pointing at the picture. He first pointed at the boy and said, "That was our son Max. He died pretty recently while overseas. He was a pilot in the navy, a very experienced one at that. He was deployed to Afghanistan to help with the initial invasion. During the fighting, his plane malfunctioned and went down."

Danny was speechless. "I'm so sorry," he said.

"Eh, it's not your fault," Greg said. "If anything, I'd blame the people that made the plane." He chuckled a bit to try to ward off the emotion. He then pointed at the little girl. "That's our daughter Amanda," he continued. "She was in college in New York City to become a journalist. She sent us pictures every day of what she was doing. She had a bright future ahead of her, until she was struck and killed by a car that ran a red light as she crossed. I know, we couldn't catch a break. The only one still alive was our daughter Jessica." He pointed to the baby. "She's twenty-six now. She's been over in Africa helping to teach illiterate children how to read. She has no idea what's been going on over here because of the lack of electronics there. We send her postcards to tell her about current events, but other than that, she has no link to what's going on over here. Mary loves that girl like no other, but she's never home."

"It seems like you two have been through a lot," Danny sympathized with Greg.

"Yeah, so have you. Just like you, we've just learned to deal with whatever life throws at us. I envy you though.

You seem to be able to deal with all of this a lot quicker than we ever could. There's nothing like losing a child. Nothing can explain the pain you feel when you get a letter or a call saying that your child's gone. The worst part of it was that we couldn't even be there to see them in their last days. The best we got was a call from Amanda only an hour before she was killed."

"I'm so sorry you guys had to go through that," Danny said, not breaking eye contact with the picture.

"Yeah, I'm just sorry for Mary. She's had nightmares ever since. She always dreams of seeing her child die. She wakes up crying saying that she saw Amanda getting crushed by a car, or she was sitting in the plane with Max as he saw his death coming. It was awful to have to comfort her through, but I stuck with her through it. It's been calming down now, thankfully." He took a pause and looked up at all the pictures.

"The hardest part of leaving this place is leaving the memories," Greg continued. "Mary and I were first married while we lived here, we raised our kids here. It's an awful feeling leaving a home you've lived in for fifty years."

"Fifty?" Danny asked with shock.

"Yeah, I know I'm old. Don't remind me." Greg chuckled a bit. Then he began to tear up. "Danny, I've seen a lot in this world. I've seen every political event you can name, I've seen people in grief, I've seen reasons for grief, but this is probably one of the hardest thing's I've ever had to do. I try to stay as strong as a I can, but when you have to make sure you put your spouse over your own emotions, it takes a toll. She's all I've got, and it tears me apart inside to see her in grief. I know this will kill her inside to have to do, but it's something we've got to do." Greg began to sob. Danny put an arm around the small old man to try to comfort him. "Danny, make sure you appreciate everything you get, and enjoy every second you get to live. When you're at a point I'm at where it literally kills you to leave a place you've lived, you know you've been surrounded by enough love to crush you when you have to leave it. In the end, though, I can say that I can look back and have no regrets with how my life's gone."

Danny was starting to get emotional at hearing this man speak through his tears. Greg looked over at Danny and said, "Well you go help everyone else. I'm going to sit in here a bit longer to say goodbye." Danny got up slowly and gave Greg a pat on the back to try to pep him up. He closed the door as he left and walked to the kitchen. Adam was standing there, looking as emotional as Danny.

"Man," Adam said, shaking his head. "These people have been through a lot."

"Yeah," Danny said. "Greg told me."

"Mary broke down while she started packing," Adam said. "It's crushing to have to see, but she said she'd finish up and be out here in a moment. I guess we'll just put the two boxes we have out here into your house." Danny and Adam picked up a box each and walked them back to Danny's. They chose to put them into the master bedroom so the old couple could get a bed to sleep together in. They then walked back to the couple's house and saw them and John standing in the kitchen, enjoying a last cup of coffee.

"Well, we're all set," Greg said. He had his arm around Mary who was still wiping tears from her eyes. All of the lights were turned off in the empty home+. Greg and Mary said goodbye to most of the pictures and took their family picture that Danny saw with them. They left out of the front door and locked it to never look back. All five of them walked back to Danny's full of emotion to wait for the others. It was a rough night, and one that all of them wished would just end as soon as possible.

CHAPTER TEN

CHEERS TO THE NEW FAMILY

Danny sat in his basement for about an hour waiting for everyone to return to his house. Upstairs, Greg and Mary were getting everything moved in with Adam's help. He had talked to them enough to calm them down from earlier. Though they had left their home behind, their memories and their new friends were keeping them going.

Champ was going around the house making sure everything was cleared out of the rooms where people would be sleeping. Even after clearing out every room that was available, there were only three bedrooms and the living room. It wasn't much at all, but being able to keep the government from breathing down their backs would make it worth it.

John was making sure the rooms downstairs were cleared out to make way for whatever they would be used for. He didn't move quickly since he'd spent the entire day working on things already. He had gotten the radio working perfectly and had gotten Danny's old generator working again to power the house. Having someone that was good with technology would prove to be an invaluable aspect of their lives.

Danny was the only one sitting around doing absolutely nothing. He felt like the only unskilled person in a group full of talented individuals. The only skill that he had was being there to lend another pair of hands when someone needed an errand boy. He wanted to help the cause, but for now, he'd have to wait for his chance.

Group by group, everyone that would be living at Danny's arrived with their few belongings. Danny, along with everyone else around the house helped them to move their things into their new rooms. It was a boring hour of helping people put the sheets and blankets on their beds and organizing clothes. The occasional picture hanging was the only thing that warded off the headaches cause by monotony.

"We need to figure out what to do with everyone that doesn't have a bed," Adam said to the group. "Danny, did your parents have any mattresses laying around?"

"There's one against the wall in the basement," Danny told him. "But other than my parents' old bed and mine, that's about it."

"Damn," Adam said as he rubbed his head. "We've got about six people without beds. So what are we working with?"

John told him, "We've got the full-sized master bed, Danny's full-sized, and two other beds from my house and yours that are full-sized."

"Alright," Adam said. "So we've got four full-sized, and what size is that mattress in the basement, Danny?"

"It's a full," he told him.

"Alright, so we've basically got five beds, but fifteen people. The only thing I can think to do would be cut all of the beds in half. Couples are going to have to squeeze together. That will give us ten beds. Are we all in agreement?"

Most people nodded in favor of the idea, but Gary spoke up, "Look, my wife and I can't try to squeeze ourselves into a small bed. We're old. If you want, you guys can grab the mattresses from our house. We've got our full mattress and three cots."

"Sounds great," Adam exclaimed. "Alright, Champ and I will grab those. Everyone else just sit tight and start meeting each other."

"If any of you want," Champ told the group. "I brought a bunch of beers. They're in the fridge upstairs." With that Champ and Adam left the house and headed next-door.

The group all sort of looked at each other awkwardly for a while. Greg asked, "Well should we pull up some chairs and get to know each other?"

"Sounds great, honey," Mary told him with an arm around his waist.

"Alright, everyone get a chair," Greg commanded. Everyone in the group grabbed a folded chair from the side of the room and pulled them up into a circle. Danny grabbed his heater and put it in the middle of them. John came back downstairs with a case of beers for the group. Danny sat between Amanda and Greg.

"Should we start without the others?" John asked.

"I'm not trying to stay up all night, no offense," Greg laughed. "These old bones need to rest at some point."

The group laughed and then looked awkwardly at each other once again. "Well I guess I'll start," Greg said.

"Well, I'm Greg Wathen," he began. "I'm eighty-two or something like that." Everyone laughed at his elderly humor. "Well I'm the husband of Mary here." He put his arm around Mary and she smiled. "Before all of this riffraff, I was a partner at a law firm in Boston. I've been in law for the past fifty or so years. I've seen the scum of the earth and I've unfortunately had to defend quite a few of them. Even more unfortunate, I was good at what I did. I've set rapists and murderers free all for the sake of money. When you really think about it, I guess I'm no better than the guys down in D.C. I'd really do anything to make more money. I took on more cases that I knew I could win, but nobody else wanted to take because of who they had to defend. To be honest, being a lawyer was the best and the worst thing that ever happened to me. I've made thousands upon thousands of dollars by being the best lawyer I could possibly be. Then again, it's the only regret I've ever had haunting my mind. I've seen the families of a dead daughter burst into tears when they hear the 'not guilty' verdict. I've even been attacked by fathers enraged by what I'd done. I've even been threatened with a weapon multiple times.

"I guess when it comes to what I bring to the table, I have a few qualities I offer. I'm familiar with the law and how they do things, so I guess if any of us get into trouble with the law and aren't shipped right off to some unknown prison, I'll be there to get you out. I'm definitely not easily intimidated with weapons anymore. I've seen so much in my life that nothing really scares me. With all of the regret I have from my job, I'm looking to do good by God before I leave this world. I don't know how I'm going to do it, but I'm putting all my chips into this and hoping I don't go broke before I pass. It's a great pleasure to meet all of you and I'm excited to be here to help out."

The group clapped for Greg and looked to Mary. She began to speak. She looked like she was feeling better than she had. "I'm Mary Watson, the wife of the lawyer." The group chuckled a bit. "Well I've been retired for the past thirty years. Before that I was a secretary at Greg's law firm. That's of course where we ended up meeting. One of those typical employee and secretary fall for each other stories I guess." The group smiled.

"Well, when it comes to what I bring to the table, I'm a lot like Greg in the fact that I want to do right, and I'm willing to do whatever it takes to make sure the Committee won't fail or anything. I know a lot of random things from my years of being a housewife so I guess that will help me to be a sort of mother figure for this group. I'm an amazing chef, or at least that's what Greg tells me."

"The best," Greg said before everyone's laughter.

"Aside from that, I'll just be here to help out. If anyone needs anything or just someone to talk to, I've been around for a while and I'd love to help out."

Everyone clapped for Mary and then turned to the next person in line. It was a younger guy, maybe late twenties. He had a clean-shaven face and buzzed hair. He prepared to speak, just before Champ and Adam came in the back door. The whole room turned quickly to see what had happened and saw Champ carrying a full-sized mattress on his own and Adam behind him with a couple of twin-sized mattresses. They threw them on the ground and Adam walked back out. "He'll be getting the other twin and then he'll be back over," Champ said. He pulled up a chair near Amanda's parents and Rob and grabbed another beer.

The patient young guy next in line finally got his chance to tell his story. "I'm Brandon Stevens," he started. "I'm twenty-eight and I was a marine before this all took place. I'd served the past ten years of my life overseas and I came back once Stone got elected. I was in a situation similar to Danny's where my brother had been taken, accused of being some big conspirator against the government. I joined up with the Committee the second it happened and I'm here to give everything I'd learned in the military to help this cause.

"Overseas, I'd seen things that have made me someone that isn't phased by any ounce of violence or tough decisions, what have you. I've seen a lot of things that I wish I hadn't but I don't really care to discuss. All I can really say is that like Greg, I'm looking to find a way to change the image the military's given me so that when I get to St. Peter, I can at least tell him that I tried my hardest to be the best person I could be."

Applause followed and the eyes moved on, just as they had for the past interviews. The next was a large black man, who seemed to be the same age as Brandon.

He was more muscular that anyone in the room and looked like something was constantly going through his head. "I'm Sam White," he said. "I'm the same age as Brandon. I served with Brandon overseas and I've had the same experiences. I guess the only thing that makes me different is that I'm still feeling a lot of effects from it. I can't sleep without seeing the things I've seen over and over. I can't watch a movie without a constant reminder of the things I've been exposed to. Hell, I can't even eat a bowl of cereal without gunfire filling my head. But don't let the demons I've got keep you from accepting me. I'm only looking to help this group advance towards its goal and I'll be here the entire way there."

It was clear Sam was dealing with more than a lot of people in that room were dealing with, but he seemed much more trustworthy than the other strangers. Everyone clapped and tried to get things moving as quick as possible. Next in line was John. Adam walked back into the house and put the last mattress on the floor. He attempted to be as quiet as possible to not interrupt the introductions, but of course he tripped over a mattress and dropped his chair. He quickly recollected himself and sat in the circle.

John began telling about himself after Adam finished humiliating himself. "Howdy, I'm John," he said. "I'm thirty and I'm a resident of rural North Carolina. Well . . . not anymore, but you get the idea. I was an eagle scout so I bring a lot to the table in terms of talent. I can fix almost anything and can do a lot of other stuff, pretty much whatever will need to be done. I've worked on farms my whole life with my family and friends so I'm not much of a pushover. I don't have much to regret. I guess I just wish that I could've brought my family to Massachusetts with me. But, it's great to meet all of you and I look forward to helping out with whatever is needed."

Applause, eye turns, continuing. The next was a woman that looked to be about the age of Brandon. She had long brunette hair and a smooth complexion. She wasn't exactly bad to look at, if that helps in a description. "I'm Dr. Ashley Kaitlen. I'm, well, a doctor. I've practiced surgical procedures as well as diagnosis in hospitals throughout Boston. I keep getting moved around because different places seem to need me more than others. Now I'm on the run, so I can't exactly go back to work for the time being."

"Thank God we've got a doctor with us," Adam laughed. Everyone else joined in.

"Yeah, I try my best," Dr. Kaitlen laughed. "Well I'm pretty good at what I do, so if anyone here gets sick, injured, killed, I'll be the one telling you what happened and how we might be able to fix it. Unless we're in the death category in which there's not much I can do. I have a weird sense of humor so bear with me. I was actually orphaned at a very young age. I have pretty much no family and the ones I do have were in no condition to help me, or they simply didn't want to help. My parents passed, one from sickness, the other from a lack of health insurance so he ended up dying of a mortal wound because he refused to go to a hospital. That's really what got me into medical stuff. It was hard, but I'm sure that I've made my parents proud. All I want to do now is to make sure that nobody else is lost because nobody was around to help."

Dr. Kaitlen seemed to get a lot more applause than some had gotten previously. It was probably her astounding story of success. A young boy was next, probably a high-schooler. He looked a lot like Charlie which was pretty eerie for Danny and Amanda. "I'm James Artur," he said. "I used to go to high school around here, but my parents took me out because of all of the protests and stuff. I don't really know what to say. I played lacrosse for the high school team, which I was pretty good at. I ran too, but wasn't so great at that. I guess when it comes to helping out I'll do whatever I'm told to. I don't know what those things would be, but I'll be here to help."

The group clapped. Greg and Mary looked overjoyed that there was a kid here for some reason, then again, old people always get happy when they see "youngsters." The next guy looked to be James's dad, judging from the similarity anyways. He was sitting with his legs crossed and wearing a flannel shirt. He didn't really look like he was much of a force when it came to anything involving physical activity. It took a long time of looking him over for Danny to realize that he was the manager of the coffee shop he'd delivered the package to. Small world. "I'm Alan Artur, James's dad. I'm thirty-four and I was an accountant and coffee shop owner before joining the group. I'm excellent when it comes to numbers and anything involving computers. So if we're ever faced with problems involving those two things, I'd be the one to call on for that. I've never really been exposed to violence, other than being a kid. I'd gotten beaten up a lot, but now I make a lot of money, so I got the last laugh.

"My wife was taken by the police a month or so ago and it's been hard on James and I. She really held us together, and nothing feels right without her being here. I had loved her ever since we met in high school and never stopped. We had our rough patches and stuff, but it never changed how we felt about each other. So just because I don't look like much, I'm willing to fight tooth and nail to get her back."

Applause, especially from the women inspired by his Hollywood love for his wife. Danny thought, "Well, he can always pick up one of these women if he never found his wife." He felt bad for the thought, but still chuckled a bit. Humor's the only way to survive a difficult situation in his book.

Champ was next to speak to the group. He opened another beer in preparation for his speech. "Well, I'm Chuck Bruce, most just call me Champ. I've been a security guard for a lot of big name people when they come through Boston. I usually just stand guard at clubs and stuff when there's not a big concert going on. I drink a lot and I get in trouble for it, but I'm not really worried about it anymore. I've gotten myself under control, and my tolerance is higher than ever." He was slurring his words which made the group chuckle whenever he began another sentence. "I'm here to make sure we take Stone down and I can see my brother again. I'm Danny's uncle too, I forgot to mention that. But I'll be making sure that this place is locked up tighter than the president's bunker so I hope you all feel safe that I'll be here. I look forward to getting to know you all and getting to take this big journey together." Champ took great joy in the applause and almost fell out of his chair.

The next person was Adam. Danny always found it odd that he looked a lot like a lead singer of some band he had heard. If he could sing like him too, that would just be too much to handle and everyone would probably believe they were the same person. "I'm Adam, and I'm twenty-eight," he said. "I've seen all of you before and I know you all have seen me. I guess you all already know a bit about me, so I'll try to figure out what else I can really say." He took a quick pause. "I actually grew up in California and came to Massachusetts in order to pursue a job opportunity in band managing. I'd say I'm a pretty good leader and I'm not afraid to speak my mind which actually has gotten me into trouble before.

"I've been pushed around by cops many times because of my openness. I was actually put into prison before because I got into a fight with a lead singer from a band I managed because I didn't like the way he was treating the fans. I don't like to see people get pushed around and I never let it happen. I had seen too many of my friends get bullied and I eventually just got fed up with it and started standing up for them. Slowly, they started getting the confidence they needed to stand up for themselves. Lead by example, you know? So you can guarantee I'll make sure nobody tries to mess with us and nobody in this group will have to feel like they're any less than someone else, especially when it comes to cops."

Rob gave Adam a pat on the back while everyone was clapping. "Oh damn. I forgot you were a cop, Rob," he said. Everyone laughed.

"It's alright, I'm not really into that being a cop stuff anymore," Rob said. "I'm just one of you guys." Rob was a big Latino guy. He had a bit of a beard, and there was always a smile on his face whenever they saw him. "Well, as Adam said, I'm a cop. My name's Robert Martinez, but most people just call me Rob. I've served with the Boston Police Department for about fifteen years now. I'm a very trusted person in the force and it's gotten me into a good spot with pretty much everyone in the force on the east coast, so I'll be the one to let everyone know what's going on in the department. If police are ever headed here, you'll know a day before it happens.

"As a kid, I messed up a lot and got into a lot of fights. I abused drugs until I was eighteen and finally wanted to change myself. I broke off from the friends I had and joined the police department. I, over time, became a lot happier of a person since I was free from addiction. I've seen what it can do to people and it's made me want to steer clear of it altogether. When it comes to the point that I have to choose between losing my job or staying with the Committee, you can guarantee I'll still be here."

Adam then gave Rob a pat on the back and laughed. The group clapped and went to Amanda's mother. "I'm Rosa, Amanda's mother and Steven's wife. I've been a newspaper journalist most of my life. It doesn't pay well, but with the kind of money that Steven's been making, I could do what I loved without worrying about money. I've covered many political events so I've naturally grown to love politics, at least until now. I can't stand politics now, unfortunately. I'm very good at coming up with ways to persuade people to join things or to believe things so I can help to get us more members. Other than that, I'm just a cheerful person and I hope to pass that onto you all."

Amanda's dad started up without skipping a beat. He always did seem like a complete ass the few times Danny had met him. "I'm Amanda's father Steven," he blurted out. "I was a self-made entrepreneur until I became a stock market broker. I've always been extraordinary at what I do. Whether it be trying to sell things to people in order to make some money, or working on Wall Street, I've been great at it. I can persuade anyone of anything so when it comes to us trying to increase membership, I'll do all I can to help come up with new ideas on it. I came from a wealthy family in Alabama and have continued my family's fame as a wealthy group. I'm a businessman at heart, and I'll use that to push this group in any manner that I can."

Amanda started after letting her dad get the applause nobody believed he deserved. "I'm Amanda, I'm twenty-one and I used to go to the University of Massachusetts. I've loved politics my whole life, so naturally I became a poly-sci major. I had hoped to one day become the first woman president, but now I've lost all faith in politics, so I know that one's not happening for quite some time. I was one of the first in my school to immediately believe that Stone was behind the murder of Marshall and when the whole world sees it, I'll be able say that I believed it all along. I don't know what real qualities I have to offer, but I'm pretty smart. I had a three-eight before I left college. I really just look forward to getting to know all of you."

Amanda was given her applause, unlike her mom who had been cut off. Danny was the last one in the group to speak, but he had spoken to them all in the meeting earlier that night, so he didn't see much reason behind saying a lot. "Well I'm Danny Bruce, I guess you all know that already. I'm a twenty-two year-old student at a college near Boston, or was. I never really enjoyed politics, so I can rest knowing that I still have an excuse to hate them. I don't really know what else to say, but welcome to my home. It's all of our homes now so don't worry about making a mess or anything. I'm just glad I got all of you here and not a load of nut jobs."

Everyone laughed and Rob said, "Well you did get Champ." The group laughed even harder while Champ wagged a finger at Rob.

"Well then," Adam said. "Let's all get a beer and have a toast."

Everyone began reaching for the beer box. The seventeen-year-old looked at his dad who shook his head a bit. "Come on, Alan," Brandon said from across the room. "We're all adults now, and we're celebrating. Let James have just one beer. He'll probably hate it anyways."

The group laughed and encouraged it. Even Greg was yelling, "Give the kid a drink!"

Alan finally said, "Alright, alright. Just this once." Everyone cheered. "Damn, your mom would have my head."

The laughter eventually calmed down and everyone stood up. "Alright," Adam said. "Here's to making new friends and becoming a big family in one of the worst of situations and to great success in the future."

Everyone cheered and clanged their cans together. They opened them up and took a long gulp. As expected, James hated it and gave his can to Champ who now had about three beers in his hands.

It wasn't long before the group was blackout drunk. James had already gone to sleep in his bed upstairs and the elderly couple joined him soon after. Champ was strolling throughout the basement with a beer box on his head screaming complete nonsense.

Danny sat in the corner laughing about everything that was happening when Amanda approached him, clearly drunk. "Danny," she said. "I'm glad that we're here together and I just wanted you to know that."

"I'm glad you're here too, Amanda," Danny said, realizing how drunk she was.

"I'm really sad that Charlie isn't here," Amanda said. "I miss him a lot."

Danny couldn't help but share in the sadness, but his inebriation kept him distracted from it. "I miss him too," he said.

"How are you going to say that's two cups?" Steven yelled from across the room at the table the group had turned into a beer pong table.

"It's two cups," Brandon said to him.

"That's bullshit," Steven argued. "I'm done with this game. I knew it was a mistake playing in the first place."

"Why are you being such an asshole?" Brandon asked. There was conflict already going on in the house. It was like the first episode of a new "reality" show.

"Just calm down, guys," Sam pleaded.

"No fuck this guy," Brandon said in his drunken ramblings. "He's been shooting me shitty looks all day and I'm sick of it. Asshole wouldn't even let his wife get her applause earlier."

"Don't tell me how to treat my wife you cocky child," Steven demanded. "I'll treat her how I want to."

Brandon's fist flew through the air and just clipped Steven's nose. He still dropped to the ground in fear as Sam held Brandon back. "I should go check on my dad, shouldn't I?" Amanda asked with a drunken grin.

"I guess," Danny said with a laugh. Amanda attempted to get out of her chair, but quickly slipped and fell to the ground.

Dr. Kaitlen was looking at Steven's nose as he yelled about retribution. "Just put pressure on it for a bit and you'll be fine," she said.

"I want him out of here!" Steven said. "He's not a good guy!"

Adam was in the middle of the room with Rob watching and laughing at the situation. Normally they would probably be the ones to keep peace, but they were too intoxicated to avoid laughter. Rosa was with Dr. Kaitlen looking at Steven's nose and trying to calm him down.

Danny stood and said, "I'll get a towel!" with as much might as he could muster. He felt like an adventurer going on a voyage to an unknown land.

Danny sprinted up the stairs and began searching for what he'd already forgotten about. He went to the kitchen and got a cup of water to avoid a hangover and walked to his room to look around some more. He heard a rustle from James's bed and realized he had woken him up. "Oh, I'm sorry, man," he said. "I'll leave soon and then you'll get to sleep and dream and whatever other stuff people do when they sleep."

It wasn't long before Danny collapsed on his bed and passed out. James couldn't help but laugh before he went back to sleep.

CHAPTER ELEVEN

DIRTY WORK

"Anthony Darrell, the man accused of assassinating Presidential Candidate Stewart Marshall, will be seeing the courtroom for the first time today. The trial begins at two this afternoon in Washington D.C. Protests against the man, as well as some against President Stone have already been gathering since midnight last night. The trial's predicted to go on for only a couple days as the evidence against Darrell piles up."

Danny awoke to the rustle of everyone else in the house around three in the morning. He could hardly remember what happened, other than the pulsing headache and Amanda lying halfway in her cot. Danny couldn't even put together the pieces of the night that got him in his bed in the first place. He leaned up and looked around. James was in his cot at one end of the room sound asleep. Danny looked at his phone, and was immediately confused by the time.

John walked in slowly as if he was attempting to allow everyone continue to sleep. This was until he announced, "Come on everyone, time to get up. Everyone else is getting ready." Danny attempted to get out of bed. He pulled the sheets off of himself and laid them to the side. He then proceeded to fall face first on the floor. Amanda had similar troubles. She had to be physically shaken by John in order to actually wake up. He thought she was dead for a moment, but was relieved to hear an annoyed moan. James got up rather quickly. His lack of drunken debauchery the night before left him well-rested, even with only a few hours of sleep.

John left the room, feeling accomplished. Amanda followed after a few minutes of stumbling to find the things she would need to get changed. She picked some clothes out of her suitcase stumbled to a room down the hall where most of the women were getting changed.

James walked to the doorway and turned the light on while shutting the door. Danny's eyes felt as if light had hit them for the first time in years. Danny sat back on his bed attempting to make out anything in the room. All he could see was the bright light that he wished would just go away. The only thing he could really make out was the silhouette of James as he stared at Danny's suspicious behavior. Danny began looking around the room at other recognizable items as James began picking clothes out of his suitcase.

"Ugh," Danny muttered. "Try to warn me next time, man." Danny forced himself back up and started picking out his clothes.

"Sorry, Danny," James said, obviously embarrassed.

Danny looked at James with a forgiving, yet somewhat frustrated look. "It's whatever," he said. James took off his shirt to put on a new white one. Danny looked over and noticed several tattoos throughout James's torso. "You've got tattoos?" he asked James.

James looked over at Danny and then lifted his arms as if he had forgotten they were there. Danny could make out several different black and grey tattoos, the most interesting being one of some sort of horseman that filled half of James's ribcage. He was sitting on a black horse with a dark background. "Oh yeah," James said. "I've been getting a ton this past year with the money I've been making at my job."

Danny examined them bit carefully. It looked like they were really well done, but thought about how James actually got it. "I thought you were only like seventeen," he said.

"Yeah," James said with a shrug. "My friends know a place that doesn't I.D. so I just got them done there. I just have to make sure not to let my dad see them and I'll be fine. Then again if he sees them, there's not much he can do now."

Danny envied him for having tattoos, but questioned the integrity and reasoning in getting several tattoos that he had to hide anyways. It seemed pretty counterproductive. James covered his tattoos again and Danny began changing as he realized what today's events would entail.

Today was the big day: step one of the big rebellion thing. They'd be driving down to Washington D.C. that early morning to steal a bunch of cop cars and break out someone accused of assassinating a presidential candidate so that they could find evidence that the current president hired the gunman in order to take over the power of the most powerful man in the country and then everything would be peachy and a bunch of people would want the president out and there would be some big rebellion in which thousands would probably die in order to stop the United States from plummeting into chaos. Easy enough.

Danny finished getting dressed and walked into the hallway. Amanda and the rest of the women in the house were walking out of their changing room laughing and talking about their lives through their fatigue. All of the guys were already on the couches in the living room passed out after getting ready for the day. It felt almost as if they were taking a family vacation that they had to wake up early for. Everyone had book bags and such at their feet for the trip there. Adam was the only one truly functioning enough to be freaking out about the crucible they would soon be undertaking.

"Does everyone have food in their bags?" Adam would yell from the kitchen. Nobody would respond in a comprehendible manner and he would assume that was a,

"Yes." Everyone sat or stood in the living room, leaning on whatever item seemed to be the most comfortable one in the room.

"Alright, everyone," Adam said as he walked into the room of activists struggling to stay awake. "Here's the deal. There are four cars that will be escorting the main prisoner vehicle. Rob will already be driving the one in the front with one of his cop buddies that had also joined the Committee. He also called me and let me know that the car all the way in the back will be driven by a cop that is a part of the Committee along with another one of Rob's old friends. That just leaves the main vehicle and the two cop cars closest to the prisoner transport vehicle."

"So what's our plan?" Alan asked. He was obviously very worried about the upcoming ordeal. He was holding James like he was going to float away if he lessened his grip at all.

"Well," Adam continued. "We'll need two people per vehicle, and four in the prisoner transport vehicle. Two in the front seats and two with the prisoner. So that adds up to eight people. We've got fourteen so we need to figure out exactly who we're going to be bringing and who will be staying behind."

Everyone looked around in a confused manner. They had assumed, for the most part, that they would all be joining in on the ordeal. With the incentives of safety and sleep on the line, staying behind didn't seem like a bad idea. The nerves were driving everyone to think of a reason they could give that would be persuasive enough to secure them a spot in the safety of the safe house.

"Well Mary and I won't be of any help if we go," Greg said. "We'll just end up getting in the way."

"And there's no way that I'm letting James go," Alan said. James looked down at the ground and turned red. Alan wasn't ready to give James any responsibility before this ordeal, and he obviously wasn't ready to now. It was now very clear why he would be as rebellious as to get a body full of tattoos behind his father's back.

"Alright so that leaves eleven of us," Adan announced. "Rosa and Amanda, are either of you going?"

Amanda and her mother looked at each other and mumbled for a bit. Rosa announced, "I'm definitely not, and I don't think Amanda is either."

"Mom," Amanda said. "There's no reason I shouldn't be involved. I know what I signed up for."

"It's not that, I just won't let you get hurt," Rosa said.

"But you'll let everyone else get hurt?" Amanda asked. "There's no logical reason to keep me behind. I can handle myself and I can be of some use to the rest of the team."

"What would you do, Amanda? Hijack someone's vehicle? Are you so certain of yourself that you're willing to say that you can do that?"

"I'm certain enough of myself to say that I have the same chances as every man in this room of getting out of there alive."

Rosa was silent. She looked at Amanda as if she had just told her mom that she's been addicted to coke for a year. "I mean," Brandon said to break the silence. "We'll need someone in a car nearby to relay information back and forth to the safe house and to the police cars. I don't see the harm in letting her at least do that."

"See, mom," Amanda said. "I can still help and I won't be in harm's way."

"I'll go with her if you'd like," Dr. Kaitlen said. "I should be there anyways in case someone gets hurt."

Rosa looked at Amanda with great tribulation. She finally said, "Fine, but you'd better be careful."

"I will be, mom," Amanda told her. "I love you." She smiled at her mother.

"I love you too, baby," Rosa told her in a sweet voice. The two gave each other hugs and looked back to the room of people. Amanda's persuasion had secured her another small victory.

"Well then," Adam started again. "I believe we're all set and ready to go. We'll take two cars so that Amanda and Dr. Kaitlen will be able to drive them back and we won't be leaving cars in D.C. Alright, so Champ and I will be taking the two officers driving the main vehicle. We've already discussed our plan for incapacitating the officers in their homes. We got lucky because the two live alone in their separate homes so it won't be hard to keep ourselves inconspicuous. The rest of you will probably have a harder time. Sorry about that. Brandon and Sam, you'll be driving the car behind the prisoner transport vehicle. Here's details about your officers." Adam handed the two a piece of paper with the officers' names and information on it.

"John and Danny, you'll be getting these two officers," Adam handed them a piece of paper with the information of the two officers that would be driving the car in front of the prisoner vehicle. Danny looked at his assignment. The guy was pretty scrawny, no way he got through the police academy easily. He was only nineteen and five foot nine. The guy had a girlfriend that he lived with. His girlfriend has work an hour before the officer so this would be pretty easy for Danny. All he had to do was get into the house in that hour of time and take out the officer.

"Alan and Steven, you'll be getting the prisoner and making sure he stays calm the entire time," Adam continued. "You'll just need to reassure him that we're trying to break him out. Make sure he feels comfortable all the way until we get inside of this building later. If he decides to resist, beat the hell out of him until he stops. Does anyone have any questions?"

"How should we go about taking down the officers without killing them?" Brandon asked.

"Well the best way I see is to knock them out in some way and tie them up in their own homes," Adam responded. "Then you grab their clothes and IDs and we'll be all good. With the chaos that will be caused around that courtroom, they'll be trying to get the prisoner out of there safely too quickly to ask us a lot of questions. Once you get the cars, we'll meet up behind the courthouse with Rob. Since Rob's the superior officer there, everyone will be on the same page. They'll leave everything to Rob. Then we wait for the trial to be over and we get the hell out of Dodge."

Seemed easy enough, then again, everything's easier said than done. Everyone gave hugs and handshakes to those that had the privilege of staying back at the house. Greg saluted the two soldiers in the group as they walked away. Everyone felt a great deal of excitement, but also a great deal of fear. None of them had ever had to knock out a police officer and steal his car, nor have they ever thought of doing so. All of those people that would attempt to break someone out of prison always seemed so insane. Now that the shoe was on the other foot, it made sense, in a really crazy and dangerous way.

Danny sat in the back seat of one of the vehicles. John and Adam crammed into the back with him. Champ was up front driving and Dr. Kaitlen was riding shotgun. When one really looked at a car full of these people, it became so clear how different everyone was. They all came from different backgrounds, yet they could cooperate enough to attempt an act of treason together. It was a beautiful thing.

The long ride from Massachusetts all the way to D.C. would be a horrific one. Adam was asleep, seemingly before he was even in the car. Danny tried to join him, but the pure magnitude of what they were about to endure was keeping his eyes from staying shut. John was the next to go. He continuously leaned on Danny, putting him in that weird position where he wanted to say something, but didn't want to wake John up and anger him before they had to steal a cop car together.

Danny looked out of the window at the highway. The road was surprisingly busy considering it was about four in the morning. Danny looked at the cars that would pass. The drivers all focused on the road, completely unaware of what the people in the car next to them would be doing today. It just goes to show how little one can tell about someone simply by looking at them. For all Danny knew, the judge for the case could be in the car right next to them. They blended in perfectly with the commuters. It was almost funny.

The road whizzed by much faster than Danny would have liked. Part of Danny didn't want to do this in the slightest, but another told Danny that it had to be done for the sake of his family and the Committee. The white lines on the road flew by in a constant pattern. The pavement never looked blacker than it did this morning. The trees were eerily still. The sky was black, lighting up only when a plane would occasionally fly by.

Champ was focused on the road as if he was driving on a tightrope. Dr. Kaitlen was checking her bag to ensure that she had everything if the situation took a turn for the worst. She pulled out gauze, then returned it. Then a set of tools would leave the bag, only to find themselves replaced quickly afterwards.

Danny looked back out to the road. The same white lines. The same still trees. The same ominous sky. The monotony of it all was maddening. The entire scene was one of pure fear. Danny's arteries were working overtime. It was the fear of the unknown that shook his foundations. Going in with absolutely no idea of what would happen. They had a concrete plan, but even the best of plans could result in disaster. If something went wrong, there were no lifeboats waiting for them. It was one hundred percent efficiency, or one hundred percent failure. The racing thoughts combined with the exhaustion threw Danny into a restless slumber.

Danny found himself sitting in front of his house. The sky was as black as the highway. The grass was as green as it would be on a spring day and the air smelled of smoke. Danny turned around to look at his home. It wasn't boarded up anymore. The house was in perfect condition. The siding shined though there was no sun and the windows were clean and transparent.

The front door was agape. Danny looked in and saw his parents in the living room laughing and watching television. Plates of food sat in their laps. The living room was spotless as it had been before his parents were taken. Danny felt the comfort he had felt long ago in his home. Danny felt as if he was in heaven, as if nothing could hurt him.

As he sat on the front steps, Danny looked out to his front yard. The grass still held the green brightness that it had before. The sky was still just as black. The clouds were circling into each other. A storm was brewing over his neighborhood. Bits of light would occasionally appear in the clouds, then vanish. The booming of thunder was faint, but eerily distinct.

Danny's eyes moved down from the clouds back to his yard. At the front edge of his yard, there were now figures. One was definitely a human of some sort, but Danny couldn't make out who it was. Next to the human were a few dogs sniffing at the ground. They seemed like harmless dogs looking around for a good spot to sit. Danny took a moment to blink. When his eyes opened, the figures were motionless. Danny felt a fierce presence. It was as if all of the eyes in the world were fixed on him, none of them concerned with blinking.

The grass began to change from the bright green to a darker color. The clouds moved fiercely and the sounds of thunder became louder. Another sound began to enter Danny's head. It was hard to make out, but it sounded as if someone was screaming half a mile away. Danny looked down his street, but saw nobody.

His eyes fixed back on the figures. They were closer now, but still completely motionless. Danny could make out their eyes. They were piercing into his soul. They too were completely motionless. "Hello?" Danny yelled out. The human finally blinked. The person began to slowly creep towards Danny. As it moved, the ground became darker behind it. The figure began to contort. The screams became louder.

The human jerked sporadically. It moved closer, quicker. The human was now on all fours. Its spine shot out from all parts of the back. Bones in the legs and arms snapped to make themselves visible. The figure was now running. The screams felt as if they were right next to Danny now. The ground continued to darken. The creature and the dogs were now in a full on sprint towards Danny. He attempted to stand, but simply fell to the ground. He looked up to the sky. The bits of light that shown were now a blood red. His eyes returned forward to catch the sight of the creature pouncing, ripping its teeth into Danny's neck. Danny's screams were dwarfed by the ones he could hear in his head. Danny watched as the flesh was ripped from his body and his blood flew to the sky.

"Wake up, Danny!" Danny heard as he felt a hard shake. He gasped and looked around. He had returned to the car with everyone staring at him. John was no longer asleep and Dr. Kaitlen was no longer checking her inventory. Champ looked into the rear view mirror and asked, "Are you alright, Danny?"

Danny looked outside. The sky was brighter now, and the clouds were gone. The highway was no longer present and the sound of the car moving along the road was the only sound he could hear . . . They were clearly in Washington D.C. now. Danny looked around and realized that Adam was no longer in the car. "Where's Adam?" Danny asked.

"We already dropped him off. We're almost at John's guy's house," Champ told him. John grabbed his book bag and put it on. He was sweating, but looked surprisingly calm. Champ pulled up in front of an apartment building. John got out and walked in front of the building. Champ pulled away quickly and started down the road. "So are you okay, Danny?" he asked.

"Yeah," Danny said. "Just a bad dream."

"Alright," he said. "Well get ready, we're going to your guy's place next." Danny's heart started racing. He'd never really been in a fight and now he had to do so and knock someone out. He grabbed his book bag and put it on. His heart was ready to burst out of his chest. Adrenaline rushed through his veins. His eyes focused on the car door handle, his hands covered in sweat.

Champ wrapped around a turn. "Alright, Danny. Good luck. Call us when it's done," he told him. Danny moved to the door as Champ began to slow down. His arms and legs were shaking, but he couldn't find the strength to make them stop. Danny looked at the house as they pulled up. It was a small house made up of bricks. It had a short driveway with a cop car sitting in it next to a sedan. As the car stopped, Danny opened the door and got out.

He began to walk towards the front door as the car drove away. Danny thought he would drop dead from a heart attack before he even got to the door. He looked in his bag. He didn't really have any blunt objects to use. He got to the front door. It felt as if everyone in the neighborhood was looking outside at him even though it was still early in the morning. He didn't know what he would do, but he knew he had to think of something.

Danny let out a long breath. His arms were shaking. His hand reached out to the door knob. As his hand made contact, Danny heard a commotion inside. His eyes widened and his jaw dropped. Without thinking, he ran as fast as he could towards the cop car. He ran around the car and laid down on the opposite side attempting to find sense in the situation. He looked under the car, heart pounding. Every ounce of his body was in a heavy shake.

The front door of the house opened. Danny's eyes focused. A body in a police officer's uniform made its way outside followed by yells from someone inside. It sounded like the officer's girlfriend. "You knew you had shit you had to do! Just because you have to take some scumbag to court doesn't mean you can do whatever the hell you want!"

"Sure thing, honey," the officer yelled back as he moved towards the car. The front door slammed shut. The officer was halfway to the car. Danny's mind began to race. The officer took his keys out of his pocket. Danny heard the door next to him unlock. He kept his eyes focused on the officer's pants. He was two thirds of the way there. Danny began to move his legs so he could plant his feet on the ground. Danny could hear a demonic song being hummed by the officer. His hands planted firmly on the ground, like a cat ready to pounce.

The officer was mere steps from his vehicle. Danny's senses heightened. Everything was completely vivid. He could make out every detail of the officer's pants as well as the ground under his feet. His feet stopped in front of the driver's door on the concrete of his driveway. The officer opened the door. Danny's hand moved up to the passenger door's handle. He watched as one foot moved into the car, then the other. He heard the driver's door shut. Danny let out another long breath and moved to a kneeling position.

The door ripped open and Danny flew inside. The officer looked over quickly and opened his mouth to say something. Before he could speak, Danny's fist hit the officer hard in the mouth. He felt a sharp pain on his knuckles as the punch connected. The officer's head flew to the side and hit the door hard. Danny climbed into the car and began punching the officer hard in the temple and cheek. The officer's hands went up to defend himself, but Danny's nervous fury caused his punches to fly through the officer's guard.

Danny was in a fury of fear. He moved his hands as quickly as they would move, for the fear of stopping and a counterattack ensuing became his prime concern. He watched the blood fly from every punch, but he never thought it was enough. He never had anything against this man before, but he was set on doing damage.

The officer slumped back into his seat. His arms were hardly defending him at all. Danny's eyes were wide and his lips pushed in towards his teeth. His fists stopped flying in order to assess the situation. The officer's face was clearly ravaged and blood dripped from his nose and mouth. Danny moved quickly and unbuttoned the middle of the officer's shirt. The officer's eyes were in a haze. His eyelids attempted to open in order to make out who the attacker was, but the officer couldn't summon the strength to open them.

Danny removed the shirt from the limp body. He started to undo the officer's straps on his flak jacket when the officer's hands grabbed at Danny's wrist in a weak attempt to stop him. Danny looked at the officer's face. He was clearly enraged, but was unable to completely open his eyes. Danny hit the officer once more in the jaw. The officer's arms dropped. He was clearly unconscious at this point.

Danny moved quickly to get the officer's clothes off. His eyes kept moving from the officer to the front door of his house. It had been five minutes by the time the officer's clothes were off. Danny pulled the bloody officer from the car and dragged him to the sedan. His body was heavy. Danny looked around the neighborhood to see if anyone was watching. He was all clear, or at least he hoped he was. He constantly expected a group of police cars to fly into the driveway and arrest him.

Danny grabbed the officer's handcuffs and put them onto the officer's wrists. He opened the driver's door of the sedan and popped the trunk. He dragged the officer to the trunk and started to lift him. He was scrawny, but he weighed a lot. Danny got the unconscious man into the trunk and went to his bag. He pulled out duct tape and put a piece over the officer's mouth. Danny shut the trunk and ran to the police car.

He threw the officer's clothes into the passenger's seat. The keys turned and Danny flew out of the driveway. He drove down the road a bit and parked. Danny quickly began to take off his clothes as quickly as he could as he could. The frustration of removing his clothes quickly got to him and Danny's nerves worked at an alarming pace. He threw his clothes all over the car and threw on the officer's clothes in a fury. Once the uniform was on, he began to look around to make sure there was no blood on it. Luckily, it looked as if he had gotten everything off before the officer had a chance to bleed on it.

With everything finished, Danny leaned back into the seat and took another long breath. His heart was finally starting to slow down and his limbs began to settle. He reached for the police radio and turned it to channel 26, the one that Dr. Kaitlen would be using. "Dr. Kaitlen, this is Danny," Danny said into the radio.

There was a long pause. Danny started to get worried. "Roger, did you get everything?" Dr. Kaitlen's voice came through.

A sigh of relief left Danny's mouth. "Yeah," he said.

"Alright, well everyone's set and moving to the courthouse," she said.

"Ok, I'll head there now," Danny told her. He was almost in disbelief that everyone had pulled off their jobs flawlessly. Danny began the drive to the courthouse. His mind was filled with thoughts of what he had just did. His only hope was that the officer wasn't found before they had gotten the prisoner.

The ten minute drive seemed to be over within seconds. Danny saw the large crowd in front of the courthouse. It was around seven now. The trial was about to begin. Danny pulled into the parking lot next to the courthouse where the other police cars were sitting. Danny was overjoyed to see everyone standing around the cars. Their heads moved to look towards Danny.

Danny pulled into a spot next to another car. He got out of the car with a huge smile on his face. Rob walked towards him to be the first to congratulate him. "Nice job, Danny," he said as he gave Danny a hug. Rob reached into his pocket and pulled out an ID. "Here you go," he told Danny as he handed it over. Danny took a glimpse at it. It had his face on it, but had the officer's name and information on it. It looked really well done.

"Who made these?" Danny asked.

"John did," Rob told him. "Pretty good right?"

"Definitely," Danny responded. He looked around. "Where *is* John?"

Adam walked up. "We're not entirely sure," he said. "He radioed in to the doc, but he hasn't gotten here yet."

"Is he okay?" Danny asked.

"We're definitely gunna hope so," Adam said. Danny looked at everyone else. They looked worried, but happy that they'd done their part. They must have felt as happy as Danny that the hardest part was over. All they had to do now was wait for the trial to finish up.

An hour went by and John still hadn't shown up. The group was beginning to get worried. "Alright, where the hell is this guy," Brandon asked.

Rob walked to his radio. "John," he said. "What's your position." Everyone gathered around the radio and listened in. They all had worried faces on and some were even shaking a bit. There was a long silence. "John," Rob repeated.

" . . .I'm almost there," John said over the radio. Everyone let out a sigh of relief. Danny looked around the parking lot. He saw a police car jetting towards the lot. John's car flew into a spot. Everyone began making their way towards the vehicle to congratulate him. John opened his door and everyone started cheering. John stepped out and looked at the group in a way that none of them would be able to forget. His skin was white and his eyes were wide. His hands were shaking at his sides. Then the group looked at his uniform. It was drenched in blood.

"Holy shit," Rob said. "Are you alright?" He ran to John and tried to put his arm around him.

"I'm fine," John said, still as white as when he got out of the car.

"What the fuck happened?" Brandon asked.

John looked down at the ground in fear. "I killed him."

The group collectively let their jaws hit the floor. "What are you talking about, John?" Rob said as he backed away from John.

"He tried to pull his gun on me and I grabbed it from him," John explained as he sounded to be near tears. "I don't know what happened, I just know that I ended up accidentally shooting him." The group became angered. "I swear to God, Rob, I didn't mean to kill that guy."

"But the point is you fucking did," Brandon said. "You fucking killed him and now we're all dead." Brandon moved towards John.

Sam grabbed him from behind and stopped him dead in his tracks. "Calm the hell down," Rob yelled at Brandon. "We'll be fine."

"How the hell do you figure?" Brandon yelled. "There's blood all over him. There's no way that he can go into the courthouse like that."

Rob stepped back and put his hand on his chin, deep in thought. It was true, there was no way that John could go in with blood covering him. If he didn't show up, however, then the officers inside would ask questions. Adam walked to the crowd. "Rob, is there any way that you could tell the officers that John couldn't make it?" he asked.

Rob thought a bit longer. "I could try to tell them that he called out of work today, but I don't know how well that would work," Rob said. "They would probably just tell one of the officers at the courthouse to ride with Danny and I'm not going to risk that. There's no guarantee that the officer would join us. Chances are he would call the station and turn us in."

"Well then what can we do?" Alan asked.

"I don't know, but we've gotta get to the vehicles," Rob said.

"But what are we gunna do about John?" Adam asked.

"Well," Rob said. "There's no way that he can come with us looking like that. He'll just have to get into the doc's car and ride back with her. We'll just have to chance this one. Are you okay with that, John?"

John was still as pale as a ghost. "I guess so," he said. "I'll go call her." John walked back to his car and started calling Dr. Kaitlen on the radio. His words were slurring together and his hands were shaking. Danny had never seen someone as scared as John was at this moment.

"Well let's get in there," Rob said. The group of cops and false cops started their walk to the courthouse. There was a mob outside yelling towards the courthouse. People were going crazy. It looked as if they might end up ripping each other apart just to get their energy out.

The group walked to the back alley of the courthouse. There were two officers standing there with assault rifles. Rob led the group. "Hey guys," he told the officers.

"Hey," the officer on the left said. "Do you all have your ID's?" One by one, each member walked up and showed the officers their badges and ID's. Danny's heart was racing by the time he got to the officer. He looked nervously at his ID as the officer looked it over. He was scared to his very depths, but he tried to keep his composure. The officer stared at every detail of the ID. He must have found something wrong with it and Danny knew it. He'd just screwed up and now he was going to die. "Go on in, rookie," the officer said. Danny had had too many scares for the day.

Everyone went in without a hitch. "Where's the last guy?" the officer asked.

The tension in the air grew as everyone's nerves started to get to them. Nobody could come up with anything to say, and every time they thought of a possibility, they realized that Rob would have to do the talking. Rob looked at the officer as naturally as he could and said, "Well he radioed in to me and told me he would be late."

The officer looked at Rob with a confused look. Rob stood like a statue. He showed no emotion whatsoever. The officer licked his lips and raised his chin. The group stared at the two with anxiety. Suddenly, a gunshot rang out at the front of the courthouse. The two officers started to run towards the front. "Get to the cars!" the officer yelled to the group. "We'll cover you!"

Everyone began sprinting to the back of the courthouse. The four cars and the prisoner transport vehicle were waiting there for them. Everyone split up and got into their vehicles. Danny jumped into the front seat of his car in front of the prisoner transport and waited. They sat anxiously, all of them staring at the back door of the courthouse. After a few more seconds, a group of officers came running out with the prisoner in shackles. Alan and Steve opened the back door of their vehicle and helped throw the prisoner in before getting in as well.

Rob's vehicle pulled out and so followed the rest of the group. Before they knew it, they were leaving. As they passed the front of the courthouse, they could see the crowd sprinting into the streets like ants from a crushed anthill. There was an officer laying face down on the sidewalk in front of the courthouse in a pool of blood.

The gunman was halfway into the courthouse's front door when he turned and noticed the group driving away with the prisoner. Danny looked at the man from his car. He looked at the man's eyes. They were wide and dilated. His mouth was halfway open. He'd obviously realized what he was doing, but he seemed to have a sort of resolve. His eyes were constantly fixed on something, never looking at surroundings.

The man's arm raised. His hand held some sort of pistol. Danny didn't know what kind. He'd never been around guns. The man's eyes were fixed on Danny's the entire time. It was as if every ounce of the man's soul was pouring into Danny simply through a gaze. It was as if the man wanted to tell Danny "I had to."

Danny's concentration broke when the man began firing. It turned out that it definitely wasn't exactly a semi-automatic pistol. Bullets flew around the caravan. Danny's sense of time slowed significantly. He ducked down as far as he could while still being able to see over the steering wheel. Rob was speeding up, so Danny did the same. The rest of the group followed suit.

Danny heard bullets hit his car. He had no idea where they were hitting, he was more focused on getting as far from the courthouse as he could as quickly as he could. As they got to about four hundred meters from the courthouse, Danny returned his attention to the gunman for a moment. He managed to just catch the man putting the gun into his mouth and pulling the trigger. Danny pushed the contents of his stomach back down with all of his might as he concentrated on the road again.

The group sped to a parking garage a few blocks away. Time was of the essence. Officers were no doubt on their way to the courthouse to make sure everything was under control. John had his police car parked at the entrance to keep civilians out. He moved his vehicle and the group headed to the lower level of the garage. Dr. Kaitlen and Amanda were waiting there with the two cars the group had taken to D.C.

They parked their vehicles and jumped out. "Alright everyone," Rob yelled. "Wipe off every part of the car that your hands touched. We can't leave anything for the cops to follow." Everyone started wiping down the insides of their cars as quickly as they could. Danny violently wiped his steering wheel, seatbelt, radio, everything.

As he wiped, Danny looked up and saw the one and only Anthony Darrell, the man that shot and killed Stewart Marshall. Anthony climbed out of the back of the prisoner transport vehicle with chains on his hands and feet. He was wearing a nice grey suit from the trial. He had a smug smile on his rough face. He walked around as everyone frantically cleaned their cars whilst looking around filled with paranoia.

"Shit!" Brandon yelled from his car. "There are fuckin' security cameras all over this place." Danny looked up to find a camera pointed directly at him on a support beam near his car.

"Damn, I'll take care of it," Steve said. He ran off to an office nearby in the garage. Danny got out of his car and closed the door, content that it was clean enough to keep any blame away from himself. Brandon and Sam had already finished. They had grabbed the weapons from their cars and were standing near their car talking. Alan had done the same and was standing next to Anthony.

Danny reopened the door to his car and looked inside. He couldn't find anything in the car. All he had was the pistol on his belt. He thought for a moment and looked for the handle to open the trunk. Danny crouched down and searched under the steering wheel and found the handle after searching for a few seconds. He made sure to wipe it back down and walked to the trunk.

Danny opened the trunk and was taken aback by his discovery. He found a handy little assault rifle. Danny took a peek through the scope and pointed the gun around. Brandon walked over to look at the gun with Danny. "That's an M4," he said. "That's a fine gun. Definitely get's the job done." Brandon chuckled a bit to himself.

Rob and the other officers finished up on their cars and walked to the prisoner transport vehicle. The rest of the group followed. "Alright, let's all load into the cars and get out of here," he said. "These other officers will be staying in D.C. to join the chapter here." Rob walked towards the exit with his cop buddies laughing and shaking hands.

"I got it!" Steve said, running back to the group. "I found the tape for the cameras. We're all good."

"Alright," Adam said. "Then let's get the hell out of here."

Everyone started jogging to the cars. "Wait," a voice rang out. Everyone turned. It was Anthony. "Who are you guys?"

The group looked at each other. "We're cops," Adam said.

Everyone started towards the cars again. "No, you're not," Anthony said.

"Yes we are," Brandon said. "Now get into the van."

"Then why were you wiping everything down and taking the security camera tape?" Anthony asked.

Champ was getting impatient. "Look," he said as he walked towards Anthony. "It's either get in that van or you can stay here and wait for the real cops to get here." Champ stopped and turned back to the cars. "Your choice."

Anthony chuckled. "Well hell, if you're not cops then you're fine by me." He followed the group.

Amanda, Dr. Kaitlen, John, Danny, and Adam got into the sedan. Alan, Steve, Brandon, Sam, and Anthony got into the van. Rob ran back to the group and hopped into the van as well. Everyone sat tightly in their vehicles holding their new guns and frantically looking around for police.

The two cars sped out of the garage. Cop cars were speeding to the courthouse past them. Adam was looking out of the window towards the courthouse. He looked worried. "We need to get out of D.C. before they realize that the prisoner isn't still on his way to the station."

"What'll happen when they find out?" Amanda asked from the driver's seat.

Adam looked at the floor behind Dr. Kaitlen's seat and said, "They'll set up checkpoints on every street out of the city. As more time passes, they'll set up checkpoints further and further from here. We need to make sure that we beat those checkpoints."

Danny looked back at the road behind them. Dr. Kaitlen turned on the police scanner to listen in. The radio was buzzing about the courthouse. The entire car was silent as they listened for any indication that they had figured out that the prisoner wasn't in police hands anymore. The Truth Committee had begun their attack.

CHAPTER TWELVE

GOT 'EM

"The prisoner's in police custody," Rob said over the radio. The convoy would need all of the time they could get and Rob was trying to buy some.

"10-4. What's your current location?" the radio answered back.

Rob was quiet for a moment, looking blankly at the radio. He licked his lips and took a breath before saying, "We're a few blocks away from the courthouse. I'm not completely sure where we are though. The gunman shot at our vehicles, but nobody's wounded."

The group was now about a mile from the courthouse. They were driving as quickly as they could towards the D.C. border into Maryland. The roads of D.C. were filled with people. It seemed as if it was the middle of rush hour, and the cars constantly clogged the streets, slowing the group's advance.

Danny peeked around Amanda's seat to look at the road. It looked as if traffic was clearing up a bit, but they had lost too much time already. Danny could just barely make out the Baltimore sign. As the group pulled off of the road onto an exit ramp, Rob came over the radio.

"We need to step on it," Rob said.

Dr. Kaitlen picked up her microphone for the radio and asked, "Why? What's up?"

"The police found the cop cars," Rob said, almost mumbling.

Everyone's hearts dropped. Amanda's foot pressed harder on the pedal and Rob's van followed. Danny began looking all around the vehicle, looking for any sign of a police vehicle. He looked at cars on their sides, in front of them, even ones that were still on the highway. His paranoia hit a point that he thought every car was against them and it wasn't helping his nerves, or his heart. They sped around the turn of the exit ramp towards Baltimore. From there, they'd head north until they got back to the safe house in Massachusetts.

The group was nearing the D.C. border. Those not driving gripped their weapons as tightly as they could, praying for a miracle to get them out of the city. Rob came over the radio again, saying, "They're setting up checkpoints on the D.C. border now." More bad news.

"Dammit, we're done," John yelled as he hit his door.

Adam was speechless and Danny continued to look around for any sign of cops.

"What the hell do we do then?" Dr. Kaitlen asked Rob.

"I don't know, maybe the checkpoints aren't set up yet," Rob said.

"We're not exactly going to speed towards the border on a 'maybe.'" Dr. Kaitlen told him.

"Well what other choice do we really have?" Rob yelled into the radio. Dr. Kaitlen was taken aback. Everyone was. They heard a breath on the radio followed by Rob's voice. "Look, I don't know what else we can do. We're all still in uniform, we've got guns, and we've got one of the biggest criminals with us right now. There's nothing we can do but hope they haven't finished the checkpoint. If they have, we'll have to run it. We'll take the lead once we get off of the exit and ram anything that tries to stop us."

Danny definitely didn't like the sound of that plan. His paranoia was taking over. Every car he looked at seemed like a cop car. Every driver, every passenger, they all looked like undercover cops. Everyone knew that they had Darrell in their vehicles. Everyone knew that they were the ones the checkpoints were being set up for.

They entered the final stretch and the van took the lead. There would be no more exits between them and the D.C. border. The concrete in the middle of the highway signaled that they wouldn't be turning around. It was just this last half mile, then they'd find out how things would be turning out.

Amanda clenched the steering wheel as she stared blankly at the back of Rob's van. Nobody in the car could see around to tell what was going on. They could guarantee that Rob was probably too scared to talk to them at the moment. The van didn't seem to be slowing down, so that was a good sign.

Amanda looked down at her speedometer. Down to forty they went. The blood started pumping. Down to thirty. The group in the car began looking around to each other. They started saying their prayers. They gave each other looks of despair and clenched their guns. Adam's hand grabbed Danny's shoulder. Danny looked at Adam. He looked distraught, and defeated. Down to twenty.

The group looked hopelessly at the van in front of them. Amanda rolled her window down and stuck her head out. She pulled it back in and said, "Yup, they're here." Another crushing blow. They prepared for the worst as they continued to advance towards the end.

Down to ten they went. There were about twenty other cars until they would be getting to the checkpoint. "We'd better get changed before it's our turn." The car full of people started getting undressed as quickly as they could. Danny grabbed the drawstring bag he had left in the car with his clothes and ripped everything out. He shoved his pants on and pulled his shirt down. Only about five cars at this point. Unfortunately, Danny got changed a lot quicker than John or Adam did. John was in the middle of trying to get his pants right side out and Adam was still trying to figure out where he had put his clothes.

"Are you sure my clothes are still in here?" Adam yelled.

"I didn't touch anything in here!" Amanda yelled back.

"God dammit," Adam yelled as he continued to search frantically.

The group was about three cars behind the checkpoint. Danny knew it was the end. They'd have to fight their way out, and that would only result in their loss in the long run. He looked hopelessly towards the van in front of them. His mind raced, but it all came to the same conclusion of failure, until the back door of the van opened and closed in a flash. Danny couldn't believe what he was seeing.

Brandon was hunched down behind the van with his assault rifle in hand. He didn't look the least bit worried. He looked ready. "No," Adam said quietly. "Brandon, get back in the fucking van." He waved to Brandon for him to get back.

Brandon looked up at the people in the car. He simply smiled and gave a quick salute. He reached into his officer uniform. Out he pulled his dog tags. He looked at them for a moment and began to mutter. Danny could do nothing but watch. Brandon gave his tags a quick kiss and put them back in their place. He looked to the sky and said his last prayer. His head turned to the car once again. He looked much more serious now. His mouth muttered the word, "Drive."

He peeked out from behind the van and started walking towards the checkpoint slowly. A couple officers that came to view looked over at Brandon. One of them put a hand out and said something. Brandon pulled out his police I.D. The officer squinted, then after a short pause, backed up. He turned his head and began to walk towards the vehicle in front of the van. The officer that had been standing next to him did the same. They both began to pick up their pace.

Brandon gave a final look to the car, and a nod. He then turned and opened fire on the officers. At that cue, Rob sped his van through the checkpoint. Amanda was in shock and her foot slammed onto the gas. The occupants of the car watched as Brandon shot everything but the police officers. His shots were off by a few meters. It was almost as if he wasn't aiming for the officers. Then it hit them, he wasn't trying to hurt anyone, only to be a distraction.

Amanda's car flew through the checkpoint behind the van. Other cars around them did the same to get away from the gunfire. They had no time to look back to see how Brandon was doing. It was a way of saying "goodbye" that left them all with a bad taste in their mouths and a few headaches. All they could do once they got through was stare at something other than what was behind them. Nobody wanted to see what was happening to their friend.

Danny no longer felt worried of what the police would do if they caught them. Nobody did. It was like losing a piece of your family, only every emotion you'd feel in those months of your loved one's downfall were felt in a matter of minutes. It was a feeling of utter disbelief along with the crippling sadness of losing a piece of your heart. It wasn't something any of them signed up for.

The road in front of them no longer looked like a path to destruction. It was a road to heaven that their friend had paved for them. The constant fear of the unknown disappeared and only hope joined them for the ride. The only emotion riding along that would certainly haunt them for the rest of the drive was the feeling of disgust that they couldn't do anything to help their friend. Everyone knew the necessity of what Brandon did, but nobody could come to terms with it.

Danny looked out of his window. Trees had a new glow to them that Danny hadn't seen in a while. The green was one that someone would only see if they had faced the end and made it out alive. He could only hope that Brandon had a chance to look at how beautiful the world was becoming before leaving.

The hours left in the car ride home were some of the longest imaginable. No music, no conversation. Nothing but the raging thoughts they were experiencing joined them for the ride.

"Alright, we're coming up to the house now," Rob's voice came over after a few hours. "Pull up around back and then Alan and Steve will drive the cars to a garage down the street."

"What garage?" Dr. Kaitlen asked the radio.

"It's at Alan's house," Rob answered.

"Ah," she responded. "Alright, see you there." She returned the radio to it's position. "Alright, Amanda. You heard him." Amanda was unresponsive. Dr. Kaitlen just hoped she heard her so she wouldn't have to prod at a distraught shell she'd become.

The vehicles pulled around to the back of the safe house and parked. Danny got out on his side and looked forward to the van. Champ got out of the driver's seat of the van and immediately looked back at Danny. He looked tired. The day obviously took a lot out of him. Champ walked to Danny and hugged him. "I'm sorry you had to see that," Champ told him.

Danny's mind raced as he felt his last family member's hug around him. "Why him?" Danny asked.

Champ pulled back, "What do you mean?"

"Well," Danny paused. "Why did everyone decide that Brandon should have been the one to die?"

Champ was taken back by the question. He took a moment to exhale and collect his thoughts. "Well, he volunteered," he said.

"And nobody stopped him?" Danny asked.

"We tried Danny. Trust me we did. But you have to understand, Brandon has a different mindset. We all do. I guarantee there were people that wished someone other than themselves would be the one to die. It's human nature. We're a cruel kind, but not Brandon. Brandon volunteered before anyone had even presented the idea. We saw the checkpoint coming and Brandon seized the opportunity."

"He couldn't wait for a different idea to come around?"

"He's a soldier, Danny. He does what needs to be done for the greater good and won't give it a second thought. He jumped out of the van before we were even ready for it. He gave us a 'good luck' and jumped. He always knew what his goal was in whatever he did with us. I wouldn't expect him to have any regrets, just resolve. If that makes any sense."

It was hard to admit that his friend dying was a good idea, but it was completely true. Just the amount of things that could have happened and the amount of things that didn't toyed with Danny's mind. "I guess so," Danny said. Champ gave him another pat on the shoulder.

Attention turned to the back of the van. Rob opened the door and went in with a fury. "Hey, hey! Watch it!" Anthony said as he was yanked out.

Rob threw him onto the ground. "Get up," he demanded.

"You know," Anthony said. "I wouldn't expect you to be such an asshole when you're expecting to get paid."

Rob pulled him off of the ground. He dragged Anthony into the basement of the safe house and threw him to the floor. "I'm not worried about getting paid," Rob said. "I'm worried about who paid you."

Alan ran by Champ before driving off and said, "Please make sure Rob doesn't kill the guy. We need some concrete evidence before anything like that happens."

"Why can't you tell him?" Champ asked.

"That guy scares the shit out of me," Alan answered. "You've got this."

Alan walked off to the van and Champ shook his head. Steve got into the car behind the van and the two drove off. The rest of the group followed Champ and walked into the basement. Amanda and Dr. Kaitlen headed upstairs to see how the rest of the group was doing. Rob sat Anthony into a nearby chair. "Now, we know that you were paid by Stone to kill off Stewart Marshall," he said. "We just want proof from you. If you make this easy, we won't beat all hell out of you."

"What the hell are you talking about?" Anthony answered.

Rob turned around. He looked up to notice Sam standing in a corner of the room watching what was going on with a look of disgust. Rob walked to Sam slowly and prepared to speak to him.

"I know what you're about to ask," Sam said. "The answer's no"

"Well," Rob responded. "I just wanted to know if you wanted to do this, seeing how your friend died to get him here. I just thought it might make you feel a bit better."

Sam looked up and said, "The last time I tried to get revenge, it bit me in the ass. Nothing good comes out of it. You can have your fun."

"Do you think we shouldn't even be doing this?" Rob asked.

"Of course we should be. He knows things that we need to know. I'm just saying that I'm not the one to do it." Sam looked back down to the floor. Rob nodded and walked back to Anthony. Champ was now sending strong blows to Anthony's head with both fists. Every hit made a loud thud that sent pain through every spectator's soul.

Champ backed off for a second so Rob could get a few words in. Anthony's lip was deeply cut and bleeding profusely. His left eye was beginning to swell up and he was clearly out of breath. "All you have to do to make this stop is tell us how to prove that Stone paid you for the assassination," Rob told him.

Anthony drooled on himself and said, "Did you ever think that maybe I wasn't paid to do it?"

Nobody had anything to say for a moment. "Then why were you seen coming out of the prison with the secretary of defense?" Danny asked.

"Because he wanted to interrogate me himself," Anthony answered.

"Outside of the prison?" Danny continued.

Anthony looked up at Danny and laughed. "Let me guess, government killed one of your friends?" he asked.

"Parents actually," Danny answered.

Anthony chuckled to himself. "So, your parents disappear and now you think that beating the shit out of me is gunna get them back. Is that it?"

"Nope," Danny answered. "Doing that is gunna get us the information we need to get the rest of the nation to help put the right people in power." Alan and Steve got back from dropping off the vehicles and walked into the basement.

Alan looked around, "Is James in here?"

"Nah," Adam answered.

Alan walked up to the crowd of people. He nudged past Danny and stopped in front of Anthony. He looked at him with a blank stare. The room became extremely quiet as Alan stared the man down.

"What's up?" Anthony said with a cocky smile.

Alan looked at the floor for a second, then delivered a hard kick to the side of Anthony's head. He dropped to the ground with a hard thud and let out a loud gasp. As his mouth opened, it spilled blood onto the floor around his head. "That's all I wanted," Alan said before he made his way up the stairs. Amanda and Dr. Kaitlen followed close behind to avoid the violent spectacle.

Anthony rolled around until he could sit on his knees. He spit blood onto the floor and looked up at the crowd around him. "So where do we go from here?" Anthony said with another cocky smile. "Are another one of you going to take your anger out on me? Blame all of your problems on a criminal just because it's easier than accepting that this shit happens and has been happening for years? Your loved ones tried to overthrow a fucking government, and you're surprised they aren't here anymore? And all you can think to do about it is kick the shit out of someone that didn't do anything to you!" Anthony paused and spit at Champ's feet. "And I'm the fucking criminal."

"You killed a presidential candidate," Steve said. "That's a bit more severe than what we're doing."

"Is it?" Anthony asked. "I killed someone that leads an organization that brainwashes assholes like you. You have no idea what that man could've done when he got into office. You're beating down a fellow citizen because you're frustrated about shit that you don't understand."

"Listen," Adam said, kneeling down. "We don't want to do this, but we know that Stone or someone under him paid you to kill Marshall. We just want a way to prove it to the rest of the world. We want to overthrow the people that keep us hiding in this basement. We want to create a country that doesn't have to be led by a tyrant. You can understand that, right?"

Anthony spit up a bit more blood. He looked up at Adam, "Who was that guy that shot those cops at the checkpoint?"

Adam paused and said, "That was Brandon. He was a friend of ours."

Anthony nodded and asked, "Did anyone pay him, or did he just think it was the right thing to do?" Nobody spoke. "That's what I thought."

Champ stepped forward and said, "We know you're lying to us. You were paid in some way."

"Why don't you prove it?" Anthony asked.

The room sat in silence while Anthony smiled to himself. Nobody could think of how to prove that Anthony was guilty. At the same time, some of those in the room began to doubt if Anthony was even guilty at all. For a while, it seemed like they could have completely over thought the situation.

"So what did you use to kill him?" a voice asked from across the room.

Anthony looked up and saw Sam walking towards him. "Why?" Anthony asked.

"Just wondering," Sam said. "Guns have always interested me."

"It was a P90," Anthony answered.

"Ah," Sam said as he looked at the ground. "So were you ever in the military?"

Anthony looked confused and answered, "No. I couldn't join because of a heart condition I have."

"My cousin had the same thing happen."

"Where's this going?" Anthony asked suspiciously.

"I'm just trying to have conversation. I'll leave if you don't want it." Sam began to walk towards the stairs, everyone watching in silence. He stopped at the bottom and turned back to Anthony. "So how does a man get a P90 without being in the military?"

Everyone's eyes opened o a much wider point, especially Anthony's. He looked at the ground and then turned to face Sam. "I bought it," he said.

Sam chuckled and said, "You bought a gun that's illegal for a civilian to own in the U.S.?"

Anthony began to stutter. "I bought it from a guy I know that brought it home from war," he answered.

"Was he in the military?"

"Yeah."

"That's also pretty suspicious considering they aren't standard issue and soldiers aren't allowed to bring those home if they are issued them."

Anthony looked at the ground to collect his thoughts. "He stole it," he said.

"How?"

"Why are you asking me all of these questions?" Anthony was getting frustrated.

"I was just wondering."

Anthony shook his head, "He snuck it in his suitcase."

"They search your possessions before you leave to ensure that you're not bringing home contraband. Trust me, I was a soldier. You're not bullshitting me."

Anthony stared at the ground. "So," Rob started. "How'd you get the gun?"

Anthony continued to stare. Rob broke his concentration with a solid punch to the nose. When Anthony looked up to the ceiling, everyone could tell that his nose was severely broken. "Alright!" Anthony yelled. Everyone backed away for a moment. "Listen, if anyone finds out I talked, I'll be a lot worse off than if I just didn't tell you anything."

"Just talk to us," Rob said. "You'll be fine."

"Bullshit," he said. "I'll be dead within a day."

"How can you be so sure?" Rob asked.

"You're so sure that they can orchestrate an assassination, but you don't think they could find me and kill me?"

"Well . . . " Rob started. "We'll keep you safe."

Steve walked from behind the crowd. "No we're not."

Rob turned around, "Says who?"

"Me," he said. "I'm not having some wanted criminal hanging around me or my family."

"He's just another guy," Rob said. "He deserves the same protection we're getting from each other."

"Bull shit!" Steve yelled. "He killed a man that didn't deserve it. He's not staying here, especially with all of the attention he's already got on him."

"You're not the one calling the shots here," Rob said as he stood up and walked to Steve. "And don't you ever yell at me again," Rob pointed to Anthony, "Or you'll be looking a lot worse than him in a few seconds."

"You think you can intimidate me, asshole?" Steve asked.

Champ walked between the two and said, "Stop acting like damn children."

"Everyone get upstairs," Adam said. "Give James a gun and get him down here to watch this guy."

"Now you're going to tell a kid to watch this murderer?" Steve asked.

"Just get the hell upstairs, Steve. He'll have a goddamn gun," Adam answered. "Alan!" he shouted upstairs, "Are you fine with your son watching this guy?"

Alan came to the top of the stairs and said, "I mean, I guess so. Is he gunna have a gun?"

"Yeah, we'll give him one of ours," Adam yelled back up.

"I guess that's okay then," Alan responded. Champ grabbed his gun from the side of the room and brought it to James. He handed the pump shotgun over and headed upstairs with the rest of the room following. James went the rest of the way downstairs with a look of discomfort on his face.

The group began sitting around the room or standing next to those seated. Amanda, Greg, Mary, and Dr. Kaitlen walked in as well. Adam walked to his side of the circle and began, “So should we let this guy stay with us?”

“Hell no!” Steve yelled. “Why would we want to keep this guy around?”

“We can’t just throw him into the streets,” Rob said. “He’ll die out there.”

“We don’t have enough supplies for this guy,” Dr. Kaitlen said. “I would be fine with keeping him here, but he’ll put a hole in our supplies. Not to mention I’ll have to fix whatever damage I heard you guys doing to him down there.”

“See!” Steve said. “Even the doctor agrees!”

“What does Rosa think?” Rob asked. Probably not the best move.

“Well . . . ” Rosa began. “I don’t see why he can’t stay.”

“It doesn’t matter what she thinks,” Steve said.

“How do you figure?” Rob asked.

“She’s my wife and I’m not going to let her side with a criminal.”

“You know,” Mary said from the loveseat with Greg. “I know if Greg had ever talked like that, I would’ve knocked him out back in the day.”

Adam couldn’t help but chuckle. Steve shot him a glare and said, “It doesn’t matter how I talk to my wife. That’s why she’s *my* wife.”

“We’re not going to bicker about this right now!” Champ yelled. “We need a damn decision!”

“All I know,” Steve said. “If he stays, I’m leaving and taking Amanda and Rosa with me.”

“But Dad,” Amanda started. “I want to stay.”

“Well then let’s hope that these people don’t start siding with dirt,” Steve said.

“You can’t start bargaining with your damn family,” Champ said.

“Yes I can,” Steve let out a grin.

"You know that if you walk out that door, you walk out to the world with completely nothing," Adam said. "You gave up your home. Remember?"

"Then we'll find somewhere else to live," Steve said. "It's better than living with a criminal."

"You don't think people can get a second chance?" Sam asked.

"Not when they've killed people that didn't deserve it," Steve said.

"What constitutes 'deserving it'?" Sam asked.

"Well . . . If they've hurt or killed someone that didn't do anything wrong," Steve said.

"You know how many people I've killed?" Sam asked. "Twelve. I've hurt plenty more I'm sure. Do you think that I believe everyone I've killed deserved it?"

"Of course," Steve said. "You were in a war."

"I was in a war where you couldn't tell who the bad guys were and who the good guys were. I left after my squad and I killed a family of five that had done nothing other than live their normal lives. None of them had done anything to hurt anyone, and we killed them. I could blame it on bad intelligence from headquarters, but it certainly will never get the images of shots from my gun mowing down a kid that ran through the wrong door at the wrong time. It's a mistake that I will never be able to come to terms with, but I try my damned hardest to be the best person I can be. Are you going to tell me that I should get going too?"

Steve was speechless. The rest of the room sat watching him and waiting for an answer. Champ gave Sam a pat on the back. "Well," Steve started, staring at the ground. "I guess not, but he knowingly killed someone that didn't do anything."

"I knew those kids didn't do anything," Sam said. "But I still shot. You need to learn to forgive people that only want to help."

"Well . . . " Steve mumbled.

"So this is great an all," Alan said. "But, has everyone forgotten that this guy is the most wanted man in the U.S. at this point? If he stays, we'll have cops here in a few days. Not to mention, if he was working for Stone, how do we know that he isn't still doing so?"

"Alan's got a point," Adam said. "We have no idea if we can trust this guy."

"Is there any possibility of him ever being trusted?" Sam asked. "We should at least give him a chance."

"His chance can be getting us the proof we need," Danny pointed out. "I think we've forgotten why he's here in the first place. How about we do that and then we worry about this?"

"Right," Adam said. "We'll discuss this another time. Let's get back down there." The group reluctantly got out of their seats and walked downstairs. James was standing a few meters from Anthony and looked relieved that the group decided to join him. Anthony was still laying on the floor with blood covering his face.

Adam knelt down near Anthony and helped him up into the chair. "So here's the deal," Adam said. "You show us that we can trust you, and maybe you'll be able to stay."

"I don't want a maybe," Anthony stated. "I want a definitely. I'll die out there."

Adam shook his head. "We'll do all we can, but you have to understand our hindrance," he said. "You worked for someone that we want impeached."

Anthony stared at the ground. He was still out of breath from the beating he had received. After a bit of thinking he looked up and said, "The only proof I can think of would be the bank transfer for the payment I got from Stone's offices."

It felt as if thousands of pounds were lifted off of the group's shoulders. They all smiled and began looking at each other with the dumbest, and most excited faces any of them had had in a while. Danny was particularly excited that they were one step closer to getting his family back. He felt so much closer than the beginning and it was a huge relief for him.

"Awesome," Adam said. "So do you have some sort of proof of the transaction at your house or online?"

"Well . . . " Anthony started. He looked at the ground again. "It's in an account that I have to be in person to access. Not even the tellers can access it legally without my presence. If they try, they'd be thrown into a federal prison for a while. Given the circumstances, there's next to no way to get the proof you'll need." The thousands of pounds were reapplied to their shoulders. "I'm sorry. It's all I can think of for concrete proof."

"God dammit!" Champ yelled as he turned away. The rest of the group had similar reactions.

"Then what do we do?" Alan asked.

"John," Adam said as an idea burst into his mind. "Can you hack into the bank's network?"

John was taken aback, "I mean, I can hack normal networks, but you're talking about a bank. I can't hack a bank's network even if it's only for paperwork."

"Damn," Adam said. "So there's basically no way that we can get to it?'

"Not legally . . . " Anthony said. He had just gotten some sort of dastardly thought. It got the group a bit on edge, but a bit excited at the same time.

Danny thought about it for a second. There was no way to get to the paperwork unless Anthony was there. The tellers could access it, but the federal government would be notified and the person would be arrested pretty quickly. Then he realized it. "So we get it illegally and forcefully," Danny said.

The rest of the room looked at him. They had confused expressions on their faces at first, but as they thought about it, it became much clearer what Danny meant. Amanda was the first to realize it, "You mean we basically rob the place?"

"Exactly," Danny said. "We get in, get the paperwork showing the transaction, then bring it back here and put it on the internet."

"What about the cops?" Steve asked. "They'll be at the bank in seconds if they realize what we're doing."

"Have the cops been something that we've been scared of yet?" Danny asked. "You heard him. It's the only concrete proof we can get."

"But what if people don't believe it?" John asked. "The entire world didn't believe the picture. How do you think they'll believe a piece of paper."

Danny's plan seemed to be shot down. He thought a bit harder about it, trying to think of something. "What if we send it straight from the bank's computers to all of the major news networks?" Amanda asked. "There's no way it could be fake at that point."

"Is that possible, John?" Adam asked.

John thought about it and said, "I don't see why not. I've gotten paperwork e-mailed to me from them before. I'll just need to get to a computer and do it as quickly as I possibly can. So we can avoid the police."

"What if you can't do it in time?" Rob asked.

John paused and became very serious. "Then I either die or go to prison for a long time," he said.

"I'm not risking that," Adam said. "We've already lost someone because of horrible planning. There's got to be a perfect plan for this."

"I'm just saying," John continued. "I'm willing to make the sacrifice to get this out to the public. It will make our stand so much stronger. The entire country will be on our side."

"Then how can we make sure that you don't have to suffer?" Adam asked.

"All I can think is for me to do it as quickly as I possibly can," John responded.

"What if you're just really calm about it so that nobody panics and calls the police?" Champ asked. "Just tell the teller what you want for them to do, and then get out of there once they do it."

"There's no guarantee that they'll actually send it," Adam said. "He won't be able to see the computer from the other side of the glass."

"Then we'll have to get in there and get it done quickly and efficiently," Danny said.

"Is it the only way?" Adam asked.

"It seems like it," Rob answered. "I can't think of any other way."

Champ butted in and said, "We could dress up like the cops and make them to do it. We've still got their clothes."

Adam turned and pointed out, "I doubt that they'd just do it without asking questions, but if we all got in there dressed as police officers and someone calmly asked a teller to do it, then they could watch them do it and we could be there to make sure everyone stays calm if something goes wrong."

"Works for me," Champ said. "Anyone opposed?"

Greg spoke up, "Do we all have to go?"

"Definitely not," John said. "I'll need to be there to ensure that they do it correctly. I'll just need a couple other people. We'll go to the bank nearest us. Which bank is it Anthony?"

"Cedar Federal or something like that," he answered.

"Well where the hell is that?" Champ asked.

"There's one about a half hour from here," Mary said. "I've gone to it plenty of times."

"How easy do you think this would be to pull off, Mary?" Adam asked.

"Well," Mary started. "I've only seen one guard in there at the most. His name is Jerry or something. He's usually only in there when Gary, the manager, isn't there."

"Then we'll have to make sure that Gary will be there then," Champ said.

"Well then," John said. "I believe we've got some e-mails to send tomorrow."

"Alright," Adam said. "Get Anthony some food and water so we can go upstairs and relax for a while."

"I'll get him some," Mary said. The group headed upstairs and Mary grabbed some food that had been left over from that day's lunch. She went downstairs alone as the rest of the house sat upstairs and thought about the day. It had put a load of stress on them and she wanted to give them time to themselves.

She sat in front of Anthony and held some food in front of him. "Here," she said. "Eat up."

Anthony looked down at the mixture of food on the plate. "What is it?" he asked.

"It's a bit of roast with a gravy I made and a bunch of delicious herbs," she said.

"How do I know it's not poison or something?" Anthony asked.

Mary shook her head and took a bit of the food. "See, it's fine," she said.

Anthony took a bite and swallowed the food. "I'm sorry," he said. "I'm just really scared right now."

Mary fed him another bit of food. "Don't worry," she said. "We're all really nice here. And if anyone tries to hurt you, I'll keep you safe."

Anthony laughed. "Well thanks," he said nervously. He took another bite and quietly asked, "So what's going to happen to me?"

Mary looked down at the food and shrugged her shoulders. "I honestly don't know," she said.

Anthony frowned and dropped his head. "So I'm probably going to die," he said.

Mary was taken back by the statement. She knew that something like that probably would happen, but she couldn't tell that to someone that was obviously in fear. "Well I'm sure that you'll be fine," she said. "If they ever tried to kill someone that didn't deserve it, and you don't seem like you deserve it, I'd stop them."

Anthony smiled. "I hope so," he said.

"Mary," someone shouted from upstairs. "Come on up! We're about to eat some dinner."

Mary turned to Anthony and patted his cheek. "I'll check on you in a bit," she said before leaving. Anthony looked down at the plate of food and tried to eat some more. Something about his behavior wasn't adding up, but the group had too much on their plates to be concerned with it at the moment. They would be invading a bank tomorrow, and it was scaring the hell out of them. Hopefully, it would be the one plan that actually went right.

CHAPTER THIRTEEN

COUNT YOUR BLESSINGS

"Anthony Darrell, the suspected murderer of Presidential Candidate Stewart Marshall, has escaped from police custody. During a shooting at the courthouse in which his trial was taking place, Darrell was transported from the prison by more than ten suspected accomplices disguised as police officers. The police vehicles they used were found in a parking garage shortly after. The officers whose cars were stolen were all reported to have been incapacitated in some way before their uniforms, vehicles, and weapons were stolen. One officer, Thomas Ivarez was murdered in his home before having his things stolen.

Police will be searching homes randomly through an executive order from President David Stone in an attempt to gain a lead for the case. This order is causing protests from demonstrators saying that this order is unconstitutional and it violates the fourth amendment. Nevertheless, police are asking that anyone with information contact their local police station. They also ask that nobody attempt to confront Darrell or his unknown accomplices."

The exhaustion of the day's events allowed the group to sleep with ease. They took turns watching Anthony throughout the night, though each of them dreaded waking up and standing around to keep an eye on the gunman and occasionally even having to get him something. The idea of keeping him there was becoming less and less favorable as time went on.

Danny began having twisted nightmares again. He was in front of his house again, looking out at the clouds and the green grass. Like before, he saw a human-like figure standing at the end of his yard with dogs sniffing at his feet. The figures stopped like they had before and began coming closer. The human figure began snapping its limbs again and charged Danny.

This time, however, Brandon walked out in front of Danny, surrounded by seven other people that he didn't recognize. Danny attempted to yell, but nothing came out. Brandon and the other people walked closer and closer to the charging figures as if they didn't know the figures were there. Danny stared at Brandon's back and could only watch. Brandon turned and looked at Danny. He gave him the same salute that he had before he charged the police. Without any warning, the human figure leapt through Brandon's torso, ripping through his body and pulling out vital organs as the dogs around the figure did the same to the people around Brandon.

Then Danny woke up, just as he had before. His bed was soaked with sweat and his entire room felt like an oven. He looked around the room slowly, as if he was stalking prey. Amanda and James were still sound asleep. Danny was frozen in fear from his nightmare. The images were fresh in his mind and continued to cycle through as if it was a horror movie. When he finally found the courage to lay back down, he couldn't fall asleep. His fear overwhelmed him and any thoughts of going to sleep seemed completely out of the question.

Danny decided to leave the room to get something to drink. Maybe some cold water would help him to fall asleep in his furnace of a room. He stood up slowly to avoid waking Amanda and James. His feet moved to the quietest spots on the floor until he was at the door. It opened and Danny made his way to the kitchen.

He grabbed a cup from the cabinet and filled it with water. Once he filled his cup with cold water, Danny made his way to the living room and sat on a couch. He took a sip and let his mind wander. Things were happening way too quickly for him to ever adapt to them. After such a small amount of time, he went from going to school every day and living in his safe home to living in a boarded up house with a bunch of people he didn't know and no parents to keep him safe.

He took another sip and continued to think to himself. The images from his dreams made their appearance again. The violence of the scene flooded into every crevice of his mind. He couldn't think of anything other than the flesh ripping from Brandon's torso. Danny was so lost in his mind that he didn't even notice someone walk into the kitchen until the sound of the water turning on threw off his concentration. He looked towards the kitchen, waiting to see who would come walking out.

After about a minute, Danny heard a sigh and then saw John walk from the kitchen. John stopped and looked at Danny. "You couldn't sleep either?" he asked with a very serious face.

"Nah," Danny responded. "Too many nightmares."

John walked over to the couch next near Danny's and nodded his head, "Same here, man."

The two sat in silence drinking their waters. They both stared at the ground thinking hard about whatever was on their minds. After about one awkward minute, John broke the silence. "What do you think of this whole situation?" he asked. "I don't think I've ever actually asked you how you feel about all of this." The truth was that nobody ever really had. He was pretty much forced into it.

Danny thought hard about what he would say. "I don't know," is what ended up coming out. To recover from his stupid introduction, he said, "Everything's been moving so quickly, it's hard to really know. I've felt every emotion that a person can feel in such a short time, it's just hitting my mind pretty hard."

"You can say that again," John responded. "A few months ago, if you asked me where I'd be now, I'd never say that I'd be in a situation like this. I had a solid job working around the technology I loved, and now I'm doing the same thing for a bunch of rebels in a boarded up house. It's a really unpredictable situation. Every night I wonder what the next day's going to bring. With Brandon dying just yesterday, my mortality's starting to coming to the front of my mind."

"Are you scared?" Danny had no idea why he asked it. It just came out and he felt like an idiot immediately.

John looked up at Danny with a face even more serious than the one he walked into the room with. "To be honest, I'm scared out of my mind, and taking someone's life didn't make it any better."

"Then why would you offer to do that bank job?" Danny asked him.

"After seeing how quickly Brandon moved to save us, there's no way that I couldn't. You saw how effortlessly he did that for us. I guarantee that he was just as scared as I am now, if not more so, but he knew what had to be done, regardless of the chance of his death. It inspired me. I realized that I'm not the only one on this planet anymore. We're always so concerned with how *we* feel, what *we* think. It's time for us to think of others, you know? For us to move from our selfish thoughts and start to treat everyone as a whole. We're a species under attack, and until we can think of ourselves as a whole attempting to survive, we're dead. That's it."

"That makes a lot of sense," Danny responded. "I've still gotta say though, you're extremely brave for what you're planning on doing, and I want you to know how much I appreciate it. You're potentially starting this revolution with the move you're making and I'll be praying that you make it back so I can shake your hand at the end of this."

John smiled and said, "Thanks, man. You have no idea how great that feels to hear. I hope I'll be able to shake your hand at the end of this too."

Danny began to feel tired again. "What time is it?" he asked.

John walked to the kitchen and looked at the microwave. "It's about four," he answered. "I should probably try to go back to sleep."

"Yeah, me too," Danny said as he stood up. He gave John a handshake and said his goodnight. They walked to their rooms and went to sleep. Danny was able to fall asleep much easier now that he had heard all of that from John. A good bit of encouragement can definitely push someone's nightmares from their mind.

Before he knew it, Danny was waking up to the conversations taking place in the kitchen. Something smelled amazing and it pulled Danny from his blankets very quickly like there was a rope from the kitchen to his nose. Hopefully it wouldn't all be gone by the time he made it there. Danny looked around his room on the way out. James and Amanda were already gone. He opened the door and walked out as quickly as he could while still acting natural.

Champ was sitting on the couch shoving food down his throat. He attempted to say, "Good morning, Danny!" but instead spit food all over himself and laughed like a toddler. Adam, who was sitting next to him with a plate of his own food, complained about Champ spitting on his eggs.

Danny walked into the kitchen where Mary was cooking up some eggs. She turned to Danny and smiled her sweet old woman smile and said, "Good morning, sweetie! How do you like your eggs?"

Danny rubbed the back of his head and answered, "Some scrambled eggs would be great, if you wouldn't mind."

"Alrighty," Mary responded. "You can go talk to everyone and I'll call you when they're ready." Then she smiled at him again and went back to cooking.

"Thanks," Danny said. "Did you sleep well?"

She smiled again. "Honey, I'm old. I get the best sleep of my life every night." Mary let out a little laugh. "How about you?"

"Eh, I guess it was an alright night," he answered. "Had a few nightmares."

"I'm sorry to hear that," she sympathized. "You know, they say that if you face a nightmare while you're in it, it makes you a lot stronger when you wake up. My mother would always tell me that. Then every time I had a bad dream, I would fight whatever would make it bad and when I woke up the next day, I would feel like I could take on the world. So if you have another bad dream, just try to make it better by fighting off the bad parts and you'll feel great! Hopefully it will even stop you from having nightmares."

"Thanks, Mary," Danny answered with a laugh. He had no idea what she was talking about, but there was no reason to be rude about it.

"You remind me so much of my son," she said. "He was always very, very polite. He loved scrambled eggs too!" Danny smiled, but couldn't help but feel guilty knowing that he had reminded her that her son was no longer around. Mary looked down at her pan. "Well your eggs are ready!" She poured the eggs onto a plate. "Thank you for keeping me company!" she said as she handed him the plate.

"Thank you for the eggs!" Danny said in response. He walked to the couch near Champ and Adam and sat down. James was sitting on the other end eating a piece of toast.

"Morning," Adam said.

"Good morning," Danny responded.

"Sleep alright?" Adam asked.

"Kind of," Danny said.

"Yeah, I had one of those nights too," Adam told him. "You know, James and I were just talking about high school."

Danny laughed. "I remember high school," he said. "Were you having fun there?" he asked James.

"Other than doing sports, not really," James laughed. It was the first time Danny had ever heard James actually laugh. It kind of shocked him in an odd way.

"Did you know I used to run track?" Champ said, very proud of himself. "Ran the mile!"

"I've had to run that before," James told him. "It sucks."

"Have you ever won?" Champ asked.

"I've never won the mile, but I've won other events," James said. "I've only run the mile a couple of times."

"I would win in the mile all of the time," Champ said. "I was probably the best on my team."

"And I'm sure that you could still run just as fast," Adam said sarcastically.

"Shut the hell up, before I make you another plate of eggs out of your balls," Champ said. "I could beat you in a race any day."

"Is that so?" Adam asked. "If we weren't hiding in here, I'd say we should go for a run."

"We'll get a chance some day," Champ said. "And then you'll see."

Danny finished up his eggs and walked back to his room to get changed for the day. In a few minutes the group would be meeting downstairs to talk about the day's plan. He was excited, but very nervous at the same time, just as he'd been the day before. He had no idea if he'd even be going, but part of him really wanted to. He picked out some jeans, a v-neck, and a hoodie to keep him warm. It was only about fifty degrees outside. Once he finished, Danny walked downstairs to join the group that was already starting to talk about the day.

"So what's the plan, John?" Adam asked.

"Well," John started. "I've been thinking about this all night and we definitely need to make sure that we can be as discrete about this as humanly possible, as we mentioned before. So what I'm thinking is I'll go in there with two others that will be disguised as police officers."

"Why two?" Dr. Kaitlen asked.

"Two just seems like a likely number," John responded. "If one officer went in with me, it just wouldn't seem like we were actually trying to get some important information off of their computers. It would just look suspicious, you know?"

"It's like if one officer went to investigate suspicious activity," Rob said. "Someone would expect at least two officers so they'd have backup."

"Exactly," John said. "Plus, the tellers know that they aren't allowed to look at Anthony's account. So if two officers go in and I go in with some suit that would make me look like a federal agent, then chances are they'll take us seriously and won't interfere."

It made enough sense so far. "Now, even though we should be able to do all of that without conflict, in case there's a conflict, we'll need people there to help us," John said. "So I'm thinking we'll have a couple of people in there concealing weapons. Any volunteers?"

"I'll do it," Mary said.

Greg immediately intervened and said, "No way. There's no way you can do that."

"Why not?" Mary said. Her nice old lady smile had disintegrated and turned into a very serious frown.

"Because you're too old for this!" John said. "You can't handle yourself in a gunfight!" The truth had come out.

Mary became very offended. It was something that nobody expected to see out of her. “I’ve been on this earth for longer than anyone else here, other than Greg,” she pointed out. “I’ve seen enough to make me a stronger-willed person than you could ever imagine. Besides, I signed up for this, I’m willing to help, and I’m going to help.”

“Mary, please,” Greg pleaded. “Nobody said that you can’t help. You just need to help in a way that’s appropriate for your skill set.”

“They know me at that bank, Greg. I don’t think you’re realizing that. They would never expect for me to have a gun or to be up to no good.”

“She’s got a point, Greg,” Alan said. “Nobody’s going to think someone her age or someone that’s been banking there for years to do something like this. She’s the perfect person to go.”

Greg looked at Mary with a defeated face. He was beaten by his elderly wife. “Greg, I’ll look after her,” James said. This day was full of people acting out of character.

“James, you’re not . . . ” Alan started.

“Dad, I’m going,” James said.

“You’re too young, they won’t believe you‘re there to do business,” Alan responded strongly.

“Mary’s right, dad,” James said. “We signed up for this, and we need to do our part. I’m tired of being in the background. I’m a part of this whether you like it or not. When they took mom, this became my mission. If you want me to let her down, then keep trying to keep me from going. You *know* that she would want for me to follow my heart, and that’s what I’m going to do.”

“Your mom wouldn’t want you to get hurt,” Alan said.

“And she wouldn’t want me to be a coward that’s afraid to fight for my beliefs,” James concluded. This whole exchange reminded Danny of what his mom would tell him to do if she thought he needed to act on something rather than simply talking about it. He could relate to what James was saying and it made him want to join in on this plan as well.

"I can go too and make sure that James is fine, Alan," Danny said.

"So will I," Champ said.

"See, dad? I'll be fine. We're all in this together," James said.

Alan was still very unsure. "I guess it's time for us to let our loved ones join the fight," Greg said. "We can't protect them forever." Mary looked at Greg and smiled.

Alan was reluctant, but said, "Alright, James. But you'd better not take any unnecessary risks. You're all I've got left."

"I will be, dad," James said.

"Alright then," John said. "Danny and Champ, you guys get into your police uniforms from yesterday and make sure to grab your badges. Danny, do you have any suits here?"

"Yeah," Danny said. "My dad probably had some in his closet."

"Cool," John said. "I'll go grab one and meet you guys back here. We'll discuss the plan when we get into the car."

With that everyone in the group headed off to different parts of the house to prepare for the day. Danny went to his room and grabbed the police uniform off of the ground. It was a bit wrinkled, but he didn't really have much time to iron it or anything. It was about eleven and the bank probably closed at three, or some inconvenient hour like that.

Once he had his uniform on and his belt of fun stuff secured around his waist, he headed back downstairs. James and Mary were already there waiting.

"Are you pumped?" James asked Danny.

Danny nervously laughed and said, "I guess you could say that. I'm pretty damn nervous."

"Yeah," James said. "Me too, man. I'm just glad I'm finally getting to do something."

"Me too," Mary laughed. "I've got to side with Danny though. I'm very scared."

"I'm sure we'll be fine," James said. "I've seen John work with computers and he's really good at it. We'll probably be done in there in a few minutes. I just hope that they don't have metal detectors or anything that could help them see that I have a gun."

"They don't," Mary said. "You'll be fine. I can't even tell that you're carrying one now."

"Awesome!" James said. "I'm glad I'm wearing a hoodie. It definitely helps."

"So does having a purse!" Mary joked.

"I like how we're joking about how we conceal weapons," John said as he came down the stairs with Champ. Champ's uniform looked a bit snug on him, as did John's suit. It probably wouldn't matter though.

"Alright, let's get out of here," John said.

The five headed outside. Adam ran to the garage down the road earlier and pulled the car up to the house. "Good luck out there, guys," Adam said as he ran to the house. Champ hopped into the driver's seat and John got into the passenger seat. They started down the road and John began to explain the plan.

"Alright," he began. "I'm going to go in there with Danny and Champ behind me. I'll tell the teller that I need to see a manager. Once I get one, I'll tell him that I need to investigate a breach into Anthony's account. The manager will probably get freaked out that someone looked at the account and shouldn't ask too many questions. If he does, we all have badges so we should be fine. I don't expect him to be good at noticing fakes."

"What if he does?" Champ asked. "We always need a backup plan."

"Well then we pull out our guns and make sure that nobody does anything crazy," John said. "If that happens, we funnel all of the people to the main part of the bank and you four keep an eye on them."

"What if one of them try to fight?" James asked.

"Then you'll have to shoot them," John said. "I know none of you want to kill any innocent people, but we'd have to. We can't hesitate and we definitely can't fail. After a few minutes, I should have the bank statement forwarded to the major news branches. I wrote all of their e-mails down so it shouldn't take long at all. James and Mary, you two just try to distract the tellers."

"How should we do that?" Mary asked.

"I don't know," he said. "Just strike up conversation. Try to do a transaction."

"I do need to pull out my money so we can buy some more food," Mary said.

"Well then there you go," John said.

After about twenty minutes, the group pulled up to the bank. Danny's heart started to race. His nerves were working hard to freak him out. The bank looked intimidating. It was a two story building, but it looked as if it was used as a bunker whenever the bank was closed. The steel of the door and the spotless glass sent a wave of fear into his heart.

He tried to look inside to see how many people were there. It was only about eleven so there probably weren't many seeing how normal people need to work. Even with this thought, his paranoia warned him of the hundreds waiting for him inside.

"Alright, Mary and James, you two head in," John said. "We'll do a loop and then head in. Just act as natural as possible. You guys aren't doing anything wrong."

James and Mary got out of the car and walked into the bank. Champ pulled the car around the block. John got on the radio and said, "Alright, James and Mary are in. We'll be going in soon."

Dr. Kaitlen answered them, "Alright, good luck, boys."

Champ pulled up in front of the bank again. The three got out and began their dreadful walk into the bank. Danny opened the first door for John and Champ. John got the next and the blood started pumping. There weren't many people inside. Only a few tellers, a couple of people in line, and . . . a security guard. Danny swallowed hard.

John led the group to the front of the line. All of the people in the bank were staring the three down as if they knew that they weren't real cops. Mary was in line and looked happy to be there. James was talking to someone at a desk. He sounded nervous, but the man he was talking to didn't seem to mind. "How can I help you today?" the teller asked John with a very nervous sounding voice.

"We received a signal that someone accessed Anthony Darrell's bank account and we're here to check it out," he said.

The teller looked even more nervous now and shakily said, "Um . . . okay. Let me get my manager." The teller walked away and the three stood there looking confident, but rattling on the inside. After a few minutes, a manager came out of the back and walked around. The group turned around to greet him.

"Hello, how can I help you officers today?" he asked.

"We're here to investigate a possible breach into Anthony Darrell's account by one of your employees," John answered. He was surprisingly good at acting like a federal officer. He even pulled out his badge to show to the manager. The manager looked at it briefly, but didn't take much time to question its authenticity.

"Alright," he said. "Can I see yours, officers?" Danny and Champ showed the manager their badges. The manager nodded and said, "Alright, follow me." He was acting very nervous at this point, realizing that the officers were real and his bank was in trouble. He probably thought he was going to get fired or something. "I want to apologize for this, officers," he said. "If I knew someone did this, I would have fired them the second it happened."

"Glad to hear it," John said. Damn he was good at this. They followed the manager around the side. The manager punched in his number to the locked door and led them in. The tellers and other assorted workers there were staring at the police officers gossiping to each other. The security guard out front was the one that was sketching them out the most, though. It was clear that he didn't buy into what the rebels were saying.

They got to one of the teller's computers and John took his seat. He only had a few minutes to send the statement. Once he accessed the account, the real federal officer would be on his way. The teller reached over him and entered her password so he could access the accounts. "What's Darrell's account number?" he asked.

The teller looked confused and asked, "Don't you have it?"

John looked at her sternly and pointed out, "I'm a federal officer, not a bank teller. Now do your job." Danny couldn't get over how well John was at impersonating a federal officer. Danny and Champ stood near John and looked around to make sure everyone was calm while the teller entered the account number from a paper the manager handed her.

Then it was on the screen, Anthony Darrell's bank account. John looked at it as quickly as he could. Then he saw it. The last transaction on his bank account came into his vision. It was for $700,000. He clicked on it and read the details. It was from a federal office in Washington D.C. To make it even better, it was a Pentagon office.

John found the button to e-mail the details of the bank statement pretty quickly. He went to his e-mail and pulled out the piece of paper in his pocket. He began entering the addresses and Danny and Champ made sure that nobody was watching him do it. At one point, Champ even threatened to arrest a teller for glancing over. It was actually getting pretty fun.

However, as John took more and more time to type in the addresses, the group began to get more and more nervous. Finally, John finished and stood up. The manager walked over and John said, "My mistake. It seemed to have been some sort of glitch in the alarm system."

The manager looked relieved and said, "Alright. Well thank you for coming in to investigate it."

John nodded to him, "It's my job. Thank you for your time. Have a great day."

The manager nodded, "You too, sir."

The three began to walk to the front door. James was already standing on the sidewalk outside and Mary was putting the money from her transaction into her purse. They had done it. They got away with it. The e-mail had sent to the major news stations all over the country. They would be flying high soon.

Then a police car rolled up to the front of the bank and shot down their hope. The group froze in their places. Their eyes widened and their muscles stiffened. Danny looked to Champ. Champ's eyes were filled with as much fear as Danny's were. This wasn't going to go well, and they knew it.

They waited inside for a moment and the real federal officers walked in. They were all wearing suits and immediately approached the group. The officer in front said, "I'm officer Johnson. Who the hell are you?" The officer had two others right behind him.

"I was here investigating a breach in the Darrell account," John said.

"That's funny," the officer said. "Because that's what I'm here for."

"Yes, sir. That was just me," John said.

"Let me see your badge, officer," Johnson said to John. John pulled out his badge. Surprisingly, he wasn't shaking as much as Danny was. The officer looked over John's badge, then looked at John, then back at the badge. "Tell me officer," the officer began. "You're a federal officer, correct?"

"Yes, sir," John responded.

"Ah," Johnson said. "Then why do you have a state police badge?" John froze up. He had no idea what to say. "That's what I thought," the officer said. "You three are under arrest for impersonating police officers and for stealing classified information." The officer began to grab John's arm. John pulled back and Champ flew forward with a strong punch to the officer's jaw.

Danny freaked and pulled out his gun. The two real officers did as well. Danny fired as quickly as he could at them while Champ and John pulled out their guns. Customers and tellers began to duck down to the ground. There was the sound of screaming and gunshots everywhere. The rebels ran to a nearby desk and took cover. The officers ran back and took cover behind a wall.

The security officer began to pull his gun and Champ shot at him. A bullet ripped through the guard's leg and he dropped with a yelp. Another bullet went through the guard's chest and he twitched on the ground. An officer moved out of cover with his superior yelling behind him shooting at the rebel's desk. "Shit he's flanking," Champ said.

Mary got up from the ground and pulled the small pistol she had been concealing. She wasn't accurate, but she emptied the clip at the officer. One managed to hit him in the head and he dropped. One of the officers yelled to the other, "Call for backup!"

John came out of cover and ran to another desk, "We can't let them call backup!"

The officer not calling backup shot at John with as many bullets as he could muster. Danny stood and began to shoot at the officers as they shot back. Danny looked up and saw James crouching walking into the bank. James was walking slowly towards the corner that the officers were hiding behind. It didn't look like they had seen him yet. James hugged the wall, just inches from the officers. Danny became distracted and felt a sharp pain in his side and dropped. As an officer grabbed his radio to call backup, James flew around the corner and emptied his gun into the two officers. They dropped quickly and James froze with his gun still held up over them.

Champ stood up and sprinted to Danny. "Danny!" Champ yelled. He looked at Danny's side. There was blood pouring out of his gunshot wound. "Holy shit."

John and James ran over. Mary was already walking out of the bank. Adam ran to James and grabbed his arm. "Come on!" he yelled. "We've gotta get out of here, guys!" Champ carried Danny to the car as the others watched their flanks. Champ put Danny in the back as the rest got in. Champ started the car and flew down the road. They moved as quickly from the bank as they possibly could.

"Shit!" Champ yelled. "What the hell just happened?" Danny was on the seat yelling from the pain. James was still frozen in fear from the gunfight. "Danny," Champ said. "You just need to stay awake, we'll be there soon." John held his hand on Danny's wound as they drove down the road. They heard police sirens in the distance and picked up the pace.

"That's not how I planned on that going," John said. "That could have gone a hell of a lot better."

"Don't worry Danny, we're gunna make it out of here," Champ said.

"I'm gunna die in here," Danny mumbled. "I'm gunna fucking die." His hands were shaking as he tried to hold the blood back.

"No you're not," John said. "Once we get you back, Dr. Kaitlen's gunna fix you up." After only a few minutes of intensely fast driving, the group pulled up to the safe house. Champ pulled up and John grabbed Danny from the car. He carried him all the way to the back door of the house and brought him inside.

"Holy shit," Rob said. "What the hell happened?"

"We got the e-mail sent," John yelled. "But Danny got shot." The rest of the group came downstairs and gasped at what they saw.

"Well how did it happen?" Rob asked.

John told them the story. He said how everything went well until the ran into the federal officers. He told them about the badge and the shootout. He told them about Danny getting shot by an officer. He even mentioned how James's heroism got them out of there. "Damn, James," Alan said. "You've made me proud, boy." Alan put his hand on James's shoulder and pulled him in for a hug. He pulled back from it and looked at James's face. "What's wrong, James?"

Dr. Kaitlen came over to look at Danny. "Get him onto a table," she said. Champ and Adam picked up Danny and carried him to a table in a separate room of the basement. She unbuttoned his shirt and pulled it off. "You should have worn the bulletproof vest," she scorned. Danny ended up passing out from the pain.

Danny woke up in the middle of Dr. Kaitlen trying to fix his wound. The anesthetic that she tried to give him to keep him under had worn off. He began to yell as her hands were working on the wound. Dr. Kaitlen dropped her tools and yelped. She began frantically looking for something to put him under. She didn't have much at the beginning and now she was out. She resorted to the only thing she could do. She wrapped her hands around Danny's throat to make him pass out. After a few seconds of choking, Danny finally went under again.

When he awoke again, Dr. Kaitlen was sitting in a chair in the room. "Ah, you're up," she said. Danny tried to sit up. "Don't do that," she said. "I got the bullet out and fixed you up, but you're going to be out of commission for a while. And we're going to need to find you some antibiotics so your wound doesn't get infected. I know where to get some, but I just wanted to make sure you woke up alright."

"Ugh," Danny mumbled. "Thanks, doctor."

"Don't worry about it," she said with a smile. "Just rest up." Danny's side sent sharp pains through his body over and over. He wanted nothing more than to just fall asleep, or even just die. Anything that would take the pain away.

The rest of the group was upstairs watching the news. The anchor was on talking about a breaking news story:

"A bank statement showing a transfer of $700,000 into Anthony Darrell's bank account has citizens enraged. The statement is said to be the most concrete evidence that the assassin was paid to murder presidential candidate Stewart Marshall that has been revealed. President David Stone and other government officials have refused to comment, but protesters are gathering in Washinton D.C. and around the country calling for the impeachment of David Stone and many other government officials. Complete anarchy has taken over the country. We'll continue to keep you updated as we receive more details."

"Well, looks like shit's about to hit the fan," Champ said as he took a sip from his fifth beer.

"Hell yeah!" Adam said. "It's just a matter of time until the entire country's on Stone's doorstep." He took a gulp from his next beer as well.

John yelled from the kitchen, "Anyone want some shots?"

"Hell, I don't see why not," Rob said as he and the rest of the group in the living room walked to the kitchen.

Champ stumbled to the door of the basement and announced, "Everyone! We're taking shots!" A group of laughing people came running up the stairs to join in on the festivities.

Everyone grabbed a shot and held them up. "Cheers to our success and to taking back the country!" Adam said. Everyone tapped their glasses together and downed their drinks. A few of them coughed and the rest just shook their heads. Champ didn't seem to have any reaction to the drink at all.

Dr. Kaitlen walked up and told the group, "Danny's awake." They then all ran downstairs to see how Danny was doing. They almost tripped down the stairs on the way there in their drunken sprint. As everyone piled into the room, Danny looked up slowly at them. "Hey," he said.

"Hey," Champ said from the front of the group. "How are you feeling?"

Danny looked down at his side. It had bandages covering it with blood on most of them. "Well, I feel like I got shot," he said with a half smile. The group chuckled.

"Well it's good to know that you're in good spirits," Adam said.

"Oh shit!" Rob yelled.

"What happened?" Adam asked.

"Anthony's still here," he said.

"Oh yeah! I can't believe we forgot that," Adam said. "Let's go talk to him."

"Wait," Steve said as he brought the conversation in closer. "Is he staying? I mean, we got what we wanted. There's no reason to keep him here."

Sam rolled his eyes, "We already said that we should let him stay."

"No," Steve said. "We never came up with a conclusion. The way I see it, we have no reason to keep him. He's just a liability at this point."

"I already told you, we need to give him a chance," Sam said.

"And we did," Alan said. "And because the only thing he could think of as evidence, my son's probably going to be scarred for life."

"Hey," John said. "James went in knowing the risk."

"But if we could have found different proof then he wouldn't be like this," Alan responded sternly.

Adam intervened, "We still got the evidence. That's all we needed."

"Exactly, and now we don't need him," Steve said.

"You know that's not what I meant," Adam said.

"And we still don't have the supplies to keep him here," Dr. Kaitlen said. "If we want to be able to live on, he needs to go."

"But, Mary got more money for supplies," Greg said. "We should be fine."

"We'll be fine for a while," Dr. Kaitlen said. "But we won't be for as long as we may need to be. Medical supplies alone would cost us hundreds of dollars."

"And he'll still bring a lot of heat that we don't need right now," Rob said.

"Well how are we going to decide?" Greg asked.

"Let's just vote," Rob said. "Everyone that wants him to stay, raise your hand." Some raised their hands. "Alright and now everyone that wants him gone raise your hand." Even more raised their hands. "Danny how are you gunna vote," Rob asked.

"I'm not going to," Danny told him.

"Why not?" Rob asked.

"Because I know that he can't stay, but I don't want to be part of the group kicking him out onto the streets to die," he said slowly through the pain. "We all know that if he doesn't get arrested, he'll die. And if he gets arrested, then he might just go back to working for Stone. If we kick him out, there's no way that we can stay here anymore."

The group thought on it. It was true. If Anthony didn't die, he might just go back to working for Stone in which case he'd tell them where the safe house was. That would only lead to the group's death. However, Anthony could end up being useful to them and could become as good of a friend as the rest of them had. It wasn't an easy decision.

"Well we already voted," Steve said. "So let's get him out of here."

"But what if he does go to Stone's administration?" Alan asked. "We'll all be screwed.

"Then just kill him," Steve said. "Either way, he can't stay. We already voted on it."

"Are you willing to kill this guy that just wants to help us?" Sam asked.

"Don't act like you're better than this," Steve said. "Remember how he talked about Brandon? Remember how he treated all of us? He can't be trusted to stay and he can't be trusted to leave. It's the only way we can do it."

"I highly doubt he saw where we were from the back of a van," Sam said. "Let's just let him leave."

"If he leaves, then he'll figure out where this house is and tell someone," Steve said.

"Will you two just shut up?" Champ said. "Let's just blindfold him and drop him off somewhere. Would that work for everyone?" The group talked it out and decided it was the only humane *and* logical thing to do. Now they would just have to break it to Anthony. “Alright then. Let’s get in there and tell him,” Champ said. They walked to the other room and went to Anthony who was still sitting in the chair. His wounds had been fixed up by Dr. Kaitlen, but he still had really bad swelling all over his face.

“So can I stay with you guys?” Anthony asked.

“We’re going to drop you off downtown,” Adam said.

Anthony flipped and yelled, “I told you what you wanted! This is bull shit! I trusted you assholes! You need to stick to your end of the deal!”

“We don’t though,” Steve said. “You’re a worthless piece of shit. You’re lucky we aren’t killing you.”

“Will you just go back upstairs, Steve?” Adam said.

Champ helped Anthony up. “Adam can you go get the car?”

“Yeah,” Adam said. “I’ll be back.”

“Awesome,” Champ said. “John, radio the Boston chapter and tell them we’ll need an escort to town to drop this guy off.”

“Oh and tell them to bring some medical supplies for Danny,” Dr. Kaitlen said.

“Sure thing,” John said. He went over to the radio and told the Boston chapter. They said that they’d be at the safe house in a short matter of time. Adam walked out of the back door and began his walk to the garage.

Amanda walked over to Danny’s medical bed to discuss the news. “This is insane,” Amanda said.

“What is?” Danny asked.

“We’ve finally got the evidence to prove that Stone paid that guy,” she said. “I really never thought we’d be this far this quickly.”

Amanda sat and began telling Danny about the news on TV. He told her about the bank and they continued to talk and joke about the situation. “I’m sorry that this had to happen to you, Danny,” Amanda said.

"It's fine. I did it for a good cause, and I'm still really glad I decided to join," Danny said. "I'm sorry for ever thinking that this group was crazy, Amanda. I really owe you the apology of apologies."

"Don't worry about it, Danny," Amanda said. "I'm just glad you decided to come with me. It really means the world to me. Not to mention, you became one of the most important people that this group could have had." She looked at Danny and smiled. He became lost in her eyes and she became lost in his. The two best friends were becoming more. They were forming a bridge between their souls. They were becoming one inseparable being. Amanda began to move her face closer to seal their bond. As their lips touched, they heard a yell from the back door.

"Cops!" Adam yelled as he ran into the door. The group downstairs panicked. They began running upstairs trying to turn off everything.

"Everyone hide!" Champ yelled.

Dr. Kaitlen ran into Danny's room and shut the curtain. She grabbed a gun from the corner and ducked down. Amanda hid under Danny's bed after throwing a blanket on top of him. She whispered in his ear, "Act like you're dead. Maybe they won't mess with you." Danny was confused by that statement, but wasn't going to deny it.

As he laid under the blanket, he heard a bang on the back door. "Police! We have a search warrant!" he heard them yell. Nobody answered the door. After another loud bang, and then a silence, a much louder bang rang out. Danny heard footsteps of people running into the house. Then he heard a yell, "Stop! Put the gun down!" Then shots rang out. It scared him senseless, but he forced himself to remain as still as possible.

He heard footsteps upstairs as well as downstairs. Then he heard someone pull the curtain open, then another series of gunshots. He shook under the covers in fear. He had no idea what was going on, but continued to fake his death. Then he felt the cover get ripped off of him. A pair of fingers came to his neck. "I know you're not dead," he heard the voice of the person say. Still, Danny continued to fake it. The hand that the fingers were on smacked Danny's face and his eyes shot open.

He saw an officer with an assault rifle standing over him. He looked on the floor and saw another officer dead in the doorway to the room. Then his mouth dropped. Dr. Kaitlen was hunched over against the wall. Her eyes were open and blood covered her torso. Danny tried to hold back the vomit as well as the tears. The officer reached behind him and pulled out handcuffs. He put them onto Danny's arms and put his cuffed hands onto his lap.

"Stand up," the officer commanded. Danny's fresh wound wouldn't let him stand very easily.

"Sir, I've been shot," he pleaded.

The officer lifted Danny up and put him onto his feet and said, "You won't have to worry about that for long." He put Danny's cuffed hands around his neck and lifted him into the other room. Danny could see everyone in the house knelt down on the ground with their hands behind their backs. As he came into the room, he saw Greg and Mary being pulled downstairs. Greg was resisting and Mary was crying hysterically.

As a police officer pushed Mary, she fell down the last two steps and hit the concrete floor hard. "Don't you fucking touch her you bastards!" Greg yelled through frustrated tears. He pushed the officer in front of him down the stairs with a hard shoulder to the back. The officer fell down about five stairs and landed on the concrete next to Mary. He stood up almost immediately and pulled Greg down next to his wife.

He forced Greg to his knees facing Mary. "Fucking look at her," the officer said. He reached down and pulled Mary's head up as she laid on the floor in tears.

"Let go of her," Greg pleaded, tears pouring down his face.

Mary was sobbing. "Greg," she said.

"Don't worry, I'm right here," Greg said.

Mary tried to pull her words together, "I love you." Her tears continued to fall.

Tears came down Greg's face as he pulled a smile together for his wife. He looked at her with the smile and said, "You're the best thing that ever happened to me. I love you with all . . . " Then the officer pulled the trigger, ending Mary's life. "You son of a bit . . . " Greg began until he was shot as well.

Some of the rest of the group began to yell and sob as they saw the couple gunned down. Danny was dropped onto the ground. His side was killing him. He didn't think that his wound had opened back up, but it definitely wasn't shut all the way yet. He looked over at the group. They were lined up. Many of them were staring at the ground. Their faces were empty.

Danny watched the head officer walk across the line of people. "You're the group that tried to get Anthony Darrell out of prison? And I guess that makes you the ones that chose to go and send his bank statement to the news. Right?"

Steve looked up at them and said, "We didn't do anything wrong! All we did was stand up for our fucking country!" The officer pulled out his pistol and shot Steve between the eyes. Rosa screamed and Amanda sobbed. Rosa began to break down in front of the officer and leaned on Amanda for support. Amanda was deeply sobbing. "Anyone else want to try to explain how you didn't commit treason against your country? Please I would love to kill another ignorant patriot."

Nobody spoke. Danny looked up from the ground and saw Anthony standing with the officers, without any handcuffs on. Steve was right. He was just going to go right back. "Now then," the officer said. "Who's the one that killed the two officers in the bank?" He began walking down the line, but nobody said anything.

The officer shook his head. "So none of you will sell him out?" he asked. He chuckled. "Well luckily we've got security cameras in banks nowadays, so your nobility if for nothing," he said. He walked over to James and pointed the gun at his head. "You assholes think you can just go around trying to start a rebellion? You have no idea what you've gotten yourselves into."

"No! Please! Kill me instead!" Alan yelled. James looked up at the gun and tears began rolling down his face.

"Please," James said. "They were shooting at us! I'm sorry!" The officer shot James and the boy fell to the ground. Everything was going to hell. Everyone knew that they were going to die and their souls broke down. They felt like cows at a slaughterhouse, waiting in line to meet the fate that the one in front of them had met.

"I'll fucking kill you," Alan yelled as he tried to stand. He got to his feet and ran at the officer. The officer didn't see him coming and fell to the ground with a hard thud. With Alan's hands being behind his back, all he could do was deliver a solid head butt to the officer's head. The officer pushed him off and stood back up. He grabbed his gun and put one into Alan's head as well.

"Now then," the officer said as he regained his composure. "Who were the other three at the bank?" Everyone knew that the officer already knew. Danny knew that he, his uncle, and John were about to die. He didn't doubt that they were all about to lose their lives. With Amanda, Rosa, Rob, Sam and Adam being the only other ones besides the one that went to the bank, they were all probably going to be shot just for causing a rough time.

"Well," the officer said. "What a noble bunch." He walked over to John, put the gun to his head, and pulled the trigger. John went limp and fell to the ground. Danny's soul was ripping apart. He was watching his friends die right before him and there was nothing he could do about it. It was the worst nightmare that he could have ever had coming true right in front of him.

The officer walked to Danny next. He put the gun to Danny's head. Danny stared into the gun and gave up all of his hope. The officer's finger squeezed the trigger, and nothing happened. He was out of bullets. "No big deal," the cop said. He reached to his boot and pulled out a knife. "Traitors deserve nothing more than a slit throat anyways." The cop knelt down to Danny and blood splattered out of the side of his head. He dropped as life left him and the knife flew from his hands.

Danny looked at the door. A group of people wearing bandanas over their faces poured in with assault rifles and shot through the officers. The officers attempted to return fire, but the surprise caught them off guard and they dropped quickly.

"Check the rest of the house!" one of them yelled. He had an Irish accent. Some of the guys ran into different rooms downstairs while the rest ran upstairs. The head guy lowered his gun and walked toward the group. "Count your fuckin' blessings, mates." The man walked over to Danny who was laying on the ground looking to the ceiling. "Are you that kid whose parents were taken and you spoke at that meeting down the road a while ago? What was your name? Danny was it?"

Danny was panting. "How do you know me?" he asked.

"You're kind of a big deal around the Committee, lad," the guy said. "I don't know if you've realized it, but you and the rest of these people, well, you've inspired a lot of people around here. But right now, we're here to get you guys out." The rest of the men came running downstairs. "Alright, let's get these folks out of here." The group helped everyone to their feet. "Blindfold them to make sure that they don't know where we're going and get them into the van. I don't know which ones we can trust just yet." Danny watched as everyone had blindfolds put on and they were escorted out. Then one of the men came over to Danny and did the same to him. He was counting his blessings, along with the amount of hope he had just lost in the past few minutes.

CHAPTER FOURTEEN

ON ONE CONDITION

Danny couldn't see a thing through the blindfold. He could only feel the cold concrete of the floor beneath him. With the bodies of his friends surrounding him, it was probably best. He'd just watched the deaths of so many of his good friends, of so many people that didn't deserve it. Unlike the movies, there was no "goodbye," and no sad scene of him sitting over his friends as they died in his arms. There was nothing but the cold emptiness in his heart as he watched the brutal murders of his friends. His heart was torn open, and he had a feeling that it wouldn't be mended for some time.

His friends never had a chance. They were killed one after another without a hesitation in sight. His inability to make it stop annoyed him and frustrated him to the deepest part of his psyche. As he stared into the darkness of the blindfold, he wanted nothing more than to be cast into that darkness forever and bring a light to his defeated soul again.

Danny felt himself being lifted up by someone's hands on both sides. He got to his feet and the wound on his side began to sting worse than it had before. All he could do was let out a yelp and drop to his knees in pain. With the gash in his side, and his loss of blood, he couldn't summon the strength to move anywhere. "Can we get some bolt cutters for these cuffs?" Danny could hear the person holding him up say. After a short exchange, Danny felt his hands come free. "Don't worry, kid, we're getting you all out of here."

Danny's concern was elsewhere. "What about my friends?" he asked.

"They're coming too," the man said.

"No," Danny mumbled. "I mean the . . .other ones."

The man began pulling Danny along, "There's nothing we can do for them."

"So you're just going to leave them here?" Danny asked.

The man's voice sounded a bit more frustrated, "We have to. We just need to get you all out of here before more officers get here."

"You don't even have the dignity to honor them with a fucking burial?" Danny questioned. "Then you'd might as well just kill me now you piece of shit." Danny had lost it. He didn't have an ounce of endurance left in his body, emotionally, or physically. He wanted to fall to the ground and die from blood loss with the rest of his fallen friends. Anything was better than attempting to move on from what he'd seen.

"We're not doing that," the voice said. "You're coming with us whether you like it or not." The grip on Danny's arms tightened and he felt his feet come off of the ground. He was being carried out of his house and he had no say in it.

"Grab any weapons or food you find," Danny could hear the Irish voice say from across the room. They were more concerned with what Danny's group had stowed away than respecting what they were going through. It frustrated Danny, but there was nothing he could do to change it. He felt himself being carried along by someone he didn't know. He could still hear the mourning of some people in the group. It was only ripping him apart even more. If the gunshot wound didn't kill him, his heart would.

Danny felt the person under him stop. The slight breeze he felt on his back signaled to him that they had arrived outside. "Alright let's get him in there," the voice next to him said. "Just lay him down in the middle or something. I'll stay in there and make sure none of them take their blindfolds off." Danny could feel someone lift his legs and then the cold metal of the vehicle he'd been put into on his back. He sat on the floor and let himself fall backwards. His body relaxed itself on the floor, but the wound on his side hurt with an intensity that words couldn't explain. If he died in the back of that van, he wouldn't have been surprised.

"We need to get moving or this kid's going to die on us," Danny heard someone say. The situation had gotten so severe that they didn't even attempt to mask it.

"Where the hell are we going?" Danny heard who he guessed was his uncle talking. He sounded a bit too drunk for the occasion.

"Don't worry about it," the Irish voice rang out. "You're safe as all hell, mate. You'll see soon enough."

"Fuckin' peachy," Adam said. Nobody could say much of anything the entire ride. The people in the front would occasionally yell back to make sure that the group was fine. Sometimes Danny would feel a towel press down on his side and he'd feel another rush of pain. He was breathing heavily. It was loud enough for everyone to take notice of it.

He laid on the ground listening to the people in the front of the van talking about possible checkpoints and which routes they should take to avoid them. There would be times that one of them would raise their voice in disagreement. They didn't sound like a very professional, or well-mannered, bunch.

It seemed like one of the longest rides ever. Danny was constantly running the possibilities through his head of what would happen next. Maybe they were going to pull over and kill them. Maybe they would reach a checkpoint and the police would kill them. Maybe the gaping hole in his side would kill him. Nothing looked too bright, especially through a blindfold.

As he stared into the darkness, twisted images formed in Danny's vision. He saw horrific flashbacks of death and despair as he begged for his end to come. The pain was driving him completely insane. With every bump of the road, a new shock of pain shot through his body, and drove his mind to quit and shut down.

The vehicle finally came to a stop. Danny was assumed they were in the right place when the Irishman yelled, "Welcome to our abode, lads!" It was demented in a sense, because even with all of the man's humor, the group still knew that they could be killed at any moment. After what they'd been through, none of them were ready to trust another soul.

The back doors to the van opened and the group turned their blind heads towards the back. "Alright, step on out," the Irishman said. Everyone still able to stand walked out of the back. Danny was the only one left behind. "Oh almost forgot about you, mate." Danny laid on the cold metal floor of the van drenched in what he guessed was his own blood. He was surprisingly calm given the circumstances. "Well don't just stand there! Help the lad out!" the Irishman yelled.

Danny heard footsteps in the van and then he felt two people lift him from either side and begin carrying him. "Get him to the infirmary," the Irish voice rang out. Danny felt a temperature change as he was carried into what he guessed was another building. He could hear people talking from every side of him as he was carried in. Some of it good, saying who Danny was, which was surprising considering he didn't know that anyone knew he existed, then some were guessing how much longer Danny had to live, which caused him even more distress than being blindfolded and carried into a building full of strangers.

Finally, Danny felt his body rest on something soft. Before he had a chance to relax, he felt the blindfold come off and he was instantly blinded by the light of the room. He quickly tried to search around the room at everything around him, his eyes swinging from side to side in a panic. He could only make out what looked like it would be a hospital, but it didn't look as professional at all. The cabinets were run down, there looked to be a shortage or medical supplies, even the thing he was laying on had yellow stains from years of abuse.

He looked down at his side. There was no doubt in his mind that the wound had reopened, and might have even gotten larger. The stitches looked to be attempting to close the wound, but blood was still flowing out at an alarming pace. The shirt that he had been given after Dr. Kaitlen performed surgery on him was soaked in blood. There was someone looking at the wound and moving around quickly attempting to put more and more things on the wound. With every touch of his gash, Danny felt a shock of pain shoot up his body. He couldn't help but let out screams at every touch.

The person working on him put an IV in his arm with some, hopefully sterile equipment. The doctor glanced at Danny's face for a second and seemed shocked to realize that he was still alive and functioning. "Oh, hello," the person said. "I'm Steven Lee. I'll be the one fixing you up."

Danny attempted to respond, but could only let out a mumble. He was on the verge of passing out and he knew that it wasn't a good sign. "Alright," Dr. Lee said. "I just need you to keep looking at the light on the ceiling and keep your eyes open. Don't let yourself fall asleep." Those words solidified his fear of sleep. Danny stopped looking at Steven and rotated his head so he was looking at the light on the ceiling. His head was tilting slightly to the side due to a lack of energy. He watched the white light as if he was waiting for something to happen.

As he stared into the bulbs and essentially blinded himself, he felt a sharp pain in his side. Danny let out a large holler and cringed to get his side away from the source. "No, you have to stay still," Dr. Lee said. "I know it's hard, but you have to try your best or I could slip and mess up." Danny became even more tense now. He stared at the light and continued to cringe as much as he could without moving his side.

Whatever was happening, it took a long time to take place. It felt as if Danny would never get off of that bed. He continued to just stare at the light and bite his lip at the pain. Either his loss of blood or the meds were causing him to begin to hallucinate. He began seeing designs in the light. He could see the light expanding and expanding. It looked as if the light was going to wipe the walls of everything clean. Danny was surprised that the doctor could even continue to operate with such a blinding force above him.

Danny then realized that something horrible could be happening. Perhaps this was the light that everyone sees when they die. Danny became very frightened and summoned all of his strength to ask the doctor, "Am I gunna be ok?" His breaths quickened and he felt his heart beating as quickly as it could to pump blood throughout his body. His limbs were going cold and numb.

The doctor glanced down at Danny's head. "I'm almost positive that you'll make it through this," he said. "You've just got to stay strong and I'll take care of the rest." Danny's mind slipped up and he looked away from the light. As he glanced down to see what the doctor was doing, he became instantly horrified. The stitches were out and the doctor was digging into Danny with random hooks and knives. Blood was now only oozing out of the wound, but it was still flowing. As he made eye contact with his muscles and fat, he passed out.

Danny awoke to the doctor slapping him. His head shot up as the light filled his vision again. The room was now full of people surrounding Danny. It caught him off guard to say the least. "He's got a pulse," he heard the doctor's voice say." Danny tried to get up and was forced down immediately by a gloved hand. "Danny, can you hear me?" the doctor's voice said.

Reality seemed like such an abnormal thing. Danny's vision was hazy and he was still having slight hallucinations from the meds. He honestly thought that he was dreaming when he had first woken up. Then he heard the question again, "Danny, can you hear me?"

He figured he might as well play along with his dream, so he answered, "Yeah." Then what sounded like a stadium cheering nearly deafened the weak individual. His vision began returning to him. His first priority was to see how his side was doing. He looked down and saw bandages covering the side of his torso. What comforted him the most was that they didn't seem to be covered in blood. There were just a few red spots around where the slit of the wound was.

Danny let his head fall back down onto a pillow and he began to look around. He saw everyone from his old safe house standing around him, or at least what was left. The remainder of his family had paid him a visit while he was still in this state of confusion. They all seemed to be smiling so Danny's health didn't seem to be in jeopardy.

"How are yah feelin'?" Champ asked.

Danny looked up at his uncle's slightly bearded face and answered, "I guess I'm alright." For some reason this made the entire room bust into laughter as if it had been the funniest joke they'd ever heard. Danny would never be able to be fully conscious of what was going on at this rate.

"What happened?" Danny asked, still attempting to regain his consciousness to it's fullest extent.

"Well, you passed out on me," Dr. Lee said. "And you almost died."

"When?" Danny asked.

"It was about an hour ago when you died," Dr. Lee said. Danny's mind did a flip.

"I died?" Danny asked the doctor.

The doctor looked at his clipboard. "Well only for about a minute," he said. "It turned out that the doctor that worked on you before forgot to take the bullet out. When you looked down at it you passed out. It wasn't a problem at first, but after a few minutes your heart just stopped working. I had to revive you and you sat there with a blank face on for about an hour as I finished up. And here we are."

This all struck Danny as the craziest thing he'd ever heard. He kept looking around at everyone to make sure he wasn't just dreaming or something. He poked at his side and felt a sharp pain. He was definitely still awake. "It's good to have you back, Danny," Amanda said from his side with a smile. Her face looked tired, but she looked like she finally had found something to establish as the bright side to the whole situation.

"Is the lad awake?" It was the Irish voice again. The man behind the voice walked around Danny's spectators to take his place at the foot of the bed. Danny finally had the chance to get a good look at him. He had some combination of blonde and red hair cut in a military style. He wasn't as large as Danny had thought he'd be, but he definitely looked as strong as Danny had imagined. He was wearing a normal collared shirt with a bulletproof vest over it and he had his arms crossed. He put a hand out to Danny. "It's a pleasure to meet you, Danny," he said.

Danny attempted to sit up, but another sharp pain sat him back down. He still raised his hand up and the man walked around to meet it. "I'm Commander Byrne

O'Connor. Pleasure to meet you, Danny. I had the chance to meet these friends of yours earlier."

"How do you know me again?" Danny asked. Champ put his hand on his face. He obviously thought that Danny was being rude. Danny didn't realize that this guy was of any importance.

O'Connor didn't seem too offended, though. "Well, I was at one of the early meetings of the Committee, the one where you spoke to the group before many of the Committee's members began leaving their homes. I had visited as a representative of this chapter, and I've got to say, you inspired a lot of people in this chapter, including myself."

Danny looked around again. He was still in that same room with the same agonizing light. "Where are we anyways?" Danny asked.

"We're just outside of Boston," the commander answered. "This place used to be a hotel. We converted it to meet all of the needs of the members of this chapter. We seized it from the original owners not long ago. Since then, we've been running most of Boston's rebellious activities from here."

"How did you get the supplies to keep all of these people here?" Adam asked. "We could barely keep our own group stable due to a lack of supplies."

O'Connor got really confident at this point. "Well, we often just intercept vehicles that are carrying supplies to police stations, hospitals, or grocery stores. Sometimes we just go to the place they're delivered to or from and take what we need," O'Connor said.

"How has this place not been shut down yet?" Rob asked. "Wouldn't the police feel the need to shut something like this down as soon as possible?"

"They can't," O'Connor said. "We've grown much too strong much too quickly. Not to mention that all of our soldiers are civilians. We blend in perfectly when we're not here. And no officer would ever dare to come to this hotel. We've intercepted enough weapons to take all of Boston if we wanted to."

"Why hasn't the military tried then?" Sam asked.

"If the military struck a target on American soil, the entire country would revolt immediately," O'Connor answered. "And we have loyalist hostages that are keeping them from acting recklessly."

"Why didn't the news say that this place had been taken by your forces?" Adam asked.

"Well the government won't let the news report on that, because then it would give other groups courage or it would give everyone a good place to go if they want to join the revolution," O' Connor said. "Any more questions?"

"You really seem to have everything figured out around here," Amanda said.

"Thank you," O'Connor said. "I was in the Irish Special Forces back in the day so I pride myself on getting things done, and getting them done right. Speaking of which, I need to figure out what we're going to do with you all."

"What do you mean?" Danny asked. "I thought we were welcome here."

O'Connor chuckled and said, "I can't just let every person that seems to want to help walk in here. We'd have thousands of people flooding this place. With how many people we already have, we can only take those that will be of use to us. Not to mention that many people can't be trusted. You all should know that."

"Sorry to sound ungrateful for what you did back at our place," Rob said. "But I think we've more than earned protection from your chapter."

"And you got it," O'Connor said. "But you have to understand there isn't that much room left here."

"We kidnapped Anthony Darrell and had a bank statement proving that Darrell was paid by the president to assassinate Marshall sent to every news station in America," Adam said. "How have we not earned a spot here? You know that we're all capable of helping out."

"I know that most of you are," O'Connor said.

"What does that mean?" Adam said.

"Well," O'Connor began. He took a pause and rubbed his neck, knowing what was about to happen once he finished speaking. "Only a few of you actually worked to do those things."

"How do you know?" Champ asked.

"I have my methods," O'Connor answered. "Not to mention, I can just tell which of you will prove useful to me."

"Look, buddy," Champ said. "You owe your entire mission to us. You should be kissing our asses for everything we've done, not the other way around."

"We saved your asses, lad," O'Connor said. "That's a lot more than you can say. So before you get out of line like that again, you should remember that we could have just let you all die back there. Now do you want to state your cases for which of you can stay or do you just want me to send you all back to that fuckin' graveyard I saved you from, mate?"

Nobody liked where this was going at all. However, they had stuck together through tougher situations, so each of them had a reassurance in the back of their mind that no one would be left behind, but this didn't seem like a time when they had much control. "So let's start with you, Danny," O' Connor continued.

Danny was confused. "What do you want me to say?" he asked.

"Whatever you think will make me want to keep you here," O'Connor said coldly.

"Well, I've taken a goddamn bullet for this cause so far," Danny said. "I think that pretty much sums up this bullshit."

"I don't think any of you are realizing the severity of this," O'Connor said. "You know what, I'll just go with what my gut is telling me then." He turned to a few faces of the group. "Rosa and Amanda, you can't stay, lasses," he said sternly.

Danny's heart dropped. "You can't be fucking serious," Champ said.

"They don't serve a purpose here," O'Connor said.

"I lost my husband to all of this," Rosa said. "My daughter and I both lost him and we're still here. How do you think that we aren't going to be useful here?"

"Women are too emotional and they don't think with their logic, they think with those reckless emotions," O'Connor said. "They'll do what they want to do and not what the group thinks they should do."

"So we're not followers and that's why we should be kicked out?" Amanda asked.

"You hit the nail on the head, lass," O'Connor said. "You won't follow orders, I guarantee it."

"What makes you think any of us will if you don't let them stay?" Rob asked.

"The fact that you need somewhere to stay," O'Connor said. "I've got your balls in a fuckin' vice, mate."

Rob looked confused and infuriated. "Look, I don't have to listen to shit," he said. "If you don't let them stay, we all leave."

"It's no hair off my back, mate," O'Connor responded smugly. "I know most of you are capable and would be a great addition to this army, but I can make due without you."

Danny tried to think of some way to reason with this stubborn asshole. He had definitely let the power get to his head and he wanted to be treated like he was the commander of the most powerful force in the world. He was a god in his mind and the only way to reason with a narcissist is to attempt to offer them what they want.

"Look, sir," Danny said. "We've all been through more than you can imagine. We'll help to take down Stone and his administration as best we can and we'll do it all the way to the gates of hell, but you have to understand, we've become a family. At this point, these are the only people I know I can trust. Just give us all a chance to prove ourselves. If you don't like what you see, you can send us packing. We just need a chance to prove ourselves. I guarantee we can live up to your expectations."

O'Connor smiled at Danny. "I've always loved a good gamble," He said before laughing. Danny wanted nothing more than to hit his smug teeth into the back of his throat. "Alright," O'Connor began again. "In about a week, this army is going to be making one of its biggest moves since the beginning. We're going to start assassinating the ones leading these police officers on the raids they've been executing. Danny, I thought you'd be interested in one of the targets specifically."

"Who?" Danny asked.

"The officer that led the raid that took your parents and took you in for questioning," he said. Danny was shocked. He thought back to the smug investigator that told him to simply deal with the fact that his parents were traitors and threatened to lock him up too. That day, he wanted nothing more than to kill that guy in the police station. Now he finally had a chance.

"I'll do it," Danny said without hesitation.

"Are you sure, Danny?" Adam asked. "We can take care of it. You need to rest."

"And miss this opportunity?" Danny said with a smile. "I'll be good in a week."

"You'll still be in some pain," Dr. Lee said.

"Getting to kill that asshole will make me feel better, trust me," Danny said.

"That's the spirit, lad!" O'Connor said. "The rest of you can either take a target, or you can help out with a different assignment."

"What's the other assignment?" Rosa asked.

"Oh, it's a fun one!" O'Connor said. "In a few days, there's supposed to be a huge shipment of weapons to a military base just outside of Boston. Our goal is to intercept that shipment and get the weapons back here."

"What's supposed to be in the shipment?" Sam asked.

"Some heavy shit, mate," O'Connor said. "We're talking assault rifles, explosives, and ammunition for days. It's enough to arm every citizen in Boston. We'll be sending them to every chapter in Massachusetts. This state will be armed to the brim and we'll be ready to help take back the country. It gets me all worked up just talking about it." O'Connor was off of his rocker, but it wasn't necessarily a bad idea.

"Well then we'll think about it and let you know later tonight what we want to do," Adam said.

"Sounds great, mate," O'Connor said. "If you all want some food, head to the cafeteria. We've got some great chefs there and tonight we're serving food that was supposed to go to a five star restaurant in Boston, so you're in for a treat! See you all around!" O'Connor walked out of the room and began yelling at soldiers throughout the hotel.

The remaining people from the old safe house could do nothing but look at each other and shake their heads. "What an asshole," Champ said.

"Yeah, I know," Adam said. "But he's a hell of a leader. I'll give him that."

"What makes you say that?" Danny asked.

"Well, he knows how to keep people in line," Adam said. "He doesn't argue with anyone, he just gives orders. Judging by how many people are here and how well armed they are," Danny looked at a soldier walking by carrying an assault rifle, "I'd say he's pretty damn good at what he does."

"I guess," Danny said. "I just can't believe that we can't all stay."

"We'll find a way to get him to let all of us stay," Rob said. "We won't let this family get broken even more."

"Thanks, you guys," Rosa said. "It means the world to Amanda and I."

"Yeah, thanks," Amanda said.

Everyone smiled at each other. Their smiles were a dime a dozen recently, so any one they could share brought more happiness than any amount of material possessions could. "So who wants to get some food?" Sam asked. The group laughed at his question. They were all starving though so they nodded.

"Wait," Champ said. "What do we do about Danny?" Everyone realized that Danny had just gotten done with a surgery, as hard as something like that was to forget. With everything that was happening, they were lucky to even remember what everyone's names were.

"He's okay to be put into a wheelchair," Dr. Lee said. "Just don't stand up and sit down too much, Danny."

"You've got it," Danny said. "Thanks a lot for everything, doc."

"What kind of doctor would I be if I didn't try to help?" Dr. Lee answered. "Go get some food. You've gotta be starving and you need to get some nutrients into your body. You pretty much bled out everything you had before this." Danny laughed even though that had been one of the most morose jokes he'd ever heard.

Rob and Champ helped Danny get up and sit in a wheelchair that Dr. Lee wheeled over. "Do you have any shirts around here, Dr. Lee?" Danny asked.

"Oh yeah," he said. "I've got some white t-shirts around here. I'll grab you one." Danny adjusted himself in the seat as the doctor grabbed a shirt and brought it over. Danny put on the shirt and Champ got behind him to wheel him around.

They went into the lobby of the hotel which was right next to the infirmary. The hotel was huge. It still had its chandeliers and fancy pictures that it had before being taken over hanging througout. The walls were a bright red. The lobby of the hotel almost looked like the entrance to a palace. Everything was surprisingly clean and structurally sound. The front doors had large metal doors right behind the initial ones. The windows had huge metal shutters that could be shut whenever necessary.

The lobby was flooded with people in both civilian and the clothing of their soldiers. The soldiers wore bulletproof vests and helmets that looked like they had been stolen from the police stations. Everyone's vests had a different design on them, but they all had the same bear design in the center of them. It was the face of a bear in the middle of a roar with a red aura surrounding it. Then at the chest of each vest was the word, "Tuebor." Danny had never recognized it, but he became interested immediately.

"Excuse me," Amanda said to a soldier that was about to pass the group. "What does that word on your vest mean?" Amanda and Danny had been starting to think alike a lot recently. It was no surprise that she would be wondering the same thing as him.

"Tuebor?" the soldier asked. "It means 'I will defend.' It's from Anglo-Saxon culture."

"Oh!" Amanda said. "That's so cool!"

"That's what I thought too," the soldier said. "Where are you all going? I haven't seen you here before."

"We're trying to find some food," Champ told him.

"Oh," the soldier said. "Just go down the hall at the other end of the lobby and walk all the way down until you see the cafeteria. Better get there quick. The food's just now coming out and if you wait too long there's gunna be a huge line."

"Damn, we'd better hurry," Champ said.

"Thank you!" Amanda yelled as they began to run. Champ started pushing Danny's wheelchair to dangerous speeds. Danny hadn't had fun in a while though so he didn't mind. He just laughed the entire ride as the world flew past. Everyone else in the group were running behind and alongside laughing all the way to the cafeteria.

They flew past the artwork in the hallway and the different designs on soldiers' uniforms. Once the scent of food hit their noses, Rob yelled, "This is the only time my fat ass will ever move this fast."

The group laughed and Champ said, "I'm with yah', buddy!" They made it into the cafeteria and went to the back of the line which was, thankfully, still pretty short. They impatiently waited in line watching soldiers walking by with plates full of food. Danny looked at one person's plate and saw a steak, mashed potatoes, and king crab legs. It was going to be the most diverse, but easily the most delicious meal of their lives.

The group finally made it to the front of the line, got their food and made their way to their seats. They sat together at a table and discussed how amazing the hotel was. "This place is ridiculous," Adam said.

"It really is," Danny said. "I can't believe we get to stay here."

Then they paused and realized the conversation that they had with O'Connor earlier that day. The food suddenly seemed a lot less delicious. "Oh, we still need to figure out what we're doing for our missions," Rob said.

"This sucks," Champ said. "I'd rather just do assignments that I knew would just be for the greater good rather than doing them to get this guy to approve of all of us."

"Regardless, I'm ready to do whatever I have to in order to make sure we can all stay," Rosa said.

"Agreed," Adam said. "So what are we all thinking?"

"Well I already know what I'm doing," Danny said.

"Are you sure you want to risk that?" Champ asked.

"I want that guy dead," Danny said. "I don't care if I'm hurt, I'll get over it. That guy had my parents taken from me and my life turned upside down. The least I can do is make sure that guy dies in the most grotesque way I can think of."

"You're seeming very dark today, Danny," Rob said.

"I'm not dark at all," Danny said. "I'm happy as hell that I get to get my revenge on him after all of this time."

"Be careful, Danny," Sam said. "Revenge can make people careless."

"Don't worry," Danny said. "I'll be safe and I'll be strong."

"I sure do hope so," Sam said.

"I definitely like the idea of ambushing a convoy," Adam said. "It sounds like it would definitely be much more interesting than stalking someone to kill them. I'd definitely want to do that."

"I'd have to agree with that," Champ said. "It'll be a good shot at getting this frustration out."

"I'm not sure what I want to do," Rob said. "I don't really want to kill another cop, but then again the convoy that we ambush could be a police convoy. Not to mention how dangerous all of this is."

"Oh yeah," Champ said. "It's gunna be dangerous, but it's gunna be worth it."

"I agree," Rosa said. "That's why I'm definitely doing an assassination."

The group was shocked at what this sweet woman just said. "Why?" Champ asked for the rest of them.

"I think I'd be good at getting close to the target without getting seen," she said. "And I definitely wouldn't be very good in an ambush." She paused. "I can't believe I'm even weighing these options. It's not something I ever thought I'd be doing."

"Same here," Amanda said. "But I think I'm on the same side you are with this, mom. I'd be better at getting close to someone and killing them rather than fighting a battle or something."

"Like mother like daughter," Rosa said as she kissed Amanda's head.

"This is the craziest shit I've ever heard a mother and a daughter talk about," Champ said.

The rest of the group had been watching them with blank stares. They were all thinking exactly what Champ had said. After a few seconds of awkward silence, they went back to eating.

"Well I'm meant for a battle," Sam said. "So I'm definitely going with the ambush. I wouldn't mind getting an efficient weapon either."

"I guess I'll have to side with you on this one," Rob said. "I'd rather fight a battle than kill a cop that I might know."

"Speaking of which, Rob," Adam said. "You should probably not tell anyone in this place what your previous occupation was. I doubt that they'd keep you around for very long."

Rob stopped eating for a moment. He looked over at Adam as if he had just had an epiphany that changed his entire way of life. "Damn, Adam," he said. "You're right. I didn't even think about that."

"I'm sure that someone else in this place used to be a cop," Rosa said. "There were a lot of cops that joined this cause."

"But we don't know that for sure," Adam said. "And I don't want to risk him not being able to stay. We're already having troubles with a similar situation right now."

"I guess," Rosa said. "I just don't want to live in fear in the place where we're supposed to be making allies. It just seems counterproductive."

"It does," Adam said. "But until we get their trust, we need to be very careful."

Soldiers that were eating around them began to become very silent. For a moment, Danny thought that they had heard the conversation that table was having. He stopped eating and looked around. They were all focusing on a television near them. "Turn it up!" a soldier yelled.

Everyone watched the television and felt immediate horror as they watched the news report.

The anchor looked tired as she spoke through the television, "The United States Army was called in to diffuse a situation in Washington D.C. today. Since the releasing of the bank statement accusing the United States government of playing a major part in the assassination of presidential candidate Stewart Marshall, thousands of protesters have shown up in Washington D.C. With the recent outrage, the army was called in to control the protesters. Rather than using conventional methods such as tear gas, the situation quickly escalated and what was reported by a witness as 'hundreds of shots' were fired into the crowd of protesters. So far there have been over two hundred protesters confirmed dead. The president has refused to comment on the situation, but today, an executive order was issued that will allow officers to search any building, person, or vehicle without probable cause. Though it has been said to directly violate the United States constitution, no talk of a stop being put to this order have come about."

The group looked at each other. None of them could fully convince themselves of what they had just seen.

They looked down at their food and thought about the situation the country was in. As they sat there, thousands of Americans were probably getting arrested or murdered without rhyme or reason. Sam was the only one able to break the silence. “That’s a line they should have never crossed.”

CHAPTER FIFTEEN

WHAT A DAY

"After yesterday's executive order, hundreds have reportedly been arrested in one night alone. Police have allegedly entered over five hundred houses throughout the night after the order and they are said to be continuing into today and throughout the week. In other news, protesters continue to advance on major cities in the United States after the shooting of hundreds of protesters in Washington D.C. yesterday. An anonymous army official said that the same may happen today if the protests get out of hand again."

Danny awoke in his hotel bed in a cold sweat. Regardless of the great condition of the hotel, the air conditioning wasn't the best. The rest of the group were still sound asleep, however, Danny didn't plan on laying in his ocean of a bed any longer.

He pulled his wheelchair up to the bed and dropped himself into it. He rolled to where he had left his white shirt and put it on. He was lucky that he decided not to wear it to bed last night.

Danny rolled to the door of his group's room and opened it, revealing the lavish hallway. There were some soldiers walking around on patrol, but not much else. Judging by the light outside, it was early morning, maybe a half hour before people would start getting up. Danny was still in amazement by the place that they had taken refuge in. It continued to surprise him that they were actually able to hold a place like this and not lose it to the police or the military. Maybe the Committee really had grown to the strength that he hoped it would.

The thoughts of the ones Danny had lost were still fresh in his mind. As he rolled through the hotel, watching soldiers joking around to each other, he still found it difficult to accept that the ones he'd shared moments similar to these with were never coming back. The only thing that still kept him going was the hope of seeing his parents again. Regardless of the hell that he'd been through in the past few days, he never forgot his main drive for putting himself through it all.

Danny rolled into the elevator and rode it down to the main floor. There wasn't much to do while he was constrained to a chair and none of his friends were awake. He figured he would just roll into the cafeteria and get a head start on some breakfast. On his way there he heard a voice call after him, "Danny?"

Danny turned around to see who would be calling after him with such enthusiasm this early in the morning. He didn't see anyone he recognized, just soldiers walking through the hotel. Figuring he was just hearing things, he turned around and continued into the cafeteria. He might have rolled about five feet before a hand grabbed his shoulder.

He looked up and saw a soldier that he didn't recognize. The guy was about the same age as Danny. He had blonde hair and seemed to be one of the scrawniest soldiers occupying the hotel.

"Aren't you Danny Bruce?" the soldier asked.

"Yeah," Danny said awkwardly. "Who are you?"

The soldier saluted, "Private Thompson, sir."

The greeting caught Danny by surprise. This entire hotel experience was proving to be a crucible for his mind. "How do you know me, and why did you just call me sir?" DAnny asked.

The soldier seemed rushed and said, "Let me grab you some food and we'll talk."

Danny was flattered, but his mind was still running circles around itself. "Alright," he said slowly. The soldier began jogging to the row of food as Danny rolled himself to a table. He tried to think of where he would have ever seen this guy, but nothing came to mind. He figured he would remember someone with bleach blonde hair that acted as suspiciously as this guy did. No matter how much he thought about it, he couldn't find a name to match the face, or a memory to match the behavior.

Before he could finish thinking about it, Thompson got to the table with a plate of waffles, bacon, and sausage for Danny and the same for himself. Danny wasn't going to turn down food, regardless of how much of a nut job Thompson was. "Thanks," Danny said.

"Any time, sir," Thompson said.

Danny took a bite of his waffle and turned to Thompson. "So you never told me why you're calling me sir or how you know me," he said to him.

Thompson laughed. "Oh yeah," he said. "Well I saw you at that meeting that the commander saw you at. The one where you gave that really inspirational speech. It's what made me want to help here at the hotel. From what the commander's said, you've done that for a lot of people here."

"Well . . . " Danny started. He had no idea how to respond. "I guess you're welcome?"

Thompson giggled again. "In all seriousness," he said. "I probably would have never joined had I not heard you speak. I had been so scared, but you were so confident when you spoke that it just made me want to help the cause right away. I don't think you realize how much of an effect you had on people. Did you?"

"No, not really," Danny said. "I just kind of said what was on my mind."

"You're modest," Thompson chuckled. Now Danny was starting to think that this guy was coming onto him.

"You know you should talk to the commander sometime. I'm sure that he'd like to properly thank you."

"I already talked to him," Danny said.

"Really?" Thompson said with a surprise. "What did you think of him?"

Danny thought back to the asshole that was telling him that his friends might not be able to stay unless they followed all of that guy's directions. "He was alright," Danny lied.

"Well why don't you go talk to him now?" Thompson asked.

"I don't know," Danny said with frustration. "I'm pretty tired."

"Then you've gotta eat!" Thompson said. "Then you'll have enough energy to do anything."

Danny was at the point where he might not be able to keep his polite attitude. The soldier's odd mannerisms were getting on his nerves. "Danny!" he heard. He prayed that it wasn't another Private Thompson character. He turned his head and luckily saw Champ and Adam walking over. He let out a sigh of relief with a smile. He waved and the pair walked over.

"Who are they?" Thompson asked.

"Friends from home," Danny said.

"Can I meet them?" Thompson asked.

Danny looked at Thompson as if he had two heads. "How'd you sleep?" Adam asked as he walked over.

"Eh," Danny said. "Alright. My side definitely kept me up for a while."

"Well at least it's a new day," Champ said. "Another great day in the Committee." He laughed at his joke and sat beside Danny.

Thompson finally looked uncomfortable rather than overjoyed. "Well I'll see you around, sir!" Thompson said as he stood up and walked away.

Adam and Champ looked at Danny in confusion. "Who the hell was that?" Champ asked.

"I have no idea," Danny said as he continued to eat his waffle. Champ picked a piece of bacon off of Danny's plate and shoved it into his mouth with a chuckle.

"That's pretty damn good," Champ said. "Want to get in line with us?" Danny looked at Champ, then down to his wheelchair, then back to Champ. "Oh yeah, I forgot." Champ laughed again. It was good that he found Danny's handicapped condition funny.

As Adam and Champ stood up, another soldier ran over to the group. "Danny Bruce?"

Danny's head went back and the breath left his mouth. He turned to the soldier. This one at least looked like he had been a soldier for quite some time. "That's me," Danny said reluctantly.

"Commander O'Connor wants to see you, sir," the soldier said.

Danny felt a bit of fear enter his body. This couldn't be good. Champ and Adam shared the confusion that he was feeling, as well as a bit of the fear. "What happened?" Adam asked.

"Why did he call you 'sir0'?" Champ asked.

"I really don't know how to answer either of those questions," Danny said. "I guess I'll meet you guys back in the room." Danny shoved a bit more waffle and bacon into his mouth and began rolling away. The other two waved to him and Danny rolled out of the cafeteria.

"Nobody calls me 'sir,'" Champ pointed out with jealously.

As he went through the lobby, many more soldiers seemed interested in him than when they had first gotten there. They would stare at him as he passed and whisper gossip to each other. It was unsettling to say the least. Danny felt as if he was heading to his death and he was the only one that didn't realize it.

Danny rolled up to the commander's office. Two soldiers were standing at the door with assault rifles. "State your business," one of them said.

"Commander O'Connor wanted to see me?" Danny said, confused.

"One second," the soldier said as he opened the door and walked inside and shut the door behind him. Danny looked around the hallway of the office. Of course, O'Connor's picture was on the wall of him in a military uniform. What a cocky ass. The door opened again and the soldier said, "Go on in, sir." Again with the 'sir.'

Danny went into the office. The floors were covered in a clean red carpet and the walls were a very clean white and yellow design. He looked to the desk and saw O'Connor sitting waiting patiently for Danny to roll his way to his desk.

"How was your first night here, Danny?" O'Connor asked.

Danny didn't see the purpose in calling him there for that. "It was alright, I guess," Danny said.

"Glad to hear it," O'Connor said. He stood up and started pacing. "Used to be one of the finest hotels in Massachusetts. Served about a million people a year. And now I control it." He let out another smug smile as he did every time he bragged, which seemed to be almost every time he spoke.

"What did you want to see me about?" Danny asked.

"Hold your horses, lad," O'Connor said. He looked at Danny and the smile was wiped from his face. "I suppose I should be quick so you can have the doctor look at your side again." O'Connor paused and walked back behind his desk. "Danny, I told you about how inspired many people were when you spoke at that meeting, correct?"

"Yeah," Danny said. "Some other guy told me that today too."

O'Connor nodded. "Told you, lad," he said. "Well, I figured I sort of owe you one, so I figured I'd repay you."

"How so?" Danny asked. He prayed that O'Connor was going to offer Danny's friends permanent residence.

O'Connor smiled. "So eager, aren't you fella?" he laughed. "Well, I want to make you a general for this chapter." Danny was flattered, but didn't see any meaning behind the position of authority. "That means other than a few other generals in the hotel, you'll be in charge of quite a few people here. You're only in training for the moment though. Prove that you can handle it and I'll make you a full general."

"Is that why people have been calling me 'sir' all day?" Danny asked.

"I guess word leaks out sometimes, mate," O'Connor said. "Anyways, you'll be let in on plans as they come through and you'll be able to suggest your own strategies. You'll be helping me in deciding how to act and you may get to lead soldiers on some of those missions. Congrats, mate!"

Danny didn't feel as flattered as he probably should have. He was still too confused to feel any other emotion. "Thank you," he said in the nicest way he could. He still didn't give a damn, but the least he could do was act like he did. If it gave him some more pull with the commander, then the title would actually mean something to him.

"It's the least I could . . . " the commander started before being cut off by the electricity going down. "Dammit," he said. Then the power came back on about thirty seconds later.

"Why did that happen?" Danny asked.

"Our generators are only so good at keeping this place up and running," O'Connor said. "I'm afraid that they're running out of juice too, lad."

"Then go get new ones," Danny suggested. "I'm sure that they sell them at hardware stores and such."

"It's not that easy, mate," O'Connor told him. "We were lucky that the hotel already had those for emergencies. But, we've been running off of those for a few months now. Buying new ones isn't going to completely solve the problem, it would only ward it off for a bit. We need a permanent solution."

"What would you suggest?" Danny asked.

"I'm not sure," the commander said reluctantly. "I'll call my other generals in here and we'll discuss it. Be back here in about an hour."

"Alright," Danny said.

He rolled himself across the room towards the door. "One more thing, mate," O'Connor said. "I had this made for you. Figured if you're gunna be a general, you'll need one." Danny turned and the commander walked over and handed him a bulletproof vest. The front had that bear head, the word, and the red aura. He turned it over and saw "Bruce" written at the top. The middle had the number 29 written as if it was a jersey.

"Why 29?" Danny asked.

"The soldiers under you will be a part of company 29," O'Connor said. "Only generals have numbers on theirs backs, though. If you want to give it a nickname or something, just keep me updated."

Danny thought of his friends. "So will my friends be getting vests?" he asked.

"If they make it in, but until then they'll get some spares," O'Connor said. "Be back in an hour, mate!"

Danny turned and began making his way out of the room again. He got out and rolled himself to the infirmary. Every conversation that he had with O'Connor seemed to be filled with more and more bull. He would always get complimented for whatever he was said to have done, and then he'd essentially be told that his achievements didn't matter, because O'Connor had the final say in everything.

Dr. Lee was already waiting for him in the infirmary. "Hey, Danny!" he said cheerfully.

"Hey, doc," Danny said.

"How's the side doing?" the doctor asked.

"It doesn't sting as badly, it just feels tender," Danny said.

"Do you mind getting onto this bed so I can have a look?" the doctor asked as he pointed to the all too familiar bed from the surgery. Danny rolled over to it and lifted himself into the bed. The doctor lifted Danny's shirt and began pulling bandages off. They pulled at Danny's skin and body hair, causing even more pain. The doctor didn't seem to care, though. He simply pulled them off like it was a race.

When the bandages were off, the doctor looked at the healing wound. Danny had to have a look too. It looked a lot better than it had the day before. It seemed to be closing up a bit. "You should be fine to walk around tomorrow without a risk of it reopening," Dr. Lee said. "Just be careful and make sure to take your antibiotics. Hopefully we'll be able to take the stitches out in a week or so."

"Thanks, doc," Danny said. Danny got off of the bed and picked up his bulletproof vest to put it on. As he dropped it onto his shoulders, he noticed the doctor looking him over.

Dr. Lee noticed the numbers on the back and commented, "The commander made you a general already?"

"Apparently," Danny said. "He's known about me for a while I guess."

"I heard," the doctor said. "Well congratulations, Danny. I'm sure you'll do great. Just don't get hurt any more before you actually get to do something." He laughed a bit.

Danny let out a chuckle and sat back into his wheelchair. He rolled himself out of the room and made his way to the elevator. He was hoping that everyone had already left for breakfast so he wouldn't wake anyone up and he wouldn't have to explain the vest this soon. He wasn't completely sure how the group would react, but he felt like they would somehow be offended by the fact that he was recognized while they still had to prove themselves.

The elevator made it to his floor and he rolled down the hall to his room. His key unlocked the door and he went inside. The group was all there getting ready for the day. It seemed that he would have to explain himself sooner than he wished.

"Hey Danny!" Amanda said from right next to the door. "How are you feeling?"

"Much better," Danny said. "I should be able to walk around tomorrow if things keep going the way they are."

"That's great news!" Amanda said. "I'm excited for you." Danny smiled at her and she smiled back.

"Danny, what's with the vest?" Rob asked as he was putting his shoes on. Danny looked down at his vest like he had forgotten it was there.

"Does that have something to do with that meeting with the commander?" Adam asked.

"What meeting?" Rosa asked.

There were too many questions going around for Danny to keep track. "I had a meeting with the commander," Danny said. "And he made me a general."

The reaction of the room was priceless. It was a combination of dumbfounded and excited. The mixture of the two in their bodies just caused an awkward laugh with a few "congratulations," coming after the laughs.

"Thanks," Danny said.

“Why did he make *you* a general?” Adam asked. Danny could sense some jealousy in his voice.

“He said that I inspired him and a bunch of others at that meeting the day we all left our houses to live in my house,” Danny said.

“Damn,” Adam said. “He’s got a hell of a memory. Does that mean that we’re all going to be generals too?”

“I have no idea,” Danny said. He left out the part where the commander said that some of them might not even be here in a little while. “He just told me that I have to meet him in an hour to talk about an energy problem here.”

“Are you talking about how the electricity went out earlier?” Rosa asked. “It went off in the middle of my shower and everything turned ice cold. It was awful.”

Rosa didn’t seem to realize the severity of the situation. Danny went over how the generators were only supposed to be meant for backup use, but they had been running for a few months straight. He also said that they would have to find a new source of energy before the power went out for good and they began to have a severe problem. Everyone ended up sitting around the room deep in thought.

“That’s a hell of a pickle,” Champ said.

“Is there any way to get juice back into the generators?” Adam asked.

“They probably run on fuel so they could probably just be refilled,” Sam said. “I had that problem once when I had to run off of my generator after a hurricane, but I doubt that a hotel would run off of generators like that.”

“I honestly have no idea how they work,” Danny said. “And I’m supposed to meet them in an hour ready to discuss a possible solution.”

“Damn,” Champ said. “Well I hope you’re ready to turn that vest in.”

Danny shook his head and mumbled, "Thanks Uncle Chuck."

Champ realized that Danny was under some stress. "Look, Danny," Champ said. "I'm sure we can help you think of something."

"Are there any power plants nearby?" Rosa asked.

A lot of the group looked at Rosa for her stupid comment. The rest looked at each other. They could tell where she was about to go with that, and knew they would have to shoot it down before her outlandish suggestion turned into a true recommendation. "I don't think that would work, Rosa," Adam said. "The state would have definitely shut off power to the hotel, and there's no way that we can get it back here unless they knew that this force was no longer here."

"And the bills have to get paid," Rob said.

"Why can't we send the power to the hotel from the plant?" Rosa asked.

"Are you suggesting that we tell the commander that he should send some people to take a power plant?" Rob asked.

"Look at how many people are here," she said. "I'm sure that this army could take a power plant and keep it up and running. Then we could get some power sent to the hotel."

"That would never work," Champ said.

"Why not?" Rosa asked. "We've done crazier things, and with a much smaller force."

As much as nobody wanted to admit it, she had a good point. It was possible for this army to take a power plant, but there were so many risks involved that it would be almost impossible to do, not to mention it might not even work. At the very worst, the force could end up damaging a reactor and killing everyone in Boston.

"Well I'm sure that the other generals will have some suggestions as well," Danny said. "I can just offer this as our suggestion just so it's in there as a possibility."

"Maybe they'll be able to refine it and make a good plan out of it and the other plans," Sam said.

"Or I'll just look like an idiot," Danny said.

"I'm thinking the latter of the two," Champ said.

"Thanks once again," Danny said. "What are you guys about to do?"

Adam was putting on a pair of shorts. "Well it turns out that this hotel has an indoor pool." He had the ridiculous smile of a kid in a candy store. "Wanna come?"

"I probably shouldn't," Danny said. "I just want to chill out until my next meeting."

"Come on, Danny!" Amanda said. She grabbed his wheelchair and started shaking it violently. "We haven't had fun in a long time. It'll do us all some good."

Danny's frustration was boiling over. His sadness combined with his anger against O'Connor was at a point that couldn't be contained. He was never known as an angry person, but with the way things had been going, that was going to change.

"Are you guys not even aware of everything that's been happening?" Danny said sternly. "We've lost friends and family, we've got an all out war coming soon, and the army could come here at any point in time and kill all of us, and you guys are worried about going to a goddamn pool? I have a fucking bullet wound! How the hell do you expect me to do that? And stop shaking my fucking chair!" Amanda backed up in shock. Everyone in the room stopped what they were doing and were now staring at Danny. Danny's stress finally got the better of him. "Fuck!" he yelled. He turned his chair around and went back out of the room.

Danny rolled down the hall as quickly as he could. How could they have the ability to celebrate and have fun with all that they'd been through, especially Amanda. She saw her father get gunned down right in front of her and she wanted to go swimming. They were so deep in their own blind minds that they thought that this was some vacation that they were on. Danny looked at the soldiers he passed and wondered how his friends could become so lost from their purpose.

"Danny!" a voice called after him. Danny didn't even glance. He wasn't in the mood to be talking to anyone. "Danny! Dammit stop!" Danny slowed down to humor the voice behind him. A hand grabbed his shoulder and commanded him to stop. Danny saw his uncle come around to his front and kneel down. "What the hell was that about?" he asked.

Danny was reluctant to even speak. He didn't want to blow up again. "I'm just stressed," he said.

"You don't think we all are, Danny?" Champ asked. "We all know what has happened, don't think that we could ever forget."

"Then how are you guys over it enough to want to go swimming in an occupied hotel?" Danny asked.

"I don't know. Do you think we should just wallow in our sadness and have a big pity party? If that's what you want then by all means come back to that room where Amanda's now crying and everyone's thinking about the things that you just reminded them of!"

Danny started to feel remorse, but was still full of anger. "I didn't mean to blow up like that," he said. "But this isn't the kind of thing that we should be doing when we should be trying to get revenge for our dead friends and should be trying to rescue the ones that aren't dead yet."

"Danny, we've been focused on that the entire time. We just need a break from all of the seriousness so we can realize that we're still alive and we need to live on for the ones that can't. We can't just sit in our room and talk about the good times all day and think up ways of getting revenge! We'll reach true insanity if we start doing that."

"No we won't. We'll actually get something done," Danny commented. He was as stern as his uncle had ever seen him. Danny watched as his uncle's face went from anger to despair at the end of his nephew's statement.

"This war's changed you, Danny. This isn't the nephew that only used to care about being happy. You've gotten so enveloped in this 'purpose' that you're talking about, that you've turned into just another soldier trying to save something that can't be saved."

"What are you talking about?"

"Those people are dead, Danny. That's it. You can't somehow bring them back by being some big valiant badass. You need to accept it. Like Sam's said, revenge is only going to drive you to insanity. I think you should talk to him. Until then, you need to take a good long break from that room. Those people are the friends that we're still fighting for, not against." Champ stormed back to the room. As he opened the door, Danny could hear Amanda crying and Adam yelling. It hurt, but it wasn't something that would stop him from focusing on his mission of finding his real family. Danny headed for the elevator and went back to the main floor.

Danny rolled around the bottom floor of the hotel for the longest time. The walls of the hotel seemed much more demented. The bright colors were turning into a dreary, dull color. The pictures on the wall mocked him and everything he was fighting for. He stormed off and went outside to get a break. He saw the outside of the hotel for the first time. It was a huge building. The entrance had a concrete roof above it with sandbags and soldiers on top of it.

Danny rolled around near the entrance for a while trying to blow off steam. He couldn't believe what his uncle was trying to tell him. There was no time for rejoicing in a time of such sorrow. They were in a war, not a wonderland of happiness where they should be looking for something fun to do.

"Sir," someone said behind Danny. Danny was ready to hit that blonde kid in the face if he was standing there. It would be a great way to get his frustration out. He turned around and saw a grizzled guy that looked to be a few years older than Danny. He had a brown beard and aviator sunglasses. "Sir, you look pretty pissed," the guy said. "Do you want a cig?"

Danny looked down at the cigarette that the soldier was holding in his face. Hell, he'd never tried them, but this was as good a time as any to see if they could calm him down, "Sure," Danny said. He put the cigarette in his mouth and the soldier lit it for him, "Thanks," Danny said as he blew out his first cloud of smoke. It burned his lungs and throat. There didn't seem to be much of a purpose in those things, but it was better than giving himself a heart attack.

"I'm guessing by your face that you don't smoke, sir?" the soldier said.

"Nah," Danny said. "I'm just fuckin' pissed."

"Sir," the soldier said. "Can I speak freely?"

Danny never heard anyone ask him that. It made him feel powerful, but also caused an immense confusion. "Hell, I'm not much of a general. Say what you want."

"Well, sir," the soldier said. "What's bothering you?"

"Just everything," Danny said.

The soldier chuckled, "I've been there before." He lit a cigarette of his own. "Then again this isn't exactly a time where people can be all that happy, unfortunately."

"That's what I tried to tell the people in my room that are trying to go swimming after our friends were killed right in front of us yesterday," Danny said as he took another drag.

The soldier thought for a second and asked, "Well, what's the right way to deal with grief?"

Danny didn't understand the question. "What do you mean?" he asked.

"Well," the soldier said through another drag. "How are humans meant to deal with sadness?"

Danny thought about it for a bit. "Well," he started with a pause. "We're supposed to remember the friends we lost and try to do the best we can to make sure that they didn't die in vain."

"No, no," the soldier said. "You're talking like a military guy. If you lost someone before all of this, what would you do?"

"I'd definitely be too upset about it to go play in a pool," Danny responded.

The soldier took another drag, "Why does it have to be that way?"

Danny was confused again. "I don't follow," Danny said.

"Well," the soldier said. "Who said that we were supposed to react that way? If there is a heaven and our friends are looking down at us, then why would we show them us in our worst state? Why shouldn't we put on a show? Why shouldn't we let them know that we're doing okay? If I died, I wouldn't want my mother to be in tears for the rest of her life. I would want her to live on and make her life the best that it possibly could be. I wouldn't want to watch her cry. I'd much rather watch her have fun."

Danny looked down at his cigarette. It was burning quickly. Trails of smoke were streaming off of the end, forming designs in the air. The smoke seemed a lot like the smoke of a gun that just shot into one of his friends.

Then he paused in his thought. He really was fucked up. "What's your name?" Danny asked the soldier.

"I'm Mike, sir," the soldier said. He offered a hand for Danny to shake and Danny accepted.

"Thanks for the cig, Mike," Danny said. "And . . . thanks for talking to me."

Danny started to roll himself back inside. "It was a pleasure, sir," Mike said. "Hopefully we'll be able to smoke another cig sometime." Mike chuckled. It even made Danny chuckle a bit. Maybe that guy had a point.

Danny rolled himself into the hotel and headed to the commander's office. He didn't know if it had been an hour yet, but it sure felt like he'd been rolling around for even longer.

He was let into the office and saw several people standing in there. "There's my cripple!" O'Connor yelled. What a hilariously unfortunate joke. "I'm just joking with yah', mate," he said. "Let me introduce you to my other generals." He led Danny to the first man on the left. He was definitely only a few years older than Danny. He was extremely cheerful looking which made Danny a lot more comfortable. "This is Lieutenant Thomas Donley. He's the one making sure that we've got enough supplies and leads missions that secure more of said supplies."

"Nice to meet you, Danny," Thomas said as he shook Danny's hand. "I've heard a lot about you. It's great to be able to put a face to the reputation."

"Nice to meet you too," Danny said.

O'Connor led Danny to the next guy. He was much older, probably late thirties. He had one of the biggest beards that Danny had ever seen in his life. He was probably one of the strongest people Danny had ever seen as well. "This is Lieutenant Jacob Adams. He handles defense," O'Connor said.

"How yah' doin'?" Adams asked.

"Pretty good," Danny said. "Nice to meet you."

"Likewise," the deep voice answered.

O'Connor led Danny to the last man in the room. This guy was smaller than the last, but still looked much stronger than Danny. He was probably a bit younger than the last guy as well. "This is Lieutenant Taylor Michaels. He's in charge of intelligence," O'Connor said.

"It's a pleasure," Taylor said.

"Same," Danny said. He was running out of clever introductions.

"Well let's get down to business," O'Connor started. "As you guys know, we're running out of power and need to find a more reliable source than those generators we've got."

"Speaking of which," Danny started. "What do those run on?"

The group turned and stared him down. It was obvious that they thought that was common knowledge. "It's gasoline," Taylor said.

O'Connor looked ashamed. "Anyways," he continued. "What are some ideas?"

"We get more fuel," Thomas said. "Easy solution. We just find the next gas tanker driving down the highway and hijack it. We bring it back here and we've got power for a good long while."

"But that's a temporary solution," Jacob said. "Not to mention that it would be way too big of a risk to go steal something as combustible as a tanker and bring it back here, and the government doesn't take kindly to its fuel being stolen, so they'll have more incentive to attack us."

"We're already in a battle," Thomas said. "What does it matter if we steal one more thing from the government? We've already taken all of the stuff we have here and we've been doing fine."

"That doesn't change the fact that it's a temporary solution," Taylor said. "We'll eventually run out and then we'll have to risk our lives again."

"That's why I believe we should get solar panels," Jacob said. "We'll have as much power as we need."

"Where the hell do you think we'll find enough solar panels to run an entire hotel, mate?" O'Connor asked.

"I don't know," Jacob said. "I'm sure plenty of buildings in Boston have 'em. So we'll take those."

"So you want to go into a huge city and just take the solar panels and get out?" Thomas asked. "We'd lose every soldier that we send into that city. Then we'll have even less here."

They were bickering like children. "What about a power plant?" Danny budged in.

The group looked at him. "Are you fucking serious?" Taylor asked. "I was led to believe you were a lot smarter than that."

"Yeah," Jacob said. "We don't have the tools to build a power plant."

Danny no longer felt like an idiot once Jacob spoke. "I mean why don't we take over the power plant that was supposed to be sending this place power and make them?" Danny said.

"That's way too much of a risk," Jacob said. "We'll have a lot less soldiers here if we send them all on some hopeless mission."

"We'll have even less if we don't have power," Danny said.

"Look at this guy," Thomas said. "I like how this guy thinks."

"Are you serious?" Jacob asked.

"Think about it," Thomas said. "We'll have all of the power we need, and we'll be able to control how much power goes into Boston."

"But the government would definitely take actions to take the plant back," O'Connor said.

"But once we get the supplies from that military convoy," Thomas started. "We'll be able to arm every person in every chapter of Boston and the forces against us in Boston will be so overwhelmed that they won't be able to stop us. It's a lot more likely that they'll just give up the city. Then we've got a much larger base to work with."

"It's fucking nuts, mate," O'Connor said. "But it sounds like it'll work pretty damn well. Are we agreed on this plan?"

"I fucking love it," Thomas said. "One of the best and most ballsy plans we've ever had."

"Same here," Taylor said. "I can get some guys into the plant soon so they can start seeing what we'll have to deal with."

"Do we have guys here that can run a power plant?" O'Connor asked.

"Hell yeah we do," Taylor said. "A bunch of people in my unit have experience with that sort of stuff."

"Then I definitely want a part of this plan, lads," O'Connor said. "What about you, Jacob?"

Jacob was rubbing his beard. "Well," he said. "I think it's definitely risky, but with the shipment coming in, I think we'll be alright. And I've been dying to get out of this hotel and do something, so I'm a hundred percent down with this plan if we get it figured out perfectly."

"Then we're in agreement," O'Connor said. "Taylor you get your guys into that plant to start gathering information, Thomas you make sure we get that shipment, and Jacob you start making sure you get the troops ready. Danny, you can take a break and come by tomorrow for your assignment. Nice job guys. That's probably been the quickest meeting we've ever had." The group laughed and they left the office. Danny got a few good pats on the back from the other officers and made his way to the elevator. Then he remembered that he's not welcome in there.

Danny went to turn and the elevator opened. Just when he thought he'd be able to avoid confrontation with his room and keep his mood up, Sam was in the elevator. "Just the guy I wanted to talk to," Sam said.

"Sam," Danny said starting to back up. "I'm sorry for how I acted in there this morning."

"Why are you backing away?" Sam asked. "Do you think I'm going to hit you?"

Danny realized he looked like he had just seen a ghost. He stopped backing up and tried to compose himself. "No," he said. "You just caught me by surprise."

"Danny," Sam said. "Your uncle told me that you're getting obsessed with revenge and I should talk to you."

"Nah," Danny said. "I'm fine." He wasn't fine, he just didn't want to talk to someone after how he had acted.

"Come on," Sam said. He started walking to the cafeteria. "I'm hungry as hell." The two went to the cafeteria, Danny a lot less voluntarily than Sam. They got their food and went to a table. Danny rolled up to the end and Sam sat near him.

Sam began eating and looked at Danny. "So you want revenge for our friends?"

"Of course," Danny said. "Don't they deserve it?"

Sam swallowed his food. "Well, they do," Sam said. "But we need to do so in due time."

"Why can't we at least start working on it?" Danny asked.

"Because it will control your entire life," Sam said. "Trust me. I've seen soldiers that saw their friends die in battle become obsessed with trying to kill as many of the 'enemy' soldiers as possible and it drives them insane. Revenge turns humans into monsters. It's normal to feel it, don't get me wrong, but if that becomes your primary reason for acting, it will take control of your mind."

"How do you know it'll happen to me?" Danny asked. "I just think we should be working towards this cause instead of trying to have fun."

"Letting loose in a situation like this is the only thing that keeps us human, Danny," Sam said. "If we become obsessed with the mission, then we'll go insane. Back when I was in the military, I've seen kids just like you go completely nuts after their friends die. You've just got to do what you can and when you can't do anything, just chill out and enjoy your life. Live in their memory, you know?"

"I guess that makes sense," Danny said.

"Cool," Sam said. "And if you ever need to talk, you've got a room full of people up there that want to help. Never forget that."

Danny had become so overwhelmed with everything, it seemed that he had forgotten how to enjoy the life that he still had. He was obsessed with trying to get revenge and Sam completely called it. Maybe he really should just sit back and enjoy the life he has in their memory. "Thanks, Sam," Danny said.

"Any time," Sam said. "Now eat your damn food before I do." Sam chuckled.

The two sat in the cafeteria shoving food in their faces without conversation for a while. Danny looked at the clock and saw that it was still early afternoon, even after everything he'd been doing that day. He began to think about what people in the room were doing at this point. "So, is anyone still mad at me?" Danny asked.

Sam looked up from his food. "I'm not sure," he said. "You did kinda make a spectacle of yourself, so I wouldn't doubt it."

Regret began filling Danny's mind and pushing his other thoughts to the side. "I guess I should probably apologize," Danny mumbled.

"Yeah," Sam said. "You probably should."

"Well are you almost done?" Danny asked while looking at his now empty plate.

Sam began shoving more food down his throat. "I'll be done when I'm done," he said. It sounded like something that his uncle would say. "Doesn't mean you can't go ahead. I'll probably be getting seconds." He was chuckling through his food.

"Alright," Danny said. "I'll see you up at the room, man."

"Indeed," Sam responded. Danny rolled himself out of the cafeteria and into the elevator. He got to his floor and rolled to the door. He stopped in front of it and began listening closely to see what was happening inside. As he suspected, there were people inside talking. He took a deep breath and opened the door to the room.

As he entered, the room became drowned in a deafening silence. Everyone in the group looked at Danny, and then looked away quickly to avoid making eye contact and sparking up a conversation. It was clear that Danny would have to say something before anyone would say another word. "Hey, guys," Danny announced.

It was mostly silent, other than a quiet, "Hey," from Champ.

Danny looked around. Nobody was actually doing anything productive, they just didn't want to look as if they were feeling as awkward as everyone else in the room was. Danny mustered up the courage and announced, "Look, I'm sorry for how I acted earlier. I'm just really stressed out and I took it out on you guys. I know you guys are probably still mad, but I just wanted to let you know that I love you guys and I'm sorry that I would let my stress get the better of me."

Amanda was quick to speak. "You don't think the rest of us are stressed?" she asked demandingly.

Danny was immediately taken aback. It definitely wasn't the reaction he was expecting to get. "I know everyone is," he said. "But I handled it the wrong way and I can admit that."

"Do you think that just admitting it is gunna somehow make up for being a dick?" Amanda asked.

"Amanda!" Rosa yelled. "Don't you talk like that!"

"Why?" Amanda asked. "You know it's true." She turned back to Danny. "You treat us like shit and you expect us to just forgive you? This isn't some nice fairytale story where you can just say you're sorry and everyone hugs one another and gets over it, Danny. You had no right to act like that to any of us."

"I know," Danny said remorsefully. "I can't make you forgive me. I can just let you know how sorry I am. I don't know how to make it up to you guys, but I will in any way I can."

Amanda began storming towards the door. "You can't make up for treating us like that." She pushed past Danny and flung the door open, leaving the room. Rosa chased after her, trying to discipline her daughter for her foul language.

And so Danny was in a room full of tension. The rest of the group had stopped what they were doing and were staring at the ground or other objects around them. "You guys know I never meant to act like that," Danny said.

"Well, you did," Adam said. "We're all stressed out about what's been happening, but the only thing that's keeping us going are the times that we can sit back and laugh with the people we still have. When you came in here and ruined a moment like that . . . " Adam paused. "That's just something that no one deserves."

The remorse was hitting Danny hard. He couldn't say a word. He just sat in his chair trying to think of what he could say to make everything go back to how it used to be. Danny wanted nothing more than to just have the revolution end so he could go back to living the life he knew and loved. He wanted to go back to his boring life with his boring family and go to his boring school and hang out with his boring friends. It was becoming way too much for someone to deal with.

Then he realized what he had been missing. Everyone was feeling that same thing. The people that they had there were their only grasp to the past. The familiar people and fun times when they could cut back reminded them of how they were able to live before all of this had started. Given the circumstances, all they wanted was to enjoy the time that they could before they'd be thrown into further chaos. They just wanted to clench to the part of them that was still human.

Danny started to break down. He'd destroyed the only bridge to normality that he still had. He just became another soldier fighting a war. He lost the part of him that made him different from the rest. With the burning of the last bridge, the last string of his will snapped. The thought of continuing to live a life like this without anyone to turn to was killing him. He was just the asshole in a room full of friends.

He left the room and rolled as fast as he could down the hallway. He didn't dare to look back. No voice would reel him back in and no grasp would hold him there. He didn't know where he was going, he just knew that he needed to get away.

He made his way to the main floor and then to the front door of the hotel. He didn't think, he just flew past the soldiers at the front door. "If you need anything, our radio frequency is 101.1!" Mike yelled from the door. Danny paid it no mind and continued to roll out.

He rolled until he couldn't see the hotel. He turned back and saw only the trees and the road leading to the hotel. He turned back forward and continued to fly down the road. Without warning his escape turned into a hell. The soft sound of the wind brushing his worries behind him turned to the sound of shouts. The way to freedom became barricaded with his worst fear. His hopes turned to despair.

Police officers were running into the road from the trees around him. Before he knew it, he was surrounded by officers in bulletproof vests, balaclavas, and helmets. Their assault rifles all pointed at their one target. They shouted for him to put his hands in the air, and he did as quickly as he could. The deepest fear that could be felt filled every bit of his essence. Danny had no idea of what to expect, but he knew that he wasn't getting out of this one.

CHAPTER SIXTEEN

DEEPEST NIGHTMARE

"Put 'em up asshole!" was the clearest thing that Danny could hear. His mouth was agape and his skin was white. He heard the guns around him cocking, ready to fire at the slightest twitch of Danny's body. The circle of people closed in on Danny quickly. Before he knew it, he was stood up from his chair with his hands cuffed.

"Can you walk?" an officer asked Danny.

Danny wanted so badly to just say no and pray that they would show him mercy. Maybe him being in a wheelchair would cause them to pity him. But his fear drove him to answer the question as honestly and quickly as he could so he could keep his skull intact. "Yeah," he said very clearly. The officers grabbed him and started pulling him into the forest off of the road.

They were almost in a full sprint. Officers constantly surrounded Danny and they ran and ran. Danny had no idea where they were going. Every tree looked the same as the last. The fury of aesthetics began to blend together into a horrifying masterpiece. Several times Danny would fall and be yanked back up. Those were the only moments that he had a chance to look around himself, searching for something familiar, but he had lost all normality the second he left that hotel.

It seemed like they had ran for only a short time. The fear made Danny lose track of time easily. He was no longer concerned with the outside world and everything happening in his direct vicinity became his only concern, yet he had no control over how any of it played out. Several times, he thought about simply attempting to run and hope that he could avoid the officers, or take a bullet and spare himself the fate that they would choose for him.

The group came to a gravel road. On that road was a police van waiting for them with several officers surrounding it. Danny was swiftly thrown into the back without a concern for his health. Had it not been for the bulletproof vest, his wound probably would have opened back up. Then he remembered. He was still wearing the vest that showed he was a general in the Committee. If they recognized its significance, he was a dead man.

The ride was a bumpy and scary one. Nobody was in the back of the van with him. All he had to enjoy were the silver metal walls, floor, ceiling, and back doors. He was the only imperfection in the van. The constant color was driving him insane. He couldn't find a moment to rest as the van would bounce occasionally and slam Danny's body to the floor.

Not only did he feel like a prisoner in the van for the entire ride, he felt like a prisoner of his own mind. He manifested every possible horrific scenario that could possibly come out of what had happened. He imagined arriving to their destination and a bullet being put between his eyes the second the door opened. He imagined them stopping in the middle of nowhere and his body never being found again. Maybe he would get the chance to live a bit longer as they tortured him to the point that death seemed like a paradise.

The constant rumble of the van was stifling. From the shakes came noises of shouts and screams. Some of them sounded like his, others sounded like unknown beings. Danny was quickly finding out what it felt like to be completely insane.

Every time the van stopped, Danny's life flashed before his eyes. He remembered the hotel, and all of the people in it. He remembered all of the friends that he left there and the ones that he had hurt. He remembered his mom and dad and thought that at least if he died here, maybe there was a chance that they would be able to rejoice in the fact that they were all together again. Then the van would begin moving again, throwing Danny into further insanity.

Before Danny knew it, the back doors flew open and he was being pulled out with unrelenting force. The intimidating lights of the building they were approaching were blinding him. He couldn't see a highway or anything nearby. All reality seemed to be limited only to this one building in the middle of the trees. It seemed like a twisted dream, but as he was battered to increase his speed, it became apparent that it was simply a sick reality.

They got to the front gate and things began to slow down and Danny was able to start analyzing things with a bit more clarity. The officer to his left slid a card that he had and the front door unlocked. Then they came to a bright lobby. On one side, there was a sort of window with an officer behind it. The other side, a blank brick wall.

The officer behind the window had a short conversation with the officers and the door blocking their advance unlocked and an officer next to Danny opened it. Then the monotony began again. They walked through hallway after hallway. All of them looked the same as the last. The same blank brick stacked on another blank brick. They rounded a corner, and saw the same hallway that they had just seen. The only abnormality they would ever see would be an officer walking through one of the hallways. The pure unfamiliarity combined with the repeating sights was a maddening combination.

A door in front of them was opened and things entered an entirely different realm of fear. Every worry that Danny had in his mind began to come true. On both sides, there were cells filled with people. Some cells were cramped with people, while others had only a few crying prisoners in them. Every face in every cell had the same hopelessness to it. The depression of their expressions worried Danny. The true horror was the emptiness in every pair of eyes he connected with. He didn't see a person in any of them. He saw only a hopeless soul begging for death. Any sort of freedom from the horror of a life they were living would be a relief and a reward.

The noises he could hear were the ones of crying and screaming up ahead. The people in these cells nearby were already at the end of their wits and they didn't complain. They knew it was a pointless battle. The noise of screams became more and more evident with every step. Danny prayed to be thrown into a cell. They might be filled with brokenness, but he didn't want to see what the screams were coming from.

Yet with every step, they became closer and closer to the screams. It was like a nightmare. Danny knew where he was going, but he continued to try to trick himself into believing that he would just be thrown into a cell. It was the hope in him that they hadn't yet broken. As the screams became louder and louder, Danny knew that his hope wasn't going to be maintained.

The screams intensified as they stepped closer and closer to the source. The faces of the people in the cells became more and more demented. They all knew what was going to happen to Danny and he had no way of knowing what they knew. Their faces went from blank and hopeless to very pitiful. The screams were now deafening. The echos filled the ears of everyone at the end of this hallway and the fear in the expressions of those in cells became more evident. Some even laid on the ground and cringed trying to get away from the sound.

Danny's deepest fear came to fruition as the door they had been approaching for what seemed like days finally opened. There were no cells with bars. There were only heavy doors that allowed no sights to be seen from the outside. It was the fear of not knowing that now began to get to Danny.

They went to a door near the end of the hall. As Danny feared, they approached a thick metal door. It opened and Danny lost all hope. The officers brought Danny to the middle of the room and removed the cuffs from his hands. The officers removed the bulletproof vest that he was wearing and sat him in a chair. His arms and legs were strapped to the chair which was bolted to the floor. The officers then left as quickly as they had entered.

Danny was now left to his thoughts again. His unknowing began to play tricks on his mind again as he thought of what could possibly happen in the near future. It was like waiting for the doctor to come in, but you knew that your doctor planned on executing you once he walked into the room. As time passed, Danny went from not wanting the doctor to ever come to begging for something in the room to change, even if it was his executioner coming into the room.

He searched the room for something new to see, but it all quickly became familiar to him. He saw nothing but brick walls all around him. The ground was the same boring concrete. The door that he had stared at for any amount of time remained the same unmoving gate to hell.

As Danny was about to reach the point of complete insanity, someone finally walked into the room. Danny immediately realized who he was looking at and became enraged. "I had hoped we wouldn't meet like this again," the man said. "I had hoped that I had talked some sense into you."

Danny stared down the same officer that had locked up his parents and tried to convince him to leave the Committee. The same officer that he was meant to kill in only a few days. The irony drove Danny's insanity to an entirely new level. "Where am I?" Danny demanded. "Why are you here?"

The officer cackled. "You remember when I warned you of what would happen if you continued to play for that team?" the officer asked. "Well this is what I was talking about." The officer walked to the bulletproof vest that was lying on the ground. Danny looked at the officer and knew that the man knew exactly what it was. "So you're a soldier for them now?" He seemed amused by it as if it was a picture that a child drew for their father.

"Who the fuck are you?" Danny asked. "How do you keep finding me?"

"You can just call me Brad," he said. "If you don't tell me what I want to know, it won't matter very soon anyways."

Danny's fear rose and rose to the point that he thought his heart would stop. "What do you want to know?" he asked.

Brad just laughed. No response. No anything. He just walked to Danny and began relentlessly punching him as hard as he could in the face. The first connected with Danny's nose and he could tell that the officer had broken it. The next hit his jaw and sent him reeling. He tried to move his face any way that he could to avoid another hit. Brad hit him no matter which way he turned. The punches got to the point that Danny couldn't even feel them anymore. The punches had no sign of ever stopping until Danny's face was a bloody pulp. Eventually a punch connected in a way that knocked Danny unconscious.

He began to have his same nightmare as he had before. He was in front of his old home sitting down. He looked out and saw the same demented figure and the dogs. The only difference was that Danny put a face to the figure this time around. It looked like Brad, only much more demonic. The eyes were large and dilated. Blood dripped from his mouth until he turned into the creature that ate the life out of Danny just as it had every time before.

Danny awoke to a painful shock in his neck. He let out a scream as he came back to consciousness. The shock stopped and Danny felt pain in every nerve of his body. He looked down to his legs. Blood was steadily dripping from his face. No part of his face was free from pain. It was the worst agony that Danny had ever been in. Possibly even worse than the gunshot.

He had prayed that it was all just a nightmare, but he returned and Brad was loving it. He walked around to the front of Danny and held up a tazer. "These things are fuckin' great aren't they?" Brad walked up and gave Danny a solid shock right to his chest. Danny let out another scream. Brad connected with Danny's legs, and even once on his cheek. Danny just prayed that one of them would stop his heart.

"What the fuck do you want?" Danny pleaded as he attempted to regain the functions of his limbs.

"I want to know how to get into the hotel," Brad said. "I want to know their plans, I want to know where they keep their supplies, I want to know everything you know, kid."

"What makes you think I know any of that?" Danny asked. "I'm just a fucking soldier."

Brad laughed. "We both know that isn't true," Brad said. "I know that you're a general. I know that you met with the commander and his generals today. I know every thing that you could possibly have done. So don't you try to fucking lie to me." Brad gave Danny another series of punches to the jaw. He was a complete wreck and he knew it would only get worse.

"I swear he hasn't told me anything!" Danny yelled. "He just made me a general recently. We haven't gotten to talk about anything!" Danny panted trying to collect more words to reason with the psychopath in front of him. Brad simply smiled and didn't muster a response. He left the room and left Danny to his thoughts once again.

Danny began to struggle to get free, but to no avail. He wasn't going anywhere. However, his hope hadn't been broken. It had become the one glimmer of light that his soul reached out and clenched to. He knew that there was no way he could die there. How could he even imagine death as an actual thing? It had always been more of a concept than a real thing.

Then again, what if Brad came in and killed him off? It would be so simple. Danny had seen death all around him. He knew how easy it was for someone to be ripped from the world, and how little effort it can take.

Brad reentered the room. "I suppose I can't make you tell me anything," he said. He reached into his pocket and pulled out an eyedropper. "But I can sure as hell make you see what it's like to be in a true nightmare until you decide to talk to me." Brad approached Danny with the eyedropper and grabbed Danny's face.

Danny began yelling, "What are you doing?!" but Brad didn't feel the need to answer him. He simply opened Danny's eyelids and began putting drop after drop of whatever was in the eyedropper into his eyes. By the time he had finished, half of the bottle was gone.

"Now then," Brad said as he backed up with a smug smile. "I don't think you'll need that chair, so I'll let you walk around this room a bit and stretch out." Brad pulled a gun from the back of his pants and took the cuffs off of Danny's wrists. He backed up slowly and exited the room. He turned back once more and said, "Every day you don't want to talk, you'll relive the hell you'll be going through tonight." Danny was in utter confusion, but he quickly began having other concerns.

As he looked around the dark, dimly-lit, room, he began to notice that things weren't how they were supposed to be. The walls began to change in color and the floor quickly became very unstable. Danny began to become very scared. He decided that maybe the chair would be the best place to stay.

He sat in the chair attempting to collect his thoughts. He was trying to piece together what had just happened. His face had been beaten brutally, then Brad left, then he put a bunch of liquid into Danny's eyes, and then he left again. Nothing was making much sense. Danny figured that things would have been a bit worse than they ended up being.

Danny dabbed at his face. He pulled his hand down and noticed a profuse amount of blood. It seemed that every part of his face that he touched yielded more blood than the last. Danny dabbed and dabbed, but the blood only added up. His hands were drenched in the red liquid. His heart began to race. His face was most definitely disfigured.

Every touch brought more and more blood to Danny's hands. He watched as the blood began to run down his arms and drip onto his legs. He stood up and turned to the chair to see if he could get a reflection from the metal. He knelt down and looked at his bludgeoned face. He raised his hands to his face and touched the wounds. He didn't feel any pain, he just noticed how odd the wounds on his face looked. It was almost as if he could simply take off the imperfections.

His fingers worked quickly picking at his wounded face. He saw bits of skin that he just needed to get off of him. He worked and worked until it seemed that he had only made the situation much, much worse. His face was now gushing blood. He tried his damnedest to force the flesh back onto his face and the blood back into his system. He was yelling and pushing at his face. He was experiencing pure terror. The more he pushed at his face, the more the problem seemed more evident. He was watching his face fall apart as his hands moved to push the flesh back into place. Then Danny heard a tap at the door and looked up. His head felt clearer. He looked back at the chair and saw that his face was wounded, but it wasn't falling apart.

Danny returned to the chair attempting to figure out what had just happened. Then he thought of his face again and it bugged him. The thought of the wounds brought back the memory of his wounded side. He lifted his shirt and leaned back in the chair. He examined the wound closely. It looked like the stitches might be ready to come out and Danny figured that he'd might as well do it himself. He began to pull at the ends of the strings. He couldn't feel any pain, so it seemed that it would be time for them to be removed.

He tugged at the stitches until one end of them became undone. He pulled at the string that held his body together until it seemed to be coming out slowly. His wound looked to have opened and blood gushed out. Danny's mind flipped and he tried to apply pressure. He had heard somewhere that such a thing worked and he figured he might as well try or he'd bleed out. He pushed with all of his might and watched as the blood continued to flow. He pulled his hands back and watched as it seemed the gap between his flesh only widened. He looked at his organs and went into shock. He yelled for help, but no one came. He pushed and pushed until he heard a tap. He looked up and didn't see anything. His eyes returned to his side. The wound was fine and still stitched up other than a single loose stitch on one of the sides.

Now Danny was becoming very paranoid. His body seemed to be falling apart, and then he would be back to normal just as he was before. He looked over his body quickly, examining it for wounds. His heart began to ache. He didn't think anything of it and continued to search his body. As he got past his arms, his chest pounded harder.

He ignored it and checked his legs. The pain in his chest became more relevant.

Danny gripped his chest and tried to push the pain back. As he increased the tension, it felt like more and more strength was being applied. His chest was heavy. Some force from the room was applying all of its strength right to his chest. He concluded that a heart attack was the only thing it could be.

Danny sat back in the chair and gripped his chest. He yelled for help again, but none came. He fell to the floor and struggled to keep himself alive. He began to pound his chest to restart his heart. His fear had gotten the better of him, and it cost him his life. He tried to calm down while simultaneously pounding as hard as he could on his chest. The pain only increased more and more. His heart was being pulled out of his chest and he couldn't stop it. Then he heard a tap and looked for the source once again. His chest felt relieved of all of the pain and Danny stopped pounding. All he did was look around the room for the source of the tapping.

Nothing was adding up. Danny had to get up and look for where the tapping was coming from. He looked into the darkness at each of the walls. He looked at the dim light above the door. There didn't seem to be anything around the room that could make a tapping noise. Danny began to run around the room looking at every wall. None of them felt right. There was something watching him. He saw nothing, but he knew that something saw him. His fear increased and he began yelling for the eyes to stop staring. He ran around the room as quickly as he could trying to find the person staring him down. He punched walls attempting to scare the source out of hiding. Then he heard that tap and his head reeled. It just looked like a dark room.

Danny was going completely insane, but he knew that something was watching him slowly lose his sanity. He got into a dark corner and hid his face. He didn't want the eyes to watch him. He occasionally raised his head and looked around slowly so his movement wouldn't attract attention. The walls were morphing. He saw a figure in every corner. The sources of the tapping were coming to life. He became overwhelmed. He was outnumbered from every side. His only reaction was the flow of tears. He couldn't scream, the figures would know exactly where he was. He watched as they grouped together from all sides. There were at least a hundred of them. They filled the room more and more before it seemed that Danny wouldn't be able to breathe. He gasped for air in the thick darkness. He was near suffocation. This would finally be the moment that he died. His head went into his arms and he cried hysterically. Then he heard a tap and his head shot up. The room was empty and the figures had disappeared. It was just him and a chair.

There was no way that he could continue to take this. He had no idea what was happening and it was frustrating. He had to search the room again. The light began to burn his skin and he knew that the tapping had to be caused by that. He ran to it and punched it with all of his might. His fists ravaged the outer casing of it until there was complete darkness. Then a tap. The light was out and everything seemed to have gone back to normal. He tried to tell himself that he was fine and that none of it was real, but his mind didn't believe a word of it.

Danny tried his hardest to force the door open. He had to get out of this demonic room. It was the only chance of his survival. If he couldn't leave, he would be defeated by his own mind. The door wouldn't budge, but there had to be some way to get out. He punched and kicked as hard as he could at the door. There seemed to be no movement. He tried the strongest kicks that he had, but they yielded no results. His head was the only weapon he had left as his hands had become bloody and useless.

He slammed his head into the door with all of his strength several times until he could no longer feel the pain. He continued to force his skull into the metal door until his strength diminished and he was on the ground. He had killed himself. His mind won, and his soul had been given the chance to enter paradise.

As he laid on the ground with no strength left, he saw himself float up. He was finally done fighting the war that he had been thrown into months ago. He never had to worry about the country again. The police couldn't get him where he was going. The best part was that he beat insanity. Sure his body was gone, but at least he would be done with the pain and everything would make sense soon. He saw the light that he had waited for. He greeted it with a smile. Danny's arms opened and he reached for the light. His hand seemed to be so close to touching it. They always said stay away from the light, but death was so much more appealing that the prison that was his mind. Then he heard a tap. He blinked and looked at the light again. It seemed to be Brad and some sort of doctor. The doctor was snapping to get Danny's attention as he examined Danny's eyes.

"Damn, only ten minutes and he managed to knock himself out," Brad said. "Is he gunna be okay?"

"Oh yeah," the doctor said. "He's got hours of this left. We'll just keep an eye on him." Danny felt a soft slap and watched the light and the figures leave the room. He had hours left? His hope was diminishing. Nothing mattered. All he knew was that his mind had taken control and there was nothing he could do.

Danny began to wonder what had gone into his eyes. He rubbed them in an attempt to get the liquid out of them. His hands never seemed to get any wetter. What a damn shame. But Danny wasn't going to accept defeat. He continued to rub and rub until he finally felt the liquid.

He pulled his hands back as he smiled wildly. Then the horror hit him. It was blood.

He rubbed his eyes more and only more and more blood came out. He was scared and the doctor had just left. He prayed that the doctor would return now. He had not a care in the world if the doctor was on his side or not. At least if he came Danny would finally know if he was going to be okay. He pressed on his eyes to keep the blood inside and he heard a tap. His eyes opened and he noticed the same dark room.

Danny couldn't take it any more he went to the door and felt around for the handle. He found the handle in the darkness of the room and pulled. He hadn't expected what would happen next. The door opened.

His mind must be tricking him. He pulled even more and only saw the brightness of the hallway. It was only as dimly lit as it had been when he walked it, but he recognized it. The familiarity brought the greatest amount of joy to his heart. He left the horror of the room. It felt like everything cleared up. He had left a flooded room and he could breathe again.

He looked down both ends of the hallway and realized that he was still on dangerous turf. He decided that he would just start running until he hit freedom at the end of one of the hallways. He ran through the hallway and saw more and more of the same doors. He could see the end of the hallway where there was some sort of sign, but it didn't seem to be getting any closer. He moved from a jog to a full on sprint. He ran and ran, but the sign was still miles away. He turned his head and looked at the walls. They were a blur to his speed, but he could still tell that they were all the same. Danny hit something hard and dropped to the ground. His eyes shot to the ceiling and the blur had become distinct surroundings.

He picked his head up and looked at the obstacle. What else would it be, but Brad? Brad looked at Danny in horror. "That's where you've been you son of a bitch." Brad jumped onto Danny and they rolled around. Danny got the upper hand and sat on top of Brad delivering haymakers to every inch of his body.

"What the fuck did you do to me?" Danny yelled. All he could hear was deafening laughter. He hit harder and harder to make it stop, but to no avail. "Answer me you son of a bitch!" Danny stopped the punches and stood up. Brad laid on the ground with blood dripping from his face.

He still had the smug smile on his face and he let out a few chuckles. "Do you know how long you've been here, Danny?" he asked.

Danny's mind wandered. He had only been there for at the most a couple of hours. "Two hours?" Danny stated, still very unsure.

Brad let out the loudest cackle that Danny had ever heard. Brad almost rolled around on the floor in his pure excitement at Danny's answer. He managed to stop his laughter and said, "You've been here for over a week." The clarity returned.

Danny's confusion turned to fury. He jumped back onto Brad and began hitting as hard as he possibly could. "You son of a bitch! I'm going fucking insane because of you!" Danny yelled. He punched and punched as hard as he could. Then he remembered what Brad had on him. He stopped the punches and looked at Brad's face. He was clearly very tired and his face was a complete mess. Danny laughed and turned Brad over and grabbed his gun.

He turned Brad back to his back and pointed the gun at his face. Brad didn't say anything, he just began his laughter again. It became louder and louder. Danny's ears could hardly stand it. His thoughts became jumbled. He held the gun in front of him and aimed closely. The laughs became unbearable. He threw the gun to the side and jumped onto Brad. He choked him as hard as he could, but still heard nothing but laughter. The laughs began to mix in some screams. Danny forced Brad's esophagus to close up. He applied even more strength until he watched Brad's eyes lose their spirit. It was a look of pure terror that Danny would never forget. They went from the bright blue that intimidated Danny's inner soul, to assuming a lifeless gray in moments. Then Danny looked up and saw an officer standing watching the entire thing. The man's mouth was open and his skin was white. "What the hell have you done?" he asked. Danny grabbed the gun and fired at the officer. As the body dropped, things became much quieter. It was almost a deafening silence.

Danny had to reach the sign. He reached into Brad's pockets and pulled out a card, a key ring, and another magazine for his gun. He got up and ran as quickly as he could towards the sign. He was finally making progress quickly and his spirits were lifted by the advance. Danny's throat let out a series of joyful laughs. He couldn't believe that Brad was dead and now he could finally make his way out. He had everything he needed and the sign was getting closer. The constant doors were coming to a finite number. He watched as the hallway began to end. The madness of it was slowing down. Danny got to the sign and read it. It read, "Communications Room," and had an arrow pointing right. As he read, his thoughts became manageable and quiet.

He ran towards the close staircase and shot up it. He entered a room that had about three people in it. They all noticed Danny and stood up slowly. They all had the same expressions of the officer that Danny had just seen. Danny laughed and flew at the nearest person. The man had been wearing glasses and Danny shattered them into the man's eyes. He ran to the next man and put the gun to his head. He was in a mad fury and couldn't be stopped.

He pulled the trigger with a smile and watched the blood splatter. He stood slowly and looked at the last guy. His skin was as white as Danny could ever imagine it getting. He slowly advanced to the man. "Please, don't kill me," the man pleaded. Danny laughed.

"Where's the fucking radio?" Danny asked. The man couldn't speak. He simply pointed a few feet to his right. Danny's eyes didn't leave the man's, but he knew where the radio was. He fired a single bullet into the man's head and saw it leave the back of his skull. His eyes widened and he looked around the room. There was blood everywhere. It looked as if a psychotic killer had a workshop there. Danny took a deep breath and collected his thoughts.

He walked to the radio and put in the frequency that he remembered Mike saying. The good old 101.1. He picked up the phone for the radio and said, "This is Danny. Can you guys come get me?"

He heard no sort of pause before someone said, "Where the fuck have you been? We've been trying to find you for a few weeks." So it seemed to have been a few weeks. No worry. He would just catch up when he got back and things calmed down again.

"I'm in a prison," Danny said. "But don't worry. I killed the one that tried to kill me. I made him pay. He won't be bothering anything anymore."

"What are you talking about?" the voice asked.

"Don't worry," he said. "He won't get to you. He's dead. I watched him die. I choked that asshole until his eyes lost every bit of life that that fucker ever had." Then he heard a bit of static on the radio. He looked at the station and saw that it was indeed 101.1. His thoughts calmed own and he pondered what he had just said.

"Alright we tracked your signal," the voice said. "We'll be there in an hour at most. Try to get outside and we'll find you. Grab a radio and get the hell out of there. Over and out." Danny went to the first man he killed. The sight of his face was horrific. It looked like something had eaten at his eyes from his skull and filled his face with glass. He reached down reluctantly and grabbed a radio. He put it into his pocket and got on the move again. He ran back down the stairs and looked around. He saw a red exit sign that are used for fire emergencies and ran as quickly as he could towards it. The arrow pointed left and he ran left. He saw cells filled with people. They all yelled as they saw him run by. The yells were deafening and brought terror to Danny's heart, but he paid it no mind. He had to keep running. They pleaded for his help and he continued to run. He didn't care what happened to them, he had to leave. Then an outreached arm grabbed Danny's shirt and pulled him closer.

"Please help me!" the voice yelled as others began coming closer to the bars. Their arms were outstretched and each of them looked like another demonic figure attempting to pull him into their hellish realm. Danny tried to get the hand off of him, but he couldn't and the figures were only getting closer. Danny grabbed the arm and yanked it to the right as hard as he could. Then to the left. He ripped it every which way that he could until he heard a very loud snap. His eyes widened and focused. He watched the arm as the man fell back. A bone was snapped and was sticking out of the man's arm as he let out a horrifying scream and blood spurted from the wound.

Danny looked at him, and ran in fear. He didn't know what had just happened, he just knew that nothing good would come out of him staying there. He made his way to some courtyard dividing two buildings. He guessed that the one he had just left was the prisoner building, because as he ran towards the next exit sign, Danny ended up in a kitchen. In his horror, two officers were in there with a cook trading bits of conversation. Danny knew he had to go through them and ran at them full speed. His gun fired and took down one officer immediately. Another bullet ripped through the cook's arm and another through the other officer's leg. They all dropped to the ground and yelled in agony.

Danny looked at the officer. The officer reached for his gun and Danny reacted quickly. He grabbed the officer's arm and immediately looked for something to stop the man. He found only the cook's knife on the ground and Danny stabbed at the officer's hand. He heard more screaming. The sounds were deafening. He wanted nothing but for them to stop. He saw the burners on the stove and walked towards them. He took his own shirt and threw it to the fire. The shirt caught quickly and began burning everything around it. The fire spread quickly and the chef screamed, "You've killed us all you psychopath!" Danny's eyes widened at the shout and his head looked around.

The officer on the ground was crawling towards his gun, attempting to end Danny's rampage. He saw Danny watching him, but continued his attempt to crawl to his savior. Danny walked to him slowly and began laughing. The officer's eyes stared at Danny with as much terror as everyone else's had.

Danny stomped on the man's bloodied hand and grabbed the man's arm tightly. He ripped the officer from his spot on the floor. He held the knife tightly and put it to the officer's throat. "Please, don't do this!" the officer screamed. He yelled and yelled as Danny let out cackles. The officer had tears running down his face and Danny ran the knife across the man's throat. He watched the blood gush out and continued to move the knife.

As he stood over the body, he couldn't help but laugh at his success. He was a one man army and he loved it. He was completely invincible. As the fire grew, Danny's thoughts quickly adjusted and the clarity of the bodies almost made him vomit.

The kitchen was igniting quickly and Danny ran for the next exit sign. He ran through the next door and found himself outside. It was as if every bit of anxiety that he had felt in that place flew off of his body. The only thing keeping him from freedom were the trees in front of him. The trees seemed as scary as they had been when he was being forced to run through a forest that long, long time ago.

Every tree showed off a new type of fear. They led to a darkness that rivaled any nighttime fear that Danny ever had. His mind flew wildly from thought to thought. What if he ran in and he lost himself in them. Then again, nobody would be able to find him in there. He could hide in there until the Committee got to him. But his fears were keeping him from going any further.

The trees reminded him of the insanity that he felt in the initial room. His fears were coming to life in front of him. He saw the figures that invaded his dreams all of those nights. He saw the wolves running at him from the trees. His heart raced as he braced for the wolves to leave the forest. He watched as they advanced and his heart pounded harder. He heard the growls and felt the stares. His heart pounded and pounded out of his chest. Every pound throwing him into a larger state of fear. Then the alarms of the prison he was in went off. Danny turned and looked at the flames shooting from the building. He turned back to the forest and ran as fast as he could. He didn't see any wolves, only freedom.

As Danny ran, he made a call on the radio. "I'm in the forest next to the prison," he said. "Where do I go?"

"We're only about a five minute walk from you Danny," the voice said in the radio. "Just keep running from the prison and you'll reach a dirt road. That's where we are." Danny rejoiced in the thought of freedom being so close.

Each footstep seemed faster than the last. Danny heard the alarm getting quieter and quieter. All he heard were the deafening sounds of the creatures around him. He couldn't imagine the darkness in front of him, but his eyes dilated perfectly so he could see where he was going. The sounds became louder, but he loved it. They threw him into a fury that made him feel as if he was only increasing speed. His body flew past trees and the creatures of the night. Danny began to laugh as he ran.

It seemed as if he was running for days, but he loved it. Every step brought him a new amount of joy. He was racing and so was his mind, but it was the greatest euphoria. He never even saw the end of the forest until he reached it. He flew through the edge of the forest until he saw a huge clearing and a dirt road in front of him. There was the car waiting for Danny. Outside of it were Champ, Adam, Dr. Lee, and Amanda. He was never so happy to see them, and the second he laid eyes on them his eyes widened and everything seemed much clearer.

The group didn't seem as happy to see him. Their eyes were wide and their skin white as snow. Danny ran to them and Champ grabbed him, but not in the way that Danny had expected. Champ held Danny's arms behind him as Dr. Lee frantically looked through the trunk of the car. He brought out a needle and it scared all hell out of Danny. He hadn't gotten out, he was only getting another dose of insanity.

He fought as hard as he could against "Champ's" grip. The apparent Adam ran in and held Danny as well. The needle got closer and closer to Danny's neck. He fought as hard as he could, but as the needle entered, his strength diminished. He didn't know where it was going, but it was simply gone. His head reeled back and he looked to the stars. The sky seemed clearer than it ever had. He looked back down and looked at the scared face of Dr. Lee. His mind no longer wandered, and his insanity had ceased.

Back to reality he went, for the last time.

CHAPTER SEVENTEEN

BACK TO REALITY

"Danny?" Champ said.

"His eyes are starting to go back to normal," Dr. Lee said.

Danny starting looking at everyone. He was now in the back of the car with Champ turned around from the passenger seat looking at him. He turned to his left and saw Dr. Lee feeling the pulse in Danny's arm. Amanda was on his right and looked very worried. "Where am I?" Danny asked.

"Thank God," Champ said. Everyone let out a sigh of relief, except for Danny who was still as confused as could be.

"What happened?" Danny asked. His entire body was aching.

Amanda had a towel and began wiping Danny's torso with a pale face. He looked down and saw blood covering his entire body. He was still wearing his pants from before, but they were also soaked in blood and ripped in several places. His side hadn't opened up which was about the only good news. "We were hoping that you could tell us the same thing," Adam said.

Danny attempted to collect his thoughts so he could tell them his story. "It all started when I rolled out of the hotel in the wheelchair," he said.

"Why did you do that?" Amanda asked. "Was it us?"

Danny shrugged and said, "I was just stressed. I figured I would blow off some steam outside, but when I went down the road leading to the hotel, some people in, like, SWAT team gear came out from the trees and led me on this huge way through the forest until I got to a van.

Then they put me in and I ended up at that building back there."

"We were wondering about that too," Adam said. "Why was that place burning to the ground?" Danny's heart stopped. He didn't recall what had happened in any way. He tried and tried, but nothing was coming up.

"I don't know," he said. He looked at Dr. Lee who then passed a worried glance to Champ. "I just remember being put into a room and tortured. Then Brad put something into my eyes."

"Who the hell is Brad?" Champ asked.

"He was the cop that took my parents in," he said.

Everyone in the car took a step back in their minds. They were trying to figure out if they had understood Danny correctly. "How do you know?" Amanda asked. "Are you sure that you didn't have him mistaken for someone else?"

Danny looked at her and couldn't really come up with a valid reason. "You're just going to have to trust me," he said. "I just know it was him. I remember him from the day I was taken into the police station and he told me that I would basically never see my family again. That smug smile he had all of those days ago, it matched the one that I saw from that guy in the prison perfectly."

Amanda could hear the passion in Danny's voice. His confidence was apparent and it caused her to put a lot of trust into what he was saying. "What happened to him?" she asked.

Danny tried to collect his thoughts again. "I can't remember that well," he said. "All I remember was the way his eyes changed when he died."

His voice was very cryptic every time he tried to recollect on what happened. "How did he die?" Amanda asked shakily.

The vision of Brad's eyes changing and his life leaving his body were the only things that Danny could actually recall. He remembered just watching the life leave his once blue eyes. "I don't know," he said. "But I think I did it."

"Why do you think that?" Amanda asked quickly. "You're not making any sense, Danny."

"The radio guy at the hotel told us that you were saying really messed up shit," Champ said. "Like, stuff about how someone was dead and you killed them. You kept just restating the fact that someone was dead and they wouldn't be hurting anyone." Champ paused as Danny's fear came back. "Was that about Brad?" he asked.

Danny's mind flew. He remembered holding the radio in the communication room. Then he remembered looking around and seeing blood all over the room and becoming horrified. "Danny?" Amanda said, giving Danny a shake. Danny's eyes widened and he looked at her. She looked worried. "Are you okay?" she asked.

"Yeah," he said. "I was just trying to think." He was trying his best to remember, but nothing was coming. "How long have I been gone?"

Champ looked at him very seriously. "How long do you think you've been gone?" he asked.

Danny thought about it. It couldn't have been that long. "I guess about a day?" he said. Glances shot around the car and mouths dropped. Adam even slowed the car a bit to register what Danny had just said.

"Did you say a day?" Adam asked.

"Yeah?" Danny said.

Adam looked at Champ with his mouth still agape. Champ looked at Danny and said, "You've been gone for three weeks, Danny. Almost a month." Danny's mind reeled. It felt as if his mind had taken a punch by Adam's words.

"Are you serious?" Danny asked.

"Yeah," Champ said. "O'Connor sent people out to search for you, but nobody knew where you were.

Speaking of which I need to call back into them." Champ turned on the radio in the glove box and took the phone. "We got Danny," he said.

There was a long silence and then a joyful voice that said, "Great job. Bring him on home."

"Roger," Champ said. "And send out some troops to secure the perimeter at least a mile down the road. Danny said that he was ambushed only a bit down that road so there are definitely some people around our perimeter."

"Alright," the radio said. "We'll lock down the hotel and search the perimeter. Thanks for the heads up. Over and out."

Champ put the radio back on the hook. "So do you remember anything other than what you told us?" Champ asked.

"I really don't," he said. "I just remember the room I was in. Then there was some other random stuff. I remember that there are a lot of prisoners in there though."

"Well, well," Adam said. "We'll have to let O'Connor know when we get back. Until then, Danny, I think you should take a nap. You're probably tired as hell."

Danny realized that he could have been awake for days on end. It didn't sound like a horrible idea. "Alright," he said. "Wake me up when we get there."

Champ turned around and let out a worried smile. "You don't know how happy I am that you're alive," he said.

"I'll bandage you up a bit once you're sound asleep," Dr. Lee said.

Danny smiled. "It's great to see you guys again." He put his head back and drifted off. He saw a deranged man running through hallway after hallway slaughtering everything in his way without discrimination. Every person that dared stand in the way were quickly killed in the most horrific manner possible.

The man went up a flight of stairs only to find more prey. Danny watched as the man brutally tore a man's eyes from his skull, shot another several times even when he was obviously gone from the world, and the last had his limbs ripped from his body. Once the man was satisfied, he walked through another door.

Danny watched as the man walked out to a grassy lawn in front of an oddly familiar house. There was a boy sitting in front of the house watching the man walk towards him. As the man got closer, he began snapping every bone in his body until he was in a four-legged sprint towards the boy. The boy tried to run into the house, but the creature jumped on top of him and began slashing at the boy's throat with its deformed hands. Danny watched the boy struggle to get free. Then he saw the face of the boy and awoke in a terror. The man had ripped Danny apart in front of his home.

Danny awoke in the back of the car with a yell. The rest of the group jumped violently and turned to Danny. He looked like he had seen a ghost. "Danny! What happened?" Amanda yelled shaking him. He looked at her and couldn't speak. The fear that he'd experienced stopped him from saying a word. That nightmare seemed to enter his mind every time he closed his eyes and he didn't know what it meant.

He finally mustered up the strength to shakily say, "I'm scared, Amanda." She looked at him with equal amounts of fear. Danny had never been one to get scared at anything, let alone admit it.

"Don't worry," she said. "We're almost at the hotel."

Danny looked through the windshield and saw the road to the hotel. They were getting close. He watched the trees to see if anyone would jump in front of the vehicle and take them all to the hellhole that he had just escaped. He watched the trees as they shook violently with the wind. Every tree seemed to be taunting Danny. It put a fear into him that he didn't understand. It was nature, and it put the fear of God into him.

The hotel was visible in the windshield now. The group rejoiced at the fact that they were getting Danny home safely. Amanda put her arm around him to try to portray the happiness that they were all feeling, but Danny was expressionless.

They pulled up to the hotel and began getting out of the vehicle. A group of soldiers headed by Commander O'Connor had gathered at the door to see the approach of their rescued general. They clapped and cheered at the sight of Danny getting out of the vehicle. Dr. Lee had to support Danny's advance to stop him from dropping to the ground from exhaustion.

O'Connor approached Danny with a large smile and hands clapping. "Welcome back, mate," he said. "Let's get you to the infirmary so we can get you patched up and caught up." O'Connor led Danny and Dr. Lee through the hotel. As Danny passed soldiers with his limp, they gave him pats on the back and cheers aplenty. Any other time, he would have loved the attention, but the fear was still great within him.

As he passed, it seemed as if every face was mocking him. The eyes of every soldier he passed seemed to be searching him for a weakness. Everyone was out to get him and he knew it. He wasn't taken by coincidence, he was taken because he let his guard down. He wasn't planning on letting it happen again.

The doctor led Danny to the same bed that he was always fixed up on and helped him get onto it. He immediately started looking at Danny's face. "Man," he said. "You really had a number done to you."

"Don't worry, Danny boy," O'Connor said. "We'll get those fuckers back. That is if you didn't do enough to their strength already."

Danny felt another wave of confusion. It seemed to be a big theme in his life. "What do you mean?" he asked.

"How do you not know?" O'Connor asked. "Champ said that you burned that fucking prison to the ground after you got out, or at least he thinks it was you. We're sending some soldiers up there soon to see what the damage is. Can you remember which part of the prison the fire was started in?"

"Not really," Danny said.

"Well then we'll have to get on that," O'Connor said. "All I know is that you burning down that prison will have saved a great deal of people that would have been sent there. You're a damned hero to the Committee."

"Are the prisoners okay?" Danny asked.

"So concerned with the people, eh?" O'Connor joked. "Well from what I've heard, that prison was split into an officer side and a prisoner side. If you burned down the right one, you'll have saved a lot of people."

Danny took a pause. "So you knew about this prison?" Danny asked.

"Well, we did," O'Connor said. "But we didn't have the resources to shut it down, unfortunately. However, you have my word that we'll be shutting it down permanently soon enough."

Danny felt a great deal of pride for what he'd supposedly done, but the confusion wasn't ending, nor was the fear. Being told all of this continued to scare him immensely considering that he couldn't remember a bit of it. He feared for the lives of the prisoners that could have been killed, and even more so, he was afraid of O'Connor's knowledge of the prison. He'd known about it all along, and nobody ever thought to shut it down because they were too concerned with their own comfort. The flaws of this army were beginning to come to light, and Danny was in no condition to deal with it.

Then he was gripped back to reality as Dr. Lee touched a sore spot on Danny's face and made him jump. "Oh, sorry about that," Dr. Lee said. He continued to work as O'Connor continued to boast as though he had done what Danny had.

"Now we can get on with our plans," O'Connor said. "We were waiting to get you back before we attacked the power plant, but now that we've gotten you back, we're ready. We'll be attacking tomorrow, mate."

"Sir," Danny said. "I'm fucking worn out. Can't it wait?"

"Lad, we've been waiting three weeks to do this," he said. "You'll be joining us early tomorrow morning. Hopefully they still have no idea of our attack. Then again, I'm sure you're much too strong to have given them any information while you were in that prison."

Danny's memory was jogged by the commander's words. "Shit, sir," he said. "There's a spy somewhere in this hotel."

The doctor and O'Connor looked at each other in shock. "Are you sure?" O'Connor asked.

"I'm completely sure," Danny said. "The guy that tortured me said that they knew that I was a general and knew that I had met with you the day that I was taken. There's no way they could know any of that without someone on the inside."

"Shit," O'Connor said. "I'm putting this place into lockdown. Nobody leaves until we sniff out the rat." O'Connor stormed out of the room and began screaming through the hotel to lock everything down and get everyone inside. He was in a fury at the news and he was going to get his revenge.

Dr. Lee looked at Danny and shook his head. "Now you've done it," he said. "That man's not going to let anyone sleep until he finds out who it was."

"Do you know who it could be?" Danny asked.

"No idea," he said. "But I don't like this. I don't like it at all."

"Has something like this happened before?" Danny became instantly concerned that he may have started a huge problem for the hotel.

"Only once before," Dr. Lee said. "There have been rumors before that have gone unchecked, but the time that he actually acted on the rumor, let's just say that a lot of people aren't around anymore because of it." He paused and made sure he had done a good job on Danny's face. "He even accused me of being a traitor and I'm one of the most trusted people in this entire hotel. Hell, if nobody trusted me, I could kill them while operating on them." Dr. Lee saw the worried expression that Danny was wearing. "Don't stress it though. You did the right thing bringing this up to him."

The intercom for the hotel came on. It rang out through the hotel as the voice shouted, "All personnel, gather at the lobby. Anyone unable to get there had better have a hell of a good reason. That's all." It was pretty clear that O'Connor was pissed. Danny hoped that he had actually made the right choice in telling him.

"Well I guess I'll take out the stitches from your side real quick and we'll head to the lobby," Lee said.

"Are you sure it's okay to take them out now?" Danny asked.

Lee looked at him in confusion. "It's been three weeks. They're more than overdue to come out," he said.

Danny kept forgetting that he had been in that prison for three weeks. That sad part is that he didn't remember sleeping, eating, drinking, or anything else for that matter. The only memories he had were from horrific flashbacks in his dreams or from random moments in the day.

Dr. Lee got to removing the stitches as quickly as he could. He cut them quickly and got them out swiftly. It was clear that he was feeling rushed from the impromptu meeting that was just called. He got them off and said, "You're all good."

"Thanks, doc," Danny said. "I feel like you've patched me up more times than any of your other patients."

The doctor laughed. "Yeah, probably," he said. "Now let's get out there before O'Connor rips our heads off." They walked into the lobby and saw the entire occupancy of the hotel in one room. The magnitude of participation on the rebel side finally hit Danny. There were hundreds of soldiers everywhere. Danny looked to the front where O'Connor was standing on some random box with a megaphone in his hand. The people in the front row definitely didn't look pleased about it.

The officers were standing on either side of O'Connor so Danny figured that he would go up there as well. He made his way to the front and saw Champ standing there as well. "What are you doing up here?" Danny asked him.

"Oh yeah, you've been gone," Champ reminded himself. "I was made a general for my performance in that ambush that got us the military hardware you might have seen around." Danny looked around and saw that some people were carrying much larger weapons than they had before. Some men standing by the door were holding long sniper rifles while others had shotguns. It was pretty clear that everyone was well-equipped at this point.

"Awesome!" Danny said. "I'm happy for you."

"Yep," Champ said. "Uncle and nephew working together to overthrow the government. A classic." He had himself a jolly laugh and looked to O'Connor.

O'Connor looked to be checking to see if he saw everyone in the lobby. There wasn't any real way to tell, unless he knew every person that had ever walked through the front doors of the hotel. With his paranoia, Danny wouldn't put it past him.

"Alright," O'Connor said. "I'm going to cut right to the chase. We have a traitor in our midst." The lobby started to chatter. "Quiet!" O'Connor yelled with authority. "Now I don't know who it is. All I know is that they've been somehow contacting loyalist forces and telling them about our movements, about our new general, Danny, who has been returned to us after a long amount of time in a loyalist prison, in particular." Even more chatter erupted. "So," O'Connor interrupted. "If anyone wants to leave the hotel, they'll have to run it by the soldiers at the door and write their names down and their time of departure and return. Also, all radio contact will now be monitored by our communications guys who will also be monitored by our defense lieutenant, Lieutenant Jacob Adams. If anyone has any concerns or you believe that you know who the traitor is, find me in my office and you will be highly rewarded for your efforts. You're dismissed."

The lobby began to clear out slowly. This hotel was beginning to sound like a dictator-run nation. Danny had only heard talk like that from the mouths of tyrants. It worried him a bit inside that O'Connor may be losing his head. However, he figured he'd keep that to himself to avoid conflict with the commander, lest he be called a traitor and killed.

Danny headed up to his room. It was a joy to use the stairs again and not be confined to some rolling chair. It was a freedom that he never thought that he would appreciate so much. He definitely couldn't do that for the rest of his life, he didn't have the courage to. So he found a new happiness in mobility.

He opened the door to the room and found that he was the first person to make it back. He expected that the rest of the group would be joining him shortly. The room looked a lot different than he had remembered it. There were a lot more articles of clothing than he ever remembered there being, and there were some new decorations throughout the room. It looked a lot more like a home and less like a temporary shelter from the government.

After a short time, the rest of the group came in. They were over enthused to see Danny and rushed him immediately. There were shouts, smiles, and hugs, and Danny felt a great deal of safety in being back to those that he had missed. "We're glad to have you back, Danny," Rob said. "It's been too long."

Danny laughed. "You're telling me," he said. The group had a good laugh. "So what have I missed?"

"So much," Adam said. "Champ's a general now, if you haven't already heard from him. We pulled off that ambush on the military shipment without a hitch, which got all of us a permanent place in this group. Let's see. Amanda and Rosa pulled off near-flawless assassinations which got them quite a bit of renown around here."

"I managed to kill a corrupt police chief without anyone finding him for a week," Rosa said. A rather demented thing to come out of such a sweet woman's mouth. Regardless, it was damn impressive.

"And that's about it," Adam said.

"So what happened to you in that prison?" Rob asked. "We're all really curious."

Danny tried to recall, but still couldn't. "I'm not entirely sure," Danny said. "I know that I got the hell beat out of me."

"We can see that," Rob laughed. Then he caught himself and realized that Danny might not have found it as funny.

"And I know that I apparently burned down part of the prison and had covered myself in blood somehow," Danny continued. "Everything else is a bit of a blur."

"Wow," Rosa said. "That makes what I did seem like a small event."

"Yeah, good job, Danny," Rob said with a smile. Sam didn't seem to be amused at any point in the reunion. He continuously stared at Danny and seemed to be analyzing everything he was doing. Even things that seemed so insignificant.

"Yeah," Danny said nervously, knowing that Sam was now watching him with scrutiny.

"Well we're about to head downstairs to get some food," Champ said. "You must be starving."

"I am," Danny laughed quietly.

The group stood up to get food together and catch up. Before anyone had a chance to leave the room, Sam said, "Danny, I want to talk to you first." The group looked at each other with confusion, but continued downstairs anyways, leaving Danny and Sam behind. As the door shut behind them, Sam immediately started his interrogation. "What happened in there, Danny?" Sam asked.

"I said I don't know," Danny said stubbornly. "I blanked out for most of the time that I was there."

"You don't remember the part where you burned that place to the ground?" Sam asked. "Not even that huge part?"

"No, I just remember getting beaten senseless by Brad, then him putting drops in my eyes and then Dr. Lee helping me get back to normal."

"What do you mean getting back to normal?" Sam asked.

"I don't know. I just remember not knowing what was happening, I would just come back to reality and see myself in a different part of the prison until I was outside of it and it was burning down."

Sam seemed very intrigued at this point. "And who's Brad?" he asked.

"He's the guy that took my parents from me. He's an officer of some sort."

Sam seemed like he completely figured out what had happened. "You killed him didn't you?"

Danny was taken aback. Then he remembered. He remembered standing over Brad's dead body. He didn't remember getting there, he just remembered Brad being dead. "I remember standing over his dead body," Danny said. "I don't remember actually killing him."

"So you tried to get revenge and you went completely insane, didn't you?" Sam asked.

Danny was starting to freak out at Sam's accuracy at this point. "I guess so," Danny said. "I just remember flashbacks of horrific scenes in the prison with people like Brad lying in blood around me."

"Let me tell you what happened," Sam began. "I've seen this shit happen before which is exactly the reason why I told you not to seek revenge. It's because of this very reason that it will make you go completely fucking insane." He paused and prepared what he was going to say. "This Brad guy put an experimental drug into you. It's been used secretly in the military for years to throw soldiers into a rage that will make them basically unstoppable. The drug enhances emotions and makes you hallucinate big time. You said he put it into your eyes?"

"Yeah."

"Yep, that's it. It fed on your deepest emotions, especially revenge once you somehow got out of your cell. Do you remember seeing demonic things and feeling like death was the only way you could get out?"

Danny was beginning to feel the fear that he had felt in his cell. "Yeah, how do you know all of this?" he asked.

"I've seen the drug in action too many times to not be able to recognize that behavior," he said. "And I know how people look after it's put into them. You look like you're trying to collect your memories, but you can't. You look troubled, but you don't know why. That's what it does. You're just lucky that you didn't kill yourself. A lot of people on that drug go into such a frenzy that they don't even register the fact that they're mortal and charge into death."

Danny was shocked at what he was hearing. It struck an abnormal amount of fear into him that he could have died and not even cared. He remembered the hopeless feeling that he had felt while waiting for something to happen in his cell. He could finally recall the horror of the hallucinations and the fear of thinking that they would never end.

"I'm just glad you're alright, Danny," Sam said. Sam had been one of the best sources of relief the entire time that Danny had been in this hellhole. He always knew how to talk to Danny if his mind was troubled, and Danny never had to ask for help. It was like Sam knew everything about Danny in the times that it mattered the most.

"Thanks, Sam," Danny said. "I'm glad that you're here to talk to."

"Any time," he said. "But now it's food time." He laughed and they headed downstairs to join the group. The cafeteria was abuzz about the possibly spy in their midst. Nobody trusted anyone. It was as if O'Connor had released an infection into the group that was causing an unprecedented paranoia amongst the most trusting people around. They were always watching their backs for the knife that could come from their best friend. It was ridiculous.

Danny sat down with his tray of food and ate like he had never eaten before. He piled mounds on mounds of food onto the tray and scuffed the food into his throat like he had never eaten in his entire twenty-two years of life. Plate after plate just seemed to vanish in the endless abyss that was Danny's stomach.

"You hungry, Danny?" Adam laughed.

"Dude, you have no idea," he said as he stuffed the day's chicken into his mouth.

"Did they feed you in that place?" Rob asked.

"They must have," he said. "I just don't remember ever eating anything. Or drinking anything. I guess it just happened at some point, otherwise I'd be dead."

"Or you're a scientific marvel," Champ said.

"There is always that," Danny joked as he took another chunk of chicken to the face. After another bit of chicken Danny finally felt full. "Well I guess I should go by O'Connor's to catch up on things."

"Alright, we'll probably head back up to the room," Adam said. "We'll see you later."

"Do you want me to come with you, Danny?" Champ asked.

"I forgot that you're a general," Danny said. "That would be awesome."

"Alright, let's go," Champ said as they stood up. The rest of the group headed up the stairs and Danny went with his uncle to O'Connor's office. They said their greetings to the soldiers guarding the door and headed inside.

"How are you doing, lads?" O'Connor asked.

"Not bad, sir, not bad," Danny said.

"You getting back into the mix of things?" O'Connor asked him.

"I was hoping that you could help me out with that," Danny said.

"Well, we've got that power plant that we still need to take," O'Connor said. "Other than that, we're not doing much. We got that military shipment and took out quite a few of the targets that we needed to. If we can get the power plant, then Boston will be ripe for the picking. Stage one'll be finished."

"When did you want to do this?" Danny asked.

"At any point that you're ready for the attack, mate.

Danny considered the condition he was in. Sure his face wasn't looking too swell, but he wasn't in any sort of critical condition. His face just hurt. The only worry he would have ever had about his condition would have been his side, but it had been three weeks, he'd be fine. "Can you do it tomorrow?" Danny asked as if he was making plans for a dinner date.

O'Connor laughed. "I like how you think, lad," he said. "You'll have to speak to the troops though."

O'Connor continued to laugh, but Danny's heart stopped. He never spoke to a crowd of people unprovoked. The only times he had, it was a time where it was called for. Why would he have to be the one to speak? "Why me?" he asked.

"Face it, lad," O'Connor said. "You're fit to give a speech. You seem as if you were born to speak to the people! You could move mountains with your words, boy! You're persuasive and ambitious. In my line of work, you're a trained killer, mate."

Speaking never really went wrong for him. When inspiration was needed, he was the person to deliver the movement that every broken soul needed. His recent memory loss would probably throw him off, but that was a risk that needed taking.

"Alright," Danny said. "When?"

"Today, lad," O'Connor answered. "They need their time to pray for a safe trip."

Of course. Everything had to be done that minute. It was the story of Danny's life. "Ok," he said. "I guess let's go then." The generals took their steps through the hallway. Word had spread quickly, and the soldiers were ready gathering.

The lobby was filling rapidly. Soldiers ran from their rooms to watch their new general speak to them for the first time. The stairs and second story were filled with people watching their future begin. The three walked past soldiers in the crowd. With each face they passed, the room began to quiet. The wave of silence was intimidating. The eyes of the soldiers saying, "Don't send us to our graves."

The combination of hopelessness and pure endurance flooded the room. The soldiers drowned in their own sorrow, but drank away with their pure will to never stop. It was a feeling that could crush the soul, but gave the opportunity for a leader to be made.

Danny and O'Connor approached the front, and stood on their own wooden boxes. They held their megaphones tightly at their sides, the anxiety building to a crushing weight. O'Connor lifted his hand against the pressure of failure.

"Soldiers," O'Connor said with the shakiest voice Danny had heard from him. "We're here to speak to you about the coming endeavor. Tomorrow we'll begin making our change. With the return of our general, I figured it would be best for him to speak to you."

Danny felt the grips of the eyes of the broken gripping his throat, begging him to save them. His hand went up in a slow, almost creaky motion. The megaphone became condensed with his nervous breath. Yet, the words still made their way to their ears.

"As most of you know, I've been gone for the past few weeks. Over those weeks, I saw the enemy that we were fighting, and it was a good reminder of why we chose to fight back in the first place. We're fighting a government that stole our families from us, stole our homes, stole our possessions, and, the very worst, stole our hope from us."

"We all joined this fight knowing what we were going into, knowing what we were fighting for. It's the people against the establishment that's tried to hold them down. We were lied to, and it was only through our endurance and dreams of freedom that we were able to shed the light to the rest of the world. As we speak, citizens around the nation are rising up and taking the steps needed to take back their towns, states, and soon enough the country. However, they lack what an army needs: a spark. Ladies and gentlemen, tomorrow, we will deliver that spark." The crowd's cheers flooded the lobby.

"You may be scared, and you may be wondering if you'll even live to see the results of our actions, but I must ask, why be scared of doing what you know is right? Why hesitate in the slightest if you know that we'll be bringing hope back to the American Dream? I beg you, don't be afraid. Don't let the bastards that attempted to spread only fear to its citizens be your downfall. Tomorrow, I want us to stand tall and proud before that power plant. I want us to charge head on, knowing that we'll be the saviors of our own lives. Because once we're done tomorrow, we'll have given the nation the spark it needs to overcome the monster that we've been fighting since it made the mistake of stepping on the people that were meant to rule it!"

The soldiers' hearts were pounding at their restoration. They cheered, their strength returned, putting their hope back in the fight. They looked forward to the next battle. O'Connor gave Danny a pat on the back and they returned to their rooms. The cafeteria filled with the songs of battle. Those that returned to their rooms stared through their windows, knowing that the sun would rise if they fought through the night.

Danny's room filled with celebration. The fight no longer seemed like a crucible, it looked like a chance to change the world. Their voices roared with excitement. The time to enjoy their dreams had come and they prepared themselves for tomorrow. The sorrows of the past could no longer catch them, they could only fuel them. Every soul in the hotel became charged with excitement for tomorrow.

As they drank, Amanda asked Danny, "Do you want to go outside?"

Danny's inebriated state led him to join the expedition quickly. "Sure," he said. They took the walk down the stairs to the lobby of the hotel. The hotel was filled with shouts from every corner. It was clear that the rest of the soldiers were joining in the celebration.

As they made it to the door, they were stopped by a soldier. "Sign the paper and put the time," he said as he passed them a clipboard. Danny drunkenly wrote his name and the time and Amanda followed. The soldier reclaimed the board and radioed the names to someone. Then he said, "Alright, you can go out."

They walked outside and found Mike sitting on a ledge smoking. "Hey, guys," he greeted them.

"Hey, man," Danny mumbled.

"Looks like you guys are enjoying the celebration," Mike said with a chuckle. Danny and Amanda joined him on the ledge and looked out at the night's landscape.

Danny's mind wandered as Amanda and Mike began talking. It seemed that they had become good friends since Danny had been gone. They talked about events that had taken place in the past few days that Danny clearly had no recollection of.

He looked into the night and his mind became lost. He looked at the trees covering the road and watched as the trees moved with the wind. They seemed to be moving closer as they shook and it took Danny by surprise. Then he began realizing what was happening.

"They're coming," Danny mumbled.

Mike and Amanda looked over at him. "What?" Mike said.

"They're fucking coming back for me," Danny said as he fell from the ledge and started backing up.

Amanda looked out into the darkness. "What are you talking about, Danny?" she asked. "There's nothing there."

"They're right there!" he yelled as he tried to run backwards. He dropped and continued to back up as quickly as he could. "They're gunna kill me."

"There's nothing there," Amanda said. "Just calm down."

They saw nothing, but Danny saw his worst fears. He looked out and saw the hordes of loyalist soldiers coming to the door of the hotel. They had the same gear as the day he was taken and it scared the hell out of him. Then he saw Brad at the front. Of course he hadn't killed him.

"That son of a bitch is back," Danny said.

"I'm going to get him inside," Amanda told Mike. "Come on, Danny." Danny continued to yell as he was pushed through the front door. His screams filled the hotel as he was led back to his room.

"We're all dead," he kept telling Amanda. She was obviously horrified by the words that were coming out of his mouth, but she refused to let them get to her.

"We just need to get you to bed, Danny," she said.

"They'll fucking get me there too," he said. "You don't understand."

She pushed him through the door of their room with worried soldiers standing in the hallways watching. She pushed him to his bed and begged him to sleep with all of her might. It took the entire room comforting him to get him to finally pass out from exhaustion. The celebration had ended as quickly as it had started. They could only hope that Danny hadn't shaken the soldiers' souls too much for them to fight the next day.

CHAPTER EIGHTEEN

STAGE ONE

"Despite the military's action, protest's have been continuing throughout the country. Thousands of Americans have now been arrested in what's being called 'The largest violation of civil rights in the nation's history.' As police continue to search the homes of those suspected to be dangers to homeland security, the protests have only grown. Several anarchist groups throughout the nation have assassinated political figures that the groups have called 'corrupt.' Along with the many assassinations, citizens have begun blockading their towns with weapons stolen from military outposts, police stations, and gun shops. To add to the chaos, power has been cut off from major cities as a method of neutralizing the uprising. The president released a statement today saying that the actions of these groups will not go unpunished."

The morning of stage one was one of over preparation and excitement. The fear of failure had turned into a fervor of courage and happiness. Soldiers passed each other throughout the hotel, pumping each other up for the step that the group would soon be taking.

The cafeteria became packed with soldiers readying themselves for deployment. Tables became crammed with guns and ammunition. Every empty space was filled with another soldier and their choice of fuel for their spirits. Men and women alike became one. Every individual shared the happiness in believing that they would soon be making a difference for those that couldn't join them.

Danny's room wasn't in this boat. With Danny's fear getting the best of him the night before, the group's heads became filled with worries for Danny's health. He hadn't been back for more than a day and his obvious paranoia regarding the loyalist army had taken their minds off of the mission. Nevertheless, they had to work to maximum efficiency and had to put the issue to the back of their minds.

Danny ran through the hotel with Champ and the other generals, making sure that everyone had taken the necessary precautions before the battle. Champ went around singing battle songs with the troops while Danny made sure that those whose heads were still filled with doubt were quickly expelling their fear. Lieutenant Donley made sure that each soldier had the ammunition and rations needed for the occupation, Lieutenant Adams prepared the group that would be staying behind to defend the hotel, and Lieutenant Michaels had gone ahead to scout out the group's target. O'Connor was locked in his office mentally preparing himself to send off the soldiers. As expected, he wouldn't be joining them.

The citizens of the nation were prepared for their first encounter with loyalist soldiers. Their guns were loaded and their bags were packed, but most importantly, their minds were ready. They were ready to take back the nation that they had once called home, so they would hopefully never have to worry about infringement on their rights again.

As the hotel approached complete preparation, towns across the nation were repelling any force that attempted to imprison those wrongly accused of being "terrorists" or "anarchists." The supplies from the large military convoy, as well as convoys throughout the nation had been distributed to those that wished only to keep their homes safe. The citizens that had been oppressed for standing up to corruption were fighting back. Though their supplies were running low, they refused to lay down and accept defeat before help arrived.

Towns united on the simple principle of freedom. Now that there was irrefutable evidence against President Stone, his administration, and the representatives that betrayed the people by refusing to remove him from office, the people were preparing themselves to take matters into their own hands.

They faced an enemy like none other. Those of the corrupt administration were standing strong behind their countless brainwashed soldiers. Those that believed in the people rather than the government left their platoons in secrecy and joined their families in the fight. Those that saw the crime in arresting those that had done nothing more than ask for a corrupt man to be removed from power left their stations and joined the fight. The few in the government that had tried to remove the corruption from the establishment that was meant to defend the people and failed, found a new way to have their voices heard.

O'Connor left his office to wish the soldiers luck. He stood in front of the readied crowd with his megaphone. "Citizens of the nation," he began. "You've taken one of the biggest steps in retaking this nation from cowards by standing here now. Soon, you'll be heading a few miles out to retake the power necessary for life in this nation. They've cut power to the water, so that citizens will go thirsty, they've cut power to the citizen's homes, so that they will remain in the dark from the rest of the nation's uprising, and they've attempted to cut the nation into manageable pieces by ensuring that loved ones' calls would go unanswered. Well ladies and gentlemen on the nation, today we show them that while they may be able to cut power to our homes, they'll never cut into the power of the people!"

The hotel erupted in cheers for the mission. They rapidly filed out of the hotel into the vehicles that awaited them. Group by group, the soldiers filled their vehicles to await their arrival. The lieutenants and the other generals of the hotel's army began to read their orders to the citizens that they would have to lead.

Danny's group sat in the back of a van. They were all younger than him, other than Mike, who he had already met. They looked at him with hope and awaited the commands that he would read to them.

Danny held the paper that O'Connor had given to every general after they had decided on the best course of action as a whole in front of him. He read the commands loudly so that every ear in the van would hear him. "We're to take positions around the power plant as the generals around the plant ask that the people inside surrender peacefully through megaphones," Danny said. "If they refuse, then our order is to neutralize any opposition. The biggest thing here is to ensure that those that wish to assist us in the fight are not harmed, so be sure to check your fire. Once the power plant has been taken, the technicians will get the plant up and running and will send power to the citizens of Boston."

The group nodded and readied themselves for the mission. "How do you think this is all going to go, sir?" a soldier that Danny had been introduced to as Buck said.

There was a bit of doubt in Danny's mind about the mission, but nothing severe. "I don't think that they'll give up the plant peacefully if that's what you're asking," he said. "But I know that the opposition that we'll face won't be too powerful. They're made up of people that like being commanded by the government, so I doubt they have much resolve. They're trained, but we're too large of a force to fail."

"Do you think any of us are going to die, sir?" a soldier by the name of Samantha asked him.

He had to be honest. "More than likely," Danny said. "But there's nothing to fear. We'll make sure that anyone that is taken in this battle weren't taken in vain. We'll continue our mission to ensure that we can celebrate those that gave their lives for the nation."

"What if they just disable the entire plant in a way that we can't fix, sir?" Mike asked.

This hadn't really been a thought in Danny's head, but there was no way that they could fail. They had some of the smartest individuals that the country had ever seen with them. Rocket scientists, engineers, doctors, and the technicians that ran power plants before the war had joined them. "We've got the power to make sure that doesn't happen," Danny responded with confidence. "There's nothing that our technicians can't fix."

The van came to a halt. Without skipping a beat, the back door flung open and the group flew out. Danny looked out and saw the power plant. It was much bigger than he could have ever imagined. The smokestacks of the nuclear power plant seemed to reach the heavens. Smoke poured out of them, creating a cloudy sky over one side of the plant.

Danny looked around the plant. Vehicles had pulled up to every side of the plant and soldiers stood ready to open fire. Behind him, snipers had taken positions on closest high ground that they could find. Everyone stood ready for the next part. Danny and the other generals held their megaphones high. Danny looked down to the paper he was given and began to read along with the other generals.

"Attention workers," the megaphones pounded towards the plant. "We are not here to harm you. Leave the power plant now, and we promise that you won't be harmed. You have five minutes to comply, or we open fire."

The generals lowered their megaphones, and the hearts got to pumping. Every soldier stood with their guns raised. Sweat dropped from their faces as nerves and heat began to take their toll. None wanted to shoot, but they each had accepted the fact that they may have to. They just hoped that nothing would explode, causing a nuclear disaster.

The first minute passed. Nothing happened. Through binoculars, Danny could see the workers and soldiers in the plant looking out to the horizon and talking. None of them were concerned with running the plant anymore, just what to do about the current situation they found themselves in.

The second passed. Still nothing. The citizens checked their guns to be sure that they would be ready to fire. The people in the plant were visibly frightened. It was starting to look like they would give up easily. However, as the time went, it seemed that they wouldn't give up.

The third minute came and went. A few workers finally began coming out of the plant, but some were still remaining. Those that surrendered were patted down and guarded by some of the citizens taking the plant. The nerves in them were still rattled, but they seemed much calmer once they saw that they really weren't going to die.

The fourth minute ticked by. Things began to get scary. Only one minute stood between the soldiers and the plant. The order was given to begin moving in slowly. The soldiers stopped at their new spot and waited.

The fifth minute. Some workers and a few soldiers guarding the plant came running out with their hands in the air. They were given the same treatment as the ones before them, however, it seemed that some of their colleagues weren't going to join them.

The order rang out from one general, onto the next. "Move in! Take the plant!" was shouted from each general. The soldiers took up full sprint towards the plant. There were only about four hundred yards to go. They planned to flood the plant as quickly as possible. Then the unexpected, yet obvious, happened.

Shots rang out from the plant and began ripping through soldiers. Those that survived the first round of bullets came to a halt. People scrambled for whatever cover they could find, while others, the more fearless, or the less witty, continued to charge.

As the shots continued to ring out and soldiers continued to fall, fire was returned. The snipers behind the troops began firing at any target they could spot. Danny's ears were ringing and his heart was pounding. He sat behind a small rock that he was able to find. It didn't cover nearly enough, but his adrenaline didn't notice.

He fired two shots from his assault rifle. He had no idea if he was actually hitting anything, but it had to be doing something. He wasn't doing any good here, and some of the other soldiers were already halfway there.

Danny threw caution to the wind and allowed his adrenaline to take control. He was in a full on sprint towards the plant. Each step seemed to take him further than the last. His surroundings became a blur. His feet bobbed and weaved between debris and pushed his body faster and faster.

He threw up his rifle and fired a few more shots as he ran. Those behind him followed suit. He was halfway there. The other soldiers were trading fire with those that were defending the plant from the perimeter. He felt so open to fire, but his heart told him to keep pushing.

The citizens' lack of training was coming to light. So few of them had ever held a gun before this, and it caused them to fire wildly out of fear. The shots from the plant were accurate, but few, and those from the citizens were random, but great enough to do the damage they needed to do.

Only a hundred meters now. He could make out the figures of the soldiers defending the plant and fired wildly at them. He was too close to stop now, and much too close to not fire. His clip emptied, and he reloaded. His hearing was giving up on him as the noise of shouts and gunfire became a background music to his mission.

Before he knew it, Danny was standing in front of the gate to the power plant. He hopped the fence with his fellow citizens and found himself in an unfamiliar place. His eyes searched in order to gain an idea of where everything was. Danny watched as soldiers around him fired and fell. The mission was turning into a bloodbath.

Soldiers ran into the plant with no regard for their own lives. Their guns fired, but their minds didn't register it. Danny saw soldiers from both sides breath their last breaths. Standing by wasn't helping the cause, and his adrenaline kicked in again.

Danny flew into action and fired with everything he had. The plant was now swarming with soldiers from the hotel. There was hardly any room to breathe, but it was better than being alone. Without him even noticing, the action had moved away from Danny. He found himself staring into the labyrinth of machinery wondering where the opposition went.

The soldiers around him realized the same and they all made their way into the plant. Danny and the soldiers around him went into another section of the plant. They crept around corners until they found themselves standing face to face with a group of workers and soldiers. They seemed to have taken refuge in the last place they thought would be safe from attack.

Both groups stared each other down in what would be the longest split second of their lives. Both cut off their thoughts and attempted to register what they were seeing and whose side they were on. Danny made eye contact with a soldier from the plant. The man's eyes were wide, but determined.

The soldier raised his gun and attempted to fire. Shots rang out and pierced the man's chest. Danny held his gun steady as the shots dropped the man in a split second.

Those around the fallen soldier forced their hands into the air as quickly as they could, lest they be gunned down as well.

"On the ground. On the ground!" Danny shouted as he and his squad made their way to the group. Their guns were focused on the remaining opposition, ready to snuff them out if any movement became evident.

Danny was the first to reach the group. He held his gun to the face of the soldier that stood next to the one that had fallen. It was the first time that Danny could actually see the fear in someone's eyes. It almost gave him a thrill. He loved being the one in complete control of the situation. He held the decision in his hands: life or death. He couldn't help but smile at the man whose life he had shaken.

His squad began escorting the opposition from the plant to the vans outside. As soldiers of the Committee began running into each other and constantly coming to the point of almost blowing each other to bits, they soon realized that the plant had been taken. Cheers roared from the plant. Soldiers rejoiced in their success.

Danny felt his voice roaring with the others. They had done it. The first stage of their plan had been completed to the utmost success, and in such a short amount of time. Danny found himself hopping up and down like a maniac. He'd killed a man, and he was happy about it, they all were.

Then it began to hit him. Not everyone had made it. Danny ran around frantically to check for any gunshot survivors. Too often, he came across his own fellow citizens. The cheers quickly became to quiet as everyone began to realize the same thing. They searched frantically for family members, friends, or just fellow soldiers.

The only noises that could be heard were those of soldiers yelling for someone they were searching for, or mourning for one that they found. A sort of depression had replaced their celebration. Danny watched as one man held his wife in his arms and cried deeply. Another turn of the head, and he was watching two soldiers carrying a dead comrade from the plant.

It was a grizzly sight, and nobody was prepared for it. They thought it was going to simply be a successful battle and a celebration, but war is much more than that. With the success that they had, the pure brutality of the situation took hold over everything. If they weren't vomiting or crying, soldiers were helping to carry the ones that couldn't see the victory out of the plant.

Danny climbed a ladder to get a view of what was happening outside of the plant. It was the same situation. Soldiers were trying to figure out what to do with the ones that had fallen. As Danny watched, he saw the vans speeding towards the plant. They were in too much of a hurry considering what had just happened.

"Get inside now!" a voice rang out near Danny. He watched the vans pull up and the survivors as well as the loyalist soldiers that had been captured sprinting out of them. The gates opened and soldiers poured inside. Danny wasn't sure what was happening, but he knew it wasn't going to be good.

He watched as the sky seemed to fall apart around them. Explosive after explosive rained down from the sky onto the grounds surrounding the plant. Regardless of the nuclear catastrophe that could ensue, planes dropped countless amounts of bombs on everything around the plant. Those that couldn't make it inside quickly found themselves in flames. Only more gruesome content for the day.

Soldiers hunkered down behind the walls. Danny dropped down from his high spot to join them. On his journey through, he ran into Champ who was getting his soldiers into a nearby building. Champ looked up and noticed Danny immediately. "Danny!" he yelled. "Get inside!"

Danny ran past Champ and took refuge in the building with countless others. Those still outside attempted to find shelter wherever possible. "Shit," Champ said. "We weren't ready for this."

"What's happening?" Danny asked frantically.

"The military's rolling in," Champ said. "They're dropping bombs on everything outside of the plant. Soon enough they're going to come to the front door."

Danny's heart was racing. All of their hard work was only going to land them in their graves. There was still a substantial amount of soldiers left, but they wouldn't have the strength to fight off everything that the military had. Sure they had the military's guns, but they didn't have the artillery, planes, or tanks that the military had.

The soldiers sat in this building listening to the bombs drop outside. They each began to reflect on their lives as they waited for the end. "What are we supposed to do, sir?" a soldier yelled at Danny.

He had no idea. He was hardly even an adult and he had to make the decisions that could possibly lead them all to their graves? His mind still raced, though. He tried with every ounce of his mind to think of anything that could get them out of this situation.

He said the only thing he could think of. "We can't do anything against the planes," he said. "But they aren't going to drop anything on the plant unless they want a nuclear explosion wiping out everything around here."

"So do we just wait?" a soldier asked.

Didn't seem like a bad idea. "Yeah," Danny said. "We'll keep a watch outside to see what's happening. Do we have any snipers with us?" A few hands raised and a few mouths sounded off. "Alright, you all get outside and find a high spot," he said. "Make sure to lay low in case the military brings in snipers of their own. Keep your eyes peeled and shout if you see anything." The snipers made their way outside and to high spots of the plant.

"What do we do if tanks start rolling in?" Champ asked.

Danny pulled him aside. "I don't know," he said. "But we have to get ready for it. We're not going to die here."

Champ smiled. "You've grown up so fast," he said. Danny returned the smile.

"Alright, let's get the perimeter secured," Danny said. Soldiers rushed out of the building and took up spots around the perimeter.

"Get anything we can use and start putting up a barricade around us," Champ yelled to the soldiers. Everyone in the plant joined in. Anything that wasn't bolted down was carried to the outside of the plant and put up as a part of the new wall. Pieces of metal and wood became the only thing between the soldiers and whatever the military was going to throw at them.

"Danny!" a voice rang out. Danny turned around and saw Lieutenant Michaels running over.

"What's up?" Danny asked. A bit casual, but formality wasn't their biggest concern.

"We've been talking to the prisoners," he said. "They're telling us that they've been expecting something like this for a while."

Danny was enraged. "How the hell do they know every move we're going to make?" he asked.

"Maybe there actually is a spy in our midst," Lieutenant Michaels said. "But right now we need to get ready. The soldiers we captured said that there's a military base not far from here that's been readying tanks and helicopters for something like this to occur."

"Then what do we do?" Danny asked.

"All we can do is make sure we're ready," he said. "Or at least as ready as we can actually be right now. The technicians are working on getting power to Boston as well as the hotel right now. It shouldn't take too long."

"Well you're not expecting to just leave when the power's up, are you?"

Lieutenant Michaels seemed nervous at the question. "Well, no," he said. "But I just think that if we can get the power up it'll be one less thing to worry about."

"I guess you've got a point," Danny said. "Do you think that the plant will be safe or do you think that the military would actually drop bombs on us too?"

"I honestly don't know. I know that if I was in their shoes, I wouldn't be too happy about my power plant being stolen. So I don't think that they'll hold much back, but I don't think they're dumb enough to bomb the plant. We have prisoners and a nuclear bomb."

Danny began to think. They had prisoners and a potential nuclear holocaust within a few meters of them. "Get the prisoners to the walls and make sure that they can be seen from outside!" Danny yelled to some soldiers.

"Why?" Lieutenant Michaels asked.

Danny smiled. "If they think that we'll kill them, then maybe they'll hold back," he said. The stress of the situation was driving him to threaten the lives of people that he didn't even know, but it made him the leader that they needed.

Lieutenant Michaels nodded. "It's better than nothing," he said.

The prisoners were still heavily frightened at the ordeal, some definitely more than others. They were positioned near the wall and just about a story above it. Next to each one, a couple of soldiers stood to make sure that they stayed in that spot.

Like clockwork, everyone's worst nightmare came over the horizon. Soldiers watched as tanks began to roll in with other army vehicles following. Danny estimated it at about twenty tanks in total and he couldn't get a clear count of the others. The vehicles took their spots around the power plant, much as the rebels had shortly beforehand.

The standoff began. The rebels stood at the wall, ready for whatever would happen. The prisoners shook, simply hoping that the rebels would let them leave. Danny's mind was focused, but his search for what to do next continued without direction.

"Rebels!" the soldiers in the plant heard from the vehicles. "Allow the prisoners to leave and you will be unharmed."

Then there was silence once again. "Well let's let them go!" a soldier yelled. "If we do then maybe they'll leave us alone."

"Do you really think that?" Champ asked. "The second we let them go we lose our protection. Once there's nothing that they have to watch their shots for, they'll get a hell of a lot more trigger happy."

"But it's better than pissing them off," another yelled.

Lieutenant Donley and Adams walked up. "We need to talk about this," Donley said.

"What's to discuss?" Adams asked. "If we give them back, we die. Easy as that."

"But maybe not," Donley said. "If we let them leave, then maybe the military will leave. They can't be that worried about one power plant."

"Oh yes they can be," Champ said. "They're trying to control a nation that's on verge of an all out war. Whoever controls the power controls the country. Right now, we have that power."

There wasn't much to it. If they let the prisoners leave, it would be just like the battle they had just gone through. The soldiers outside would move in and kill off the ones waiting to die.

"We're not giving them back," Danny said. "There's no way we can until we get something we want."

"What do we want?" Donley asked.

"We want them to leave," Danny said. "Let's tell them that if they leave, we'll let the prisoners leave. By that time, we'll be able to have backup here."

"I don't know what kind of backup will help us, but whatever," Donley said. "I guess it's better than just sitting here."

Adams gave a soldier a megaphone and led him up to a higher position. He gave him the order and got down to watch the scene unfold. The soldier held the megaphone to his mouth and said, "If you leave, we will let the prisoners go." He lowered the megaphone and the group in the plant waited for a response. Moments passed until the soldier's head burst and he dropped.

None of them had seen anything like it and it left them in horror. They weren't kidding around, and they'd just proved it. They had to think of something to do before another shot would kill another soldier.

"If you wish to surrender, leave the plant with your hands raised and we will not fire," the military ordered back.

Soldiers began to look to each other to figure out their next course of action. They had planned on taking the plant, not all of this. The situation had gotten out of hand very quickly and they should have seen it coming. Their poor planning was about to end their lives.

A group of soldiers began making their way to the gate of the plant. "I'm not dying here," one of them said. "At least we know that they'll show us some mercy if we surrender."

Adams picked up the megaphone from the dead soldier's hand. "If anyone attempts to leave, shoot them in the fucking head," he said over the megaphone. "You're courageous enough to fight for this, but not enough to keep it? We didn't fight for nothing. You either stand by your convictions and fight, or you walk away a coward and die. Your choice."

With that, Adams dropped the megaphone and cocked his gun. Those around him did the same. The group that had attempted to leave took that as an act of hostility and raised their guns. In seconds, the plant was split, with separate groups aiming their weapons at each other. Some tried to reason with their friends, but no one was ready to listen.

One half of the group was ready. They had gone into the mission with the mindset that they would get the mission done so that they could hope for a better future. They took the power plant so that they could help to retake the nation.

The other group was having second thoughts. The idea of dying for a simple establishment wasn't appealing to them. Sure they would like to live without a corrupt government, but it wasn't something that they could control. All they wanted was to return to their homes.

Explosions began ringing out from outside of the plant once again. Were they firing on the plant? Soldiers ran for cover as they imagined an attack taking place. The stages of fear that they had just endured were repeating themselves. Soldiers looked to they sky, but saw nothing. Danny climbed a ladder partially to see what was happening and couldn't believe his eyes.

The tanks were turned on each other firing away. Shell after shell landed on their targets and caused massive explosions. All around the plant, clouds of fire and smoke floated up into the air. Nothing was making sense, but the enemy was being cut down. That's all that mattered.

Tank after tank burst into flames until the firing ceased. The tanks that remained began moving towards the plant. Soldiers readied themselves for a fight. Each took shelter behind something praying that a stray shell or bullet wouldn't be the end of them. The end was coming and they all knew it.

"Don't shoot," they heard from outside of the walls. "We're on your side." Danny and a whole pack of others looked out to the tanks. Soldiers were getting out as the other vehicles pulled up and the soldiers did the same. It had to be a trick.

"Drop your guns then!" A voice yelled out with many supporting shouts behind it. The military troops put their guns on the ground and continued to advance with their hands up. They all approached the main gate of the compound. Danny wasn't going to miss this for the world. He sprinted towards the main gate as it opened. He and the other generals were surrounded by fellow soldiers as they awaited the arrival of their guests.

The supposed opposition walked to the gate. One man walked in front of them and spoke for the group. "We're not here to fight, we're here to help," the man said.

"What are you talking about?" Champ asked.

"Do you think that all soldiers are on the government's side?" the man asked. "We're tired of killing and imprisoning other citizens. We didn't sign up for that. We joined so we could defend the people, not put an end to them."

"How can we be sure that you aren't just going to kill us when you get the chance?" Donley asked.

"We just blew up the tanks that were here to kill you," the man said. "Not to mention we haven't tried to kill you yet." The guns of the Committee were still focused on the military men and women. "Can you please stop pointing those at us?" the man asked. "I swear to you we're only here to help."

It was a hard decision to make. "What do we do?" Danny asked.

"We let them in," Adams said confidently. The generals turned to him in confusion. Adams wasn't the kind of person to trust anything that could be a danger to the well-being of the Committee.

"How are you so sure that they aren't going to kill us?" Michaels asked.

"It's just a hunch," Adams said. "But they've more than proven themselves."

"We knew which of us were going to join the Committee before we got here," the military man said. "We've planned on doing this since we were told that an attack was planned here. I'm sorry if we're hard to trust, but believe me, we're only here to make sure that this place stays in the people's hands."

The air was still uneasy. "Then I guess we'll have to trust you," Danny said. The other generals had no disagreements.

The military man smiled. "Thank you," he said. "I'm Colonel King by the way. We'll get back to the tanks and watch the perimeter. I'll radio back to base and tell them that the plant's been retaken to buy some time."

The generals watched as Colonel King made the call and gave them a confident, "Mission accomplished." He told the base that they would be making sure that no further attacks were coming and thus would remain at the plant. They would be told to return sooner or later, but until then, the military base was none the wiser.

Troops headed back to their tanks and took positions around the plant. They looked out to the horizons, ready for anything. The rebels' hope became bolstered with the confidence that the military's hardware brought. Whenever the troops got a chance, they looked at the tanks in wonder. Was there anything that they couldn't do now that they had those on their side?

Danny radioed in to O'Connor to tell him the status of the mission. "Sir, we've successfully taken the plant and are now attempting to get the power restored in Boston," he said.

"Fuckin' right!" O'Connor shouted over the radio. Danny could only imagine the kind of celebration that O'Connor would be having at the hotel. "How long until the power's back?" O'Connor asked.

"Not sure," Danny answered. "Hopefully soon. I'll go check on them and get back to you."

"Thanks, Danny," the commander said. "Over and out." Danny made his way to the main building of the power plant. The door opened to reveal the most technologically advanced thing that Danny could ever remember seeing. He'd opened a door to an observation deck for the reactors. It looked like a huge pool, but probably quite a bit more radioactive.

He walked to the next door to his left. He opened it and found himself in the control room with the technicians. The multiple knobs and switches threw him into a temporary daze. There was no way that anyone could possibly know what all of those controls did.

When he came back to his senses, Danny approached the technicians to figure out the status of the power. "How's it going, everybody?" Danny asked.

The technicians stood up in a frenzy and saluted him. After all of the times that that had happened, Danny still wasn't used to it one bit. "Power should be online shortly, sir," a technician said.

"Do you have an estimation?" Danny asked.

The technician ignored him for a moment with a quick hand raise to silence him. After a couple more flicks and turns, the technician turned around with a crazy smile on his face. "The power's on!" he yelled. He grabbed a female technician that he had been working with and hugged the life out of her. "We did it!" he yelled as he threw the woman around like a rag doll.

Danny called O'Connor on the radio to give him the news. "Commander, it's Danny," he said. "The power should be back online now. Is it back on at the hotel?"

"Hell yeah it's back on, lad!" O'Connor yelled into the radio. "Thank God I don't have to use this piece of shit battery-operated radio ever again." Without giving Danny a "goodbye" or anything, the sound of the radio being crushed and disabled came over on Danny's end. Just a bit overjoyed.

Danny left the technicians to their celebration to tell the soldiers. He made his way to the balcony of the building he was in. When he arrived, he looked out to the soldiers. They were casually talking about life and the mission. Some of the soldiers that had come with the tanks were mixing themselves into the Committee's army.

Danny smiled and grabbed the phone that controlled the speakers in the power plant. He turned the speakers on and made the announcement. He tried to serious himself up and said, "Attention soldiers, the power's back in Boston!" The troops' screams could be heard all the way in Boston.

Danny watched from the balcony as the lights in Boston's buildings lit up. It was easily one of the most beautiful sights he'd ever seen. The light seemed to start from the highest floor of the tallest building and move its way down to the town houses, then across the city to every house, office building, and even police station. As it was turning to night, this would be known as the first time that Boston saw the light of the revolution.

The plans were made to keep a solid percentage of the soldiers in the power plant so that they would be able to keep it under rebel control. The tanks and the soldiers that came with them agreed to remain there and offer their assistance. With that, the rest of the soldiers of the Committee rode back home in what vans they had left.

As the soldiers arrived back at the hotel, the festivities were already underway. They walked inside and were greeted by a lit up hotel and excited occupants. Everything had a new light to it, in more ways than one. Things seemed to look up more than they had. With their first taste of victory, the soldiers only became hungrier, and as they drank and celebrated, their hunger only increased.

CHAPTER NINETEEN

HEARTBROKEN

"As violence increases across the nation, we are sorry to say that this news station will be off of the air until the station is cleared to broadcast once again. Best of luck to everyone out there, and be safe."

"Bullshit!" Champ yelled at the television. "We get our power back and now I can't even watch the damn news."

"Champ, we've got a radio," Adam said. "We'll just get our news from the other chapters around the country."

"Which chapters can we actually contact, though," Champ responded. "I know of the few in Boston and the one in D.C."

"Well just because we can't contact them doesn't mean that they're not there," Danny said.

"Shouldn't we consider our lack of communication with the other chapters a problem?" Sam asked.

The group pondered it. "What do you mean?" Danny asked.

"Think about it," Sam said. "We haven't contacted any other chapters about missions, or even simply current statuses. For all we know, we could be the only chapter still around. Now that the news won't be coming on anymore, we aren't going to have any way to know what the other chapters are doing."

"I mean, I guess so," Danny said.

"But, it's not on our list of priorities," Champ said.

"And why not?" Sam asked. He leaned in closer. "I think that O'Connor's just doing it to keep his influence high amongst the soldiers here."

The majority of the group were surprised by Sam's accusation's, but Rosa seemed to understand Sam's point. "I could definitely see that," she said. "The less leaders there are in this revolution, the more strength the few leaders will have. It makes a lot of sense."

Danny didn't want to believe it. "Look," he said. "O'Connor's an asshole, sure, but he wouldn't do something that would hinder our strength just to gain a bit more power. I don't think he's like that."

"Then why hasn't he attempted to get a solid connection to the other chapters?" Rosa asked.

"I'm sorry, Danny, but they're making crazy amounts of sense," Amanda said. "Maybe it's time for us to look into it ourselves."

"If we do that and O'Connor thinks we're doing it behind his back, we'll be considered traitors," Adam said. "It's not worth the risk."

"Not to mention that there's no way for us to set up that connection without the resources that O'Connor has at his disposal," Rob said.

"How would you recommend setting up the connection?" Danny asked Sam. He was genuinely interested, but simply didn't think that it was possible.

"A radio station," Sam said. "We somehow get access to a broadcasting station and get someone to send news to the other chapters. It would be like watching the news, but with the revolutionaries."

A radio station for revolutionaries, it wasn't a bad idea. A source of information regarding the national effort for a revolution that would broadcast nationwide. People across the country could listen in and hear about the successes of chapters across the country and learn about what the government's doing to stop it. Even people that aren't already assisting in the revolution would listen and, with some luck, would join the effort.

"So how do we do that?" Danny asked.

"Is there a broadcasting station in Boston?" Sam asked.

"I have no idea," Danny said.

"Yeah, there is," Adam said. "I went to it a lot when I was still managing bands back in the day. The only problem is that it's not like the power plant. It's in the middle of downtown Boston."

"Damn," Sam said.

"Weren't we trying to take Boston anyways?" Amanda asked.

"That was the general plan," Danny said.

"Well then when we take Boston, we set up the radio station," Amanda said. "Because I don't see how we would have another chance to do it other than then."

"Hell, as long as nobody tries to drop bombs on us again, I'm fine with that plan," Champ said.

"Speaking of which," Danny said. "We need to go talk to O'Connor about stage two."

"What's stage two?" Sam asked.

Danny was out of his bed now and was searching for a cleaner shirt to wear under his vest. "We're getting some more hardware." Danny began to change shirts.

"From where?" Adam asked.

Danny turned and smiled with his new shirt on. "The best place I can think of," he said. "A military base."

The group had a simultaneous gasp at the idea. "Are you nuts?" Amanda asked. "How would we take a military base after just recently finishing that battle for the power plant by the skin of our teeth?"

"Easy," Danny said. "We cut off their power."

"How would that help?" Rob asked.

"The same way it helped the government suppress the Boston citizens by cutting off the power," Danny said. "They won't have hot water, or running water if we cut the power to the pumps. Not to mention the fact that they won't have power going to their lights or anything defense-wise like electric fences."

"So you want us to get a group to go into a military base where they have all of the big guns and just take the base so we can use all of their guns for whatever we want?" Champ asked. "I like this plan."

Danny smiled. "Thought you would," he said. "We just have to see what O'Connor thinks of it."

"Then let's not keep the good ol' commander waiting," Champ said. They said their goodbyes to the room and headed downstairs in their bulletproof vests. The hotel was still on lockdown from the mole, regardless of the celebrations the night before. Many soldiers were visually suffering from the amount of partying they had done after the mission.

Regardless, the halls of the hotel seemed more like one of a military outpost than it had before. With most of them having just tasted battle for the first time, the soldiers had a greater professionalism to them. Their stances resembled those of guards at an army base and their gaits were those of dignified officers. Each held their weapons as if they had gone through the boot camp of the country's finest.

New faces began showing up, begging to be a part of the new nation. Families that had lost some of their numbers to oppression went through the now extensive screening process that had been put into place. They were interviewed ten times at the very least by various generals as they searched for the motives, the skills, and the backgrounds of the newest recruits. The new warriors were then trained behind the hotel in guerilla tactics and basic weapons training. If this wasn't considered a military base yet, it would have surprised anyone that had stepped foot in the hotel.

Champ and Danny made their way to the main floor and past the families trying to reason with the guards.

Danny watched as one family was turned away. The father's previous police officer status had limited his ability to make it in without scrutiny. His wife refused to allow the family to split, and the guards sent them back out of the door. Danny caught only a glimpse of the children that cried behind them.

The system seemed to be corrupting, but the officers' paranoia could not be said to be unnecessary. They were in a war against an enemy much more physically powerful than themselves and any leak of information could prove to be detrimental to the revolution. The government that looked to regain control would certainly use any tactic necessary to take down the leaders of the revolution. The captured military officers and loyalists that remained inside of the hotel under constant guard were the only things keeping the hotel from being demolished. That was the only piece of information that the generals were happy the mole told their superiors about.

The pair entered O'Connor's office as he was drinking his morning scotch. Despite his reputation as an experienced drinker, it was obvious that the commander had been fatigued from the celebration. "How are yah' doing, lads?" O'Connor asked.

"Not bad, sir," Danny said. "We came to discuss stage two with you."

O'Connor sighed. "We have bigger problems than stage two right now," he pointed out.

"Like what?" Champ asked. "Oh . . .sir."

The commander walked to his desk and sat down to examine paperwork. "Well, we've still got the mole," he said. "Then that prison we thought you burned down, Danny, remember that?"

"I remember you telling me about it," Danny said.

"Oh yeah, the memory loss," O'Connor said. "My mistake, mate. Well, turns out that the fire was stopped before the building could collapse. Now my sources tell me that the prisoner building is being used to house both the officers and the soldiers. Based on past examples, I'd say that they'll start executing prisoners soon to avoid overcrowding."

A lack of comfort was causing a lack of morality, what a surprise. It was always a downfall amongst human beings. If those in charge weren't as fulfilled as they could be, they drill, kill, and fill their pockets. War hadn't been a thing of valor or justice for quite a while.

"Well then what do you suggest we do about it?" Danny asked.

O'Connor put his head into his hands in an attempt to push the hangover out of his head. He pulled them back to only get another shockwave of migraines and nausea. "Ugh, how are you two feeling today?" he asked.

"I couldn't find any booze by the time I got inside, so I'm fine," Champ said.

"And I didn't drink much," Danny said. "I was more worried about sleep."

"Great," O'Connor said as he envied their condition. "Then I want you to get a team together, get to that prison, kill the officers or take them prisoner if at all possible, and get the prisoners out of there. Let them go back to their homes and refer them to the other chapters in Boston. They need a few good men over there and the help they provide will help with stage two. Once they've settled in there, we can get on with stage two."

"Sounds good to me," Danny said.

"I'm definitely not opposed to that," Champ agreed.

"Right," O'Connor said. "I'll have some vehicles sent to the front. Get a team together and you'll be briefed on the way there. In the meantime, was there anything about stage two you wanted to discuss?"

"Well, sir, I thought it would be a good idea to take the military base just outside of Boston before attacking Boston," Danny said. "We could give the guns that we get there to citizens in Boston so we'll have the entire city covered with rebels."

"Doesn't sound like a bad idea," O'Connor said. "But how do you think we could pull that off?"

"We cut the power to their base and attack when they're weak," Danny said. "Like the hotel, the generators can only operate for so long. We just have to cut the power and wait."

"Alright," O'Connor said. "I'll get the other generals in here and discuss it with them. Until then, go take that prison for me."

"Thank you, sir," Danny said respectfully as they left. Mission after mission, that was life for a soldier.

The core of their squad would be made up of those that they knew they could trust. The ones that had come to the hotel with them would be choice candidates. The rest would just have to be those that hadn't destroyed their bodies the day before.

They arrived back at their room. Danny looked at the time and realized that they had only been gone for about ten minutes. What a spot of luck. It would still be daylight for quite a bit longer. The drive was only about a half hour, so they had some time to make sure all of the necessary preparations were made.

"Alright, guys," Danny said. "We're going to my old prison to get the rest of the prisoners out. Who wants to come along?"

It wasn't something that they had expected to hear that early in the morning, but it got them pumped up. They hadn't gotten many chances to make an impact and rescuing their fellow citizens was the kind of direct effect that each of them wanted to be able to say they made on the revolution.

"I'll go," Sam said. "I'm pretty curious to see this place."

"I'll go too," Rob said.

A long pause after Rob spoke was a prime spectacle of how tired everyone still was. "Anyone else?" Champ asked.

"Eh, I guess I'll go too," Rosa said. "I haven't done much while I've been here and it's time that I got to work on that."

"Then I'm going too," Amanda said.

"No, I want to do this without having to worry what will happen to you," Rosa said.

"But, mom . . . " Amanda started.

Rosa cut her off. "Trust me, Amanda," she said. "I won't be able to focus if I know that you could be killed. Just let me do this."

Amanda hated the thought of not being able to see her mom to safety, but this was one of the only times that she had seen her mom standing her ground from any debate that could possible erupt. She was solid in her decision and it was time for Amanda to accept it. "I guess," Amanda said. "Just please be careful. I love you."

"Love you too, Amanda," Rosa said as she kissed her daughter on the cheek.

A warming moment before a battle, but it was taking their minds off of the task at hand. "Alright, then let's get going," Champ said. "I want to get back at a reasonable hour tonight."

"Yeah," Rob said. "I'm still pretty tired from yesterday. It's about time I got a good night's sleep."

The group set out of their room and went to the lobby. Champ stood on the balcony over the lobby with a megaphone. "Whoever wants to go take a prison and free some citizens, meet us outside," he announced. Short and simple, just the way Champ liked it.

Surprisingly, a large amount of soldiers bolted for the door. Not something that would've been expected from the worn-out army. By the time that Danny and his friends made it outside, the front lawn of the hotel was filled with soldiers. Probably about a hundred at the very least.

"Looks like we're gunna need to be a bit more selective," Champ said.

"Backup is never a bad idea," Rob said. "Just bring a small squad to check things out and then have the rest of them rush the prison shortly after."

"Overwhelm them with numbers," Champ said. "The people's greatest strength is their numbers. Let's do it."

"Alright, I'll tell them," Danny said. He stood on a van and announced to the crowd, "We'll only be bringing about twenty soldiers in at first to get an idea of what to expect and cause the guards there to get cocky. After we've been in the prison for fifteen minutes, I want the rest of you to come inside based on information that we'll be supplying and get the job done. Understood?" The crowd nodded and a few raised fists. "Alright then, let's do this," Danny finished.

Soldiers piled into their civilian vehicles. Each was handed a weapon as they got in and they made sure it was loaded. They sat in the back of vans as they drove off, each of them fully prepared for the endeavor. Compared to the power plant, this would probably be a piece of cake.

"We've gotta get in and gather as much information as we possibly can before an altercation," Danny said. "We'll scan the outer perimeter to find a good entrance. During all of this, we'll be radioing the next team to give them the information. Then we'll head inside and start the fight."

"Danny," Sam said. "With your permission, I'd like to operate the radio. I don't think I'll be too great with a gun today anyways because of the hangover."

"Sounds fine to me," Danny said. He handed the radio over to Sam and gave him a brief explanation of how to use it. Sam was obviously amused by the lesson.

He'd been in the military for years, chances were he knew how to operate a radio.

The road was becoming very bumpy, a sure signal that they were close. The van came to a halt. Danny and the other nineteen of them got out of their vans to begin the mission. "Alright, the prison is right through these trees," Danny said. "We'll split into groups of five and approach from different sides. Remember to radio in to the main squad with anything that will help them out when they attack."

Danny went into the trees with Champ, Rob, Rosa, and Sam. The other three squads split up and ran through different parts of the forest. Danny began having flashbacks of the forest when he had run through it at night. It looked much more beautiful now than it had before, or at least it did.

"The fuck's that smell?" Champ asked.

Rob froze. "Probably that," he said. He pointed to a group of people with bound hands and bullet wounds in their heads. It was clear that the prison had begun executing prisoners already. The gruesome sight was sending Danny into further horrific flashbacks. He saw the excess amounts of gore that had filled his mind after the stay in the prison. It was clear that this wasn't going to be an easy mission. He snapped back into consciousness and addressed the situation.

"We've gotta move," Danny said. "Be on the lookout for any guards that are taking prisoners out here." They continued their run until they could faintly see the prison in the distance through the trees. Their hearts began their thumping as the group slowed their advance. The biggest worry in Danny's mind was that one of the other groups would give away their position and begin the assault too early.

Right away, Sam began radioing in their position and everything that they were looking at. He detailed the forest, how far the forest was from the walls of the prison, and all possible entrances as well as dangers of each entrance. He was being more observant than anyone in the group. Some of the things he pointed out were so hidden that they shocked the rest of the squad.

Before long, there was nothing left for Sam to radio in. The radio still buzzed with talk from the other squads reporting in on their sides. “Well should we move closer?” Rob asked.

Danny looked around the prison. There were a few guards on patrol, and about the same amount on the rooftops. He could see where there had been fire damage to the building, and how the guards tended to avoid it when on patrol. Even with this weakness, there was a guard covering every aspect of the prison.

“I don’t think so,” Danny said. “There are enough guards outside of the walls to kill us off. I think we should just stay put until the rest of the soldiers show up for the battle.”

“That’s not a bad idea, but I think you have other things to worry about,” a voice said from behind Danny.

“Shit,” Champ said.

Danny turned around to see a group of about five guards pointing their guns at the group. “Get up, now!” a guard yelled. The rebels dropped their guns and stood up. “Now get inside.” Without asking questions, Danny and his friends moved to the prison. Chances were they were going to be taken to interrogation rooms and by the time they got there the army would have showed up. Then they’d have a force inside and outside.

While Danny’s heart raced, he wasn’t scared of the situation. He’d been in this place before and almost burned it down. However, as they entered the main corridor with prisoners on both sides of them, horrific flashbacks began to enter Danny’s mind once again. He saw the twisted expressions of the prisoners as a painful reminder of what he'd been through.

"Stop here," a guard said in the middle of the hallway. The rebels looked around at the prisoners watching them. The guards pushed them up against the cages and patted them down for weapons. Danny listened as Champ just started to laugh.

"So how did you find us?" Champ asked humorously.

"Didn't take much effort," a voice said. Danny turned and his smile quickly faded.

"You mother fucker," Danny said. "I killed you! I watched you die!"

Brad stood with a smile on his face. "Do I look dead to you, Danny?" he asked.

"What are you talking about, Danny?" Champ asked.

"I killed him!" Danny yelled as he pointed at the head guard.

"Um . . .I don't think you did, Danny," Champ said.

"Danny!" a voice cried from the cells. Danny turned and his mind did another flip. He couldn't believe what he was seeing. "Brian, it's Danny!" the voice cried again. Danny's heart was clenched in what he was seeing.

"Mom?" he said. He looked into the cell and saw his mom standing there watching him. She looked as if she'd had the life poured back into her only a short time ago. Since being in the cell, she seemed to have aged quite a bit, but she had the energy of a child in this moment.

Danny's mom approached the cage and tried her best to hug him. "My baby," she cried. "I can't believe it's you." She kissed Danny's cheek through the bars as many times as she possible could.

Danny's throat felt like it was closing up. "Mom," he cried. "I'm so happy to see you."

Danny's dad ran to the bars and gripped his child as tightly as he could. "Son," he said through tears. "I knew I'd see you again." Brian had grown quite the beard during his time in this prison and he'd lost quite a bit of weight. He seemed to be trying his hardest to hold back tears, but seeing his son again brought more joy to him than one could imagin.

"Fucking heartwarming," Brad said as he ripped Danny from the bars. "It's disgusting." He pulled a pistol from his side and pointed it at the bars.

"Don't you fucking dare," Danny yelled as he tackled Brad to the ground. He delivered two solid punches to Brad's face before he was ripped off by a guard. Champ attempted to grab the guard that held Danny back, but he too, was ripped off, by someone that he'd never seen coming.

Champ turned and saw that Sam was holding him back. "What the hell are you doing, Sam?" Champ questioned. Another guard grabbed Champ to hold him still. Sam backed away and walked to Brad.

He looked into Danny's eyes and said, "I'm sorry."

"You didn't really think that we would just have some random guy in the hotel to spy for us, did you?" Brad asked.

"How could you do this to us, Sam?" Danny asked as he struggled against the guard's grip.

"You operate blindly, Danny," Sam said. "I always told you to never go after revenge, but that's all this war has been about. You only look to kill a man to get revenge for him killing another. Don't you see that it will never stop? Men will continue to kill each other, regardless of who's in charge. It's the world we live in, and it's human nature. We all desire to be on top, but no one ever realizes that it won't come to an end."

"How long have you been doing this?' Danny asked.

"Since I joined the Committee," Sam said. "Brandon had done it too, but he weakened. He grew to love you all and decided to stand up for you all at the checkpoint that I had called for. We tried to stop you from getting the prisoner out, but Brandon's heart got in the way of his mind. Then I tried to get you all captured at your home, though I didn't expect for them to begin killing everyone off. Then the team that I had waiting on the hotel road had finally gotten you and you got out, but not today, Danny."

"You fucking asshole," Champ said. "We let you into our protection, and Danny's home. We trusted you. We treated you like family and you do this to us?"

"I didn't want it to be this way," Sam said. "I wanted to do what I could to make sure that you were only taken into police custody and released shortly after, but you all had to keep going further every day. Believe me, I had every good intention, and I even began to like you all too, but a revolution is not what this country needs. It would only throw us into anarchy until another group took control. Nobody will every see eye to eye on everything and it's crazy to think otherwise. We'd just be thrown into another war."

"This is fun," Brad said. "I have a great idea. Sam, kill Danny." He handed Sam a gun. Sam took it slowly, obviously still having some sort of connection with Danny.

"For the love of God, kill me instead," Marisa yelled from the cell. She shook the bars and seemed like a ravenous animal.

"No mom," Danny said.

"Dammit, Danny. I'm not losing you again," Marisa told him. "Please just let me take the bullet."

"This is stupid," Brad said. "Just kill someone, Sam."

Rosa stood in front of Sam. "Please, Sam," she said. "You can't do this. We still love you and you can still turn this around. Just remember what we all had. Remember what you can still go back to if you just put the gun down."

A shot went off and Rosa flew to the ground in a puddle of her own blood. Brad stood behind the trigger with a smile on his face. "Dumb bitch," he said.

Rob tackled Sam hard to the ground. In the same moment, Danny broke free and took Brad back to the ground. Shots began to ring out in the hallways of the prison. Danny stared only at Brad as he delivered blow after blow with fists and elbows.

"Danny! The rest of our guys are here!" Champ yelled. Danny took a quick glance off of Brad and watched as the rebels ran into the prison and went down every hallway. Gunshots banged through the prison as the rebels spread like a fire.

Danny looked back down to Brad and the mess that his face had become. It looked as if someone had taken a hammer to his face multiple times. Danny stood up and looked around. Sam laid dead on the ground with multiple bullet wounds. The rest of the guards were in the same state. Rosa laid peacefully on the ground beside them.

His eyes returned to Brad. He was on the ground spitting up blood and attempting to clear his eyes. "You know that this isn't going to end, right, Danny?" Brad asked as he attempted to let out a laugh, but only released more blood.

"It will this time," Danny said. He grabbed the gun from Sam's body and emptied the clip into Brad's chest and skull. He watched as the life left Brad's eyes once again. He stared at the body to ensure that he didn't see any hint of life that could possibly be left in him.

"Danny?" he heard from the cell. He looked up quickly and noticed that his parents had been watching the entire time. He went back into reality once again.

He searched the guards' bodies until he found a key ring to the cells. He went to his parents' cell first and immediately grabbed them as the doors flew open. As prisoners ran past them and joined the fight, Danny and his parents seemed suspended in time. The rest of the world became a blur to them in this moment. No noise could pull them from each other. The tears dropped and dropped as the family had finally been reunited.

"Danny!" Champ yelled. It suddenly pulled Danny out of the moment. He turned as Champ yelled, "We're not done yet! Grab a gun and let's go!"

Danny turned to his mom and dad. "Just get out and I'll see you when we're done here," Danny said.

"Danny," his mom said. "Please just come with us. I want to know that you're okay."

"I can't," Danny said. "I need to get to the rest of the prisoners."

"Why can't you just leave this?" Marisa said. "We're together again. Can't we just go back home?"

"Mom, I'd be going against everything that you and dad had ever taught me if I turn back now," Danny said.

"He's right, honey," Brian said. "Let's just get out of here and meet him outside."

His mom was reluctant, but she sighed and said, "Just please be careful. I love you, Danny."

Danny hugged his mom as tightly as he could and said, "I love you too." His dad walked to join.

Danny turned and gave his father a hug as well. "Get back safely, bud," he said through tears. "You've made me prouder than I ever could have been, Danny."

"Thanks, dad," Danny said. Brian pointed down the hallway and Danny ran in that direction. He began opening cell after cell telling people to get outside or join the fight. Some grabbed a weapon from a fallen guard, others ran outside, still others sat in their cells too afraid to leave.

As Danny continued to run through hallways, he began to realize that he had made it to every one as he passed the same soldiers and the same dead guards. "Danny!" Champ yelled. Danny ran up to meet him.

"Is that all of them?" Danny asked.

"Sure is," Champ said. "Let's get outside and see your parents." The two started on their way out of the prison laughing about their success. Then the gunshots started again, only this time they were outside. They ran as quickly as they could outside. Prisoners were scattering into every part of the woods as some of them laid on the ground. Soldiers of the Committee shot up at the walls of the prison and killed the last of the guards that had attempted to kill everyone from the rooftops.

"Dammit," Danny said. "How many are down?"

"Only about four, sir," a soldier said.

"Danny," Champ said.

"What?" Danny asked. Champ pointed toward a screaming woman kneeling over another person who had been hit. The fear hit Danny when he realized that it was his mom screaming. The sound of his own mother's scream was something that gripped his inner soul and pulled it as far down as it could budge. It was a sound that wouldn't leave his head any time that day.

He ran through the grassy field to the person lying on the ground. His father was spitting up blood as he laid staring at the sun. His mother cried profusely. "Dad!" Danny said as he tried to hold his father's head up.

"Danny," his dad said as he turned his head to him. "Danny, I'm dying."

"No, dad," Danny cried. "I just got to see you again. Please, you can't give up. I love you, dad."

"I love you too, Danny," his dad mumbled. "I wish that you didn't have to see me like this. I wish that we could have gone back home and seen the end of this war. All I want is for you and your mom to be happy and safe."

"I'll be the happiest kid in the world if you just don't give up on me, dad," Danny said as the tears fell onto his dad's bloody chest.

His dad smiled. "And I'll be the happiest dad in the world if you don't give up on what you've been fighting for," Brian said. "You've become a man, Danny. I'm just happy that I got to see you . . . " His sentence was cut off as a rush of blood came out of his mouth.

"No, dad!" Danny screamed. He pushed on the wound as hard as he could to stop the bleeding. His dad's coughs stopped and Danny continued to try. "Dad, please!" he screamed. "I can't lose you again." He pushed and pushed on the wound, but his father's heart had stopped and broken Danny's into pieces. He fell back onto the ground and cried. He looked at the sky and saw a nightmare in the sun. The once beautiful sky taunted him.

Danny's mom came to his side and held Danny tight. "It's okay, baby," she said. Danny grabbed his mom as tightly as he could. Their tears flowed seemingly endlessly. "It's all going to be okay," she told him as her sorrow continued to break her down.

Champ walked up slowly. Tears fell down his face as he looked down at his dead brother and crying family. He knelt down next to the two broken souls and held their shoulders as he dropped his head. Danny's dad, Marisa's love, and Champ's brother had left the world.

Soldiers gathered as they began to notice what had happened. It pulled hard on their hearts and even drew the tears out of many of the prisoners that were watching. A prisoner came over to the mourners and looked down to Danny who was now knelt over his father. His tears had subsided, but his face was still filled with remorse.

"Hey . . .Danny?" the prisoner said. Danny turned to see the tired face of an older prisoner. He put his hand out for Danny to shake. "Thank you for coming for us, and for what you've given up," he said. "We owe you and the rest of the Committee our lives, and we'll go back home to Boston to join you in the fight."

Danny looked up at the hand, and accepted it and even forced a smile through his sadness. The crowd smiled, even though they knew the sorrow that Danny and his family had gone through. The only advantage was that they had freed hundreds that would be more than happy to assist in the revolution. Though Danny had lost his father, he'd gained the support of hundreds. The fire in their hearts had been ignited.

Soldiers and prisoners took the time to help the Bruce family to bury one of their own, along with the other prisoners that couldn't make it. It was a long ordeal, but it was necessary for them to keep their morality. It was difficult for Danny to say goodbye, but with his family close, it became much simpler than it had to be. He said his final words to his dad's grave and turned back to the rest of the group.

The prisoners walked away, and the others began to head through the forest towards Boston. It wasn't far, but it would be a hike. However, it would be much easier than what they had gone through. At least now, they knew that they were going home.

"What are you going to do?" Danny asked his mom.

"I'm going with you, Danny," she told him.

Danny shook his head. "I can't let you do that," he said.

Marisa tried to grab a hold of him. "Please, Danny. I just want you to come home. I can't lose you again," she said.

"Mom," Danny said as he tried to back away. "If you come with me, there's a very big chance that I'll lose you. Please, just go to Boston. We'll be there soon, I promise."

His mom's face didn't have any fight left in it. "Please," was all that could leave her lips.

It was painful to see her this way, but it was for the best. "Mom, I promise, I'll see you again soon," he said. "But there's a fight that has to be won. I have to make dad proud."

She looked down to the ground. She'd been defeated. Marisa looked up to Danny and forced a smile. "I love you, Danny," she said. "Just please be careful."

He gave his mom a hug. "I will be, mom," he said. "I love you so much." Feeling his mom in his arms again and being able to tell her that he loved her was the greatest reward that Danny could have ever gotten from that mission. It gave him the drive that he would need. As he walked back to the van and rode it back to the hotel, he rested assured that he would have the strength to make his father proud.

As they pulled up to the hotel, Champ pulled Danny to the side to talk to him. "Are you going to be okay, Dan?" he asked.

Danny's soul was crushed, but his resolve was keeping him going. "Yeah, I'll be fine," he said.

Champ smiled. "You really do remind me so much of Brian," he said. "I know that he's watching you right now and he's more than happy with the man that you've become. I know you'll continue to make him proud."

"Hey guys," someone said from the front of the hotel. It was Mike. Apparently he was on guard duty for the night. He walked up and looked to Danny. "I heard what happened, sir. It's a damned shame," he said.

"Yeah," Danny mumbled.

"Well here," Mike said as he pulled his cigarettes out. "I was about to smoke. Do you guys want to join me?"

"Hell yeah," Champ said with a lot less enthusiasm than he usually used for the phrase. "I think we need something to calm us down. You care for one, Danny?"

It couldn't possibly hurt him any more than the loss did. "Sure," Danny said.

The three sat on the front ledge of the hotel and began their smoking session. The first pull relieved a ton of stress from Danny's shoulders and helped him lighten up a bit. "Well, what do you plan on doing now?" Mike asked.

"Not sure," Danny said. "I guess we're just preparing for Boston."

Mike nodded. "Looking towards the future, eh, sir?" Mike joked.

It helped Danny smile a bit. "My mom's waiting for me there," he said. "I'm just looking forward to taking Boston so I'll know that she'll be safe."

"I hear yah', sir," Mike said. "I have family near Boston. I want nothing more than to get them out of that fucking place. The government's been sending troops there to put down the protesters and retake parts of Boston that rebels have been trying to isolate from the rest of the city. Lost half of my damn family to this war."

Danny realized that in the grand scheme of things, maybe he was the lucky one. "Damn, I'm sorry to hear that," Danny said.

"Yeah, it's painful, but I just look to make sure that I keep my head up and get the job done, sir," Mike said. He took another drag and turned to Champ. "So are you related to Danny, sir?"

Champ didn't seem very used to the "sir" thing either. "Yeah, his uncle," he said.

"Damn," Mike said. "So were you his dad's brother?"

Champ took a long pause. "Yeah," he said. He took another pull to choke down the pain.

Danny put his hand on his uncle's shoulder like he did whenever Danny was upset. It didn't seem to help. "He meant a lot to you, didn't he, sir?" Mike asked.

Champ's wall of frustration was beginning to crumble and let his emotions out. "More than I could ever describe," Champ said as tears began to make their way out.

Mike took another pull and looked forward. "I lost a brother too," he said. "One day, just before I joined the Committee, my brother tried to stop me from getting arrested at a protest. He did nothing more than push an officer that was sitting on me, practically breaking my arm. The officer stood up and shot him right there in the street. Never even had a chance to say goodbye."

"Me neither," Champ mumbled.

Mike looked to the grizzled face as tears ran down it. "There's nothing like losing someone that's been there for you your entire life to bring you back to reality," Mike said. "I know that it took me a long time to get used to it, you know? To get used to that feeling of not having your brother to get you out of trouble, or just to talk to. You know though, I feel like my brother's still with me. I feel like he's still there to protect me and for me to talk to whenever I need him. A brother never leaves another brother, even in death."

Champ began to break. "But I let him get shot down in the middle of fucking nowhere."

"And I let mine get shot down by a fucking pig," he said. "I let some piece of shit kill him because he was having a bad day. He died helping me and I don't think I could forgive myself for it. But you know what? I can't blame myself for what happened. Like I said, a brother never leaves another, and I know I would have done the same thing. If you had died and your brother was in the situation you're in now, I know he'd act the same way, because brothers love each other in a way that some will never understand. You just have to live on in the beauty of knowing that you understand and that your love for the best friend that you ever had won't die because of some asshole with a gun."

Mike started to tear up himself. "Thanks, man," Champ said.

"You know, sir," Mike said. "I could beat myself up every day because I got my brother killed, but the thought of getting back at the assholes that allowed it to happen without penalty is a hell of a motivator."

Danny thought back to Sam's words. "But you can't let revenge take over your mind," Danny debated.

"Sir, if I can speak freely," Mike said.

"Sure," Danny said.

"Fuck revenge, I want justice," Mike responded. "My brother wasn't killed by another soldier, he was killed by a coward with some power. That's exactly what happened to your father. I would never say that I'm searching revenge. I just want the motherfucker that let it happen to get what he deserves and that's exactly what should be driving you two. Don't beat yourselves up because you could have stopped the situation, beat the ones that caused a good man to die because they didn't agree with their actions. Our brothers were revolutionaries. They're the ones that will drive this army to the gates of the White House. I for one look to honor their sacrifice. It's up to you two to decide if you make this a loss, or a motivation to do what they would have wanted."

Not revenge, but justice. Danny shouldn't mourn the fact that he could have stopped it, he should use his father's death to push him to carry on what his dad taught him. Champ had similar thoughts. Sure his brother had been taken from him without any farewells being said, but it should only drive him to make sure that the person that made that happen should pay.

"For a young guy, you're pretty damn smart," Champ said.

"Thank you, sir," Mike said.

"Well, I've got to go inside and break the news to Amanda," Danny said. "I completely forgot until just now."

"Sister?" Mike asked.

"No, she lost her mom today too and she doesn't know it yet," Danny said.

"Well if you need anyone to talk to, I'll be out here, sir," Mike said.

Danny began to walk away and turned back. "Hey, Mike," he said.

Mike looked up from the cigarette he had just thrown onto the ground. "Yes, sir?" he asked.

"You don't have to call me 'sir.' You've been more than a friend for me," Danny said.

Mike laughed. "I just know a lot about loss, but thanks, Danny," he said.

Danny and Champ headed into the hotel and upstairs. As they opened the door, Amanda rushed the door. "Danny, where's my mom?" she asked. "Rob won't tell me."

She had to approach it that directly. Danny looked in her eyes. They were so full of hope, and he was about to be the one to destroy it. "Hey, Rob and Adam," Champ said from the door. "You want to go get some food?"

"Sure," they said. They stood up and left the room with Champ.

Danny took this time to sit down on his bed and take off his shoes. Amanda sat next to him. "So where is she, Danny?" Amanda said with worry in her voice.

Danny reflected back on the moment that Rosa hit the floor with disgust at the situation. "She stopped my parents and I from being killed," Danny said. "A guard told Sam to kill either me, my mom, or my dad when we found out that he was a traitor. Your mom stood in front of the gun and the guard shot her."

Amanda's mouth dropped and her eyes filled with tears. "Are you serious?" Amanda asked with a shaky voice.

"Yeah," Danny said with hope. "Your mom's a hero, Amanda. She gave her life willingly for people she hardly knew. I know it's going to hurt you to have lost her, but I just want you to know, so many people owe their lives to her. If I could change it, I would have let the bullet hit me, I swear, but the fact that she took it so bravely . . .it was amazing, Amanda. She had no ounce of fear. She was only concerned with my parents' and my safety and I would give anything to thank her for it."

Amanda's tears began to fall and her lip began to quiver, but she smiled. "I never knew how brave she was," Amanda said. "It's pretty inspiring." She tried to wipe the tears from her eyes. "I'm sorry about your dad, Danny," she said.

Danny smiled. "Thank you," he said. "If you ever need someone to talk to, I'll be here forever."

Amanda chuckled. "I love you, Danny." Her eyes widened as she realized what she had said. Danny had the same reaction. For a moment they just sat there trying to figure out if they both heard the same thing. The heartbreak no longer took a seat at the front of their minds.

Danny laughed and wore the largest smile that he'd had in a while. No matter how much he fought it, it remained. "I love you too, Amanda," he said. They fell into each other's arms on the bed and became the comfort that each of them had needed through the war. For one night, at least, their minds no longer carried the burdens of sorrow and worry. The young minds cleared and the hearts became full, as the sun slept behind the horizon.

CHAPTER TWENTY

SNEAK ATTACK

The nights were rough on Danny. Every night that he slept, he dreamt only of his father. He dreamt of talking to his dad and laughing about what had happened in their day. He dreamt of the fishing trips that he and his dad would take during the summer off of the Massachusetts coast. Then he had horrific nightmares of the day that his dad was taken from him, all because he told him to wait outside instead of leaving the war like his mom asked him to.

Champ didn't seem to have the same enthusiasm that he'd always had. Knowing that he could someday see his brother again was the only thing that kept him going. Now that he was gone, that hope was gone. Nobody had seen the motivation that Brian had given him, but now that the motivation was gone, people began to take notice.

Amanda began to look towards the others for support much more than she ever had. The loss of her parents left her with no one to seek advice or love from, and she filled the gap with those that were still alive. She, like the others, was still very distraught, but simply having someone to speak to was more than she could have ever wanted.

After the prison had been taken back, the soldiers had regained even more of their fervor, but the ones that had seen Danny's reaction to the loss of his father were still shaken up. The generals that had heard the news seemed concerned with Danny and Champ's will to continue, but some had other worries.

O'Connor hadn't handled the news of the traitor very well. "I shouldn't have trusted your friends as much as I had," he told Danny. "Why shouldn't I kick the rest out of here and save myself the risk of another traitor?" Danny and Champ had to fight to keep Rob, Adam, and Amanda in the hotel.

"Sir, I can personally speak for all of them," Danny said.

"I'm sure you would have told me the same thing about Sam," O'Connor told him. The rest of the lieutenants arrived to discuss the situation. "Good you're here," O'Connor said.

"Rumors are spreading that the mole was found, sir," Lieutenant Donley said. "Tell me it's just a rumor."

"Unfortunately, no," O'Connor said. "It was one of Danny and Champ's friends. He'd been feeding information to the loyalist forces since he joined the Committee."

"Is he still alive?" Lieutenant Adams asked.

"No, he was killed in the prison," O'Connor answered.

"Then what's the issue?" Lieutenant Donley asked.

O'Connor was becoming flustered. "The issue is the fact that our defenses were breached because we trusted too easily," O'Connor said.

"Do you expect to just stop trusting people that want to join the cause?" Danny asked.

"No," O'Connor said. "I've given everyone in this facility a test to ensure that I can trust them, but it seems that the tests were too easy. So, I'm going to make a new test."

"And what would that be?" Danny asked.

O'Connor pulled some papers out of his desk. "Our operatives in the military base have told us that the base is struggling considering their lack of supplies and power," O'Connor said. "This means that we're ready to attack. To ensure that the ones attacking can be trusted, I want every soldier to cut an ear off of a loyalist soldier and bring them back."

"Are you serious?" Champ asked.

"Is there a problem with that?" O'Connor asked.

"We're not fucking barbarians," Champ said. "Not to mention that there aren't enough soldiers in that base for this, and that not every soldier in there deserves that."

"If they're still stationed in that outpost, then they're a threat to the citizens," O'Connor said. "Anyone that threatens the wellbeing of the American citizens deserve nothing less."

"How are you so sure that they're all loyalists?" Danny asked.

Lieutenant Michaels intervened. "We have some of our best spied in that place," he said. "Trust me, everyone in that place is a loyalist. That's why they're still staying in the closest base to Boston. They're preparing themselves for an attack to completely secure Boston. The only thing stopping them is their lack of supplies and power, both of which we control."

"So what do we do if someone tries to surrender?" Danny asked.

"It's pretty simple," O'Connor said. "You kill them. We're not taking prisoners on this one."

That answer stunned Danny. "How are we not going to allow mercy to anyone that we can sway or at least get information out of?" he asked. "We'll be no better than the government that has been killing our citizens off."

O'Connor rubbed his head. "Lad, the only reason we kept anyone alive was for the protection," he said. "Once we have that base, we'll have access to weapons that can take out any threat that comes our way and we'll have no more need for the information that our prisoners have given us."

"Then what do we do with the prisoners that are here now?" Danny asked.

O'Connor simply tilted his head at Danny and said, "I think you all have a base to take."

"Come on," Lieutenant Michaels said. "We have to discuss the plan of attack."

Danny turned and glared at O'Connor on his way out of the room. "Have fun, mate!" O'Connor yelled to him. Something had to be done about him. O'Connor was completely out of control. He could be potentially killing American citizens simply to avoid his paranoia.

They were walking to the lieutenant's room to discuss what would be done in the military outpost. It wasn't going to be an easy day, and Danny was already distracted. He'd only spent about a week without a mission, but it was a week that he needed. He'd just gotten the thought of his father to the back of his mind and now the concern of O'Connor's tactics took its spot at the front of his mind.

What was there to do? O'Connor ran one of the strongest chapters in the country. Betraying him would come with a heavy price and it would probably never work. The soldiers put all of their hope into him and he'd become invincible from it. He certainly couldn't be reasoned with, that was for sure. Danny was left with no options.

The group arrived in Lieutenant Michaels' room. It looked very little like a hotel room and much more like a serial killer's room of obsessive pictures and newspaper clippings. The walls were covered in different pieces of information that the spies had acquired. Each of them were categorized as things such as "strengths," "weaknesses," "leaders," and hundreds of others. It was a wonder that Michaels could keep any of it in order.

Michaels pulled more papers out of a desk buried underneath bags and ammunition boxes in the corner of the room. He pulled a chair from the desk and began to look over his notes. "I think the best way to go about this would be a nighttime attack," he said. "During the day, snipers will be keeping lookout using the daylight, but if we attack at night, they'd only have the searchlights to guide their shots on a normal day. Fortunately, their power's out and according to the spies we've got in there, they've only got enough power in their generator until about eleven tonight by their estimates."

"So you want us to sneak an army into the base?" Danny asked.

"I guess kind of," Michaels laughed. It was clear that he was one of the only generals that had a sense of humor anymore. "We're going to put our snipers throughout the area surrounding the base. When we give the signal, the snipers will fire and take out the military's snipers. Then we move in and hop their walls."

"How do you propose that we hop the walls?" Champ asked. "They're made out of concrete and they're at least ten feet tall, probably more."

Michaels smiled. "Have you ever watched one of those medieval movies where all of the soldiers put up ladders and jump the walls of the castle?" he asked.

"So we're attacking a castle now," Champ said.

"Don't be a smartass," Michaels said. "We're going to bring our own ladders and get over the walls. We'll sneak as many soldiers in as we can before we're noticed."

"We just intercepted a shipment yesterday that was meant for that base," Lieutenant Donley said. "It had the fuel that they were aiming to use on their generators as well as ammunition for their tanks. The way I see it, they've used all of their fuel to power the base, which means that they've probably been siphoning the gasoline out of their tanks so we won't have to worry about those. However, since we've got those supplies, we can operate the tanks once we take the base."

The plan was sounding pretty flawless, but an aspect of it still bothered Danny. "So we just get in there and kill everyone?" Danny questioned.

"Those are the orders from the commander," Michaels said.

"Are we actually going to kill everyone, even people that want to surrender?" Danny asked.

"They're orders," Michaels said. "As much as I don't want to have that, we need to."

Danny was disgusted. Everyone in that place had been brainwashed into thinking that they had to obey this one guy. The entire purpose of the revolution was to be free, and now they were following someone else's orders like always.

"So once the base is captured, we'll have to call to the plant on the radio so they'll direct the power there," Michaels said. "Then we'll move to begin distributing weapons to the people of Boston and we'll attack to take the city tomorrow."

"Tomorrow?" Lieutenant Adams said. "Shouldn't we give everyone a chance to rest?"

"If we give ourselves a chance to rest, then we give the loyalists time to prepare," Michaels said. "Right now, they're attacking citizens to get them under control. They're weak, but if they figure out that we've taken a military base nearby they'll call for military reinforcements from places throughout the country."

"Haven't they been getting those reinforcements anyways?" Lieutenant Donley asked.

"Yes, but at a much slower rate," Lieutenant Michaels said. "At the moment, the rest of the country is in unrest as well so the military is needed throught. If they find out that an all-out attack is coming to this one city, we'll have military forces coming from every part of the U.S."

"So are we even going to bother coming back to the hotel after the attack?" Danny asked.

"Thanks for mentioning that," Lieutenant Michaels said. "We'll all be staying in the base until the attack tomorrow. We need to make sure that it isn't recaptured overnight. Are there any other questions?" Just a silence while everyone tried to come up with a reasonable question. "Alright, then get ready and we'll leave at nine tonight."

The generals left the room to spread the word. Everyone had already known that the attack would be today, they just didn't have all of the details straight. Outside, the vans were being loaded up with equipment as they had been before the other missions. Soldiers began going back to their rooms to load their guns and check their bulletproof vests for damage.

Danny headed outside to see if Mike was on duty. Soldiers flew past him to spread the news of the nearing attack and prepare. A few times he was almost pushed to the ground. As he left the hotel, he signed in with the soldier guarding the door for O'Connor's anti-mole policy.

As Danny walked outside, he saw Mike sitting on the ledge in front of the hotel smoking a cigarette like always. "Hey, Mike," Danny said.

Mike turned quickly. "Oh, hey, Danny," he responded. He gave Danny a handshake and a cigarette.

Danny lit his cigarette and began the conversation. "What have you been doing so far today?" he asked.

"Not much," he said. "Pretty much just been watching people load these vans and chillin'. How about you?"

Danny took a long drag and attempted to blow smoke rings. "Not much," he said. "Just found out the details for the attack tonight."

"Oh yeah," Mike said. "I heard about that. How's that going?"

"Everything's pretty perfectly planned to be honest," Danny said. "It's pretty surprising considering our plans are usually to simply attack head on."

Mike laughed. "There's power in numbers," he joked. The two sat in their own thoughts as they felt the slight breeze blowing through the air. “So what do you plan to do when we get to Boston?” Mike asked.

“Definitely need to go see my mom,” Danny said. “I don’t know what else. We were planning on setting up a radio station for the citizens since the news isn’t on anymore.”

“Yeah, those assholes,” Mike said. “That’s a pretty good idea, though. It would be a great way to help everyone in the country stay updated to what’s happening. Who’s going to run it?”

Danny hadn’t thought of that much. “I’m not sure,” he said.

“I mean, not to be pushy or anything, but I’d be willing to do it,” Mike said.

“Really?” Danny asked. He was kind of confused and hesitant about that. He thought he could trust Mike, but did he trust him enough to be able to run the one station that would be sending news to the nation?

“Yeah,” Mike said. “I’ve wanted to be on the radio my whole life. I know how to work the equipment and everything, and if you’re concerned I give you permission to pull me out of there any time you want.”

“You wouldn’t mind having to leave the hotel for good and having that much responsibility?” Danny asked.

“Not really,” Mike said. “Keep this between you and me, but I really don’t like the leadership around here. I think once we take Boston and the rest of the country starts mobilizing to retake the rest of the land, I’d rather just be in Boston to hear the stories and retell them to everyone listening. It sounds like a lot more fun than guarding this door.”

He had a point, and it was refreshing for Danny to hear that someone else was questioning the leadership of the hotel. Mike seemed like the chill kind of guy that would be fit for something like running a radio station, and there weren't many other choices out there. "I guess that sounds good to me, man," Danny said.

Mike was overjoyed. "Awesome!" he said. "I promise I'll do great, man. Thanks a lot."

"Sure thing," Danny said. "Are you going on the mission tonight?"

Mike shook his head. "Nah," he said. "I'm going back on guard duty later tonight. Best of luck to you, though."

"Thanks," Danny said as he shook Mike's hand and walked back inside. He headed up to his room to talk to the group a bit before they had to leave. As he entered, the mood was pretty similar to how it had been all that week: depressing.

Rob was just waking up as Danny walked in and Adam was making some dinner with food he'd gotten from the cafeteria. It smelled delicious, but upon further examination, it turned out to be a disgusting combination different kinds of chicken, multiple condiments, and rice. Amanda was reading and Champ wasn't back in the room yet.

"What's up?" Danny asked as he walked in.

"Getting ready to eat!" Adam said. "You want some?" He held the plate holding the unholy creation in Danny's face.

Danny gagged a bit and said, "Nah, I ate a while ago."

"Suit yourself," Adam said.

"How was the conversation with O'Connor?" Amanda asked.

"Pff, pretty damn pointless," Danny said.

"Why? What was he saying?" she asked.

"He was basically just telling me about how we shouldn't have been trusted, how we need to have a new test for people to prove their loyalty, and about how we're no longer taking prisoners. He's gone off the deep end."

"Jeez. That guy's nuts."

"That's what I'm saying. It's starting to worry me."

"Why?"

"Because who knows how far he's gunna go? At any point, he could turn on any one of us and call us a traitor. He's gone mad with power and it's a danger to everyone here."

"What are you going to do about it?"

"What?"

"What are you going to do about it? Are you just going to accept it for how it is and move on or are you going to try and change it?"

"I don't know." Danny thought long and hard about it. Was there anything he could do? "I want to change it," he said. "But I don't know what to do that could get him to lighten up without him flipping out and having us killed."

"I guess that is quite the pickle, isn't it?" Amanda asked.

Danny looked at her and smiled. "Yes it is," he said. She returned the smile. Who knew that her smile could completely illegitimate a serious situation.

"What did he say about me?" Rob asked.

Danny turned around to see him. "Nothing," he said. "Why?"

Rob shook his head and pulled the blankets back onto himself. "That guy's got it out for me," he said. "Asshole."

"What makes you say that?" Danny asked.

Rob sat up. "I don't know," he said. "I've just got a feeling that he suspects something's weird about me."

"Don't worry," Danny said. "We wouldn't let him try to accuse you of anything."

Danny laid back on his bed and let his mind wander. It was great to just lay down every once in a while and let the thoughts find their way in and out of his brain. Such a simple thing, but such a luxury when you're being constantly battered with twists and turns. Before he knew it, he'd fallen asleep.

His thoughts conjured up images of his father. Danny and he were outside of their old house trying to change the oil in Danny's car. His dad was under the car attempting to get the filter off after Danny had tried and failed. His dad always was much stronger than he was.

His dad eventually came out from under the car with the filter held high in victory. Brian stood up and said to Danny, "You want to smoke some cigars and drink some scotch?"

Danny laughed. "Of course," he said. "The best way to end a hard day." His dad laughed at Danny's unexpected rhyme.

"Alright I'll go get the scotch," Brian said. "The cigars are in the garage." Danny walked into the garage as his dad walked into the house. He grabbed two of his dad's fancy cigars from the box that his dad always kept on top of the fridge. He went to the front step of his house and sat to light his cigar.

As he lit the cigar, Danny watched the flame as it rose when he exhaled and caught the paper as he inhaled. He pulled the lighter and sat back with his cigar, watching the designs as they formed in the smoke.

It wasn't long before his dad showed up with the scotch. The two sat taking swigs and smoking their cigars in front of their house, simply enjoying a beautiful day. The sun was out and the grass was looking greener than ever. Danny looked up at the clouds in wonder.

His eyes descended and noticed that a cloud must have blocked the sun for a moment. He took another puff of his cigar and looked out to the street. There was some guy walking his dogs on the sidewalk. Danny watched the man pass and wave to Danny and his dad. Danny waved back and the man stopped with his animals.

Danny's dad said, "How are yah' doin'?" but the man was unresponsive. He walked towards the house. Danny couldn't see his face and it really bothered him. He attempted to focus, but it wasn't getting any clearer, that is, it wasn't until he blinked. The second Danny's eyes opened, the man was only feet away. Then the horror struck him.

"You aren't making this easy," Brad said as he smiled at Danny.

Danny shot out of bed. His head ascended in alarm and he fell right out of his cot. The rest of the group were startled by the yelp that Danny let out. He looked up from the ground at their faces. It wasn't long before he realized how much of an idiot he'd made himself look like.

"What the hell?" Champ said. "Again?"

"Are you alright, Danny?" Adam asked.

Danny looked around the room. It seemed like everything was back to normal. He gave himself the traditional pinch on the arm to ensure that he was indeed awake. The jolt of pain informed him that he was.

"Yeah," Danny said. "It was just another nightmare."

"I tell you what, Danny," Adam said. "You should see someone about those nightmares when this is all over."

Danny reflected on what he'd just seen. He was still too scared to make any sudden movements as he tried to collect his thoughts. It was only a dream, but the reality of it was frightening.

"What time is it?" Danny asked.

Adam checked his watch. "It's about eight-thirty. We were actually about to wake you up so we can get downstairs and get ready."

Danny finally had the courage to stand up. He grabbed his bulletproof vest and put it on. After finding his gun under his bed, he made sure that it was loaded and ready to go. His extra ammo, he packed into his pants' pockets. Not very professional, but it hadn't failed him yet.

The group completed their checklist of things they needed and headed to the downstairs of the hotel. It was already pretty dark outside and soldiers were gathering in the hotel lobby. The humidity of the outdoors was seeping in through the front doors and making the soldiers very uncomfortable in their layers of clothing.

Danny and his friends stood in the crowd for close to ten minutes before it was their turn to get into their van. The packed in and the ride began. It would be about an hour ride. Once they arrived at their destination, they would have to take the walk about a half mile to their vantage point.

Danny checked his bag that he'd brought for everything. He had his binoculars, a pistol, and a radio. He looked his rifle over to make sure that nothing was out of place. Over preparation was a common thing in his life recently. Ever since everything that could possibly go wrong went wrong every time, he'd sort of adapted to it.

He wanted nothing more than to take a nap on the way there. However, there were two downsides to that: he'd be tired for the mission, and he might have nightmares that would freak him out too much for the mission. It was scary how he couldn't even close his eyes without the fear of his mind's manifestations keeping him from falling asleep.

The soldiers arrived at their drop off point and got out of their vans. This was when Danny realized how large their group truly was. It seemed like they had more people this time than they had for the mission at the power plant. If he had to guess, Danny would say that there were about two hundred and fifty people. It was quite the group to have to sneak into a base.

Lieutenant Michaels huddled the group together around him and began to explain everything. "Alright," he said. "When we get to the point that we can see the base, we'll stop and wait for their lights to shut off. When they do, we'll move to the walls with the ladders and start hopping in. Don't attack until either everyone's in or you're in a situation where there's no other option. Everyone got it?" The group nodded. "Alright, let's move."

Danny was crouched with the rest of the group running through the area. It seemed that nobody had been there in a while. Figuring in the fact that almost every shipment that was meant for them had been intercepted by the Committee, that probably wasn't unlikely.

As he looked to the sky, Danny realized that the moon wasn't even out that night. It was an ingenious night for a sneak attack. He could hardly see the person in front of him, let alone anything more than ten meters away. Once the lights went off in the base, the snipers wouldn't be able to shoot anything. What a plan this was.

The group went over a hill and saw the base ahead. They all laid side to side to form a huge wall of soldiers all facing the same target. Danny pulled out his binoculars to get a better look at the base. He looked at the snipers that were standing in their towers, their eyes following the searchlights.

The walls around the base were intimidating. Chances were that the ladders would just barely reach the top. The only thing that Danny wondered was how they'd get down on the other side. The wall was maybe twelve feet high, and that didn't seem like a very fun jump to have to take. Through some problem-solving, Danny figured that they'd have to put a ladder on both sides. Damn he wished that nobody would see them.

Anticipation was building in the troops. They were all waiting for that moment when the generators would run out of gasoline. Each gripped their gun, waiting for the moment that they would get to pull their triggers. Their minds prepared their bodies for a rough night.

The fear of being seen before everyone could get a good position was a common thing. At any point, a sniper could see them and open fire, ruining the entire plan. That, or they could get a few guys inside, only for them to be mowed down and then get everyone outside of the gates killed as well. It was a game of trying to decide which way they'd rather die.

Danny's eyes were locked on the searchlight nearest them. It wasn't at all close to shining on them, but he wanted it to go out with everything he had inside of him. It was like watching the clock while waiting to get off of work. Every second seemed to take forever and you knew that the second that the signal came, you were off.

The light went out. There was a moment of hesitation. Maybe the light would come back on or something and they'd be caught. It was the longest five seconds that any of them had experienced. Once it hit five seconds, the line rose and did their crouch run all the way up to the walls.

Danny's calves were killing him, but with the adrenaline pumping, he didn't even notice. They only had to travel about two hundred meters until they reached the walls. With each meter that they traveled, the walls looked even larger than they had a few meters back. At the rate they were going, it seemed that the walls were going to be too much for them to handle.

The eyes of the soldiers were fixed just above the walls, where the snipers were trying to figure out what they were supposed to do. Some walked down from their towers to attempt to fix whatever problem the lights were having. They all probably knew that they were out of fuel for the generators, but there was no reason that they couldn't hope. With what was about to happen, the lights were the least of their worries.

The soldiers reached the wall and spread themselves around it. The ones that had carried the ladders that miserable two hundred meters put them up quickly, but quietly. Soldier after soldier climbed the ladders. Lucky Danny ended up being one of the first ones over.

As he climbed the ladder, every step that he took raised his paranoia. He knew that the next step would be the one that got them caught, and then he was fine. When he reached the top, he hardly even took a moment to look at the base from up high. The most that he saw in his split second of sight were the tanks nearby. The lack of light had basically blinded him, so he wasn't even sure if he'd seen tanks or a building.

He made his way down the ladder cautiously. Soldiers were coming in from all sides of the base and hiding until the attack began. It was insane that none of them had been shot at yet.

Danny made his way to the corner of the building that they had taken refuge behind and peeked around the corner. He still couldn't see anything. It was insane how there was literally no light at all. There was no moon, no stars, no anything. Danny could have closed his eyes and nothing would be different.

In a little over five minutes, people stopped climbing the wall. Danny pulled out his radio and called the other lieutenants. "Everyone ready?" he asked.

"All good over here," Adams said.

"Yup," Michaels said.

"Yeah, we're ready," Donley responded.

"Yeah, let's do this," Champ said.

"Alright," Danny said. He dialed the frequency for the power plant and said, "Turn on the power at the base."

"Roger," the radio responded. It hadn't been agreed upon beforehand, but they needed some light so they could shoot at their targets. Danny stood on his toes up until the second the lights turned on.

As the base lit up, the yells of the rebel soldiers could have been heard from miles away. Danny flew around the corner and saw a group of soldiers only a few meters away.

He pulled his rifle up and shot the first in the side, then the chest and he dropped. The next went down quickly as well. The last of the group only had his gun up halfway when Danny sent a bullet through his chest.

He continued to run. He took cover at the bottom of a guard tower and decided to make his way up. The barrel of his rifle guided his path the entire time. With every step, his gun pointed towards the top of the current incline.

As he rose, the sniper's rifle made a booming sound just above him. He was shooting at the rebel soldiers. Danny ran up quietly until he saw the back of the sniper. He put the gun to the back of the sniper's head and fired. The sniper's body stiffened and he fell over the side, with his rifle remaining in the tower. The physics of it was horrific.

Danny looked down to the rifle and picked it up. He looked into the scope in wonder. It could zoom in so much further than any scope he'd seen. He looked to the other towers and systematically began shooting every sniper he saw. With the amount of gunfire in the base, none of the snipers realized that the one before them had been shot until it was too late. Considering Danny's lack of accuracy, it was probably a good thing that they couldn't pick out his shots.

The attack was much shorter than the one on the power plant had been. The shots stopped and Danny looked out to the area surrounding the base. That's when he noticed a soldier trying to run for it. There was no sense in killing the guy, he'd already given up.

"Shoot him, Danny!" a voice yelled. Danny looked down to see lieutenant Adams yelling up at him. Dammit. Now he had to shoot the guy. If he didn't, O'Connor would definitely be told. Danny raised the scope to his eye and focused in on the soldier. The guy couldn't have been any more than eighteen. Danny watched the kid's back and led his shot. The trigger came back and he watched the bullet puncture through the soldier's torso and hit the ground in front of him. He dropped quickly and remained motionless.

Danny lowered the gun with disgust and started walking down the stairs of the tower. He made it to the bottom and saw the sniper he'd killed lying at the bottom. It was much more gruesome than he'd expected. It wasn't like a movie or video game where the body was just sort of there. There was a bone sticking out of his arm and his neck had obviously been broken. The bullet wound was large and had blood steadily gushing from it, even though he'd been dead for a few minutes. It wasn't something Danny wanted to see every mission, or ever again for that matter.

"Well, get your ear," a voice said to him. It was Lieutenant Adams once again. He was holding a knife out to Danny for him to perform the ritual. Danny shook his head and took the knife. He lowered himself down to the body and took a moment to figure out which way he was going to go about it. The body was already starting to smell unlike Danny could have ever expected it to.

Danny lowered the knife with Adams standing over him. The edge of the blade touched the back of the soldier's ear. The mere touching of the knife to skin was enough to make Danny's spine shiver. He took a deep breath and turned his head. The knife started to move rapidly, though the cut didn't come quick. Danny clenched his eyes closed and rubbed the knife across the ear as quickly as he could until he felt it detach from the head.

Danny looked down and almost vomited at the sight of what the side of the guy's head had become. He looked up at Adams's ignorant smile. Danny held the ear up to him and Adams laughed and took it from him. The ear was placed gently in a bag full of fresh ears and Danny's name was checked off on some list that Adams had. Danny walked away in disgust to find his friends.

Soldiers were sprinting around the base looking for the supplies and basically getting a feel for how the base worked. Engineers were getting to work on the tanks, filling them up with gasoline and ammunition. Others were hopelessly looking for an ear to cut off. The base had turn into the place of a massacre. The soldiers had been butchered and their bodies were being mutilated. It was sick.

Danny spotted the rest of the group walking towards him. He raised his hand to them and they approached. "Hey guys," Danny said.

"This is fucking sick," Champ said. "I can't believe this shit. Not only were we told to kill every last soldier in here, we have to cut off their fucking ears?"

"Yeah, I don't like this," Adam said.

"This is what I've been talking about," Danny said. "O'Connor's out of his goddamn mind."

"I definitely see that now," Adam said. "Well what do we do now?"

Danny looked around. He saw a soldier vomiting on the ground and a couple of other soldiers joking around with ears in their hands. "I just don't know anymore," he said.

CHAPTER TWENTY-ONE

BOSTON

Danny and his group walked around the Committee's new military base, observing the horror that the rebels had created. The soldiers had done their job, but unlike the mission at the power plant, they had gone much too far this time. Blood covered every inch of the ground in the base. Every soldier that had defended the base could be found mutilated in some corner of the base.

Soldiers were working on throwing the dead bodies over the wall of the base while the engineers were finishing up on the tanks. Many soldiers were forming a line to a supply building to receive more ammunition or a new weapon. The entire time, Danny and the rest of his friends simply watched as those with morality vomited and those that lacked it moved along as if nothing was out of the ordinary.

A soldier was running straight for their group. Chances were that they were going to be asked to do something else for the Committee. Sometimes it seemed like they were the only ones ever asked to do anything.

"Lieutenant Bruce?" the soldier asked Danny.

"Yeah, that's me," Danny said, sounding very annoyed.

"Commander O'Connor wants to speak with you," the soldier said. "He's waiting on the radio in the new communications room.

Danny turned to his friends. "I'll catch up with you guys," he said. He jogged his way through puddles of blood to the communications room. As he entered, he noticed how much more technology was in this communications room compared to the one back at the hotel. He walked to someone working with a radio. "Hey, I heard that the commander was waiting to talk to me?" he said.

"Yes, sir," thle radio operator said. "That radio's right over there." The operator pointed to a large radio on a table in the corner.

Danny approached the radio and took a deep breath to brace himself for the bull he was going to have the privilege of hearing. "Hello, sir?" Danny said into the radio.

Some static could be heard, then O'Connor's voice. "Danny boy!" O'Connor yelled. "How are yah doin', mate?"

"I'm alright," Danny said.

"Great!" O'Connor said. "I heard about the victory. We're one step closer to taking back the country."

"Yep," Danny said. "So what did you want to talk to me about?"

"Oh, yes," O'Connor said. "I need you to go into Boston tonight and begin handing out weapons to the citizens there."

"Why tonight?" Danny asked. "I'm exhausted."

"Because the attack's tomorrow morning, lad!" O'Connor said.

"Aren't there tons of soldiers there right now trying to get Boston under control?" Danny asked. "I don't think they'll just let me come in and start handing out weapons."

"Normally, no they wouldn't, but with that base being taken, they soldiers are going to be much more concerned about an attack. Just to help you out, I'm going to have a mortar team shoot some rounds near the outskirts of Boston to distract the soldiers and hopefully move them towards the mortar fire to prepare to defend. While they do that, you drive the truck in and start handing out weapons."

"Can I bring anyone with me?"

"Go for it, lad. Just make sure those weapons get to the citizens."

"Alright. I guess I'll get started then." Danny said. He left the communication room with his mind filled with thoughts. He was running on little to no sleep. His eyelids were a constant burden to carry. His mind was beginning to play tricks on him. Peripherals became a means of insanity and his brain became his own enemy.

Danny groggily walked back to the outdoor area of the base in search of his friends. The bodies caught him off guard as if he'd seen them for the first time, and his stomach responded. Pressed down with fatigue, Danny dropped to his knees and vomited on the ground.

As he felt his stomach churn, the thoughts of his purpose began to overwhelm his mind. What was he doing with his time? Each day consisted only of running errands for a paranoid and power-hungry commander while the nation bled. The very reason that they'd decided to abandon the common way of life was evident even in the revolution. It seemed that they were facing a battle against human nature, a battle they could never win.

"Danny?" he could hear his friends calling to him. "Are you alright?" He attempted to stand, but the lack of energy allowed the ground to tighten its grip on his body.

Champ came around to Danny's front. "Danny!" Champ yelled into Danny's weakened ears. "What happened?"

Danny fought to force the paragraphs from his mouth, to let it all flood out of him, but all he could muster was, "I'm okay." It was a lie that his weakened spirit had produced. He didn't have the power to portray the thoughts and emotions pouring through him.

"Come on," Champ said. "We're getting you to the doctor."

His endurance kicked the words from his mouth. “No, I’ll be fine,” Danny said. He looked towards the truck that was being loaded with weapons. The crates seemed to weigh a limitless amount as the soldiers struggled to push them into the back of the truck. “We need to go to Boston tonight,” Danny said.

“What are you talking about?” Rob asked. “We just did all of this and he wants us to go to Boston? Why?”

Danny’s insanity began to get the best of him. “To arm the nation,” he said with a sickening grin.

The group eyed Danny for a while. “Are you sure you’re okay?” Amanda asked. “You don’t have to go, we can do it.”

“No,” Danny said. “I want to go. I want to get out of this hell and just be home. I need to get them the guns so we can be done with this.”

“What do you mean, Danny?” Adam asked.

“When we kill what soldiers are left in Boston, we’ll be free,” Danny said.

Nobody could muster any words that could possibly be used as a rebuttal to the madness that Danny was speaking. “Well then fuck it, let’s go,” Champ said with an exhausted shout. Amanda shot him a worried look. She could tell that something was severely wrong with Danny, but Danny seemed completely content with going on the mission.

“Well then let’s go,” Danny said. “I’ll throw the guns.”

“Yeah, it’s probably best if someone else drives,” Champ said. “Well then I guess I’ll drive.”

“What should we do?” Adam asked.

“You guys don’t have to go,” Champ said. “We’ll see you when you get there.”

“I want to go,” Amanda said.

Adam turned to her with as much worry as she’d had for Danny. “It’s too dangerous,” he said. “We’ll go tomorrow when there are other soldiers there to make sure nothing goes wrong."

Amanda didn't dignify Adam's suggestion with a response. She simply began walking her way to the truck as quickly as she could. Champ reasoned Adam to attempt to alleviate the worry. "We'll be careful and make sure she's safe," Champ said. Even though his words presented a visage of security, Champ was as worried as Adam was, but it would be better if someone else was there to offer conversation than to drive a truck full of weapons with a mind full of paranoia.

Champ shook Rob and Adam's hands and made his way towards the truck. Danny followed with a stagger of fatigue. Once they made it to the truck, Danny plopped into the back and began to shut the back door. Champ stopped him. "Danny," Champ said. Danny's weary eyes looked towards his uncle. "If anything goes wrong, keep that door shut." Danny smiled, nodded, and followed his response with a closing of the door. Champ shook his head and got into the truck. They pulled away with the cheers of the soldiers behind them.

"What do you think is wrong with Danny?" Amanda asked as they went down the road. The midnight moon was nowhere to be seen. The headlights and the dimly lit radio that had no stations to play were the only sources of light for miles.

Champ watched the road as he juggled the possibilities in his mind. "He's just changed I think," Champ said. "Hopefully some sleep will help him out." Champ had taken up smoking since the death of his brother and for the beginning portion of the ride, all he did was smoke cigarette after cigarette, no amount of nicotine relieving the stress.

Every turn seemed like it would lead to a checkpoint and every long road gave the feeling of someone watching them. Amanda attempted to get some sleep, but her own concerns combined with the constant cigarette smoke denied her any comfort.

The back of the truck was entirely too dark for Danny's mind to handle. He tried with every bit of his might to keep himself awake for the mission, even though the blanket of darkness was rocking him to sleep. As he drifted in and out of sleep, his fatigue-caused hallucinations were getting worse.

As his eyes shot back and forth, scanning the darkness for anything recognizable, the boxes around him began to morph into demonic beings. His fear of the unknown was manifesting itself in the blinding dark. The back of a truck became his prison, and his mind became the warden.

"Just give up, Danny," Danny heard over and over in that familiar voice that had haunted him.

"You're dead," Danny said. "Leave me alone."

His head bobbed as he fought his own body's signals telling him to let it rest. The voices continued, and did nothing but amplify as his insanity grew. "So are you, Danny," the voice rang out. "Boston will burn, and so will everything you've loved and fought so hard for. How sad."

Danny flung his fists through the air, connecting with nothing but wooden crates filled with weapons and the empty air around him. He fought what he couldn't see, but what his mind told him was there. As he fought, he heard explosions from outside.

"What the hell was that?" Champ yelled. His and Amanda's eyes turned to the outskirts of Boston. The sky was lighting up with fire as if the world itself was coming to an end. Clouds of black smoke shed through the moonlight as mortars fired shot after shot at the border on the side of Boston that neither Champ nor Amanda could see. To them, it seemed that the city was being bombed, and, due to the lack of communication between them and the other rebels, it became very real to them.

"We need to hurry!" Amanda said.

"What the hell are you talking about?" Champ questioned. "We're not going in there!"

Amanda fought tooth and nail. "We need to help them," she said.

"We'll only have a bomb dropped on us if we go in there."

Danny heard them from the back and yelled, "Let's get in there!" Champ's head shot towards the back. He wasn't sure how Danny's voice had penetrated the cabin, but the shock of it only drove him faster in his current path. There seemed to be no further questioning of what their next move should be, only forward.

Danny sat in the back and laughed at his utter insanity. He opened the back door to the truck and prepared himself to throw box after box out of the back. The lights from the streets of Boston shed light on Danny's prison and allowed him to regain most of his sanity. The wind produced from the barreling death machine was a refreshing one.

As the lights became more and more frequent, Danny could tell that they were approaching their first neighborhood. There were no soldiers in sight, but the sound of explosions from the mortars became deafening, despite the distance between the truck and the bombs' targets.

With the hands of a delirious soldier, Danny lifted a crowbar from the ground and began opening boxes to prepare them for drop off. Each was filled with something even more devious than the one before. Assault rifles, light machine guns, submachine guns, and even the occasional launcher of explosive ordinances shimmered in the dim light of the night. Danny's fatigue seemed to disappear as he opened Boston's presents.

They approached the first house. It was a small one that seemed untouched by the revolution, but the people outside seemed to have taken the damage that the house had withstood. Their eyes drooped and their mouths couldn't muster the strength to close. They looked at Danny in fear as the truck pulled up in front of the home. The family came together for protection, until Danny pushed the first box out of the vehicle.

The father of the family approached the box and looked inside. His eyes glistened as he looked up at Danny. The man reached in and pulled out an assault rifle. He loaded it in order to make sure that it wasn't a trick, but as he pulled the trigger and a shot rang out, he came to the realization that help had indeed arrived.

The man held his gun high and cheered. The ones that had stayed indoors made their way outside and those that had been listening to the destruction down the street gathered around the truck.

Danny threw box after box out of the vehicle as if he was the ice cream man throwing free treats to the neighborhood kids. As more and more guns made their way out to the public, their hopes rose and they cheered in the streets. Some got into their vehicles and prepared themselves behind the truck. The motivated voices were louder than the bombs down the street, which filled the community with the endurance they'd need to fight on.

The truck started again and the vehicles filled with excited citizens followed, providing an escort for the truck. As they moved from neighborhood to neighborhood, their presence began to become predictable. The occupants of homes throughout Boston waited in excitement outside of their homes until they'd get there chance to arm themselves. This would've seemed like an inspirational sight, but they weren't the only ones predicting the truck's arrival.

It wasn't long until the military forces occupying the city began to take notice. The occasional loyalist would be shot down by the entourage of destructive might as they attempted to stop the mission. It became a worry when one soldier began to turn into two, then three, then a vehicle filled with loyalists. Champ sped down the road in attempt to beat the loyalists to the next destination, but it was clear that they were way in over their heads.

As they drove up to a neighborhood in downtown Boston, the road and the houses on the street were completely empty. No one came out to greet the truck, not one soul. Champ continued on, attempting to figure out if they were in the right place. Before he could stop at the sight of it, a spike strip shredded the tires of the truck.

They swerved across the road and as Champ attempted to adjust his course, the truck flipped onto its side. Danny flew across the back of the truck with the boxes that surrounded him. He hit the wall with a hard thump. Before being able to regain his composure, Danny saw the boxes filled with weapons flying towards him as gravity forced them to Danny's side.

Danny did the only thing that would save his life: he jumped from the truck. As his body fell through the air, the logic behind his plan became a large question in his mind. He braced himself and hit the ground hard. His body tumbled another five yards until it came to a halt.

In the chaos, the vehicles behind the truck swerved and stopped in an attempt to avoid a crash themselves. Danny looked up from the ground and saw a convoy of about twenty cars waiting behind them, their drivers and passengers jumping out to check on Danny.

With the adrenaline pumping, Danny shot up and ran to the truck. He grabbed an assault rifle and loaded it. Surprisingly, his body felt fine. The combination of adrenaline and his bulletproof vest had saved his life.

Champ and Amanda soon joined the rest of the crowd outside of the truck. They were seemingly unharmed as well so the group's concern turned towards the spike strip. It didn't take long for them to figure out that something was horribly wrong. "Get inside!" a voice yelled from the convoy.

Like lightning, the group fled towards the houses in the neighborhood. If the front door didn't open, someone kicked it down and took refuge inside. Danny, Champ and Amanda were one of the fortunate ones that found an unlocked door. They ran inside with a few other people and took positions around the windows. The sound of glass shattering filled the neighborhood as the rest of the group followed suit.

Those inside peered out of the windows at the rooftops, the cars, and the other houses around them. There were still some people outside that were either looking for a house to take shelter in or were defending the vehicles.

Danny's eyes watched the citizens outside holding their weapons high as they awaited what would happen next. For the longest time, it was nothing. There was no noise other than the bombs that had become distant and the sound of the occasional car that would pass the parked vehicles.

They scanned their entire line of sight as if they were looking for a small detail that seemed out of place in an area that was unknown to them. The time they waited seemed like an eternity. As they waited for their doom to come, some began to believe that the strip might have been a random act, until those that didn't take refuge inside began to drop like flies.

The rooftops filled with loyalists and military vehicles took positions at the ends of the neighborhood. Soldiers poured from every direction and began to open fire on the houses. Danny dropped to the floor and covered his head as bullets ripped through their house. Amanda's fear got the best of her and she ran as rapidly as she could towards the back of the house.

"We're under attack!" Champ yelled into his radio. He yelled it countless times until some sort of a response was heard.

"We're attacking now then," a voice said on the radio. It was such a simple statement, but it put a load of anxiety on their shoulders. Who knew when they would actually arrive in Boston? How long did it take them? Danny had no clue and the fear in him began to rise.

At some point, the shots seemed to stop and the rebels took their opportunity. Barrels of rifles pointed out of the windows and shot everything they had towards the loyalists. Many dropped from the rooftops due to their lack of expectations and cover, but only a few fell near the ends of the neighborhood.

The inexperience of the citizens was becoming their biggest downfall. While the loyalists' shots were precise and deadly, the shots of the citizens were only hitting because the numerous boxes of ammunition had allowed them to fire as many times as they pleased.

The reality of the situation became evident as the house next to Danny's burst into flames after a misguided missile blew the house and its occupants into the area that had surrounded it. Danny watched in horror as men and women alike ran from the house immersed in flames. Without mercy, the loyalists on the roof opened fire and took the opportunity to gain a significant upper hand.

The battle raged on. The targets were becoming so overwhelming that Danny hardly had an idea of what to shoot. Shots seemed to come from nowhere, yet the enemies were everywhere. His head flew from left to right and so did the shots from his rifle. Any experience that he'd had went out of the window along with the inaccurate shots from his rifle.

The only advantage that the rebels had were the houses that were keeping them mildly protected. Surprisingly, however, supplies were beginning to run thin. The truck was in the middle of the road and the citizens were running out of ammunition. As they approached their last clips, the rebels began to think that the effort was hopeless.

"We need more ammo," Champ said as he shot a loyalist off of the roof across from them.

Danny emptied his clip towards the loyalist vehicle down the street and sent the soldiers scattering for cover. "I know," he said. "But the truck's in the middle of the road."

"Well it's either we wait to die or we die trying to live on," Champ said. "And right now, I'm too tired of this bullshit to give a damn about what might happen." Champ stood up and ran towards the door of the house.

"What the hell are you doing?" Danny yelled across the room.

"I'm making sure we don't fucking die," Champ said. He flew from the house and with the speed of an Olympic athlete, the beer-bellied uncle ran to the truck. He leapt into the back and took cover. The loyalists were now focusing their fire on the truck, attempting to ensure that Champ wouldn't get any ammunition out of there.

Danny's head fixed onto the rooftops. There were soldiers readying some sort of missile launcher that they were aiming at the truck. If they couldn't get it back, they were ready to destroy it. Danny's gun aimed at the rooftop and fired, but his nerves threw off his aim. He shot again and again, but his frustration only grew. After a clip was emptied in their direction, the loyalists were ready to fire at the truck.

Bullets ripped through the top of the truck, but not in the same direction as they had before. The bullets were actually coming out of the truck at a very rapid speed. They spread along the rooftops and the streets. Even the rebels had to take cover to avoid the gunfire.

Soldiers along the rooftop dropped in order to dodge the shots. Those that didn't were quickly mowed down.

Thankfully, that included the ones that were attempting to shoot a missile at the truck.

Champ peeked out of the back of the truck, his light machine gun still firing rapidly into the loyalist's direction. "Grab some ammo!" he yelled to the rebels. The group hesitated, but when they realized that most of the loyalists were dead, they ran to the truck and loaded up.

Danny came out of the house slowly and looked everywhere for any remaining loyalist soldiers. As he watched the rest of the soldiers get pushed back because of the rebels, he lowered his gun and let out a sigh of relief. The battle seemed to be over.

"Well should we get going?" Danny asked as he grabbed a few clips from the truck.

Champ was attempting to figure out how to reload his gun. "Oh, yeah," he said. "Let me get this thing figured out real quick." Danny surveyed the area, looking for any sign of a loyalist soldier. He constantly checked the rooftops as if he was playing peek-a-boo with the enemy.

There didn't seem to be anyone else to oppose them, but it was much too difficult to actually believe it. Gunfire was erupting in the streets around them, signaling that the loyalists had come back to town. Though the gunfire was distant, Danny continuously convinced himself that they weren't safe.

"Danny," Champ said from the truck. "Do you feel that?" Danny stopped his pacing and stood still. The rest of the rebels followed in his motion. They stood in the middle of the neighborhood street, surrounded by their vehicles and empty shell casings.

As he stood completely motionless, Danny began to feel a rumbling in the earth beneath him. It felt almost as if an earthquake was on its way to their very spot. There was something very wrong.

“Get the hell inside!” Champ yelled from the truck. The rebels sprinted towards the houses once again. Danny ran towards the door of the house he’d been in, but stopped himself as he went through what he’d just seen. He remembered the soldiers on the roof dropping as they were shot while taking aim at the truck, but where did their weapon go?

Danny ran back towards the truck and saw the destructive weapon that the loyalists had tried to use. He ran to it and grabbed it. It seemed to have weighed a ton, but the adrenaline allowed him to lift it for that moment. “Danny, what the hell are you doing?” Champ yelled from the house.

There wasn’t much urgency in Danny’s mind, it must have been from exhaustion. He tried to jog while carrying the heavy device, but it was a burden. The rumbling was right on top of them, and he was still about twenty yards from the house. As he turned to check his surroundings, he saw what had caused the quake.

Urgency finally came back and Danny ran for his life as a loyalist tank pulled onto the road. Champ could only watch on as Danny tried with every bit of life he had to get back to the house. His feet picked up speed and Danny threw the weapon through the window of his shelter. Danny’s body came jumping through soon after.

The shock held Danny on the floor. There was a death machine outside, but all he could think to do was stay glued to the floor and think about what else he could possibly do. He turned his head to the weapon next to him. The weapon was covered in a variety of different triggers and buttons, too many for Danny to figure out. However, it was still loaded, and would help immensely in the fight.

Champ jumped onto the floor next to Danny from his place at the window. Amanda had begun to come back to the front of the house, but she quickly ran back. It caught

Danny by surprise and he tried to get up quickly, only to be forced back down by his uncle.

Shots from the tank's machine gun ripped through the buildings alongside them. It sprayed bullet after bullet in a sweeping motion across the houses. Danny watched as light began to shimmer through the holes formed in the walls and dust spread through the air. The shots were only inches above him and each pierced the wall behind him.

This continued for what felt like hours. The same sweep of bullets performed over and over by someone that was looking only to kill whatever was waiting in the neighborhood. Then the shots stopped.

Danny looked at his uncle. They shared the same white complexion that the fear had given them. Danny began to get up once again, but an explosion in a nearby house quickly suppressed his hope for survival. The tank was now firing rockets at the houses in an attempt to finish off what the bullets failed to kill.

It was only a matter of time before a rocket crashed through the exterior wall of the house and destroyed everything that had been protecting them. Danny picked up the launcher, but could only look at it in wonder. "How the hell do I use this thing?" Danny yelled in frustration.

Champ attempted to solve the problem, but only had a similar reaction. "I don't even know what the fuck this is," he said. Danny lifted it and pointed it out of the window in hopes that he could figure it out in time.

As he pushed at the different switches and triggers, Danny could only watch as the barrel of the tank's main weapon moved towards his shelter. He frantically attempted to pull the triggers, but nothing was produced other than more fear.

"Run, dumbass!" Champ yelled as he grabbed Danny from the window. Danny stumbled to his feet and ran to the other end of the house. Champ ripped a door open and ran inside with Danny and Amanda following close behind. It was just somebody's old bathroom, but today, it had to be a bomb shelter.

They jumped towards the tub and hunched down just as they heard the tank fire. Danny could hear the distinct sound of the boards on the exterior wall crushing in as the rocket entered and exploded.

When Danny opened his eyes, he had no idea if he was dead or alive. All he could see was the blackest darkness that he'd ever seen. He couldn't breathe, smell, or even hear. The situation was terrifying, yet surprisingly peaceful. If this was death, Danny certainly didn't mind the vacation.

He watched as the darkness remained and his senses continued to fail him. A smile made itself visible on Danny's face, and he could do nothing but laugh. After all of the chaos that he'd been through, he just hoped that this was the end of it. He hoped that the missile had come through the wall and killed him off. He no longer cared about the world, he just wanted to finally have peace.

Then the light began to shone through the darkness. Danny could see the thick cloud of smoke beginning to clear. His eyes adjusted and immediately searched the room for clues to what had just taken place. He looked to his side and saw his uncle struggling to stand and Amanda lying in the bathtub coughing. The walls that had encased the bathroom were almost completely gone. If Danny hadn't known better, he would've assumed that they were in the aftermath of a tornado.

Champ pulled Danny to his feet. "Not dying today," his uncle said calmly with a smile. It seemed that the insanity had spread to him as well.

"Just let me stay," Danny's mind forced out of his mouth.

His uncle stared at him as he continued to try and lift Danny. Danny's eyes met his uncles and he saw the ecstatic look that he hadn't seen in Champ for the longest time. "And let you miss the party?" Champ asked.

"What the hell are you talking about?" Danny asked.

Champ laughed. "Why don't you get up and look to the road?" he said. Danny's interest forced him to his feet and his eyes peered over the wall that had once stood between him and the road. What he saw, he simply couldn't believe.

The tank was covered in rebel soldiers. One forced the hatch open and crawled inside. The others cheered him on from outside of it and attempted to look inside to watch the action. Some of the soldiers leaned in and helped to lift the loyalist soldier from the tank. Danny could see the fear on the soldier's face, but was happy that he would probably be dead soon.

He and his uncle approached the tank and gathered in the screaming crowd of reinforcements. The loyalist soldier laid in the middle of the group, being kicked and punched mercilessly. Danny looked at his surroundings and didn't have any recognition of them. The buildings that the rebels had taken refuge in were demolished and in them laid the bodies of many that had tried to join the rebellion. This brought a new kind of rage into Danny's soul that he couldn't remember ever feeling before.

Danny pushed through the crowd to the center to see the scum that had killed the innocent civilians. As he made it to the soldier, the other rebels backed off and began cheering Danny on. It was clear that they wanted blood, and Danny was the one that would be delivering it.

The loyalist soldier looked up at Danny with the most fear-stricken eyes that Danny had ever seen. The soldier was no more than eighteen and seemed to have never seen a battle in his life. His uniform was clean and bare. No medals or patches signifying that he'd made any sort of progress in any branch of the military were visible on his clothing.

Danny looked down on the kid with pity. This little punk had single-handedly killed more of the rebels than any other soldier had that day. However, this kid was no soldier at all. He was just another brainwashed child that had been forced into doing something he didn't want to do because of his fear of the government. He was just another sheep in the herd, and only when he was moments from death did he feel the need to show any sort of remorse.

"Please, don't kill me," he told Danny.

Danny couldn't help but laugh. The times of war had driven him to feel no sense of emotion when it came to the enemy. Though he was just a kid, he was a loyalist. "Why?" Danny asked him in a condescending tone.

The kid broke down into tears. His face was one of a broken soul, but his eyes were those of a coward. Danny could read into him easily. This kid wanted to get the hell out and then simply rejoin the fight against the rebels. He was out to get Danny, and Danny had no plans of letting that happen.

"Please, I have family in Boston," the kid said. "I just want to go home. I was forced to fight or die. Please, you've got to believe me, I'll just go home or I'll even help you! I'll help you to kill all of the people that you want! I'll do anything, just don't kill me."

Danny's amusement was criminal. He was frustrated, tired, and utterly insane. He reached out and grabbed a pistol from the hands of a nearby rebel and pointed it at the kid's face. He knelt down next to the crying soldier. "You want to go home?" Danny asked. The kid could only nod. "You kill all of these citizens, cause all of this destruction, and you want to go home?"

"Please, I didn't . . . " the soldier began.

Danny delivered a bullet to both of the kid's knees. The loyalist soldier screamed in pain. It was a scream that seemed to have been louder than the gunshots themselves. Danny stood up and returned the gun to the rebel soldier. The crowd had backed up from the sound of the shot. Danny looked at the loyalist with the most dastardly expression he could muster. "Walk home, you piece of shit," Danny said.

Danny walked away from the crowd and to the truck. Champ came running from behind him. "Danny!" he yelled. "Where the hell are you going?"

Danny turned around. "Well, we're all here," he said. "I say we go to city hall and let them know that we're taking over." The soldiers nearby cheered at the news and began boarding the vehicles throughout the street to join. Champ shook his head and got into the driver's seat of a nearby truck and the shocked Amanda that had just gotten herself out of the wreckage joined him in the front. Danny took his place in the back of the truck and they started their journey to city hall.

Fighting continued throughout the city. As the convoy reached different blocks of the city, they saw either rebel soldiers celebrating a victory, or a small battle that was quickly finished. By the time the sun was fully in the sky, every inch of Boston had been taken back and rebel soldiers were stationed throughout the city, awaiting news of an official victory.

Danny watched from the back of the truck as they passed the homes of celebrating soldiers and mourning families. Every street began to look the same. Some buildings were demolished, and yet others looked spotless. Every street had a family that had lost someone in the fight and they mourned silently as the rest of the city celebrated.

The thought of going into city hall and taking power was exciting Danny. The issue of who would take power over Boston would be figured out later in the day. The road flew from under the truck and more vehicles joined the convoy. At the rate that things were going, the convoy had a full parade by the time they reached city hall.

Danny and the rest of the rebels dismounted and walked up the stairs of city hall. Each step seemed to be even more effortless than the last. The hard part of the battle was over, now it was time to make things official.

Champ pushed the doors to the building open and the rebels poured in with their weapons drawn. Those inside that had heard the fighting throughout the night and saw it throughout their commute to work that day didn't seem at all surprised by this sight. Each of them stood to the side with their hands raised in the air.

Power filled Danny's soul. He felt as if he ruled the world in this very moment. They made their way up the stairs, right to the mayor's office. Danny passed the secretary with his uncle and shot her a wink, just out of spite.

The doors to the mayor's office opened and the rebels walked in. The room filled with about twenty rebels and hundreds more piling into other parts of the building. Danny stood at the front with his uncle and looked at the mayor.

The mayor seemed saddened, but fearless. Danny could tell that the mayor didn't fear for his life, he seemed much too content for that. He even gave Danny a smile as he had watched them approach.

Danny looked down at the mayor, who was sitting at his desk waiting to hear what Danny had to say. "Mr. Mayor, we're taking our city back," Danny said. The rebels behind him cheered him on and the mayor simply nodded and stood out of his seat. He walked around the desk and shook Danny's hand.

The mayor was aged and let a smile enter his wrinkled face. "Then I suppose I resign," he said. The crowd erupted in cheering as the mayor made his way out of the office.

The news spread through Boston like a wildfire. The entire city celebrated their victory. For the first time since the war had started, they finally had the power to keep their city safe, and to keep it theirs.

CHAPTER TWENTY-TWO

COLLATERAL DAMAGE

"This is Mike from Revolutionary Radio, broadcasting to you from the birthplace of both American Revolutions, Boston. If you're just joining us, that means that you've had enough of your government and you've joined the revolution! Congrats!

"Anyways, time for some news. Seattle, Olympia, Houston, Hollywood, and Baltimore have all been officially taken by the citizens that live there. With these new additions, that makes a total of three hundred and thirty-nine total cities and towns that have seceded from the United States.

"Also very big news, in the wake of recent events, thirteen more senators and twenty-six representatives have stepped down from their positions in the U.S. government to return home to their families. It's rumored that more public officials will be stepping down as the revolution spreads across the nation.

"From the only radio station not silenced by fear of prosecution, I'm Mike. Stand your ground."

It had been a month since the taking of Boston by the rebels and things were finally starting to feel normal. After less than a week of living under their own conditions, the citizens of Boston elected a committee to keep the city running while the revolution continued. Champ had even been elected as the city's temporary mayor.

As mayor, Champ and his advisors had managed to keep the energy flowing through Boston constantly and without interruption through communications with the power plant just outside of the city. The water flowing through the faucets of the city's homes had dipped in quality for a while, but with the rebels spreading across Massachusetts, they acquired the water treatment plants around Massachusetts and began drawing the chemicals from the water and Boston's water has never been cleaner. Massachusetts had become a safe haven for rebels across the nation and they worked together to keep the state afloat during the revolution, making it the capital of the rebel-controlled portion of the United States.

O'Connor and his men continued leading assaults on federal buildings and cities across the east coast, helping to push the revolution forward. Included in their tales of victory were the battles for New Jersey, Ohio, and their largest success: New York. No one was quite sure where O'Connor was due to his increased secrecy, but he was leading a flawless revolutionary effort. At times, his methods seemed to be too extreme, but the end result was always enough to alleviate the criticism.

Mike had taken the job as the main host on Revolutionary Radio and was running the channel with enthusiasm. His show spanned all the way from his station in Boston to the west coast and even parts of Europe and South America. He'd become a symbol of the revolution all over the nation and he encouraged many citizens to rise up. With his name topping the FBI's most wanted list, some rumored that he'd end up leading the new nation when the revolution ended.

Rob and Adam received homes in Boston for their heroism in missions of the revolution. They continued to assist the revolution in any way that they could, but most of their time was spent making sure that the city of Boston stayed afloat.

Rob commanded Boston's security force which held off any loyalist attempts to retake the city and kept crime within the city to an all-time low. The laws of the land focused on equality for all citizens and a cut down on major crimes such as assault and murder, rather than the previous laws which had been used to stop small crimes rather than the ones that mattered. With the citizens having little to no fear for their lives, Boston's people were able to focus on helping the nation.

In the midst of the revolution, thousands of companies cut business with federal companies and with areas that hadn't been taken back in the revolution in general. Those still loyal to the United States government struggled to keep services and goods flowing through the loyalist cities with the loss of large companies' support. They were in a major recession and put rebel hostages to work in order to maintain their remaining stability.

Throughout the world, citizens from all countries were cheering on those participating in the American revolution. Nations showed their support by sending donations, adding up to millions of dollars to the rebel army and the new nation. The internet buzzed with news of the revolution and the news stations of the world were in a constant chatter of revolution.

The loyalist armies were falling back towards Washington D.C., which was the only strongly fortified part of the loyalist United States left. From a distance, people could see tons of military hardware taking stations at the edge of the city in order to keep the city safe. Those that were able to get inside and make it out with their lives told stories of military forces on every street, the continuing abduction of rebels, and the construction of bunkers throughout the city.

What has Danny been doing? He'd moved to a nice house in Boston with his mom and Amanda. His mom, Marisa, had found a job with the newly-established Boston government as a financial advisor. She helped to ensure that Boston would have enough money to support itself and advised officials on trades with other rebel territories.

Amanda had been taking care of Danny for the most part, and keeping the flow of information from other rebel territories passing on to the radio station. She'd taken a liking to Danny, even though his condition had worsened.

Every night, Danny would have the same nightmare. He'd see the same old house, the same demonic figures, and even Brad. His nights were haunted with memories and hallucinations. Every morning, he would awaken as fatigued as the day before, and every night, he feared the moment that his eyes would close.

With his condition the way it was, Danny no longer played a large part in the revolution. He would occasionally offer advice to Champ or speak to citizens via Revolutionary Radio, but other than that, he was alone.

Marisa was spending a lot of her time at work, and the rest of her time doing paperwork. She had attempted to reconnect with her son, but every effort she made was met with failure and catastrophe. Any attempts to talk to her son always ended in him breaking down or speaking nonsense.

Amanda had become the closest person to Danny, but his insanity had pushed her away. She listened to his mad ramblings every night before she had to leave him to his thoughts. Every night that she left, a part of her died inside as she'd watch Danny beg her to keep him company. He feared himself in a way that nobody could ever imagine.

The nation as a whole had been in utter chaos for almost a year, but it was all coming to a close. Sixty-four percent of the nation had been taken by the rebel forces and they were moving in on D.C. quickly according to the radio report that Danny had listened to that morning.

As Danny ate his cereal with baggy eyes, his mom organized papers on the couch as they both listened to the radio. "So how did you sleep?" Marisa asked her son.

Danny turned from his spot at the table and glared at her. "Not well," he told her as he returned to his cereal.

Marisa let out a sigh as she stuffed the papers into her suitcase. "Are you sure you don't want to see a doctor?" she asked. "I guarantee they can do something for you and they might even be able to stop your nightmares."

"I'm not going to a therapist," Danny told her.

Marisa closed her suitcase and took a place at the table next to her son. She made an attempt to rub the side of his head, but he flinched at her motion. "Please, Danny," she said. "I just want to see you be happy again. I want the bundle of joy that would always brighten my day to come back." Marisa stopped and looked for some sort of reaction from Danny, but got nothing. "I just want you to be happy."

Danny stopped eating and looked at his mom. "You know it's not that simple," Danny said.

"I know, Danny," Marisa said. "But they can help you to get better."

"I know you seem to like the idea of it, mom, but I'm not a fucking psychopath," Danny said. "My thoughts are organized and my actions have been very precise. I don't act outside of what the conditions of my life have foreshadowed. If this is to be my conclusion then so be it."

Marisa sat in shock. "Your conclusion?" she asked. "Listen to yourself. This isn't okay, Danny."

"If it's not okay then maybe I should have left you in that fucking prison," Danny said.

His mom couldn't react. She simply grabbed her suitcase and left the house. Danny sat in his seat and continued to eat his cereal without a concern in the world. He looked around the room and relaxed in the feeling of everything watching him. His insanity had become his home.

"What a child you've turned out to be," Brad told him. Danny simply laughed and continued his meal.

The front door to his house opened and Danny figured it was just another hallucination. He chomped away at his cereal and listened to the voices arguing in his head. "Danny?" a voice said.

"Yup I'm here," Danny said. "Nice to meet you."

Adam walked in front of him. "Danny?" he said. "It's me."

Danny's mind reset and his eyes widened. "Oh, hey, man," he said.

Adam smiled. "How have you been?" he said. Then Champ and Rob walked in behind him. "I hope you don't mind I brought the guys."

Danny looked at them and smiled. Their expressions were similar, but seemed much more concerned. "Hey, guys," Danny said.

They nodded and said their greetings. "So we've got some news, Danny," Adam said.

After gulping down his milk, Danny asked, "What's up?"

"Do you want to explain, Champ?" Adam asked.

"Sure," Champ said. "Well, the rebels are gathering in Annapolis, Maryland to prepare for the final battle at Washington D.C."

"It's about time," Danny said with a laugh.

The group chuckled, but returned to their worried expressions. "Well, we were wondering if you'd like to join us," Adam said. "We're heading down there later today."

"So what do yah' say? Ready to finish what we started?" Champ asked.

Danny laughed. "Of course I am," he said.

"Well then let's have ourselves a drink!" Champ said.

The group opened the fridge in Danny's house. It was filled with the alcohol that Danny's mom had become connected to. They each grabbed a beer and had a toast. "Here's to the group getting back together to fuck shit up once again!" Champ laughed. Their cans clinked together and they drank the intoxicating liquid.

It wasn't long before they had all reached a high blood alcohol level and found themselves sinking further and further into their seats. "So what have you been doing, Danny?" Rob asked.

"Not much," Danny said. "Just been chillin' and doing whatever."

Rob nodded. "So . . .what does that mean?" he nervously chuckled.

Danny's head nodded back from it's own weight as he laughed. "Well, you know," he said. "I've just been thinking a lot and sometimes I like to go to the radio station and talk a little bit. It's fun I guess, but I miss all of the action."

"I hear yah'," Champ said.

Rob remained serious. "But can't you enjoy the peace now that things are almost over?" Rob said.

Danny laughed. "It'll never be over, Rob," he said.

"Can we please not go into this again, Danny," Rob said.

"Just let the kid talk," Adam said. "It's not worth it."

"No," Rob said. "We can't just keep encouraging this."

"Is there something wrong with the truth, big man?" Danny asked.

Rob was getting visibly angrier. "No, but there's a problem with constantly believing that nothing's going to get better," Rob said. "Every time we come over here, you find some way to start talking about how only more and more corrupt people are going to take power, but I don't think that you take into account that we did all of this to avoid that. We're going to be much more careful this time around. So why can't you just have faith?"

Danny smirked. "I'm sure that the founding fathers told themselves that too," he said.

"You're fucking ridiculous," Rob said as he stood to leave.

"Rob, come on," Adam said. "Just come have another beer."

"Or should I get you a wine cooler?" Danny joked. Rob continued out the door and Champ followed to talk to him.

Adam looked at the very amused Danny with a disappointed gaze. "Danny, what happened?" he asked.

"What are you talking about?" Danny asked.

Adam shook his head. "I don't know," he said. "I just feel like you've changed since the beginning of all of this. Right around the time that we got you out of that prison, I noticed that you've been acting odder with every day. It really came out when you were at that military base. I'm just worried about you, man. I just want to know if you're really okay."

Danny nodded. "Adam, I'm fine," he said as he took another sip from his beer. "I might be a bit drunk right now, but I've got my head straight. I just think a lot. Is that such a bad thing?"

"I guess not," Adam said. "But do you think that maybe you think too much?"

"There's no such thing," Danny said.

"There is when you're making connections that aren't there and you're only thinking of places where things could go wrong rather than thinking of ways to improve the world around you."

Danny pondered that thought for a moment. He let it run through all of the areas of his brain before he responded, "I don't need to think of ways to better the world, because I already know how it'll get better."

Adam decided to entertain this idea. "How's it going to get better, Danny?"

"I don't sleep, Adam," Danny said. "My connection with the world has allowed me to figure it out, but you'll have to simply wait and see."

Rob and Champ walked back into the house as Adam could think only of what Danny could have meant. Rob sat back in his chair and began sipping his beer again. "I'm sorry I stormed out," Rob said. "I just worry about you, Danny, and I guess I should let you think what you want to think, regardless of how I feel about it."

Danny smiled. "Thank you, Rob," he said. "And I promise I'll keep thinking." Danny laughed while the rest of the room remained silent. Danny wasn't even able to register the awkward feeling that the room had been given.

"So are you pumped, Danny?" Champ asked.

"Of course I am," Danny said. "Things are finally going to come to an end." He took another sip of his beer as Champ had himself another nervous chuckle.

"Well we already told your mom about all of this," Champ said. "So I guess we'll just swing by there on our way to D.C. and let you say 'bye' or whatever you want to tell her."

"Sounds good to me," Danny said. "Can we stop by the radio station to pick up Amanda too?"

Adam sighed. "I don't think Amanda's going to be able to join us, Danny," he said. "That's another reason we came here."

Danny put his beer down. "What are you talking about?" Danny asked.

Champ looked at Adam, and then to Danny. "She committed suicide, Danny," Adam said.

Danny stared at the table in silence. He let the thought run it's course through him. His stomach dropped at the words, but not at the news. "Well," Danny started slowly. "Then I guess we should just get to D.C."

Champ was saddened by Danny's silence, but offered nothing more than a casual, "I'm sorry, Danny," as they left the house.

The car waiting for them outside looked pretty expensive. It was like something that a celebrity would be seen driving.

"Where'd you get the car?" Danny asked Adam.

"Oh, I got it from a dealership nearby," Adam answered nervously.

Danny saw right through it. "You stole it didn't you?" Danny asked.

Adam's nerves began to get the best of him. "No, I didn't have to pay for it though," Adam said.

"Because you stole it," Danny said.

Adam was starting to get as tense as Rob had been. "Dammit, Danny," Adam said. "It's not stealing if nobody owns the lot."

Danny laughed. "Because we led a revolution for free cars," he said.

Adam almost responded, but Champ stopped him. They could all see the change in Danny. He'd become much more bitter than ever before, and he called them out on everything they did. They just hoped that he wouldn't talk the entire ride.

City hall wasn't too far from Danny's new house. They only drove for around five minutes or so. Danny got out of the car, but the rest of the group remained inside.

"Are you guys coming?" Danny asked.

Champ leaned out of his window. "We're going to go get some food," he said. "We'll pick you up some too."

Danny was confused. "You're not coming in?" he asked.

"You need to talk to her alone, Danny," Champ said. "You might never see her again."

Reality hit Danny like a ton of bricks. Through the entire revolution, he knew that he could die at any moment, but the thought of never seeing his mom again seemed so surreal. The thought of losing someone that at one point greeted him every morning wasn't something Danny had ever thought of.

Danny took the walk up the stairs of city hall slowly. He ran the thoughts of what he'd tell her through his head over and over. He'd prepared a script of a flawless farewell that would get everything said efficiently. With how he pictured the battle going, it would have to be a hell of a goodbye.

City hall's security seemed much larger than it had ever been before. A row of soldiers stood inside to pat down guests and check the bags of employees. It was clear that they didn't expect for their revolution to go unchallenged.

Danny had himself patted down and he walked inside. He approached the front and told the receptionist, "I'm looking for Ms. Bruce."

The receptionist looked around on her computer for a moment and said, "Alright, I'll tell her she has a guest."

"I can't just go to her office?" Danny asked.

The receptionist shook her head. "I'm sorry, but due to high security, nobody but employees can go to the offices," she said.

"Fine, I'll wait," Danny said. He walked back outside past the soldiers and sat on the stairs outside to wait for his mom. Since the revolution, he'd taken up smoking. It was a bad habit, but life seemed short. There was no reason for him to not do it, so he lit a cigarette on the front steps of city hall.

His mom walked out shortly after he lit the cigarette. She sat next to him and said, "So you're smoking?"

Danny shook his head. "I'm not here to talk about bullshit," he said.

His mom pulled a cigarette out of the pack next to him and lit it. "Stressful times?" she asked.

Danny was stunned to see her smoking. It was the first time he'd ever seen her do it. "Yeah," he said. "Stress."

"So what did you come here to talk about Mister All-About-Business," Marisa asked.

"I came to say goodbye," he said.

Marisa took a long drag from her cigarette. "You're going to D.C. with the rest of them?"

"Yeah," Danny said.

Marisa shook her head. "When are you going to stop?" she asked.

Danny nearly choked on his cigarette. "What?" he asked.

"When is this revolution going to be done for you?" she asked.

"Once we take D.C."

"Is that really when it's going to stop?" Marisa asked through another drag.

"What are you talking about?" Danny asked.

Marisa looked towards the road. "It just worries me that you've gotten so wrapped up in this," she said. "You know I'm proud of you, but this whole thing has changed you."

"I know, I get that a lot."

Marisa chuckled. "Did you ever think that maybe it has?" she said.

Danny thought about it. "Yeah, I've noticed a few changes," he said. "But when you lose everything you've ever loved, been thrown into a war, had to move around constantly, and generally just been physically and mentally abused, it tends to change a person." Danny took another drag. "Now I find out that Amanda killed herself because she couldn't take being my lifeline anymore and I've got all of this shit piling up on me and it's just crushing me down to nothing. I hardly sleep anymore and I just want to be done."

"Danny, you've done more for most of the people that we'll ever see again than anyone can say. It's just important that you don't act like you've lost everything you still have."

"Like what? I've put everything into this and I've gotten nothing. I went in with the intention to change the country and all I got was a fucked up head."

"You don't even realize it? You've still got people that love you, Danny. You've got an entire country that already owes you the world. Hell, I owe you the world, Danny. Without you, I wouldn't be here. How many kids can say that they saved their mom from the government?"

Danny chuckled. "I guess not many," he said.

"See? You're an amazing kid, Danny, and don't ever forget it. I know that you think you're being unappreciated and you think that doing this will make everything better, but you have to remember that you'll always have the people that love you."

Danny smoked a bit more of his cigarette. "Mom, can I tell you something honestly?" he said.

"You can tell me anything," Marisa answered.

Danny choked up. "I'm scared, mom. I'm really, really, scared."

Marisa held her child. It had been the first time in a long time, and it felt wonderful for her to hold him in his arms like she used to. "I know, I am too," she said. After another moment of comfort, she released him and they continued to talk. "You know, when you grew up, I was always so scared that I wouldn't see you in the morning. Every night, I checked on you to make sure you were still breathing, and every morning, going into your room was the first thing I would do, just to make sure you were okay."

She paused and took another drag of her cigarette. "Now you're all grown up and you're becoming the man that I always knew you'd become. You may not be perfect, but nobody is, and I just want to let you know, that I'll always support whatever you do, but all I want in this entire world is to know you're okay and that you're happy."

Marisa began to break down. "Mom," Danny said through some tears. "I know I never say it, and I know that I never show it, but I love you with every bit of my heart. I know that I mess up and worry you, but I just want you to know that you're the best mom I could have ever had. I'm sorry for what I've become, and I love you."

Danny gave his mom another hug. They held each other for what seemed like hours. Neither wanted to let go, because they knew that once that happened, it could be the last time that they ever saw the other. Danny would be going off to finish the war and both of them knew that he could be killed. All they wanted to do was be able to say that they didn't leave each other feeling as if they'd been unloved.

As they let go, both of them were visibly upset. Marisa was shaking and staring at the ground. "Well I guess I've gotta say 'goodbye,'" she said.

Danny nodded as he saw Adam's car pull back up. "I guess so," he said.

They stood up and hugged each other one last time before Danny left. "I love you so much, Danny," Marisa said.

As Danny's tears continued to fall, he said, "I love you too, mom." They pulled back and Danny pushed out the words, "Bye, mom," through the sadness.

"Bye, sweetie," Marisa said as she walked back to her building.

Danny got into the car trying to regain his composure, but saying all of that to his mom was more difficult than he would have ever been able to imagine. Champ gave him a pat on the shoulder as they started down the road. Danny knew that he'd just seen his mom for the last time.

CHAPTER TWENTY-THREE

WASHINGON D.C.

Annapolis was flooded with rebels. As Danny, Champ, Adam, and Rob drove through the streets of the crowded city, they saw nothing but soldiers preparing for battle. The stores had all been converted into places for soldiers to equip themselves or chat before going into D.C.

The streets were filled with other vehicles filled with soldiers and an abundance of military hardware. Adam occasionally yelled for someone to move as he checked the address that he'd been given. They were headed to an Annapolis bar to meet up with the rest of the soldiers that had come from Boston.

The numbers of the rebel army were staggering. It was obvious that the army of citizens was much larger than the loyalist forces that awaited them in D.C. Citizens came from all across the nation to join the fight, and they would certainly get their fill of action.

The soldiers looked more like they were already celebrating a victory, rather than preparing for the final battle. The sight of the masses of soldiers was enough to push the confidence of the soldiers to a new height. As they looked at the numbers and the weapons they possessed, it was apparent that there was no way they could fail.

Adam pulled up to the curb in front of the bar that they were in search of. "Holy hell," Champ said. Danny looked across the car towards the bar. The building had been filled to the brim with soldiers, so much so that there were soldiers spilling onto the sidewalk outside.

They got out of the vehicle and were instantly recognized by some citizens at the door. "The heroes of Boston" had become their title amongst the city's citizens. It was a title that none of them could get tired of hearing. Danny seemed to get the bulk of shocked expressions while the rest of the group were greeted with great admiration. His absence and sudden appearance had clearly caught the soldiers off guard.

As they entered the bar, a path was formed by those that had anticipated their arrival. They received handshakes and nudges as they made their way to whatever this path was leading them to. The cheers of the soldiers at the sight of their heroes became a deafening one. Those still outside gathered at the door to get a glimpse of what the commotion had been caused by.

Danny put on his bulletproof vest, along with the rest of his friends. It still fit as well as it had during the battle of Boston.

"Hello, lads," they heard come from the bar as they reached the end of their path.

The reuniting of people that couldn't stand each other, how wonderful. "O'Connor," Adam said.

"You know, Irish society says that when you are given so much by someone, you should at least have the decency to thank them before you leave," O'Connor said. "Yet, none of you have said one word to me." He had a grin that signaled that he hadn't been entertained by the group's departure from the hotel's army.

"We had other things to worry about," Adam said.

"Like taking control of the city that I had supplied for its revolution and not even mentioning me?" O'Connor said.

"Champ was voted in, O'Connor," Rob said. "Don't try to seem like Boston's hero when you didn't even have the courage to join the fight for it."

"Leaders don't do the fighting," O'Connor said. "They ready the soldiers to do it for them, and boy did you lads do a wonderful job."

"We can listen to you bitch all day, or we can get this show on the road," Champ said. "What's it going to be?"

O'Connor laughed. "My apologies," O'Connor said. "But I think you forget that I'm still the commander here."

"What do you mean?" Champ asked.

"I'm still the one leading all of the soldiers standing around you," O'Connor said. "That's right, lads, I'm your commander once again, and when this battle is finished, we'll just see who takes control."

"Well then why don't you get to telling us your ingenious plan, commander," Adam said.

"The plan that myself and the rest of the rebel leaders agreed upon consists of bombing all hell out of D.C. until they give up or we have to walk in and take it," O'Connor said. "It's simple, but it's bloody beautiful."

"Where are we going?" Champ asked.

"Our group will be on the eastern side of D.C. once the airport and pentagon are under control," O'Connor said.

"When do you think that'll be?" Rob asked.

"They've almost got the airport under control and the pentagon has already been taken," O'Connor responded. "So I'd say in about an hour. In the meantime, get yourselves ready and we'll be meeting here before attacking."

Danny's group left the bar and went back to their car. They got in and began cleaning their guns and talking about the day.

"So are you guys scared?" Rob asked.

"Of course," Adam said. "Then again, I get scared before every mission we do."

"Same here," Champ said. He looked over at Danny who was putting his gun back together. "What about you, Danny?"

Danny continued to put his gun together. "I'm fine," he said. He locked another piece in place.

"Are you scared?" Champ asked.

"Nah," Danny said.

"Are you feeling anything?"

"Not really."

Champ looked at Adam who had turned around in his seat. "What's going through your head right now?" Adam asked.

"A lot of things," Danny said. "Mostly how this day's going to go."

"How do you think it's gunna go?" Adam asked.

Danny put another piece into its place and smiled. "I think it's going to go perfectly," Danny said. "Not sure how I feel about how it'll end, but it'll be fine."

Champ was becoming concerned. "How do you think it's going to end?" he said.

Danny looked up. "Like I said, perfectly," he said.

The group steered away from conversation for the rest of the time they were in the vehicle. Each of them worried about Danny. He didn't seem like he had any sort of concern in his mind about much of anything. His mind was somewhere else and he didn't seem to mind a bit.

As Danny watched his fingers work, his head produced thought after thought at an alarming rate. He watched flashes in his peripherals and madness in the center. Nothing in his reality seemed real, and he was done with attempting to fight it. If he was going to be stuck in a dream for the rest of his life, he at least wanted to be able to sit back and watch it work.

"Game time, lads," O'Connor yelled from the bar. Soldiers ran from the building and to their vehicles to begin their short journey to D.C. Danny's group quickly finished what they were doing and readied themselves for departure. As the last of the soldiers left the bar, the massive convoy formed and started its drive.

As they drove down the highway, the only vehicles on the road were those of the rebel forces. As they passed each other, some hung their bodies out of the windows and joked with one another. Others boomed music in order to excite themselves.

Still, there were those vehicles that had consumed themselves in silence, the car that Adam drove was one of them. None of them seemed to have any desire to discuss the mission, or even say any final words to each other. They simply meditated on their thoughts and the sound of the tires rolling over pavement.

As they neared their destination, the sight of smoke and fire could be seen from a distance. It looked as if the attack had already begun. Word had arrived that both the airport as well as the pentagon had already fallen to rebel forces. All that would have to be done now included bombing the hell out of the loyalists and not much else.

The vehicles pulled up to a point where D.C. was barely visible. Soldiers rushed form their vehicles and ran to a nearby truck that had been part of the convoy. Each vehicle of soldiers grabbed a mortar and began setting it up. Many of them had never used one, let alone been trained to use one, but they quickly figured it out.

Rob nervously set up the mortar based on what he'd seen in a movie and from those around them. Champ claimed that he would be able to figure it out because he'd used fireworks similar to this, but in the end, none of them really knew what they were doing. If they'd blown themselves up before they even entered the city, it wouldn't have been a surprise to anyone.

O'Connor observed the group finishing their preparations. They had a total of about fifty mortars ready to fire on the city. From the sounds, it seemed that the rest of D.C. was already under heavy attack.

Through binoculars, one could see the loyalist forces looking right back at the rebels. They noticed what was coming and they took refuge inside the city. The wall that had been erected around the city would have to serve as protection for the forces that fled inside. Snipers took spots along the wall to attempt to shoot those at the mortars before they had a chance to fire.

As a nearby mortar team came under fire, anxiety took control of O'Connor. "Fire! Fire now!" he yelled as soldiers scrambled to recover from the hit they'd taken. They began firing off missiles. As each team waited for theirs to fire, they sat in the fear that theirs would blow up in their face, but as they fired successfully, the adrenaline pushed them to fire again and again.

Champ continuously loaded the mortar and the rest assisted in firing. A nearby team exploded as their loader had accidentally dropped the round in backwards, causing it to explode. Danny watched as pieces of the team were strewn around them. Nearby teams produced horrific screams of pain from the shrapnel that ripped through them. The attack was too important for them to be attended to by medics.

Snipers fired and fired at the teams, but few round hit their targets. The mortars hit the walls and the outer buildings of D.C. hard. They watched as their side of the city burst into flames. The city was beginning to look more like ruins than a once glorious capitol of the strongest nation in the world.

More and more soldiers arrived from different parts of the U.S. and set up their mortars as well. It wasn't long before they had countless lines of mortars firing into the city. The military outposts around the U.S. had supplied the rebels nicely.

As the chaos of the rounds continued, it got to the point where the shots from the snipers had ceased. As the city was constantly battered from all sides, no resistance decided to show it's face for fear of losing it. A circle of citizens with explosives had formed and they relentlessly fired on the city.

As minutes became hours and no shots were being fired on the rebel forces, O'Connor gave the order for his group to cease fire. The leaders of groups around them followed suit to observe the city. The area quickly became silent. It was so quiet, that the rebels could hear the screams of the wounded loyalists from their position.

O'Connor seized the moment of opportunity and commanded, "Attack! Kill everything that stands between us and capitol hill!"

The rebel soldiers jumped to their feet, weapons in hand, and ran towards the walls of the city. Each hoped that they'd fired enough tons of explosives into the city to stop any fire from coming from the loyalist soldiers. It soon appeared that their hopes weren't going to become reality.

Tanks fired from inside the city towards the rebel forces. The citizens scrambled for cover as their attacks were answered with bullets and rockets. O'Connor laid in a ditch and yelled towards his radio man, "Get us some air support." The man with the radio made a few calls.

Danny laid in the complete open. When the tanks began firing, he had been in an open field that offered little to no cover. He just laid with his face in the dirt, waiting for something to save his life.

He turned his head and saw Adam sprinting towards him. His eyes were focused only on that one mobile object. His mind produced ideas of what Adam could possibly have been doing. As Adam grabbed Danny and tried to yank him to his feet, it was becoming clear what Adam's motives were.

As Danny ran with his friend, the tank that had approached the group fired round after round towards them. The rebel army scattered in all directions attempting to dodge the machine. Danny and Adam hurdled dead bodies and sprinted around those that were too slow to survive. It was survival of the fittest, and they felt like Olympic athletes.

They took cover in a ditch that Champ and Rob were lying in. "What the hell do we do?" Champ yelled as they approached.

"I have no idea," Adam said. "We've just got to lay here until something happens that will give us an opportunity to actually do something."

Their ditch was becoming less and less effective as the tank only got closer. The rebel tanks had taken up positions on the other side of D.C. in order to control the airport. They were in this alone.

A boom flew over the rebels' heads. They looked up only to catch a flash of a plane overhead. The rebel's air force had arrived, and it dropped bomb after bomb on the approaching tanks. As the vehicles burst into flames, the rebel army regained its footing and pushed towards the walls of the city.

Danny huffed and puffed as he watched the planes fly overhead and drop their payload on the city. Their fire stopped any loyalist forces from firing on the rebels. They were suppressed and it had given the rebels the opportunity of a lifetime.

They approached the battered walls and began pouring in through any opening that they found. Danny's group chose a piece of the wall that had been completely disintegrated as their entry point.

Danny climbed over some rubble and looked at the city. It looked nothing like what he'd remembered it being when he had visited it as a kid. The images of everything being either demolished or in flames, came as a shock to him. He expected carnage, but nothing to this level.

As the rebels regrouped, they approached the inner city slowly. Planes overhead killed anything that would pose a problem to the rebels in the future. As they passed the burning tanks and dead soldiers, it had become clear that they had a force unlike any other on their side.

The rebels made their way through the city until capitol hill was in their sights. From the look of things, their group had been the first to reach the historic building. Their joy in finally seeing the building caused the group to become overzealous.

They charged, with all of the strength that remained in their bodies, towards the building. That's when the birds started falling from the sky.

Rockets flew from points surrounding capitol hill and shot down every plane that came to protect the rebel forces. They ran to buildings to avoid the flaming machines that were raining down upon them. Some pilots managed to fly their machines into the ground near capitol hill, but none of them had the opportunity to do any real damage. Just like that, the rebels were on their own again.

The rebel tanks had arrived, which became the only piece of hope that the soldiers clung to. As the last of their planes fell from the sky, the loyalist forces came out of hiding with every bit of strength that they had remaining. Tanks and soldiers came from every area surrounding capitol hill and did everything the could do destroy the rebels' tanks.

As the rebel soldiers took refuge in the buildings around them, the loyalists fired relentlessly on the tanks. Rockets and bullets alike hit the armored plating of the tanks, and many of them did an unexpected amount of damage. Danny had the fearful realization that they had managed to become surrounded by loyalist forces through their arrogant charge.

Danny and his group hunkered down in a small grocery store as the explosions of the battle rocked everything around them. From all of their surroundings, rounds came and hit their targets. Glass of the grocery store shattered as they were fired upon. None of them even had the ability to look outside at what was happening, due to the continuous fire.

It wasn't long before every tank that had accompanied them had been destroyed. Hope was fading. "We need to get the hell out of here," Champ said.

"Where can we go?" Rob yelled.

Champ looked around the store. It was small, but it was all that they had. "Get to the back!" Champ yelled. They ran to the counter in the back of the store and took cover. "If anything comes near those doors and it isn't on our side, unload on it."

They sat behind the counter gripping their guns in their hands. Their crosshairs focused on the glass doors in the front of the store. It was becoming clear that this could easily be their last stand. The tanks and planes that had made the battle so simple were gone. All they had were their guns and their small amounts of training.

The first loyalist came through the door and the small resistance fired. The soldier dropped quickly, but many more came. They gathered outside of the store and attempted to run in at once to overwhelm the rebels. The rebels fired with everything they had, but it was becoming clear that they couldn't contain the flood of loyalists for long.

Loyalist forces spread themselves out through the store. Danny dropped and attempted to reload, only to discover that he had run out of ammunition. The only thing that he could possibly do was pick up an enemy's gun, but they were a long way away, and they had live soldiers all around.

The group hunkered down as each of them came to the realization that they didn't have the ammunition to fire back. The loyalists' fire stopped and they sat in silence around the rebels. Champ peeked over the counter and saw a loyalist soldier only inches from his face.

The loyalist attempted to hit Champ, but he pulled the soldier over the counter. Rob sent a strong punch to the soldier's face and he grabbed the gun. As he aimed over the counter, the loyalists that had been moving in slowly stopped and scattered. Rob sent rounds into the backs of every soldier that couldn't run as quickly as the one in front of them.

Then Rob flew back next to the rest of his group. "Rob!" Adam yelled. Champ grabbed the gun from Rob and continued to hold the loyalists off. Rob had been shot in the shoulder and was bleeding badly.

"Shit, they got me," Rob said as he gripped his wound.

"Let me see it," Adam said. He pulled Rob's hand off of it and analyzed the wound. The bullet had gone all the way through Rob's shoulder and caused the area to bleed profusely.

"What the hell do we do?" Champ yelled as he continued to fire.

"I don't know!" Adam yelled. "But Rob's dying on us."

"I'll be fine," Rob said. "It's only a shoulder wound."

"God dammit," Champ said as he dropped down behind the counter. "I'm out of ammo." So they had to sit there and pray that the loyalists would just go away. They had used up their resources, the attack had failed, and now they had to deal with the consequences.

The group stood with their hands raised. The loyalist forces pointed their weapons at the group and stood their ground. It looked like they were attempting to figure out if the rebels were actually giving up.

Danny's head went down. He didn't want to look at the loyalist forces. It was like being mocked after being beaten by your rival. As he realized that he would be dying that day, he couldn't help but laugh.

His head shot up and laughter poured out of his mouth. His eyes sent fear into the hearts of the loyalists that were watching the spectacle. He had lost his sanity once again and it was sending a chill down the spines of all that watched.

Champ looked up and saw more soldiers pouring into the store. The loyalists didn't acknowledge the arrival and continued to watch the boy in front of them lose his mind. They began to approach the small group to take them in, but soon, the soldiers that had entered opened fire.

The loyalists were caught off guard completely. As they turned to return fire, they dropped. It seemed that the soldiers that had entered weren't on the loyalist side. It was almost too glorious to believe. Danny's laughter ceased as he watched each of the loyalist soldiers die in front of him.

The group stood behind the counter with their arms still raised as the rebels approached. "Don't worry, I'm here mates," O'Connor said with his cocky smile.

Adam dropped his arms and ran back to Rob. "Rob's been shot!" he yelled to O'Connor.

"Well that's a problem," O'Connor said. "I'll have a medic look at him, but you all need to get back outside. We're going to the capitol. Word is that the president has taken cover inside and I think it's time we talked to him."

Danny jumped the counter and picked up a loyalist weapon and the ammo that laid on the body. As he searched the body, he even found a grenade. He smiled at the sight and put it into his pocket for later. The rebel group left the grocery store as a medic looked over a bloodied Rob. He seemed calm, but the group still worried that he'd be dead before they even returned.

"Give 'em hell!" Rob yelled after the soldiers. They didn't respond. The concentration that had been caused from being so close to the end had deafened them as their excitement overwhelmed them. They left the grocery store and made their way through the streets.

The streets were littered with bodies and destruction. The entire rebel force had gathered around capitol hill. Just by estimation, it seemed like there were at least a few hundred thousands of people there, each of them waiting. O'Connor grabbed Champ and Danny. "We're going inside with the rest of the nation's generals, mates," he said.

They and a few other soldiers made their way to the steps of capitol hill. The leaders from each part of the nation converged with the cheers of the people behind them. As the front doors opened, they held their guns up, but those inside were ready to surrender.

The congressmen and other random political figures that had taken refuge in D.C. stared at the ground in defeat with their hands held high signaling that they'd surrendered. They moved out of the building and were given to the crowd of angry rebels waiting outside. Some were beaten, but they were all taken into custody by the new leaders of the nation: the citizens.

They made their way to the office that the president was said to be inside. There was a group of loyalist soldiers sitting outside of the door. "Danny?" one of them said.

Danny turned his attention to one of them and became instantly surprised. "Charlie?" he said. He looked at the soldier and there was no doubt that it was his friend that had been abducted so long ago in his dorm room. Danny remembered jumping from his friend's window and running to avoid capture.

"What are you doing here?" Charlie asked. "You're still with the rebels?"

"And you're with the loyalists?" Danny asked.

"Danny, it's sad that you've joined them," he said. "You know that once you all take over this isn't going to stop, right?"

Danny laughed. "I know what's going to happen, Charlie," he said. "It's just a shame that you had to be on the wrong side for all of this."

"Enough, is the president inside?" O'Connor asked.

"Yeah," Charlie said. "I'm guessing that you want to go in?"

"Damn right," O'Connor said as he approached the door. A hand reached out and stopped him dead in his tracks.

"Hey, why don't we let Danny bring him out?" Champ said.

"Hell no," O'Connor said. "I'm not letting that kid go in there."

"O'Connor, you know that kid's been a bigger figure in this revolution than you ever could have hoped to be," another rebel leader yelled.

"Yeah, let him do it," another yelled.

O'Connor glared at Danny. "Fine," he said. "Just be quick."

Danny looked at the door. His uncle patted him on the back. "It's time," Champ said with a smile. "Finish this. Bring that asshole out so we can take control."

"Make sure that he's still alive when he comes out, lad," O'Connor said. "There's a lot of information that he has that we need to run this country."

Danny nodded and walked inside. He passed Charlie and gave him a smug look that shook his confidence and rose his level of frustration to a new level. The doors shut behind him and the rebels waited. They glared at the loyalist forces that waited at the door. It was a long silence filled with tension. The only noise that could be heard was the sound of the citizens outside cheering.

They had done it. They were about to pull Stone out and they would be able to start running the nation. The last large figurehead in the loyalist army would soon be in rebel hands and he'd be spilling all of the information that the rebels required into their ears. All of the classified information in the president's head and office was going to be their's soon.

After all of the fighting, the fatigue began to hit the rebels that waited outside. They were filled with joy, but their bodies were exhausted. They held their guns tightly, but they were ready to put them down and start their nation's next page.

A gunshot rang out from inside of the office. Champ pushed past the loyalists at the door and ran inside. As the doors opened, they saw Danny standing over the body of the president with a gun in hand.

"Danny, what did you do?" Champ yelled. He looked at Danny's eyes. They were empty and bloodshot. Danny was panting and had a wicked smile on his face.

"Now the nation will fall into chaos," Danny said. He held the gun up to his head and pulled the trigger. Champ and the rest of the rebel leaders filled the room to figure out what had happened. Champ stood next to the body of his nephew in shock. Next to the body laid a grenade without a pin.

Danny had single-handedly killed the last of the loyalist leaders and in his death had led to the demise of the rebel leaders. As the grenade went off, the leaders of the revolution, and the last of the old government vanished in a cloud of fire. The citizens waiting outside watched in wonder as the building burnt to the ground from a madman's actions.x`The nation was left only to the citizens that had played their part in the revolution. Now that the revolution was over, the only thought on their mind was, "Where do we go from here?" They were left a nation of their own, but nobody to run it other than themselves.

With Danny's mind having driven him to kill every leader that had a part in the revolution, the nation was officially run by the people, but with so many different perspectives and no leadership, they would be faced with a challenge even larger than that of the revolution: they would need to save the nation from the chaos that they'd caused and Danny had ensured.